I0702769

THE STORY BEGINS

GRANT ANDREASEN

https://truequest.info

Copyright © 2023 Grant Andreasen.

All rights reserved. This book is protected by copyright. No part of this book may be reproduced or transmitted in any form or by any means, including as photocopies or scanned-in or othwer electronic copies, or utilized by any information storage and retrieval system without written permission from the copyright owner.

Cover and Interior Design by Formatted Books

Printed in the United States of America.
ISBN: 979-8-9878554-0-9 (Softcover)
ISBN: 979-8-9878554-2-3 (Hardcover)

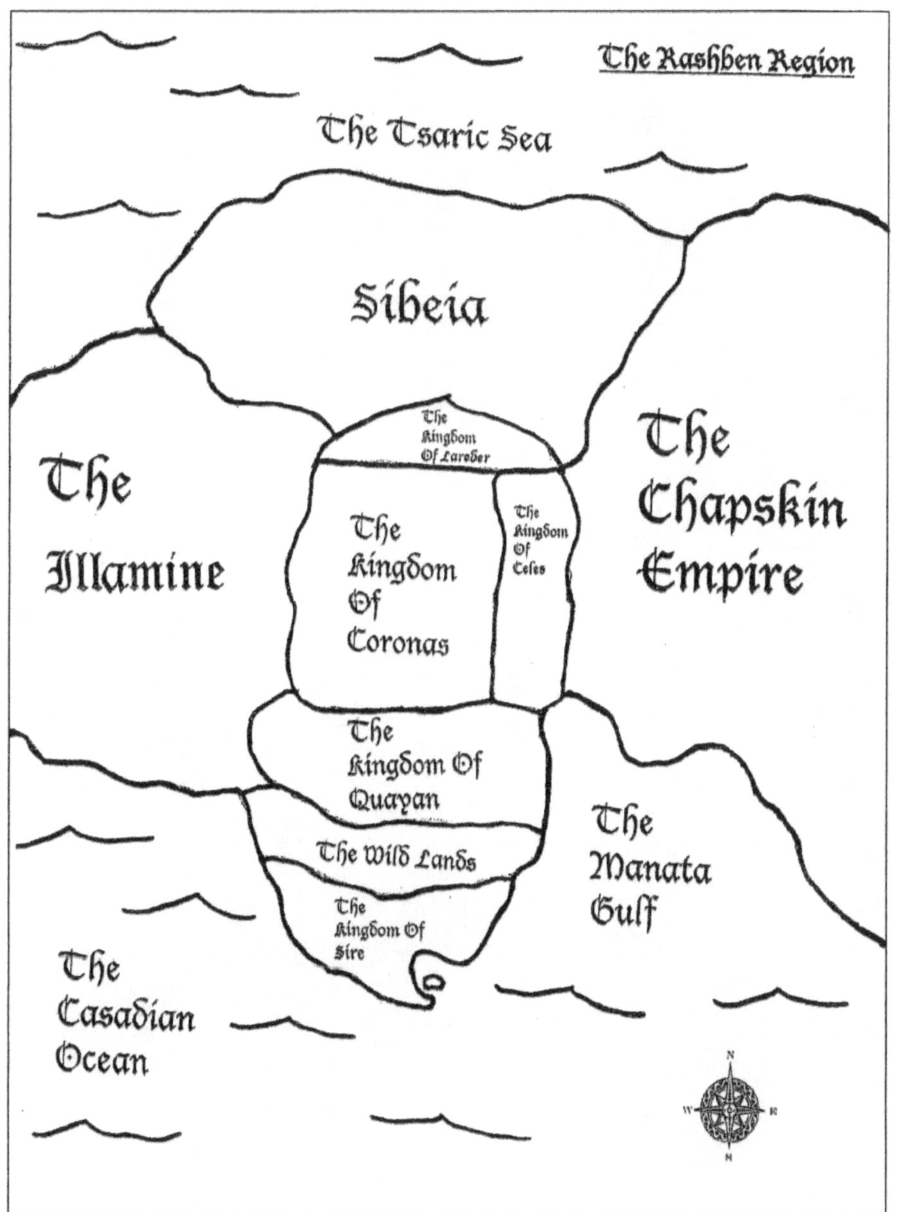

The Rashben Region
The Tsaric Sea
Sibeia
The Kingdom Of Lareber
The Illamine
The Kingdom Of Coronas
The Kingdom Of Celes
The Chapskin Empire
The Kingdom Of Quayan
The Wild Lands
The Manata Gulf
The Kingdom Of Sire
The Casadian Ocean
N
W
E
S

Deities of Calatan

The Elder Gods: Creators of the world and its many inhabitants.

Mirsha

Representation: Animals, plants, the elements.
Alignment: Neutral
Symbol: A seed with a worm wrapped around it.
Primary Followers: Farmers, hunters, miners, sailors/fishermen, nature lovers.
Ceremonies: Good weather, natural bounties.

Talana

Representation: Light, life, health, families
Alignment: Good
Symbol: Two cupped hands holding the sun.
Primary Followers: Families, unhealthy.
Ceremonies: Birthday's, reunions.

Kardok

Representation: Darkness, death, pain, hardship
Alignment: Evil
Symbol: An encircled red skull with flaming eye sockets
Primary Followers: Elderly, underground races.
Ceremonies: Funerals, executions, sacrificial homage.

The Risen Gods:	Long dead heroes whose spirits were worshiped into godhood.

Rightin

Representation:	War
Alignment:	Neutral
Symbol:	A gauntleted fist placed in front of a shield.
Primary Followers:	Warriors, protectors.
Ceremonies:	Honoring a fallen opponent.

Clowani

Representation:	Love, passion, happiness
Alignment:	Good
Symbol:	A red heart above two crossed keys
Primary Followers:	Young, lonely.
Ceremonies:	Weddings

Anthalos

Representation:	Knowledge
Alignment:	Neutral
Symbol:	A torch in front of an open book.
Primary Followers:	Politicians, scholars, mages.
Ceremonies:	Guidance

Luxar

Representation: Luck, choice
Alignment: Neutral
Symbol: Two vertical coins. Top is gold and depicts a diamond; bottom is silver and depicts a skull.
Primary Followers: Poor, risk takers
Ceremonies: Charity

Shareen

Representation: Vengeance, desire, grief
Alignment: Evil
Symbol: Eye with a bloody tear.
Primary Followers: Victims, widows, dangerously ambitious
Ceremonies: Revenge

Dargen

Representation: Crafts, music, art
Alignment: Neutral
Symbol: Quill pen in front an anvil.
Primary Followers: Craftsmen, merchants, musicians
Ceremonies: Gift giving

Chapter One

Echo blinked as a light breeze blew a small bit of dust into her eyes. Looking towards the direction of the dust, she saw a busy farmer tilling his field behind an ox-driven plow. Standing next to the farmer was a young boy with a thin reed he used to help goad the oxen forward. She smiled at the sight and thought this was how humans should be living their lives. Working with animals as a family while trying to cultivate the land for everyone's benefit.

It was a beautiful spring day, with only a couple clouds to mar an otherwise bright blue sky. Echo stood on a long stretch of dirt road in the middle of farm country. Under normal circumstances, she might have wanted to go find a nice place to sit and play her flute, but today, she had more important things to do... if her companion would ever bother to hurry up!

Looking back along the road, Echo called out, "Pick up the pace, Ontar! This is my first assignment for the Bloody Side, and I'm not going to mess it up because you're moving like a snail."

Ontar gave Echo a dirty look, but she was far enough ahead of him that he could do little more than that. This was probably a good thing since Ontar was a mountain of a man to behold. Standing at six-and-a-half-feet-tall, the powerfully built human had broad shoulders, bulging biceps, chiseled pecs, and a rock-hard abdomen. Not to be thought of as a completely lumbering brute, Ontar could also be seen as someone in his early twenties with fair skin, gentle blue eyes, and shoulder length brown hair parted up the middle.

Unabashedly pronouncing he was an experienced warrior, Ontar wore a full suit of gray plate armor and carried a helmet tucked under one arm. A blue cloak could be partially seen draped across his shoulders before getting covered by both a brown backpack and an enormous tower shield that dominated his back and upper legs.

As was common with most warriors, Ontar wore a brown leather weapon belt with a crossbow and quiver on one side and his prized morning star on the other. He even kept a dagger in his boot in case of emergencies. A precaution Echo herself engaged in since one never knew when an extra blade might be necessary.

Exerting a little extra energy, Ontar caught up with Echo. "What's your hurry?" he asked. "The thieves' guild said we'd still have a week before the nobleman tried to leave this kingdom. That gives us plenty of time to get the job done."

Echo glared at him. "Yes, but we're only sure of one spot where he'll be staying at, and if we don't get there quickly, then we might lose him altogether."

The two started down the road together. As they did, Ontar asked, "I don't see why the guild wants this guy so bad. Who cares if one of Lareder's pampered lords decides to run off with a peasant girl?"

"The girl isn't important. She's merely the reason Lord Marcain has put himself in such a vulnerable position," Echo explained. "However, his lordships bloodline is essential to our patron's objectives, which is why Narcos hired the guild to kidnap him in the first place."

"So, what do you know about Narcos?" Ontar wondered.

Echo thought a moment. "My contact said he was a necromancer who lived in a cemetery near the city of Miltus."

Frowning at the unfamiliar term, Ontar asked, "What's a necromancer?"

"A follower of Kardok, the god of death," Echo explained. "By *channeling* power from his deity, he can raise corpses and summon spirits to do his bidding."

"Well, you know some magic," Ontar observed. "Can you cast a spell that could help us if things go bad?"

Echo shook her head. "Ontar, I'm a dabbler. My power's *essence*-based and is drawn from the fabric of the world around us. However, when I do cast a spell, it's more for stealing and hiding than anything else."

A little disappointed by her response, Ontar said, "Oh well, I guess we better stay on Narcos's good side then. Did your contact happen to mention what his plans are for Lord Marcain?"

Getting a little irritated, Echo replied, "Who cares? He paid the guild to do a job, and I intend to carry it out. My family's reputation is at stake here, and I will not let my aunt regret sponsoring my membership."

"We haven't seen Searce in ages," Ontar noted. "She probably doesn't even know we're on this mission."

Annoyed by his attitude, Echo said, "Don't think for one moment that word of our task isn't going to spread. The guild put its faith in her, and she put her faith in me. Failure is *not* an option!"

Ontar knew there was no point in arguing with her. For a wood elf, Echo could be exceptionally strong-willed. Being about the same height as a human woman, it took a moment for Ontar to recognize Echo's elvish traits. Of course, the pointed ears were a dead giveaway, but not everyone would notice her blemish-free complexion, or the years of knowledge hidden in her eyes. While at first sight, Echo appeared to be in her late teens, the truth of the matter was she was well over a hundred and twenty years old.

Lacking her people's gentler appearance, Echo's sky-blue eyes were set within tight facial features that easily blended into the lean, wiry muscles of her body. Her long brown hair, parted up the middle and woven into two braids, hung behind her distinctive ears. Covering her hair was a brown leather pot helmet with studded iron bands along its rim and center.

Leather was Echo's armor of choice, and while her torso was the first place she decided to protect, she also had greaves made from it to cover her upper arms and legs. Boots and a weapon belt helped complete the leathery portion of Echo's ensemble, while a light green shirt and brown pants illustrated she *did* prefer the feel of cloth when possible.

Much like Ontar, Echo had a dark green cloak that adorned her shoulders. Sadly, it had to compete for space on her back with a longbow, backpack, and a round iron shield. Arrows for the bow could be found in a quiver on her weapon belt, which was situated near a scabbard with a broadsword in it.

Watchful of the road, Echo noticed a small dirt path that branched out from it and into the countryside. Remembering the description she had received from the Bloody Side, she motioned to Ontar, and the two headed down the path towards their new destination. It wasn't long before they saw the path led up to a small isolated farmhouse.

The structure wasn't anything special. A thatched roof covered a white walled building with wooden framework and a gray stone chimney. A wooden chicken coop could be seen towards the back of the house, with a handful of the noisy birds loudly clucking at Ontar and Echo's approach. The whole scene would have been entirely unremarkable if not for the two beautiful horses tethered to a hitching post alongside a small vegetable garden.

Echo gave a sly smile. "My goodness, I didn't know peasants rode such magnificent animals."

"They don't," Ontar replied as he placed his helmet on his head. The iron full helmet wasn't anything special. Cylindrical in nature, it was bent slightly inward around the brow to fit better. Looking out through its two small eye slits, Ontar drew his morning star and shield. Echo decided to choose a distance weapon in case there was trouble and briefly removed her backpack and shield in order to get at her longbow. Loading it with an arrow, the two slowly advanced towards the farmhouse.

Marcain was nervous. A handsome brown-haired noble in his early twenties, he certainly didn't seem to belong in a rural setting. Clad in a puffed sleeve white shirt under a green jerkin with gold embroidery, the rest of his garments consisted of a regal black cloak, which matched his pants and polished boots, and was held in place by an ornate golden brooch. Huddled inside the house with him was Lomana, his pregnant lover, and Rolit, her brother.

The young lord was alerted to Ontar and Echo's arrival by Tegas, a personal guard who had stood watch next to the window.

"Milord, we've got two armed stalkers headed towards the house. One appears to be a warrior, while the other is an elf."

Rolit looked to Marcain and said, "They aren't from around here. Your mother must have sent them to bring you back to Miltus."

"If that's true, then maybe you should go with them," Lomana stated. "I can raise our child here on the farm with Rolit."

Marcain shook his head. "No, Lomana. I will not let my mother separate us because of my title. I love you and want to raise our child together." Glancing at his guard, he then asked, "Tegas do you think you could hold them off while we make our escape?"

Drawing forth his broadsword, Tegas replied, "The odds aren't great, but I've faced worse."

With Lomana's hand in his, Marcain watched their protector open the farmhouse door and go to meet their enemies.

❧ ❧ ❧

Curious to see who had come to greet them, Ontar and Echo stopped a short distance from the building when a muscular man with short gray hair emerged from the front door, which quickly closed behind him. Clad in simple, yet well-kept clothes, the warrior wore an iron breastplate and confidently propped a broadsword along his shoulder with exaggerated ease.

"If you're looking at the horses, then I suggest you move on," Tegas warned. "They're not for sale or worth the fight I'd give you for them."

Tightly gripping her bow, Echo replied, "We're not interested in horses. We've come for Lord Marcain. Now, you can either stand aside or we'll go through you."

Adopting a battle stance, the old warrior held his sword in both hands and smiled. "Well, come on then."

If I can defeat you, then I can defeat Lydon, Ontar thought as he stepped in front of his elvish companion and proclaimed, "He's mine! Watch the house."

"But I could kill him right now with an arrow," Echo argued. Ignoring her, Ontar spun his morning star. Clearly annoyed, she merely uttered, "Fine," before standing off to one side.

Tegas charged Ontar and swung his sword when he was within striking range. Unimpressed, Ontar knocked the blade aside with his weapon and surged towards the man with a counterattack.

Stepping back, the warrior narrowly avoided Ontar's morning star. Seeing an opening, Tegas thrust his sword forward and delivered a glancing blow to Ontar's right shoulder plate. Wincing at the pain, Ontar prepared to take another attack as the warrior swung his sword straight at his head!

Using his shield, Ontar successfully deflected Tegas's blow. He then lunged inwards to direct his opponent's blade along the shield's face and towards his left side. This exposed Tegas's torso, which Ontar brutally struck his morning star in a calculated blow. The man crumpled to the ground before him, and Ontar spun his morning star, preparing for the final strike.

The strike, however, came from Tegas, who caught Ontar off guard by kicking him just below the knee. Ontar fell face first into the ground. For a moment, both men struggled to rise, but using his sword to pull himself up, the old warrior was the first one to his feet.

Tempted to help Ontar against his opponent, Echo aimed her bow at Tegas just as the farmhouse door opened. Refusing to let Marcain escape, she fired an arrow at the door and struck it dead center. Frightening whoever was on the other side, Echo saw it quickly slam shut again. Relieved to see the elf had missed her mark Tegas decided to go after her instead. Backing away from the warrior, Echo narrowly ducked a swipe from his sword as she managed to reload her bow. Thankfully, she never had to fire it.

Coming up behind the old warrior, Ontar used his morning star to bash his head in. Splattered with gore as Tegas fell, Echo said, "Thanks. I wasn't sure who was going to get the next attack off, him or me."

Ontar let his weapon droop when it became apparent the battle was over. "He put up a good fight. In all honesty, if I got to be his age, I wouldn't mind going the same way myself."

Snickering when she heard this, Echo said, "The only way you'd live to be that age is if you gave up what you're doing right now."

"We both know I can't do that," Ontar replied. "At least not yet."

"And I wouldn't want you to," Echo added before turning to the farmhouse and shouting, "Lord Marcain, we have killed your man and foiled your escape. Come out now or you'll share his fate!"

❈❈❈

An air of tension was thick within the farmhouse. Trying to hold back tears, Lomana said, "Tegas...I can't believe he's gone."

Drawing a beautiful sword from beneath his cloak, Marcain said, "His death will be avenged! I will not let them destroy our family."

"Are you mad!?" Lomana exclaimed. "Tegas was twice the warrior you are. If he couldn't beat them, then you don't stand a chance."

Marcain gave her an exasperated look. "What choice do I have?"

Focusing on the noble's regal attire, Rolit had an idea. "Let me go in your place."

"What?" Marcain and Lomana asked simultaneously.

Rolit quickly explained his plan. "Give me your sword, signet ring, and cloak. I will surrender to those monsters out there and give the two of you a chance to escape."

"Rolit, you can't," Lomana objected.

"My mother would spot your deception immediately," Marcain added.

Rolit gave them a nervous smile. "What's spending a couple of years in the dungeon when compared to giving my little sister and lord a lifetime of happiness together?"

Tears streamed down Lomana's cheeks. "Rolit, I don't know what to say."

Already removing his cloak, Marcain told his friend, "I will not forget what you're about to do for us."

"Just make sure my nephew grows up happy," Rolit replied.

Growing suspicious of how long it took Lord Marcain to show himself, Ontar and Echo advanced upon the farmhouse. Unsure if the noble would attempt to either fight or flee, they stopped when the man in question emerged from the building and slowly advanced towards them.

With his sword drawn, Rolit tried to keep his voice firm while Marcain hid behind the house's door. "Hello. My name is Marcain D'Shad, and I am the only son and heir to the duchess of Miltus. If you promise not to hurt the girl, then I will do anything you ask."

Glancing over the noble's shoulder, Ontar and Echo both saw a pregnant young woman standing in the doorway with tears in her eyes.

"You have our word, milord," Echo said.

Looking back and forth between Ontar, Echo, and Tegas's body, Rolit nodded his head and dropped the sword. Keeping her bow at the ready, Echo took a few steps towards the noble and stopped. Moving behind her, Ontar withdrew his morning star and shield before opening Echo's backpack so he could get some rope. He then went over to Rolit and proceeded to bind his hands in front of him. As this happened, Ontar and Echo both heard the noble's lover weep quietly from within the farmhouse.

Once the lord was secure, Echo shouldered her bow and searched him for weapons. Finding nothing else, the elf escorted him over to the hitching post where Ontar had untied the horses. The big warrior unceremoniously hoisted Rolit onto the lead horse while Echo slipped into its saddle. Afterwards, Ontar mounted his own mare, and the trio made a hasty departure from the lonely farmhouse.

Waiting until they were out of sight, Marcain slipped out of the shadows and wrapped his arms around Lomana. "Your brother's sacrifice will not be in vain."

Lomana quietly spoke as she wiped away her tears. "I don't know what I'm going to do without him?"

Bending over to reclaim his sword, Marcain replied, "We follow the plan and take the road south. Rolit said his friends have already agreed to help us establish a new life. All we have to do now is get out of Lareder."

Reluctantly retreating inside, Lomana said, "I'll pack our things."

It was a two-day ride across open plains before Ontar and Echo reached their destination. The trip was a quiet one. Rolit did little to aggravate his captures and, in return, he was treated respectfully. It wasn't until an afternoon meal on the second day that he decided to strike up a conversation. "Pardon my asking, but have either of you ever been in love?"

"Nope," Ontar replied abruptly as he picked through a small cloth containing his supposed dinner. One thing Ontar always hated about traveling was the nearly constant diet of jerky, hard tack, dried peas, raisins, and nuts that came in every bundle of trail rations. The first thing he was going to do when he finished this job was get a decent meal.

"I have," Echo said as she finished tending to the horses.

"Good," Rolit began as he sipped from a water skin. "Then perhaps you will understand my plight. I am someone who has chosen love over lineage. It is an act my mother doesn't understand, but truly, there are far worse crimes out there than that. Can you not grant mercy to a man who was simply following his heart?"

Echo gave Rolit a piercing look. "Everything I know about love I learned from my suitor. He was a good and brave soldier whose sole duty was to protect the ones he loved…and he died in battle while doing that," Echo's words were tinged with pain, but a moment later, her voice took a distinctly darker infliction. "On the other hand, *you* my dear lord, tried to run away with a woman whom you didn't even have the guts to fight for. Do you really think that sending a loyal guard to his death was truly the noblest way to show your love?" Echo asked.

"No," said Rolit sadly. "Tegas died while trying to give my beloved and I a chance at real happiness. Is your heart so cold that you'd let his final act of bravery be in vain?"

"An act is only considered brave if you survive it," Ontar retorted. "Failure on the other hand belongs to the foolish."

Deciding to enlighten the beleaguered noble, Echo added, "Besides, we aren't here on your mother's behalf. We've come to take you to a cemetery near Miltus."

Rolit was clearly surprised by this information. "The cemetery...why? From what I've heard, only the undead lurk amongst its tombstones? How in the world would you defend yourselves against creatures like that?"

Pointing to the weapons on his and Echo's belt, Ontar said, "Do you see my morning star and her sword?" Rolit nodded. "Well, they might not look like much, but we've spent a lot of money to have them enchanted so that we can take on anything an enemy might throw at us. Including these supposed undead."

"But why are you bringing me there at all?" Rolit wondered.

Not completely sure herself as to why Narcos would want the noble, Echo decided to be vague. "You'll just have to find out when we arrive."

Debating on whether to reveal his true identity, Rolit feared his captors would kill him if they learned the truth. So, he chose to stay silent and look for a way to escape when they reached the cemetery. Mounting up once more after they finished eating, Rolit unwillingly rode with Ontar and Echo towards the cemetery.

The sun had nearly set when the party made a stop along the side of the road. Gathering a mound of dried grass to make a fire, Ontar noticed the horses were rather skittish while Echo seemed to struggle to keep them calm. "What's wrong?"

Wincing as she tried to hold onto the reins, Echo asked, "Do you hear that?"

Knowing the elf's pointed ears allowed her to hear far better than a human's, Ontar simply replied, "No, what is it?"

"It sounds like some sort of screeching," Echo complained.

"Probably the banshee," Rolit suggested.

Echo gave him a strange look. "The what?"

"The banshee," Rolit explained. "About ten years ago, the spirit of a hideous woman appeared at the cemetery and scared away the mourners. They say her scream brings death onto any-one who hears it."

"Well, I don't know about death, but I'm sure getting a head-ache," Echo grumbled.

Ontar thought a moment. "She's probably there to warn Narcos of any intruders. I'll go see if I can shut her up so you can bring his lordship and the horses."

"You could just let me go and avoid her altogether," Rolit suggested.

"Nice try," Echo retorted before addressing Ontar. "What will you do about her scream?"

Removing his full helmet, Ontar pulled the hood of his cloak up over his head before replacing it. "There. Between my hood and helmet, I won't be able to hear a damn thing. Just meet up with me after the wailing stops."

Continuing his trek down the road, Ontar wondered what his first encounter with an undead would be like?

Darkness had descended upon the land by the time Ontar reached his destination, and a full orange moon dominated the starlit sky above him. Carrying a burning torch that he had gotten from his backpack, Ontar let its light fall upon the edge of a vast cemetery overgrown with weeds which grew sporad-ically between broken statues and a sea of faded tombstones. It was an ideal setting for any necromancer to practice their dark arts.

Adding a hint of menace to this already dismal environment, Ontar could now hear the constant wail of a banshee even be-neath his helmet and hood. With his head starting to pound, he tried to silence the evil spirit by calling out to her master.

Shouting at the top of his lungs, he said, "Narcos, hear me! My name is Ontar Liongrave, and I have captured the lord of Miltus for you!"

An eerie silence washed over the land as the banshee's wailing abruptly came to an end. Disturbed by this development Ontar switched the torch to his other hand so he could draw forth his morning star. Suddenly, off in the distance, he saw the pale glow of a transparent figure as it slowly ascended skyward from the middle of the cemetery. A hideous woman whose ghostly skin appeared to have suffered from massive burns, the banshee had both long hair and a tattered ethereal dress that blew wildly in a nonexistent wind. Turning to glare at him with glowing red eyes, her mouth opened excessively wide to reveal her sharp jagged teeth…and then she screamed!

Ontar had never heard anything more horrific in his entire life. The sound was so intense he thought his brain would burst from within his skull. Falling to his knees, he let out a tormented scream as he dropped what was in his hands and clasped the sides of his helmet. Soon, a high-pitched whine was all he could hear as he crumpled to the ground and stared off in a daze. Delighted to see how easily her victim had fallen, the banshee glided over countless tombstones until she hovered directly above Ontar. Reaching out to touch his left arm, she grinned with delight as he howled in pain.

Sheer agony woke Ontar to the danger he was in as his arm twisted and contorted in an extremely unnatural way. Thinking, *No…I will not fall before I face him,* Ontar summoned all his strength to use his one good hand to grab the torch and swing it at the banshee. Shrieking at the blow, the vile spirit watched as her own hand briefly vanished from view before fading back into existence a few seconds later. Recoiling from the attack, the banshee saw Ontar stand with the torch in front of him. Infuriated by the sneak attack, she opened her mouth and let out another soul-shattering scream, but this time it had no effect.

Unable to hear anything beyond the whine in his head, Ontar swiped at the banshee with his blazing torch. Barely dodging his attack, the wicked spirit retreated to a nearby grave where she wailed in frustration, then sunk underground. Ontar knew he couldn't pursue her, and the throbbing in his head and arm made him reluctant to try. So, he watched and waited to see where she would reappear, only to find she never did.

Instead, off in the distance, he caught sight of a shadowy mausoleum where a flickering lantern had been placed by the corner of the building. Taking it as a sign, he decided not to proceed any further until Echo joined him.

Thankfully, it didn't take long for Echo and "Lord Marcain" to arrive. Traveling on foot while holding the reins of their horses, Echo's night vision was superior to any humans, and she was able to spot Ontar with ease. Riding on horseback, Rolit shifted nervously in the saddle while searching for some sign of the banshee. Calling out to her companion, Echo thought it was odd that Ontar didn't respond until they were close enough for him to notice them. Seeing that his right arm was curled up tightly against his chest, Echo asked, "Ontar, what happened!?"

Shouting at her Ontar exclaimed, "Echo, I can't hear you! The banshee injured my ears and arm!"

"Were you able to defeat her?" Echo asked.

Staring at her blankly a moment, Ontar pointed his torch and said, "I think Narcos is waiting for us at that mausoleum!"

"Your warrior has been crippled. We should flee while we can!" Rolit urged.

"Get off that horse, you coward," Echo demanded as she pulled Rolit to the ground. Taking the horse's reins, she found a tombstone with a large crack in it and tethered the animals.

While this happened, Ontar handed Rolit his torch and said, "Here, make yourself useful," before going to retrieve his morning star.

Drawing forth her sword and shield, Echo got behind Rolit and gestured at the mausoleum with her blade. "Come on, let's go."

Proceeding through the foreboding landscape, the party eventually came upon a small square building whose gray stone pillars were covered in cobwebs and supported a domed roof. Large empty urns could be seen flanking the structures short staircase that led up to a slab of rock, which served as the mausoleum's door. Resting on one of these urns was the lantern Ontar had seen earlier, while standing next to the other one was Narcos.

An older man with short white hair and cold cruel eyes, Narcos wore a long black cloak, which hung from his shoulders over a dark blue robe that almost covered his old brown boots. Armed with a simple wooden staff, Echo noticed the necromancer carried little of anything valuable. Ontar, however, was interested in the human skull whose spinal column coiled around his waist like a belt. To him, this was the sign of a man who knew a thing or two about the dark arts.

Stopping these intruders before they got too close, the necromancer said, "Halt, I am Narcos Melador, the master of this cemetery. Who are you to come here and disturb the dead's eternal slumber?"

Echo quickly made introductions. "My name is Echo Karashenmahagensea, and this is my companion Ontar Liongrave. As a representative of the Bloody Side thieves' guild, I am here to deliver unto you Lord Marcain D'Shad of Miltus."

"I am NOT Lord Marcain!" Rolit uttered to Narcos in an anxious voice.

"WHAT!?" Echo exclaimed.

Seeing this as his only opportunity to escape, Rolit went on to say, "These thieves are trying to deceive you so they can take your money and run. Please…punish them and let me go. I am just an innocent man in all this."

"You lying son of a bitch!" Echo roared as she raised her sword to take a swipe at him.

"Wait," Narcos said as he pointed his staff at Echo. "I want to see if this man is telling the truth." Addressing Rolit, he added, "The mausoleum behind me can only be opened by a member of the D'Shad family. Push upon its enchanted door with all your might, and if it doesn't open, then I'll know who has tried to deceive me."

Seeing that something was wrong, Ontar clutched his weapon and tried to figure out what the young lord had done. Increasingly bothered by the whole situation, he noticed the necromancer had made them stop both out of striking range and on top of what appeared to be strangely loose earth.

Rolit lifted his hands and asked Echo to untie him. The elf yanked at the rope binding her prisoner and cut it, allowing Rolit to raise his torch while he strode past Narcos and up the mausoleum's steps. Pushing on the buildings cold stone door, he looked back and said, "It won't budge."

"Try harder!" Echo demanded.

Pressing his shoulder against the door, Rolit leaned against it but was still unable to get it to open. "There's nothing more I can do."

Narcos's icy gaze fell upon Echo. "Lying worms, how dare you try to cheat me!"

"Lord Marcain must still be back at the farm," Echo stammered. "There was a woman there. Let me go back and question her for you. I swear we can find him!"

"I will not let your deceit go unpunished!" Narcos declared as he slammed the butt of his staff into the ground.

Unsure of what would happen next, Echo shrieked when a skeletal hand erupted from the earth and grabbed her ankle. Bony fingers easily pierced her boot and drew blood as they dug into her flesh. Crying out as she fell over, Echo used her shield as a brace when she hit the ground only to have a second skeletal hand grab hold of its rim. Driven by pain, Echo swung her sword at the hand on her ankle and chopped it off at the wrist, causing the rest of the appendage to go limp.

Being a little more prepared than Echo, Ontar felt the skeletal hands coming from beneath him and successfully dodged their wicked grip. He then spun his morning star just enough to build momentum before using it to smash the hands as they appeared. This brave act kept the enemies closest to him and Echo at bay, but that didn't stop the ones who were farther out. Having been buried in just the right spot for an ambush, over a dozen skeletons pulled themselves out of the ground and shook off the dirt as they prepared to attack Ontar and Echo.

Terrified by the sight of these undead, Rolit used their preoccupation with his captors as an opportunity to shoot past Narcos and run out of the cemetery. Disgusted by the man's cowardice, Narcos pointed his staff and shouted, "Kill him!" prompting six of the skeletons to give chase.

Rolit felt his heart pumping in his ears as he darted around tombstones and ran for his life! The skeletons were able to keep pace but had yet to overtake him. This all changed when the banshee rose from a grave in front of him and reached out to try and take the frightened man into her wicked grasp. Rolit shouted in alarm and kept her back by swinging his torch in front of him. That, however, did not stop the skeletons who leapt on his shoulders from behind and began ripping the poor man to pieces!

Rolit's dying screams immediately motivated Echo to escape. Hacking off the skeletal hand that held her shield, she rolled out of the way of an approaching skeleton that tried to take a swipe at her. Seconds later, this skeleton collapsed to the ground when Ontar's morning star reduced its skull to dust. "We have to get out of here!" he shouted while using his weapon to shatter the elbow of another enemy.

Deflecting another skeleton's blow off her shield before chopping its leg off, Echo got to her feet and limped away from the mausoleum. Ontar followed close behind, and the two fought side by side to keep from being overwhelmed. Eventually, they managed to defeat their enemies while putting some distance between themselves and Narcos. Unfortunately, the skeletons which had killed Rolit now advanced towards them. Withdrawing his weapon, Ontar offered Echo an arm to help her run while making their escape. Together, they reached their horses and quickly mounted up. Eager to put the cemetery behind them, they rode off into the night as fast as they possibly could.

Mildly interested in the thieves' escape, Narcos was tempted to send the banshee after them, but since her deadly wail might hurt him as well, he decided instead to turn his attention elsewhere. Calling out to the skeletons, he said. "Bring the man you killed to me."

Following orders, two skeletons grabbed Rolit's corpse by the arms and dragged it back to the mausoleum. Impressed by his minions' handiwork, Narcos saw that Rolit's left eye and cheek had been torn out while a skeletal arm dangled from a bloody hole in his chest. For many, it would be considered a gruesome sight to behold. Narcos, however, dwelled amongst the dead and was quite used to seeing such things.

Raising his hand over the corpse, he closed his eyes and let his soul cry out to the god of death for the power he needed to bring back the dead. A frighteningly cold sensation ran through Narcos in a clear sign that Kardok had answered his prayers. Uttering the words necessary to harness this power, he felt the chill leave his body and pass into the one before him. Rolit's corpse tensed for just a moment…then, slowly, it rolled onto its hands and knees. Getting up to stand by the skeletons at its side, the zombie slouched as it stared vacantly at its new master.

Narcos wasted little time gathering the information he sought. "Do you know Lord Marcain?"

The zombie's voice was a slow monotone. *"Yes."*

"Would he still be at the farm the elf had mentioned?" Narcos asked.

"No," the zombie replied.

Not surprised, Narcos then inquired, "Do you know where he's going?"

The answer came easily to the zombie. *"Oneca."*

Familiar with the location, Narcos knew Oneca was a city in the Kingdom of Coronas. "And how will he reach Oneca?"

The zombie revealed Lord Marcain traveled down, *"Rabbit's…Road…"*

Having learned all he needed to, Narcos called out to the banshee, "Rinna, stop all travelers on Rabbit's Road heading towards Oneca. Do not attack Lord Marcain. I will deal with him myself as soon as I arrive."

Nodding, the banshee rose into the sky and laughed fiendishly as she flew south. Confident she would not fail him, Narcos went to gather supplies and raise a horse to begin his journey.

Chapter Two

The smell of incense and the distant sound of a children's choir helped Ontar to relax as he sat up in one of at least a dozen small beds that lined the walls of an infirmary. Arriving in Miltus earlier that morning, he and Echo sought out the Temple of Talana to heal the wounds he had suffered at the cemetery. Having placed his armor and equipment on the floor next to him, Ontar was more than comfortable wearing just a light blue shirt with black pants. Kneeling on the ground beside him, in a white robe and golden pendant, was an elderly cleric, who stretched out his arm and asked, "How does that feel?"

Ontar wiggled his fingers. "Good as new."

"And your hearing?" the cleric asked.

"Couldn't be better if the goddess herself had cured me," Ontar replied. "Although, I do think you should take a look at my friend's leg."

Sitting along the side of a bed next to him, Echo had looked at the room's other injured occupants when she heard what he had said, "No way! Ontar, you know I can recover from wounds far faster than anyone else. The last thing I need is some cleric to glance at my leg and demand I pay for services I didn't need."

"As you wish," the cleric replied as he stood up. "An acolyte will be waiting by the temple doors when you're finished."

Watching the cleric go, Echo grumbled to Ontar, "Damn acolyte cost almost as much to watch our horses as it did for you to get yourself healed."

Ontar leaned over and began the process of putting on his gear. "So, what do we do now?"

"We head back to the farm and look for the real Lord Marcain," Echo declared.

Ontar gave her an odd look. "Why? Even if we could find him, do you really think Narcos wouldn't try to attack us again after what just happened?"

"No," Echo conceded. "But I have to do something! This was my first assignment for the Bloody Side, and it ended in total failure."

Shrugging it off, Ontar said, "Everyone fails at some point."

"Not Searce," Echo began. "Her first assignment for the Bloody Side was to spy on a local lord as one of his servants. Do you know what she did instead? She stole a gown, passed herself off as a countess, and learned enough about the noble's family for the Bloody Side to blackmail them for the next *three* generations."

"That's quite an accomplishment," Ontar admitted.

Echo shook her head glumly. "Yeah, and while she was able to go on and accomplish great things, I'm stuck just trying to figure out how to redeem myself."

Fully equipped, Ontar put on his helmet and stood so he could extend a hand to her. "Don't worry, we'll figure something out."

Grabbing his gauntlet so she could pull herself up, Echo replied, "You have more faith than I do."

❈ ❈ ❈

Exiting the temple through its large double doors, they found themselves descending some broad stone steps at the center of a gray crescent structure dominated by towering columns and tall stained-glass windows. Coming up behind a statue as tall as the building itself, Ontar and Echo saw it depicted a proud mother carrying a small child in each arm. These children each held up a round crystal sun that cast little rainbows in the morning light. Standing next to this statue was a white robed acolyte who held the reins of their horses in his hands.

Taking their animals, Ontar and Echo walked down the busy cobblestone streets of Miltus. Surrounded by people who were going about their daily lives, Echo had always found human cities to be a fascinating contradiction for her. Professionally, she knew a city was the most likely place to find a patron for her more *illicit* activities. However, her elvish background couldn't help but cringe at the destruction humans wrought in the creation of such a settlement.

After all, Miltus was an immense place. Most of the city blocks were comprised of a series of narrow buildings with shingled roofs and stone chimneys that were practically built on top of each other. These structures were painted a variety of different colors and effectively utilized a diverse number of building materials in their creation. Occasionally, a couple of odd trees could be seen growing along the road, or on the lawn of a wealthier household. For the most part, though, nature was soundly supplanted by the grand development of human civilization.

Preferring not to wander aimlessly, Ontar asked, "Where should we go?"

Echo spotted a wooden signpost she'd been looking for and said, "There's a tavern on Wilgen Street called the Peaceful Repose where I was supposed to find a couple of halflings after we delivered Lord Marcain to Narcos. Initially, they would have shown me where the thieves' guild was hidden. Now, I'm just hoping they can keep me from getting expelled from the Bloody Side altogether."

"I don't think I've ever met a halfling before," Ontar mused.

"Me either," Echo conceded. "From what I've heard, they're little barefoot people who build their homes into grassy hills."

Looking around, Ontar said, "A big city like this probably shocked them when they first saw it."

"More than you know," Echo assured him as they turned onto Wilgen Street.

Reaching their destination, Echo handed Ontar the reins of her horse and prepared to enter the building. Outwardly the Peaceful Repose resembled at least a dozen other taverns Echo had seen before. Constructed completely out of wood the establishment was two stories high with a red and yellow stained-glass window on the lower level. The upper floor had some plain shuttered windows that were nestled into the buildings darkly painted framework. A small stable could be seen attached to the left side of the tavern while a hanging sign above the door depicted a sleepy little man peeking his head out of an ale barrel.

Stepping inside, Echo saw a dining hall half-filled with hungry people who ate at round wooden tables while sitting on sturdy stools. A roaring fireplace along the far-right wall accompanied a few rusty chandeliers in providing decent illumination to the tavern. Looking past a couple of serving wenches, Echo saw a prominent bar lined with occupied stools to her left. On one side of the bar was a staircase leading to the tavern's upper levels. On the other side was a swinging door whose sole purpose seemed to be to help waft in the smell of slightly burnt food coming from the kitchen.

Acutely aware she was being watched; Echo glanced at the tavern's other patrons until she spotted the two halflings she was supposed to meet up with. Tempted to go over and strike up a conversation, she diligently reminded herself Ontar still waited patiently outside with their horses. So, instead, she walked up to the bar and tried to get the tavern keeper's attention. Standing next to a recently emptied stool, Echo spotted the man pouring drinks and chatting with some thirsty locals.

Unsure of how long his conversation would last, Echo decided to interrupt him. "Hey, tavern keeper! I'll need lodging and two stalls for my horses."

Turning towards her, the man said, "The name's Gelmar. A room will cost you two copper, and the stalls are four tin."

Echo tried not to wince at the sight of tavern keeper and quickly grabbed the coins from her belt pouch. She had never found humans to be terribly attractive, but Gelmar had obviously been kissed by the ugly fairy. Short, fat, and smelly, he had greasy brown hair that fell to his shoulders. His chin was covered in stubble while his nose and cheeks were overwhelmingly rosy. A *white* apron stained with ale and grease covered the tan shirt he wore along with some brown pants and boots.

Taking her money, Gelmar turned to the wall behind him and grabbed a key off a big rack that had at least a dozen hooks with numbers on it. Handing the key over to Echo, he then barked an order at one of the nearby serving wenches who proceeded to scurry back into the kitchen. Assuming everything was taken care of, Echo left the bar and headed towards the halflings' table.

Echo took a moment to examine the two males who sat there. As their name implied, the halflings probably stood no more than rib high. Their other distinguishing features included fuzzy bare feet and hands with long slender fingers. However, the similarities ended there.

The halfling to Echo's right had a sophisticated look about him. He had short curly brown hair, spectacles, and a dark red scarf, which was wrapped around his neck. His tidy attire consisted of a faded brown jacket with breeches. A slightly darker leather vest could be seen beneath the jacket that matched his weapon belt while also covering a plain white shirt.

The other halfling seemed to be far more rural in appearance. He wore a wide-brimmed straw hat with a dirty tan shirt and some brown breeches. A little tougher looking than his companion, the halfling protected himself with some brown leather armor, which covered his torso, along with a weapon belt. Puffing on a pipe, he briefly glanced at Echo before blowing a ring of smoke into the air.

Peering at Echo through his spectacles, the first halfling became rather excited. "Oh, my goodness! Your name isn't Searce, is it?" he asked in a polite, yet articulate manner.

"No, Searce is my aunt. My name's Echo Karashenmahagensea," she replied. The question had caught Echo a little off guard, but it shouldn't have. The Bloody Side was a predominantly human organization with only a handful of elvish members. Searce just happened to be one of the most infamous of them.

"My apologies. I wasn't even aware Searce had a niece. Please, join us," said the halfling.

Feeling slightly insignificant, Echo pulled up a stool and sat down. "You haven't heard anything about her, have you? We parted ways a while ago, and I would love to know what she's been doing?"

"Last I heard, she had left her homeland to try and find a bandit in Coronas, but that's all I know," the halfling replied.

So, Lydon has returned to Coronas, Echo mused. The choice made sense since a human would be easily spotted in elvish lands. All the same, though, she still wished Searce found the bastard and made him pay for destroying their lives.

Returning her attention to the task at hand, Echo saw Ontar enter the tavern and beckoned him over so she could make a quick introduction. "And here is my partner in crime, Ontar Liongrave."

Ontar gave Echo an annoyed look before greeting the halflings and setting his helmet, backpack, and shield on the floor. Echo followed suit and, together, they sat at the table and ordered some food and drinks from a passing serving wench. Ontar immediately took notice of the girl. She had a long auburn hair with two small braids covering her ears. Her ample breasts were barely contained within a white, short-sleeved shirt and a black bodice. A brown dress matched her shoes and playfully flowed around her long legs. Suddenly, Ontar found himself to be very hungry.

Returning to the conversation at hand, Ontar overheard the halfling with the scarf say, "Well, since you've been so kind as to introduce yourselves, the least we can do is repay the courtesy. My name is Pudge, and this is Stump," he said, motioning to the halfling in the straw hat. "And we're the Hayseed Brothers."

"I see," said Echo. "So, I assume you're our guild contacts."

"Yup," replied Stump.

Ontar immediately pounced on this information. "Did they say anything about Searce or Lydon!?"

"Only that they're somewhere is Coronas," Echo stated. Ontar was obsessed with the idea of facing Lydon in combat. This notion led him to constantly prove his might by challenging their most difficult opponents in battle. Her only fear with this approach was that one day he'd meet someone better than he was and die before he got his chance at vengeance.

A little disappointed with her response, Ontar said, "Ah well...I guess you're stuck with me for a little while longer."

"Oh, the more the merrier!" Pudge exclaimed. "So, dare I ask how your assignment went?"

A sad expression crossed Echo's face. "Terribly..." she began before going into detail about the folly of her quest.

Listening with interest, Pudge waited for her to finish before saying, "Good gracious. I'll admit I expected far more from someone related to Searce. The Bloody Side will not be pleased when they hear of this."

"That's why I'm desperate for a chance to redeem myself," Echo pleaded.

Briefly pausing their conversation, their serving wench returned to the table while carrying a tray with four tankards of ale on it. Passing out the drinks, Ontar gave her an intense look that caused her to linger by his spot for just a moment before she headed back into the kitchen.

Drinking a bit of ale, Ontar set down his tankard and remarked, "Hey, this is pretty good."

"I should certainly hope so," said Pudge. "After all, it is brewed here in Miltus."

"Sip it slow. You'll need it for the meal," Stump warned as he put his pipe away. Surprised at the sudden comment, Ontar and Echo both noticed the halfling spoke with a long slow drawl. Almost like a farmer.

Getting the conversation back on topic, Pudge said, "You know the guild is going to ask a heavy price for you to retain your membership. Even then, you might have to do something extraordinary if you want to stand a chance at rising through the ranks. Fortunately, I think we might be able to help each other out."

"How so?" Echo wondered.

Pudge took a quick drink before enlightening her. "The guild has asked my brother and I to sabotage an exhibit at the city's museum."

Echo gave him a curious look. "That seems like an odd task. Why sabotage an exhibit instead of stealing from it?"

"Because the museum's guards are currently being led by a paladin from the Order of Dargen, who feels it is his sacred duty to protect the artifacts inside," Pudge explained. "Now, if we can get this holy warrior to fail in his divine task, then the museum might consider putting a less pious man in charge who could be swayed by the guild to turn a blind eye when treasures go missing."

Waiting patiently for his meal, Ontar asked, "So, why don't we just kill the paladin?"

"Because the temple can replace him," Stump replied.

"The temple's guardian must appear incompetent for our plan to work. Not dead," Pudge added.

Making her way back to the table, the serving wench carried a large platter of food and another tankard of ale for Stump. Ontar couldn't help but notice that, while handing out the meals, the wench made sure to give him an ample view of her cleavage. With a quick wink, she turned around and headed back towards the bar. Grinning to himself, Ontar and the rest of his dinning companions ate.

Echo thought her food smelled odd as she said, "I don't mind helping you sabotage the museum, but what would Ontar and I get in return for doing so?"

"A pixie," Stump replied with a snicker.

Ontar wasn't sure if he heard the halfling correctly. "A pixie? I thought they were just one of the fey folk who frolicked in the forest with animals?"

Pudge was quick to clarify his brother's comment, "Wink is no ordinary pixie. She originally belonged to the Mage Lord of Sibeia, but after he was deposed for treason, she was given to the mages' guild for study."

Ontar and Echo were leery of anything that had to do with Sibeia. This was because both of their homelands had fought in punishing wars against the hated nation. Considered to be one of the most powerful countries in the Rashben Region, it was Sibeia's skill at blending arms with magic that made it such a formidable foe. Ruled by six lords, the country's leaders were known to be greedy, conniving, backstabbers who probably didn't even hesitate to turn on one of their own.

Realizing Pudge was still talking, the two immediately refocused their attention. "...so, when Stump and I learned of the pixie, we figured she probably knew where the mage lord had kept some of his most valuable treasures. That's when we decided to break into the mages' guild and steal her."

"Sounds like a difficult job," Echo commented.

"Oh, it was," Pudge said. However, that excitement quickly turned to disappointment. "You see, Wink knows the location of a powerful magic sword called Spirit Slayer, but she wouldn't reveal its location unless we rescued her former master from a Sibeian dungeon. Afraid the treacherous mage lord might turn on us once we released him, Stump and I decided the risk wasn't worth the reward."

"And we've been stuck with her ever since," Stump grumbled.

Echo's mind whirled with possibilities. "This is just the quest I'm looking for! Retrieving Spirit Slayer for the guild would easily justify retaining my membership while sneaking the mage lord out of a dungeon would demonstrate how I could be of use for future assignments."

"Echo, are you sure you want to risk dealing with another magic user? Especially after the last one tried to kill us?" Ontar asked.

Sipping her stew, Echo replied, "If you can think of a better solution, I'd like to hear it?" Seconds later, she added, "Blech! This stew is all broth, and the rolls are as hard as rocks."

"Told ya you'd need the ale for yer meal," Stump stated in-between gulps from his beverage.

Ontar had to admit his food wasn't much better. The beans were alright, but the roast was terribly dry...then inspiration struck. "That's it! I did not travel two days just to eat this pathetic excuse for a roast!" he said in mock outrage. Slamming his hands on the table, Ontar pushed himself up and stomped over towards the bar. Suspicious of his motives, Echo watched him go and listened intently to what he had to say.

Seeing the serving wench talking to a coworker, Ontar approached the bar and got her attention. "Hello, my name is Ontar. I'm sure by now you've caught me staring at you from my table, and I wish to apologize. It's just that traveling with an elf has blinded me to the beauty of other women for such a long time...that is, until I saw you."

The wench blushed, and Echo seethed. The thought of that horny idiot using HER to bed some gullible slut was infuriating. She was definitely going to have some words with him later. Turning her attention back to the halflings, Echo told them, "We're in."

"Wonderful," exclaimed Pudge. "I was just going to go survey the museum to help prepare for a nighttime entry. Would you care to join me?"

"Absolutely," Echo said as she and the halfling stood up to-gether. "The last thing I want to do right now is watch Ontar get rejected while eating a lousy meal."

Turning to his brother, Pudge asked, "Will you be joining us?"

"Nope. I like the show right here," Stump replied as he drank his beverage.

Pudge merely shrugged. "As you wish. We shall return later."

Gathering her equipment, Echo handed Stump a room key. "Give this to Ontar and tell him the girl had better be gone by the time I get back."

Stump took the key and put it in his belt pouch. As he did, Pudge and Echo got up and left the tavern.

A few hours later, Ontar found he was extremely close to accomplishing his objective. With most of the tavern's regu-lar patrons off to work, Mirta's duties had slowed to a point where she could share a drink with him at the bar. Ontar soon regaled her with stories of his daring exploits, while Mirta talked about the unique (and often hilarious) people she had to serve.

Sensing the moment was right, Ontar asked, "So, when do you finish work?"

Mirta smiled sat him and said. "About half an hour ago."

Ontar was about to propose she join him in his room when a wench came up to her and pointed towards the tavern's entrance. "Hey, Mirta, Hargil's here."

Clearly annoyed, Ontar turned around and saw a young, lean, bald man with tattoos covering his arms standing in the doorway. "Who's that?" he asked.

"My suitor," Mirta said as she stood up to leave.

Ontar looked at her in dismay. "I can't believe this. You're going to leave *me* for *him*? What in the world does he got that don't?"

"A big cock and lots of money," replied Mirta with a laugh as she walked towards the tavern's exit. Hargil put his arm around her shoulder, and the two departed.

Ontar's shoulders sagged. *Damn tease!* he thought. Heading over to his table, he noticed Stump was blowing smoke rings with his pipe. "Looks like you got abandoned faster than a eunuch at a brothel."

"Love is a game of chance," Ontar retorted. "Sometimes you win, and sometimes you lose."

Stump snorted when he heard this. "Personally, I'd prefer to play cards. The odds are usually better, and you get to keep your dignity."

"Do you have a deck?" Ontar asked.

Standing up and waving for Ontar to follow him, Stump said, "Yeah, come on. I got them up in my room."

Eager to meet the pixie the halflings had been talking about, Ontar followed Stump up the stairs to the tavern's second level. Handing Ontar the key Echo had given him, Stump went on to unlock the door to his room, while Ontar scanned the hallway to see where he would be staying. Suddenly, he heard a small cry from behind Stump's door that caught his attention. Listening closer, Ontar heard the cry again and furrowed his brow. It almost sounded like high-pitched weeping to the perplexed warrior.

Opening the door, Stump entered a small room with two beds that flanked a candle on a nightstand near the window. Resting on the floor between the beds was an elegant golden birdcage. However, peering down into the cage, Ontar saw something that was definitely *not* a bird. In fact, the cage seemed to contain a tiny person in it that couldn't have been any larger than a foot tall.

Huddled on the cage floor with her arms wrapped around her knees and her head bowed, Ontar couldn't help but feel sorry for the poor little prisoner. While a wide brimmed green hat obscured much of her facial features, Ontar could tell she was a female thanks to the sleeveless, form-fitting green dress she wore. She even had on a cute pair of tiny green shoes that curled upward at the toe. The miniature woman had obviously been crying as she tried to stifle a whimper at the sound of the door opening.

"Is that Wink?" he asked Stump while gesturing towards the cage.

"Yeah, I suppose," the halfling said while reaching over the cage to get at some cards on the nightstand.

"What's that bastard said about me!?" squeaked a high-pitched voice as the little woman suddenly stood up in her cage. Wink looked like a beautifully tanned teenage girl. Her long dark red hair was curly, and a handful of freckles could be seen just beneath her big brown eyes, which burned with an indomitable spirit. Of course, Ontar couldn't help but notice she also had long slender legs and full round breasts, which served to remind him she certainly was no child. Sadly, Wink was forced to wear a thick golden collar around her neck, with a long chain that connected to the cages floor.

Offering comforting words, Ontar said, "Don't worry about the halflings. By tomorrow, I promise you'll be free."

Wink's eyes lit up when she heard this. "Are you serious? Oh, please, tell me you're serious. I can't stand this cage anymore."

"Eh, shut yer yap," said Stump as he took the cards and shooed Ontar out of the room.

"Will she be alright?" Ontar asked while looking down at her cage.

"Yeah, yeah," Stump said as he tried to close the door behind them.

Wink pressed herself up against the cage bars and pleaded, "Don't go, please. I need you!"

Standing in the hallway, Ontar didn't have a chance to respond before Stump shut the door to his room and locked it. Troubled over the pixie's plight, Ontar reluctantly followed the halfling back downstairs.

Chapter Three

It was a busy afternoon on the streets of Miltus. Everywhere Echo looked, she saw humans racing towards this destination or that. Street performers played lively tunes on their instruments, while draft horses pulled merchant carts towards the market. A few beggars could be seen sitting in the corners of dark alleyways not far from a boisterous city crier, who loudly proclaimed the day's events.

Echo was grateful to have Pudge at her side. The halfling easily knew the ins and outs of Miltus and was an excellent guide. Together, they eagerly discussed a fun little scam that would help them gain free admission into the museum.

Arriving at the building in question, Echo had to admit that it was a magnificent structure. Two rearing unicorn statues were placed on either side of a broad stairway that led up to a row of gray stone pillars which supported the museum's gabled roof. A number of heroic statues were placed in front of the gable, and Echo could have sworn she saw a small dome centered on the top of the building. Ready to experience some high human culture, Echo and Pudge ascended the stairs, opened a pair of tall wooden doors, and entered the museum.

⊹⊹⊹

The buildings foyer was quite large and had an artistic chandelier hanging overhead. Walking across the polished floor Echo and Pudge saw the foyer's side walls had little nooks carved into them containing various busts of important people on pedestals. Looking ahead, they saw a prominent wall with a decorative arched doorway located at its center. To the doorway's left was an enormous world map of Calatan. On the right was a detailed map of the Rashben Region. In front of the doorway was a wooden podium with a collection box on it.

Standing behind the podium was a slender old man with a stylish gray goatee and short, well-groomed hair. Assuming he was the curator, Echo saw two spear-wielding guards that flanked the museum's entrance. Wearing iron pot helmets with studded rims and leather weapon belts that had short swords in them, these guards were clad from head to toe in chain armor covered by a brown surcoat depicting the profile of a white bust on their chest.

The curator cocked an eyebrow as Echo and Pudge approached. "May I help you?" he asked in a manner a little too condescending for Echo's tastes.

"Yes, my friend and I would like to purchase admission to your beautiful museum," Pudge stated politely.

"I'm sure you would," said the curator. "Unfortunately, this is a *dignified* institution that requires appropriate attire from *all* its patrons in order to gain admittance. Attire *you* clearly lack," proclaimed the uppity human in reference to their rugged clothes and Pudge's fuzzy bare feet.

Pudge wiggled his toes, then looked up at Echo to see a twinkle in her eyes. Feigning disappointment, she shrugged and muttered, "I should have known we'd have to put up with this primitive human nonsense."

The curator was aghast. "Excuse me!" he said.

Echo smugly commented. "*My* people have learned the value of accepting the cultural differences of other races well over a thousand of years ago. It's a pity *humans* are still so uncivilized you've failed to grasp even this most simple of concepts."

The curator turned red with anger. "You have no idea of how advanced our society is." Regaining his composure, the human backtracked slightly. "I simply made the assumption you and the halfling would not be able to afford the museum's admittance fee based on your present attire.

"How much?" Echo asked.

"Two silver," the curator replied.

Echo mentally winced at the price. Two silver to see a bunch of dusty artifacts was ridiculous! However, she had a plan and smoothly moved her hand over her belt pouch. At that same moment, Pudge reached into his own pouch and pulled out a small number of coins. Echo then proceeded to pass her hand over the collection box. As she did so, Pudge inconspicuously dropped his coins onto the floor.

Turning towards him in false anger, Echo said, "Dammit, Pudge, let me handle this!"

The halfling knelt to pick up his coins. "I'm sorry, I'm sorry. I'm just so distraught by what that awful man just said."

Turning towards the curator, Echo stared him in the eye. "Don't worry about it. I'm sure that one day his people will eventually rise to reach *our* level."

Not waiting for a response, Echo moved past the curator and entered the museum. Pudge quickly followed behind her.

Fuming, the curator glared at Echo. Refusing to take his eyes off her, he spoke with a sneer to a nearby guard, saying, "Summon Yalard."

Echo reveled in her verbal victory over the curator, and it put her in a pleasant mood while she toured the museum. The building's interior was just as splendid as its exterior, with multiple exhibits featuring eloquent paintings, breath taking sculptures, and priceless artifacts. Most of which originated in Lareder.

One particular display case which caught Echo's eye was situated beneath the portrait of a king. Within it was a golden crown and scepter along with several other relics of royal authority.

"What's all this?" she asked in wonder.

"The crown jewels of King Miset. Last ruler of Miltus before it was conquered by Lareder," Pudge read aloud from a plaque on the display case. He grimaced. "It looks like the good king here was captured by invading forces, publicly tortured, and ripped to pieces by ravenous dogs."

Echo grimaced. "Ugh…that's brutal."

"Yes, indeed," Pudge noted. "It appears that Lareder's rise to power came when it led city-states like this into battle against the remnants of the Ha-Ress Empire. Sadly, it later turned on these allies in order to create the kingdom it is today."

Ignoring the history, Echo quietly asked, "So, what do you think about swiping the jewels when we come back here tonight?"

"We can't," Pudge said. Stealing from the museum would lead to a search that could implicate the Bloody Side. Sabotage, on the other hand, keeps focus exclusively on the paladin."

"Huh, a thief who doesn't want to steal…now, isn't that ironic," Echo remarked.

Pudge chuckled when he heard this. "My brother and I didn't start out as thieves. Originally, our parents owned an unsuccessful bookstore, and while I spent my time reading tomes and praying for customers, Stump was busy working at grueling jobs to support our family. Neither of us were terribly successful at what we did so we turned to more illicit activities to get by."

"I guess you do what you have to in life," Echo concluded.

"Exactly," Pudge said with a grin.

Passing by a couple of nobly dressed aristocrats, Echo and Pudge ignored their disapproving whispers and entered a hall labeled "Illamine." Standing in this place, Echo was suddenly overcome by a wave of homesickness as she saw an enormous tapestry depicting an apple tree beneath a cloudy blue sky. It was the emblem of her country, and all around her were various elvish artifacts on exhibit. While wood elves and high elves comprised the bulk of the Illamines' population, there were still a couple of trinkets displayed from the avians, fairies, nymphs, and leprechauns that also inhabited the territory.

Glancing about the hall, Echo couldn't help but chuckle at the foolishness of the museum's curator. In truth, the exhibited relics *were* hundreds of years old, but in a society where every citizen had the potential of living forever, this *collection* was really nothing more than a beautifully arranged pile of junk. Still, it was nice getting a taste of home, and Echo stood by quietly while Pudge thoroughly explored the area.

As he finished up, Echo decided to ask him. "So, do you think we'll find a halfling exhibit around here?"

"Oh, I doubt that," said Pudge. "Museums tend to cater to those races that have forged mighty empires. My people are simply content to live within those empires instead of trying to fashion one of our own."

"Well, we'll just have to show the people of this museum what happens when they ignore the humble races now won't we," Echo stated.

Pudge grinned in approval. "Yes, indeed."

Leaving her homeland's exhibit behind, Echo and Pudge entered the museum's rotunda. It was an enormous two-storied space with a domed roof and a railed walkway that rounded the entire second level. In the center of the rotunda was an immense white marble statue of a bearded merman with his trident majestically pointed upwards.

Pointing to the roof while nudging Echo, Pudge discreetly said, "The dome's constructed out of thin material that should be fairly easy for us to break through. We'll come in from up there and use a rope to reach the first floor."

Echo merely nodded as they moved around the statue. Following Pudge's lead, the two continued to their primary destination where they found a chamber with two guards standing on either side of an archway whose plaque read: "Enchanted Artifacts." Passing through the open archway, the two entered into a room with a much higher ceiling than any of the ones they'd been in before. In truth, *ceiling* might have been far too generous a term since the area above them was covered in pullies, chains, gears, and other unfamiliar mechanisms. Dangling from the ceiling at random points across the chamber were several chains with heavy hooks attached at their ends.

Suspended from four of these chains in the center of the room was an artistically crafted stone platform, which hung roughly six feet off the ground. Placed in the center of this platform was a simple gray statue that resembled a gorilla sitting cross-legged with its hands folded in prayer. A plethora of other artifacts could also be seen lining the chamber's walls for those who cared to admire them.

"What is this?" Echo inquired.

"I believe it's some sort of elaborate trap," Pudge guessed. "They probably don't activate it until nightfall."

Bending over to whisper in his ear, Echo asked, "Is this what we have to sabotage for the guild?"

Pudge shook his head. "Not exactly. Our goal is to distract the guards by luring them into this trap while we ransack the museum."

Afraid of being overheard, Echo led Pudge out of the chamber and back to the rotunda. "How are we going to lead the guards into a trap they already know about?"

"Good question," Pudge replied before Echo briefly put a finger to his lips.

Listening to the clamor of armor with her keen, pointed ears, she soon saw a man standing on the walkway above them who was unabashedly staring their direction. A warrior of stern disposition, Echo saw he wore a suit of plate armor with bits of chain covering the joints. His surcoat resembled that of the other museum guards except for the emblem on his chest, which depicted an anvil with a quill pen in front of it. A violet cape graced his shoulders, while a shield bearing his orders emblem was strapped to his back. His face was framed by a plain iron helmet that helped accentuate his brown moustache.

Motioning to Pudge, she said, "I think that's the paladin you were telling me about."

Pudge agreed, "The curator probably sent him to keep an eye on us."

"Well, he certainly isn't much of a spy," Echo muttered. "However, I think it might be good to take the hint and leave while we can."

Nodding in agreement, Pudge followed Echo out of the museum.

Watching them go, Yalard stood for a moment with his hands braced on the walkway's railing. The curator was right to be suspicious of those two. Their hasty departure upon seeing him was extremely suspicious. Leaving the rotunda, he walked down a wide corridor past two wealthy (yet curious) visitors. Finding a nearby guard, Yalard approached the sentry and said, "Rally the men. I want to double our numbers for the next few days."

"Yes, sir," said the guard as he saluted before setting about on his newly-assigned task. As the man departed, Yalard sighed and hoped his precaution would prove to be an unnecessary one.

Returning to the Peaceful Repose, Echo and Pudge entered the tavern and found Ontar and Stump sitting at a nearby table playing cards. Evidently, Stump was winning the game since he had most of the coins resting in front of him.

Approaching the table, Echo adopted a nagging tone. "That girl's not still in our room, is she?"

Ontar shook his head. "Nope, she never made it."

"She turned him down hard," Stump added while clenching a pipe between his teeth and blowing smoke through his nose.

Echo was impressed. "Huh, I guess even serving wenches have standards."

Ontar groaned as he laid down his cards. He'd been dealt a bad hand twice in a row, and now Stump was set to claim all the money he had brought to the table. That is until Pudge mentioned, "You know, dear brother, that the gods *do* punish those who cheat their friends at cards."

"Aw, shit!" Stump grumbled.

"What do you mean?" Ontar asked in surprise.

Pudge explained, "Stump's been cheating. You can always tell because when he does, he can't help but blow smoke out his nose."

"Is this true?" Ontar asked Stump in anger.

"Yup," said the halfling. He then slid all his winnings towards Ontar and collected his cards.

Giving Stump the evil eye, Ontar collected the coins and slipped them into a belt pouch. "My apologies," said Pudge. "It's terribly hard for us to find people we can trust in our line of work, and unlike my brother, I've always found it's more important to have friends you can rely on over being wealthy and alone."

Stump scoffed at the notion.

Echo interjected, "Hey, speaking of divine punishment, Pudge and I spotted the paladin leading the museum's guards. So, we'll have to be watchful for any sign of holy magic."

"You didn't do anything to raise suspicion that we might target the museum tonight, did you?" asked Ontar.

"Well, I did have an argument with the curator, but the man was a complete ass," Echo said.

Ontar sighed. "Alright, well, it looks like we might have some extra guards to deal with then." Standing, he moved away from the table. "I'm going to go catch a nap since who knows how late we'll be up tonight."

Pudge nodded in agreement. "I think I'll join you. It's always better to be fresh faced for these sorts of things. Stump, are you coming, too?"

Stump nodded. "Yeah, I'll be right there."

Echo shook her head at the other race's propensity for sleep. Heading towards her room, she tried not to disturb Ontar as he settled into bed. Setting down her shield and backpack, she rummaged through it until she found a slender wooden flute. Returning to the dining hall, Echo pulled a stool up by the fireplace, sat down, and played.

Like all elves, Echo had a natural affinity towards music, and for the next couple of hours, she played songs both merry and sad to the delight of the tavern's patrons. At one point, she had just finished with a lively tune when the tavern keeper came up to her and said, "I ain't payin' for the music."

"I wouldn't dream of it," Echo replied dryly before continuing with her next song.

Evening approached, and Ontar came down to dinner fully equipped in battle gear. Pudge and Stump followed closely behind with backpacks and a spear now in Stump's hand. Gathering for a bland meal, the party ate quietly and waited for Echo to get her equipment. Ignoring curious whispers from the tavern's other patrons the four companions stood ready for action and quietly headed out into the night.

The flickering streetlamps of Miltus revealed a relatively quiet city as the party cautiously made their way towards the museum. Taking the lead Pudge and Stump kept a vigilant watch for patrolling guards and successfully led their comrades to the building without incident. Entering a side alley next to the museum, Pudge reached into Stump's backpack and removed a rope and grapple. Tying the two together, Pudge spun the grapple in his hand before tossing it up the side of the building. Hearing the satisfying *clang* of contact with the roof, Pudge then pulled on the rope until it was taught.

While he did this, Stump slipped his spear into his belt and prepared to climb the rope. The Hayseed Brothers went first, followed by Echo.

Ontar frowned at the others' agility. He knew he was not built to go nimbly scurrying up the sides of buildings, but resigned to his fate, the big warrior put on his helmet, grabbed the rope, and made a difficult attempt at climbing up. It didn't go well. Strong as Ontar was, the dead weight from his armor, backpack, and shield were just too much for him to carry. Unable to go any further, he slowly climbed down the short distance he'd been able to cover.

Crouched amongst the brown tiles of the museum's roof, Echo looked back along the rope and whispered, "Ontar! What are you doing?"

Ontar shouted back, "My equipment's too heavy. I can't pull myself up."

Echo tensed at the noise he made and put a finger to her lips. "So, drop it in the alley and get up here."

"I'm not going to leave my stuff in an alley for some beggar to steal," Ontar complained.

Again! Echo wanted to strangle him for all the noise he made. Before she could shout back, though, Pudge moved next to her, popped his head over the side, and said, "Ontar, tie the rope around your waist and we'll pull you up."

"Are you kidding? He's going to break our backs!" Echo complained.

"It's the only way to get him up here," Pudge whispered.

Deep down, Echo knew it was a good idea, but she couldn't help but wish Ontar would lose a little of his junk for all the noise he'd made. "Alright," she grumbled.

Stump moved across the roof and tied the rope to a nearby statue. At the same time, Ontar tied the other end of the rope around his waist and held on tight as it went taught. Once this was done, Echo and the Hayseed Brothers began the grueling task of pulling Ontar up the side of the building. The hoisting took far longer than anyone really liked but, in the end, Ontar was finally able to pull himself onto the roof.

"Thanks." he said, genuinely grateful for the others' help.

"Don't thank us yet," Echo said. "You're the first one going down into the museum."

On that note, the Hayseed Brothers scrambled across the roof and stopped directly in front of the building's dome. Reaching into Pudge's backpack, Stump removed a hammer and chisel. He then pounded a small hole in the dome while Pudge retrieved the grappling hook. Curious, Ontar and Echo approached the dome to see what the halflings were doing. Moving with practiced ease, Pudge hooked the grapple and rope into the dome's tiny hole while Stump cracked a wider opening. When the hammering was done, Pudge pulled on the rope and removed the chiseled piece of dome. A sizable opening was now available for the party to squeeze though.

Ontar peered into the hole. "Hmmm. Looks like its pitch-black down there," he observed.

Echo slid her backpack down on one shoulder. "Well, let's light your way then," she said as she pulled out a torch with some flint and steel. Lighting it, she gave the torch to Ontar before repositioning her equipment.

"After you," she said, gesturing towards the hole.

Making sure the rope was still tight around his waist, Ontar went over to the opening and climbed through. Once again, Echo and the Hayseed Brothers manned the rope while lowering Ontar into the museum.

Slowly descending into the building, Ontar couldn't help but be a little disconcerted when he saw an enormous merman statue with a trident pointed straight at his head! Staying calm, he held out his torch and got a clear view of the rotunda while being lowered to the floor below.

Grateful when his feet touched the ground, Ontar had just finished untying the rope from around his waist when he saw a light coming from the corridor in front of him. Dropping his torch, Ontar drew his morning star and shield right before he heard the *snap* of a leather leash and the low growl of a vicious animal. Ready for trouble, Ontar spun his morning star the moment he saw a big black dog on a short leash come into view. The leash was being held in the left hand of a surprised guard who happened to be carrying a candlestick in his right one. Dropping the candle and releasing the leash, the guard quickly grabbed at the short sword on his weapon belt.

Seeing a stranger, the dog immediately ran towards Ontar and leapt for his throat. Ontar knew the animal couldn't pierce his armor and that its attack was based on pure instinct. Moving his tower shield in front of him, he braced for impact as the dumb dog slammed snout first into the flat piece of metal. The animal fell to the floor with a whimper.

Alerted to his second enemy, Ontar heard the guard shout, "Intruder," before charging the warrior with his sword raised. Ontar couldn't help but think how sad it was when man reflected animal in battle. As the guard surged forward, Ontar used his weapon to knock aside the tip of his blade. Unfortunately, the guard's momentum continued to carry him forward, which brought his head directly into the arc of Ontar's morning star! The poor man fell right on top of his dog while bleeding from a wound to the temple. Ontar ended both their lives a moment later. By the time Echo and the halflings had managed to climb down the rope, he had already checked the rotunda's entrances for additional enemies.

Looking over the dead man's body, Echo turned to Ontar and said, "Shit! We weren't supposed to kill anyone. Now, the city guards will be looking for a murderer instead of focusing on an inept paladin!"

Pudge tried to calm the frantic elf. "Don't worry, all we have to do is bring the bodies to the artifact room and people will think they died in the trap."

"Well, you're dragging the guard over there!" Echo told Ontar.

Taking the dead dog by the tail, Stump asked Ontar, "How long do you think we have before reinforcements arrive?"

Ontar withdrew his shield and weapon so he could grab the guard's body. "That all depends on when he started his rounds. Fortunately, I was able to take him out before he sounded too much of a warning."

"Then I suggest we utilize the time we have effectively," Pudge said as he grabbed both the candlestick and torch.

❦ ❦ ❦

Carrying their burden to the chamber where the enchanted artifacts were kept, the party saw that all the artifacts themselves had been placed on daises that were attached to hooks and pulled up by chains into the gear-filled ceiling. This left only the cross-legged gorilla hanging from its spot in the middle of the room.

Being the first to enter the chamber, Echo saw all the artifacts were in the ceiling and said, "Huh, doesn't look like we could steal anything from this room even if we wanted to."

This offhanded comment triggered a loud echoing voice from deep within the statue in front of them:

**Silence! You who seek the treasures of this place
be wary.
I am the chain guardian, and only those who display great wisdom may claim their reward.**

"Well, we're doomed." Stump stated dryly before being shushed by his brother. The guardian continued:

**If you wish to claim these riches, then name a gift
that's priceless.
That can't be bought or sold.
But by value is far greater.
Then a mountain made of gold.**

Dropping the candlestick, Pudge put a finger to his lips and slowly backed out of the chamber. Ontar and Stump did the same thing with the dead dog and guard while Echo followed behind them. Returning to the rotunda, Echo heard footsteps running along the stone floor and said, "The guards must have heard the guardian and are headed this way."

Grabbing the rope they had climbed down on, Stump said, "We have to get out of here!"

Ontar shook his head. "There won't be enough time to climb out. We'll have to hide in the museum."

"But how are we going to trigger the trap?" Pudge fretted.

"Don't worry, I know a spell that can help us," Echo told them. "Now, go!"

Watching her companions flee down a corridor opposite of the guards, Echo closed her eyes, took a deep breath, and re-laxed. As an inner peace swept through her body, she felt her senses tingle and expand to the world around her. Magic was everywhere. Pure, raw, and wild, it surrounded her as if she waded through water while being caressed by a breeze all at the same time.

Then she spoke. Her words drew in the untamed power that swirled about her. She gave it form and shaped it to her will. In an instant, she felt her senses being drawn back to the corporeal world, carrying the power she had forged with them. The magic now had a purpose, and as Echo finished casting her spell, she felt its essence washing over her. Opening her eyes, she looked down at her body and saw that it had become nothing more than a mere shadow.

Success, she thought excitedly! Examining her figure, Echo felt no different and knew that physically she was completely unchanged. However, her external appearance now resembled that of a shadow. Crouching near the dark corridor where her friends had escaped, she quietly waited as the guards approached.

Yalard held his flickering candlestick close to two ornate suits of armor clutching antique swords in their lifeless gauntlets. Reading a plaque on the wall between them, he learned the armor once belonged to two knights who had survived the siege of Miltus during Lareder's war with Sibeia. The paladin mentally cringed at the thought of what could have happened to the city were it not for the reinforcements that had arrived from the neighboring kingdom of Coronas. In truth, Sibeia's very creation was in response to Lareder's brutal expansion northward, and the realm learned a terrible lesson that nearly destroyed it in the process.

Stepping back into the center of the corridor, Yalard refocused his attention on a guard named Nelk, who approached the holy warrior with a worried look in his eyes.

"What's wrong?" Yalard asked.

Filled with a sense of urgency, Nelk replied, "It's the chain guardian! I heard him speaking from across the museum."

"Gather the men and have them meet me in the rotunda," Yalard instructed. "Let's find out who was stupid enough to rouse that thing in the first place."

Rushing towards the rotunda, Yalard, Nelk, and two other guards met at the merman statue. "Look!" Nelk exclaimed as he pointed to a rope hanging from a newly-created crack in the dome above.

"Sneaky bastard. Someone has broken into the museum," Yalard said as he set down his candlestick and drew forth a sword and shield. Seeing the other guards all held their spears at the ready, he noticed there were drops of blood scattered across the floor and asked, "Where's Sart and Bruiser?"

"We haven't seen them," Nelk confessed, "but there's a light coming from the Enchanted Artifacts exhibit."

Pointing his blade, Yalard exclaimed, "Let's go!"

Shit, they know we're here! Echo thought upon seeing the rope. Following them in her shadowy form, she knew Pudge's careful plans were about to go terribly awry.

Entering the exhibit with his fellow guards, Nelk saw Sart's body lying on the floor and ran to his side. "Sart...NO!"

Roused by the presence of intruders, the chain guardian once again uttered his signature speech. **"Silence! You who seek..."**

Hidden from view just beyond the exhibit's entrance, Echo knew that, if she was going to activate the trap, now was the time to do it. Waiting until the riddles end, she shouted, "ARMORED IDIOTS!" in an act that canceled her spell and made her visible once again. Running before anyone could catch a glimpse of her, she quickly sought out her companions.

"Who was that!?" Yalard exclaimed to the guards at his side. Realizing why the mysterious woman had decided to speak up when she did, the chain guardian loudly proclaimed the answer given for its riddle was: **"Wrong!"**

All of a sudden, a burst of activity could be heard from the roof above as the loud rattle of chains preceded the guardian's platform being rapidly hoisted up towards the ceiling. As the guardian went up, a dozen hooked chains dropped onto the guards in what appeared to be multiple attacks at once. Clutching their weapons, the men scattered while dodging this way and that to avoid being struck by the menacing hooks.

Blessed with a shield, Yalard raised it to protect himself from a hook that crashed into him. Defending against the initial blow, he groaned as the chain it was attached to came down at a pace that threatened to bury him alive!

The guard at his side fared little better. His spear was jerked out of his hands by a heavy hook just before two more pummeled him to death. Horrified by what was happening, Nelk didn't even notice when a hook swung into his armpit from behind and pulled him up to be ground by the gears above! The last guard suffered a similar fate as he was crushed beneath the platform of a heavy exhibit dropped from the ceiling.

Refusing to die in this place, Yalard uttered the spell word, "Heavy," which pulled the chain guardian down to the floor while briefly stopping the hooks it used in battle. Taking advantage of the situation, Yalard climbed out of the chain pile that buried his legs and fled the chamber as fast as possible. Devastated by the loss of his men, Yalard saw the rope was still hanging in the rotunda and swore vengeance.

Returning to the spot where he had been admiring the two suits of armor, Yalard held his sword with its tip to the ground then got down on one knee and prayed. As he did, he felt his soul desperately cry out for Dargen to give him the power he needed to defeat his enemies. The god, in his benevolence, answered Yalard's prayer, and a pure indescribable energy flowed through him.

Channeling this divine gift, Yalard cast a spell that illuminated his blade with a dull white light. That light was then surrounded by a wispy, glowing mist. Standing up, Yalard slowly pointed his sword at each of the two suits of armor. This action was accompanied by the glowing mist slowly stretching from his blade to envelop its intended targets. Raising the sword to his face, Yalard closed his eyes and concentrated. Time stood still for the paladin as the old suits of armor shuddered and moved. Stepping back while opening his eyes, Yalard watched as the mist covered suits of armor grabbed the swords in front of them so they could be hoisted in a majestic salute.

Thinking back to those who had fallen, Yalard said, "Rest in peace, my friends. Dargen has blessed me with the ability to guarantee your loss will not be in vain."

❦ ❦ ❦

Unaware of what the paladin was up to, Echo found herself running through the museum in search of her companions. Following the light from Pudge's torch, she startled them with her sudden appearance as she ran into a room filled with fancy portraits. "The paladin knows we're here! He saw the rope we used to get in. I triggered the trap in the exhibit room, but if he survived, then there's no doubt he'll have the city guards out searching for us."

"So much for sabotage," Stump said while clutching his spear in both hands.

Pudge let out a disappointed sigh as he drew forth his short sword. "Damn, I was hoping it wouldn't come to this. Now, the only way to hide our involvement is to kill the paladin ourselves."

"Which we should have done in the first place," Ontar noted.

Drawing her sword and shield, Echo said, "He still might have been killed by the trap."

"I'll believe it when I see it," Stump grumbled.

Cautiously returning to the rotunda, the party saw Yalard standing in front of the statue with two suits of armor at his side covered in a glowing mist. Angrily pointing his sword at the party, the paladin said, "Intruders beware! This museum has fallen under the divine protection of Dargen the Creator. As a vessel of his omnipotent will, I tell you now to drop your weapons and surrender yourself for judgement. Failure to do so will leave me no choice but enact his wrath upon you."

"Oh, dear," Pudge began. "Please, tell Dargen this is nothing personal but…"

Spinning his morning star, Ontar thought. *If I can defeat you, then I can defeat Lydon,* before telling his companions that, "The paladin is mine. All you have to do is finish the others, and we can get out of here."

"I have offered you mercy, but by refusing to accept it, your fate has been sealed. Prepare yourselves!" Yalard warned.

Nodding to his brother before charging into battle, Stump darted to his left and attacked one of the suits of armor surrounded by glowing mist. Moving with uncanny speed, he thrust his spear straight into the armor's breastplate. Refusing to allow it reaction time, Pudge came in along the armor's right side and slashed at its hip. The armor seemed unfazed by the attacks. Grabbing at the spear with its left gauntlet, it jerked out the weapon with enough force to push Stump back. Then, taking its sword, the armor made a downward slice straight at Pudge. The halfling dodged the blade and sparks flew as it struck against the ground.

Echo initially followed the halflings, but then veered right to face her own armored menace. Moving in for a quick attack, it was almost painful for her to see how slow the armor was when she swung her sword for a successful cut along its neckline. Ignoring a strike that would have otherwise killed a living combatant, the armor raised its sword above its head and swung down at her. Echo lifted her blade to parry the attack, and the two locked weapons in an intense battle of strength.

Yalard saw the intruders go after his armored minions and wished he could aid them, but before that could happen, the paladin was forced to contend with the menacing warrior who approached him. Ontar eagerly spun his morning star and looked fully ready to use it. Letting out a battle cry Yalard surged towards him and swung his glowing blade.

Batting aside the sword with his weapon, Ontar directed his morning star straight at the paladin's chest. Unwilling to yield an easy victory, Yalard raised his shield and blocked the attack.

Yalard knew he was up against a skilled opponent, and a part of him wanted to engage the warrior in a noble fight. The only problem with that notion was there was a slight possibility he'd lose. Unwilling to take that chance, Yalard drew upon the power of his god and said a single word, "Heavy."

Ontar's morning star immediately lost momentum and threw him off balance. Strangely enough, it seemed almost as if the weapon had suddenly gained five pounds.

Yalard was prepared for this and thrust his sword straight at Ontar's head.

Ontar barely had time to react. Fortunately, the spell had made his movements erratic, which helped him when he jerked his head away to avoid the paladin's blade. Yalard's sword clipped the side of Ontar's helmet but did little more damage than that. As Ontar regained his footing, his morning star returned to its normal weight.

Stump caught Ontar's fight out of the corner of his eye and knew the warrior could use some help. Thinking of a strategy to beat his nemesis, the halfling waited for his armored foe to strike. Not surprisingly, it didn't take long for the suit of armor to swing its sword straight at the little thief. Diverting the weapon away with the tip of his spear, Stump hoped to create a wide enough opening in his adversary's defense that his brother could easily exploit it. Moving in with his short sword pointed down, Pudge thrust it deep into the armor's knee. Releasing the blade, he stepped back as the metal monster struggled to move its leg. Readying himself for another attack, Stump couldn't help but grin at his suddenly crippled opponent.

Echo, however, wasn't having quite as much luck in her battle. She had crossed swords with a suit of armor that had superior bulk and would soon overpower her weakening arm. Changing tactics, she decided to sidestep the armor and watch as it staggered forward. Now standing behind her enemy, she quickly brought her sword down square on the middle of its back. Falling to one knee, the armor pivoted to face Echo while still holding its blade out defensively.

Focused on his own battle, Ontar took a couple of small steps back from his enemy while swinging his morning star and trying to figure out what just happened. Obviously, a spell of some sort had been cast. The only question was how to get past it. Yalard could sense the warrior's confusion and decided to make the most of it. Uttering the spell word, "Heavy," once again, he attacked his foe the moment his weapon went limp.

Ontar felt his morning star magically get heavier. This time, though, he was prepared for it and brought his shield up to defend against the paladin's sword. *That's enough of this magic bullshit!* he thought as his weapon returned to its normal mass.

Yalard observed his opponent's body language and knew the man was getting frustrated. This was good because an enemy who didn't think clearly often made mistakes during combat. Readying his blade, Yalard called upon the power of his god one more time and confidently shouted, "Heavy!"

Prepared for this moment, Ontar dropped his morning star right as the paladin's spell was cast. Clenching his gauntlet into a fist, Ontar pulled back his arm and threw a punch that connected right with the other man's nose, instantly breaking it. Yalard was caught totally off guard by the attack that left blood streaming into his moustache and mouth. Dazed, he couldn't help but feel weak-kneed.

Grabbing his morning star, Ontar spun it once before sending its spiked ball careening into the paladin's chest. This act shattered the man's ribcage and caused bone fragments to pierce his lungs and heart. Shouting in pain, Yalard dropped to the ground dead.

Upon the paladin's demise, his sword's dull white light faded away. This caused the glowing mist that surrounded the suits of armor to disperse and (much to the relief of Echo and the Hayseed Brothers) reverted their once deadly adversaries back into nothing more than lifeless shells.

Picking up his short sword, Pudge addressed his fellow companions, "We have to get the paladin and armor over to the Enchanted Artifacts exhibit. With any luck, the curator will think he and the other guards triggered the trap that caused their demise."

"What if the chain guardian tries to attack us?" Echo wondered.

"We run," Stump replied.

Leaving Echo and the thieves to carry the armor, Ontar dragged the man he just killed into the exhibit and witnessed the brutal carnage brought on by the chain guardian. Thankfully, the guardian decided to ask them its riddle before attacking, allowing them the chance to drop their burden and escape unharmed. Returning to the rotunda, Echo pulled a water skin from her backpack and washed away any blood spots she saw. Grateful to have no further incidents to slow them down, the party climbed the rope, hauled up Ontar, and fled into the night.

Chapter Four

hen is that shrieking going to end? Munker thought as he sat in the seat of a wooden, horse-drawn cart. Traveling down a dirt road through farm country, a distant wailing sound that began last night continued to get louder the next morning. Trying to keep his horse under control, he briefly glanced back at the travelers, who had paid him for a ride to the border of Coronas. The man was a richly-dressed noble while the woman lying by his side was obviously carrying their child. Telling him their names were Ole and Lena when they first hired him, Munker suspected they wanted to keep their real identity a secret. Not that he cared. Having already gone to market, the money he made now was simply a bonus for the trip back home. If he could ever get there!

Rabbit's Road was supposed to be an easy path to go down with lots of little holes at its sides for bunnies to pop out of for the amusement of travelers. Unfortunately, the wailing had scared away any wildlife, leaving nothing to watch until Munker heard what sounded like a host of confused farm animals rumbling from up ahead. Sure enough, as he drove his cart forward, he saw a vast assortment of sheep, goats, cows, and other creatures milling about randomly in the middle of the road. Three farmers and at least a dozen of their children stood in the middle of this mess arguing with each other.

Seeing that this makeshift herd was blocking their path, Marcain cringed at their smell and asked Munker, "What is going on up there?"

Munker brought his cart to a stop. "I don't know, but I'll go find out."

Watching the farmer leave them to see what was going on, Lomana said, "I don't like this. First, the wailing, and now all these animals appearing out of nowhere. Something very strange is going on here. Maybe we should turn back."

"Turn back!" Marcain exclaimed. "We've gotten scarcely more than a day's worth of travel in."

Lomana shifted uneasily as she rubbed her rounded belly. "I don't want to risk hurting the baby by going somewhere dangerous."

"My dear, I understand your concern, but Lareder isn't safe for us. We have to get to Coronas to avoid my mother's wrath, and the best way to do it is by getting past all these damn animals!" Marcain argued.

"I suppose your right," Lomana conceded. "I just wish the wailing would stop. It's starting to give me a headache."

Marcain tried holding her hand for comfort. "It reminds me of a legend I heard about a ghostly woman called a banshee, whose shrieks frightened everyone away from the cemetery near Miltus."

Fearing the worst, Lomana asked, "Do you think that a banshee could be on this road right now?"

"No," Marcain said with more confidence than he felt. "A banshee's place is among the dead not the living."

Returning to the cart, Munker said, "I'm sorry, milord, but I'm afraid we'll have to turn back."

"What…why?" Marcain wondered.

Munker climbed back onto the cart as he explained that, "The wailing sound we've been hearing only gets louder the further we get down the road. In fact, the farms closest to it have all seen their livestock flee from the noise. Now, everyone's gathered here and is arguing about who has what animal and how to get them back where they belong."

"Do they know what's causing this noise?" Marcain asked.

Shaking his head, Munker replied, "I'm afraid not."

Lomana nervously grabbed Marcain's hand. "Please, let's go back and find another route. This one just isn't safe for us!"

Frustrated by what happened, Marcain glanced at the animal-covered road and said, "Very well. I suppose we have no choice."

Turning their cart around, Munker found it was much easier to drive his horse back from whence they came.

The sun's light gently faded on what had been a pointless day of travel. Watching its brilliant hues tinge the fertile fields they passed through, Munker had been asked to find a place where they could stay for the night. Feeling confident Ole could cover any of their expenses, he saw a farmhouse with a barn just off the main road that would be a perfect place to rest should its owners choose to be hospitable. Pointing this out to his passengers, the group agreed to go ask about lodging for the night.

Narcos couldn't believe his good fortune when he saw a horse-drawn cart heading his way. Sitting by the window of an otherwise empty farmhouse whose occupants were now zombies, he had originally sent his new minions to ambush anyone coming back along the road. The fact these travelers were now coming straight to him would only make things easier. Of course, they might not be the ones he was looking for, but he had a way of finding out for sure.

Bringing his cart to a stop outside the house, Munker turned to Marcain and said, "Alright, milord, I'll leave the rest up to you."

Marcain climbed out of the cart and walked up to the door. Knocking politely, he waited until Narcos opened it. Surprised to see what looked like robed a mage with a brown leather satchel slung over his shoulder, Marcain said, "Greetings. I hope I'm not disturbing you, but my name is Ole. This is my wife Lena, and our driver Munker. We are travelers in desperate need of a place to stay for the night. If you would be willing to take us in, then I would be happy to compensate you for your trouble."

Intrigued by Marcain's regal attire, Narcos asked a simple question to unmask the noble's identity. "Well, Ole, my name is Narcos, and I might be able to help you out. After all, you do look rather familiar. Didn't I see your cart going down Rabbit's Road just the other day?"

"Yes, we were on our way to Oneca when a roaming herd of animals blocked our path and forced us to turn back," Marcain explained.

Narcos quirked an eyebrow. "Oneca, isn't that in Coronas?"

Marcain nodded. "Yes, my wife and I are traveling there from Miltus."

Got you, Narcos thought as he reached for his staff, which was propped behind the door. "Such a shame that a pack of dumb animals would keep you from your loved ones. Please, come in. I'll go help your driver settle his horse in my barn for the night."

"I appreciate your kindness," Marcain said as he accompanied Narcos back to the cart. Waving to Lomana, he then shouted, "Good news! We have a place to stay."

With Munker's help, Lomana climbed down from the cart and went to greet Narcos. Taking one look at the robed stranger, she quietly said, "Thank you for your generosity."

"It's my pleasure," Narcos replied before going to talk with Munker.

Reluctantly following Marcain back to the house, Lomana whispered, "We can't stay here."

Marcain frowned. "Why not?"

"That man is evil," Lomana warned. "His belt is made out of a skull and bones!"

"He's probably just an eccentric old wizard," Marcain argued.

Lomana shook her head. "How many wizards do you know that live in a farmhouse?"

"How many wizards do you know at all?" Marcain retorted. Watching Lomana go silent, he added, "Don't worry, my dear. He's an old man Munker and I could both overpower if we had to."

"I still think this is a bad idea," Lomana fretted.

Opening the door to the farmhouse for her, Marcain said, "You're just tired from your journey. Trust me, after a good night's sleep, you'll come to realize just how lucky we are to have found this place."

Lomana let her guard down slightly when she saw the house's brightly burning hearth, with the remains of some fresh pottage bubbling in its cauldron. Wondering if the baby would like to try some nice hot food, she replied, "I suppose one night won't kill us."

"...and I swear to you that when I saw all those animals sitting on the road, I knew the gods had sent me a sign saying I should turn around and go back!" Munker proclaimed as he walked beside his horse while it pulled his cart towards the barn.

Silently motioning for the zombies on the road to attack the farmhouse, Narcos saw that he and Munker had reached the barn's dark open entrance. "My goodness, your horse must be exhausted after such a fruitless day of travel."

Munker agreed, "Yeah, he's tired, but you won't find a better breed anywhere else in the entire kingdom."

"Oh, really?" Narcos said as a wicked grin crossed his face. "Well, let me show you mine."

Suddenly, a bright blue flame ignited from inside the barn to reveal a sinister black horse whose unholy red eyes glowed in their otherwise empty sockets. Frightened by the animal's burning mane, Munker saw that two of its legs were skeletal in appearance while three broken ribs protruded from beneath its saddle. Backing away in horror, he heard Narcos say that, "I like to think of this creature as my *nightmare*, but now it is yours!"

In an instant, the horse attached to Munker's cart whinnied in a panic and fled from the barn. Unable to stop him, Munker chased after the cart and attempted to leap onto it only to miss his mark and fall face first onto the ground. Listening to the sound of the nightmare coming his way, Munker rolled over just in time to scream as the undead horse reared and brought its flailing hooves down upon his skull!

❧ ❧ ❧

Startled by the scream from outside, Marcain ran to the farm-house's open window just in time to see the horse-drawn cart they'd been traveling on veer off into a random field. Trying to figure out what was going on, he uttered a shout of his own as a zombie shot up from under the window outside and grabbed at him! Pulling away as one of the zombie's hands ripped off his shirt sleeve, Marcain felt the other draw blood by clawing at the side of his face with its filthy fingernails. Quickly clutching the hilt of his sword, Marcain drew forth its blade and stabbed the zombie in the middle of its forehead. Much to his horror, the undead merely grabbed at the weapon, causing him to pull it back and accidentally slice off his enemy's fingers in the process.

More screaming followed as Lomana reacted to the sight of two zombie children breaking side windows and climbing into the house. Terrified of being caught in this unholy trap, Marcain flung open the door to the house and faced the finger-less zombie. Seeing that his enemy's arms were raised to grab him, Marcain swung his sword and chopped one of them completely off. Unaffected by the wound, the zombie punched him in the shoulder with its mutilated fist. Marcain retaliated by kicking it in the stomach with enough force to knock it over. He then grabbed Lomana's hand and pulled her out of the house before the little zombies could attack.

Running towards the field where the horse and cart had gone, Marcain and Lomana saw that two more zombies had joined the three inside to slowly chase after them. Watching their escape with mild interest, Narcos stood next to the nightmare and cast a spell, which caused a sphere of violet energy with a pitch-black core to appear in his hand. Tossing this shadowbolt, Narcos saw it strike Lomana with a blow that knocked her unconscious.

"NO!" Marcain exclaimed as he stopped to check on his beloved. Crouching, he could still hear her shallow breathing, but he trembled at the sight of the large indentation in her belly where the shadowbolt had struck. *My child*, he thought as rage consumed him. Clutching his sword in two hands, he let out a ferocious battle cry and charged straight at the necromancer.

Making a slight gesture with his staff, Narcos had the nightmare at his side gallop towards the young lord at full speed. The creature's fearsome eyes stared straight into Marcain's soul, and when he saw the nightmare's blazing mane, he suddenly pictured himself being burned alive by its wicked blue flames! Overcome by sheer terror, Marcain broke his charge and fled back towards Lomana.

Lowering its head, the nightmare slammed into Marcain from behind and caused him to cry out as its burning mane flared along his back and made Marcain's skin erupt in frostbite. Tumbling helplessly to the ground, he felt his vision start to go and took one last look at Lomana before blacking out.

Casually strolling up to the nobleman's body, Narcos took his sword and slid it under the nightmare's saddle. Seeing the zombies had reached Lomana's body, he waved for two of them to come over and hoist Marcain onto the nightmare's back while the rest savagely ended her life. Instructing the undead horse to, "Take him to the barn," Narcos then told the two zombies they should, "Seek out the banshee and have her return to the cemetery. Her purpose here is finished." Fulfilling their orders, the zombies and nightmare carried out their tasks while Narcos prepared to turn in for the night.

The next morning, Marcain woke up afflicted by pain to both his body and heart. He had utterly failed to protect the woman he loved, and their unborn child was now dead because of it. Wishing he could apologize to Lomana for what had happened, he looked around and screamed when he saw her standing before him. Blank-faced and bloody, her once round belly had been completely shredded open, allowing her innards to hang down below the ribcage. Repulsed by what had happened to her, Marcain couldn't help but turn his head and vomit!

Trembling as he tried to regain his composure, Marcain looked around and found he was on the straw-covered floor of a wooden stall in the barn they had passed the previous evening. Aside from Lomana, there were three other zombies in the barn, including what was left of poor Munker. These lifeless abominations were nothing, though, when compared to the nightmare that stood next to the barn's entrance. Letting out a loud whinny, its frightening presence ensured Marcain would do nothing to escape. Scrambling to his feet, the young lord waited for the inevitable appearance of his captor.

It wasn't long before Narcos entered the barn with a bowl of pottage in his hand. Setting it on top of a nearby butter churn, he said, "Eat. We have a long journey ahead of us."

Never in Marcain's life had he ever wanted to kill someone more than this man, but the nightmare standing next to him ensured its master would be protected. "Why...why did you kill her? She didn't deserve to die."

"Ah, the power to decide who lives and dies." Narcos sneered. "It is a tremendous gift those of noble birth constantly take for granted."

"It is no gift!" Marcain snarled. "The gods have placed this burden on those of royal blood to help ensure the peace and prosperity of the lands they hold."

"Ah, but you've turned your back on this sacred duty to run off with a peasant girl," Narcos noted.

Marcain clenched his fists. "Lomana tried to save me from responsibilities I never wanted! As the son of a duchess, I had to keep my vassals from quarreling amongst themselves while my mother schemed against our peers to gain the king's favor. There was no freedom or love. Only the wretched tradition of accumulating and maintaining power for ourselves."

"A power the average man could only dream of obtaining," Narcos retorted.

Narrowing his eyes, Marcain asked, "Is that what you're after…power?"

"Yes," Narcos replied. "You see, as the son of an executioner, I got to witness firsthand what power was really like. Murderers, rapists, and thieves were all brought before the baron my father served to face judgement for their crimes. Some stood defiant. Others begged and pleaded for mercy. For a boy like myself to see a grown man grovel like a sniveling toad was truly inspiring. No matter how hard they tried, though, the baron made sure their sentence was carried out, and my father was happy to do it."

Marcain gave Narcos a disgusted look. "You sick bastard. Executions are meant to serve as a warning and punishment for those who break the law."

"They also serve as an exhibition of a lord's power," Narcos countered before adding, "A power my father told me I could never possess because I was not born of noble blood. However, I soon learned that power comes in many forms, such as when I happened to witness a shorthanded cleric of Kardok use his magic to animate a dead criminal long enough for it to climb into his hearse."

Shaking his head in disgust, Marcain said, "So, you've chosen to dwell with the dead instead of the living. What does that have to do with me?"

"You are descended from an ancient knight named Eragosh, whose tomb can only be opened by someone of his blood line. Once inside, I can summon Eragosh's spirit to help me find the hidden city of Uch-na-Mach," Narcos explained.

Marcain gave Narcos a suspicious look. "Why are you seeking out this hidden city?"

Intentionally vague in his response, Narcos said, "You'll see soon enough."

"No, I won't!" Marcain declared. "I will not let you defile the spirit of my ancestors. You have already destroyed my life, and I would rather die than help you to steal any more secrets from the dead."

"Are you sure about that?" Narcos asked with a snicker.

Raising her arms, Lomana's corpse snarled as it advanced towards her former love.

"Lomana…please!" Marcain pleaded as she approached. "Don't do this!" Void of all sympathy, Lomana wrapped her hands around his neck and squeezed. Marcain attempted a half-hearted struggle but, eventually, fell to the ground unconscious.

Shoving the zombie out of his way, Narcos knelt to hear if he was still breathing. Taking the ragged gasps as signs of life, Narcos stood up and told Lomana to, "Put him on the cart. We have a long journey ahead of us."

When Marcain finally awoke, he found himself lying on the floor of Munker's cart with his hands tied behind his back and Narcos in the driver's seat. Shooting down the road at a breathtaking pace, he saw the nightmare had replaced the horse Munker had used and was easily pulling the cart without even the slightest trace of fatigue. Preferring not to draw attention to himself,

Marcain kept still during this wild ride that continued even after the sun went down. Using the nightmare's burning mane, along with the full orange moon for light, Narcos didn't stop the cart until they had finally returned to the cemetery outside of Miltus.

Shuffling past the tombstones to greet Narcos as he got out of the cart was a zombie whose appearance totally stunned Marcain. "Rolit! How is this possible?"

"He tried impersonating you after being captured by some useless thieves," Narcos replied while prodding Marcain out of the cart with his staff.

Marcain shook his head in disbelief. "I thought those thieves had been sent to retrieve me by my mother."

Pointing to the zombie, Narcos said, "Well, you thought wrong, and now he is dead. So, quit wasting time and move."

Shoved forward by the zombie, Marcain followed Narcos towards the mausoleum and up its well-worn steps. Being brought directly in front of the buildings slab of a door, Marcain stood defiant. "I will not open this for you."

"You act like you have a choice." Narcos sneered before the zombie slammed Marcain into the door and pushed against him until the slab slowly slid open.

Dust fell upon Marcain as he stumbled into a chamber dominated by a gray stone sarcophagus whose lid depicted a fully armored knight with a surcoat and cape that held a downward pointed sword. Glaring at Narcos as he entered the mausoleum, Marcain said, "You've got what you want now release me!"

"Oh, no, I'm not done with you quite yet," Narcos declared as he stood in front of the sarcophagus. Waving his staff and hand over it, he began to cast a spell that caused a low, moaning sound to reverberate across the chamber. Then…rising from its eternal slumber was a pale ghostly figure whose appearance resembled the image on the sarcophagus itself.

Speaking in a strong echoing voice, the ghost immediately asked, *"Who summons me back to the land of the living?"*

"Eragosh, I am Narcos, your new master," the necromancer replied before pointing his staff at Marcain. "And I demand you use this vessel to lead me to the hidden city of Uch-na-Mach."

"What!?" Marcain exclaimed.

"As you command." Eragosh replied as his spectral figure flew into the nobleman's body and vanished.

Feeling like he had been plunged into a freezing lake, Marcain cried out in pain and collapsed to the ground where he spasmed for the next minute. Eventually regaining control of himself, he got onto his hands and knees and quietly asked, "Why?"

For Narcos, the answer was simple. "The world has drastically changed since Eragosh was alive. By combining your knowledge with his, I can easily find where Uch-na-Mach is hidden. Now, tell me where I should begin my search?"

Marcain's eyes widened when the voice that answered Narcos was not his own, *"In the Wistwind Plains of Sibeia."*

Amused by the young noble's reaction, Narcos told the zombie next to him, "Untie Lord Marcain. Now that he is possessed by Eragosh, he will be no threat to me." Looking down at Marcain, he added, "We'll rest here tonight and head out in the morning. I want to find that city as soon as possible."

Chapter Five

A sense of nervous anticipation filled Ontar and Echo as they followed the Hayseed Brothers down several desolate city streets, which eventually led them to the Peaceful Repose. Their mission at the museum had turned into something far bloodier than originally planned, but the overall objective was still accomplished, which meant they could legitimately lay claim to the pixie the halflings had promised. Keeping a wary eye out for both the guards and any shady figures roaming Miltus at night, the Hayseed Brothers skillfully guided their companions back to their refuge at the tavern.

Relieved to have entered the establishment without incident, the party found that its dining hall was empty except for a young man busily wiping down tables. Pulling off his helmet, Ontar couldn't help but empathize with the late-night worker. He had to perform similar tasks himself not so very long ago.

"May I help you?" the young man asked after finishing his last table.

"Yes," Pudge replied. "I'd like to order a round of drinks for my friends and I."

"Sorry, sir, but the bar's closed at this time of night," the young man replied.

Pudge's shoulders dropped a little. "Such a shame. Well, I guess a nightcap is out of the question then. Shall we retire for the evening and meet up again tomorrow?"

"No," Echo said without hesitation. "I risked my neck tonight so I could get my hands on that pixie, and by the gods, I'm going to do it."

"Fair enough," replied Pudge. "She awaits you in our room." He beckoned the group to follow him. Going upstairs, the halfling took a key from out of his belt pouch and unlocked the door to his quarters.

An excited cry came from the brother's room the moment the door swung open. Practically jumping up and down in her cage, Wink called out to Ontar in her impossibly high voice, "Hey, you came back! I just knew my hero wouldn't abandon me." Glaring at the Hayseed Brothers, she stomped her foot and said, "Now, get me out of here you black-hearted bastards!"

Both halflings shook their heads in mild embarrassment. Grabbing a small golden key from his belt pouch, Stump inserted it into the specialized birdcage lock and opened the door. Wink took a couple of nervous steps back as the halfling reached into the cage and used his long slender fingers to apply a small amount of pressure on the collar around her neck. A second later, the collar dropped to Wink's feet.

Eager to finally taste freedom (and get a little bit of revenge), Wink bit the tip of Stump's finger. Cursing, he rapidly recoiled his hand and shook it in pain. Wink then took the opportunity to bolt from her cage and ran straight towards Ontar. Spreading her arms as wide as she could, the pixie leapt towards her hero and hugged his armored boot with all her might. Ontar couldn't help but blush a little bit.

Looking directly at her enormous rescuer, Wink's eyes welled up with tears of joy. "I don't know who you are but, please, take me away from all this," she said in a trembling little voice.

Bending down, Ontar scooped up the pixie and held her gently in his gauntleted hands. "My name is Ontar, and this is my friend Echo. We're here to make sure that no one will ever lock you in a cage again."

Turning to the Hayseed Brothers, Echo couldn't help but ask, "Jeez, guys, what'd you do to her?"

"Nothing," Pudge scoffed. "The little drama queen just likes to put on a show."

"What!?" exclaimed Wink angrily. "You spent the past six months interrogating me nonstop on where to find Spirit Slayer, and when I didn't tell you anything, you threw rotten onions in my cage and made me sniff them until I choked!"

Echo's mind reeled with this new information. Spirit Slayer was the key to retaining her membership in the Bloody Side, and if she could get this pixie to talk it would go a long way towards preserving her family's legacy. Addressing the halflings, she said, "Alright! Obviously, the three of you don't get along very well. I think it would be best if we parted ways for now."

"I'm afraid you're right," Pudge said sadly. "Although, I'll have to admit that I enjoyed getting to know the two of you and look forward to the next time that we can work together."

"Oh, there won't be a next time." Wink snarled as Ontar carried her out of the room.

Escorting them out, Stump shot Ontar a look and snickered. "She's yer problem now," he said with a grin.

"Good Riddance!" Wink shouted after him.

Lagging behind a little bit, Echo leaned in close to Pudge and said, "Make sure that when the Bloody Side hears word of the mage lord's escape, they know *I* am the one responsible."

Pudge nodded. "Of course."

"Good," Echo replied. "Because when I return to Miltus, it will be with the most amazing sword they've ever seen."

Already eager for that day, Pudge said, "The guild is in Morvin's Butcher Shop. Bring the blade there when you have it, and no one will ever doubt you're from Searce's line again."

Pleased to hear that, Echo bid the halflings a pleasant goodnight.

❧❧❧

Returning to their own quarters, Ontar set Wink on the bed, lit a candle, and was soon joined by Echo in casting off their bulky equipment. Curious about her new companions, Wink said, "I can't believe I'm finally free. Normally, the fey folk are just ignored by people like you. Why did you decide to rescue me?"

Ontar yawned loudly and sat next to Wink on the bed. Slowly pulling back the blanket so she wouldn't trip over it, he rested his head on the pillow and covered up. "I guess I've just got a soft spot for cute little women."

Wink blushed while Echo said, "That's a long story, and we're both very tired. Why don't we tell you in the morning?"

"Oh, I suppose," Wink grumbled as she watched the elf sit on the floor next to the nightstand. Crossing her legs, Echo then rested her hands on top of her knee's palms up. Elves had mastered the art of meditation a long time ago and effectively used it as a substitute for sleep. Personally, Wink had always found meditation to be a double-edged sword. On the one hand, it allowed Echo to completely recuperate from a long day of travel in less than three hours. On the other hand, it also shut off her senses during that period, which made her highly prone to ambush. Not that this was a big concern right now.

Licking his fingers, Ontar was about to extinguish the candle when Wink crept up beside his ear and asked, "Hey, Ontar, can I sleep next to you tonight?"

"Huh? Oh, yeah, sure," he said absentmindedly.

Clapping her hands excitedly, Wink gave him a quick kiss on the cheek before tossing her hat on the nightstand and sliding under the blanket far enough away from him that he wouldn't roll over her during the night.

"Aw, how cute. Little Onnie has a snuggle buddy," Echo teased.

"Ooh, Onnie, I like that," Wink exclaimed brightly.

"Oh, great. Thanks, *Squeaker*," Ontar growled as he used Echo's childhood nickname. Ignoring the comment, she simply took a deep breath, closed her eyes, and cleared her mind of all the evenings activities.

Wink didn't seem to notice. "Goodnight, Onnie," she said adoringly as Ontar extinguished the candle and drifted off to sleep.

The next morning, Echo awoke from her meditation to find that neither Ontar nor Wink was in their room. A quick glance of her surroundings revealed Ontar's bed had been made, and that his equipment was gone. Gathering her gear, Echo surmised the two probably went to make some last-minute preparations before they left Miltus. She had to admit it was a good idea considering it probably wouldn't be long before news spread of last night's exploits.

Slipping on her backpack and adjusting her armor, Echo did a quick check of all her possessions before leaving the bedroom and heading down to the dining hall. Striding up to the bar, she asked Gelmar if he'd seen her two wayward companions. The tavern keeper confirmed they had left earlier in the morning, and that while Ontar had dropped off his room key, the horses were still in their stalls.

Satisfied with what she had learned, Echo sat at a nearby table and ordered some breakfast. Nibbling on a meal of toasted rye bread and grapes, she took a swig from her cider cup and cursed the cook's preparation of her plate. Apparently, the difference between *toasted* and *charred* bread was something the chef couldn't readily figure out, and Echo was about to complain to a passing serving wench when Ontar and Wink entered the building.

Ontar seemed a little tired as he approached Echo's table. The weary warrior must have just finished shopping as Echo noticed he now donned a dark red headband, which was tied about his brow. Wink sat on Ontar's shoulder, clearly proud of the role she played in selecting his new accessory.

"Well, don't we look dashing," Echo said as she gestured to a chair next to her. "Have a seat. Would you like anything for breakfast?"

"Ugh, no," Ontar replied. "We ate at the market."

Grabbing a stool, Ontar sat down and placed his full helmet on the table. Moving gently, he then picked Wink off his shoulder and placed her close to Echo's plate.

"See, I told you it looked good," she said to Ontar before turning her attention towards Echo. "I wanted to give him a little token of my affection before we went out to rescue Hatch."

Ontar shook his head and grumbled, "How is it that *I* had to pay for *your* token of affection?"

"Because it was for you, silly," Wink replied.

"It's a cute gift," Echo noted. "But I'm interested in a token that's a little bit bigger than that."

Wink got the hint. "You're talking about Spirit Slayer aren't you. Onnie told me that's what the Hayseed Brothers promised in exchange for doing their work at the museum."

Echo ignored her biased tone. "Yes, but they also said you wouldn't reveal where the sword was unless we rescued a former Mage Lord of Sibeia."

"A rescue they passed upon because they didn't think the mage lord could be trusted," Ontar added.

"Onnie, don't be so mean," Wink said with a scowl. "Hatch is one of the most important people in my life, and I have to do everything I can to set him free. Big or small, no one deserves to spend their days locked away from the people they love. Especially if they didn't do anything wrong in the first place."

"Huh, I've heard that one before," Ontar said while glaring at Echo.

"Excuse me," the elf said a little defensively, "but there's always a reason behind someone's actions, and Sibeia's rulers are widely known to have betrayed each other on more than one occasion."

"Which is exactly what happened to Hatch," Wink exclaimed.

"How so?" Echo asked with interest.

Wink moved over to Echo's beverage, cupped her hands, and scooped up a little bit of cider. Taking a quick drink, she then wiped them on her dress and explained.

"As you probably already know, five years ago, Hatch was the Mage Lord of Sibeia. He was a good man who always tried to help aspiring magic users who were skilled at what they did. One of those people was a talented white knight named Sir Temas who *definitely* had the potential to become the next warrior lord if someone just gave him a chance. The only problem was the current warrior lord is a selfish old crank who didn't want anything to do with grooming a successor."

"How could a mage lord like Hatch be of much help to a knight like Sir Temas?" Ontar wondered."

"Sir Temas was a *white knight* who practiced a form of magic called *mentalism,* which allowed him to draw upon the power of his very soul," Wink explained. "While Hatch is a wizard who uses *essence* for his magic, he can still teach others how to form that power into various different spells."

Ontar smugly crossed his arms and said, "So, white knights aren't true warriors then."

"Maybe not," Wink conceded. "Which might explain why Hatch tried so hard to advance Sir Temas's career by having him lead his men on several big missions for the mages' guild. This was supposed to help him increase his standing among the troops, but then, for some reason, he went absolutely berserk and started attacking Sibeia's leaders. He even managed to kill the Harvest Lord before the army finally wiped him out.

Afterwards, the evil Warrior Lord decided to blame Hatch for helping Sir Temas and had him arrested for treason! I tried to spook the horses pulling his prison cart so that he might have a chance to escape, but then the guards caught me, and I was thrown into a cage at the mages' guild."

"Where the Hayseed Brothers eventually found you," Echo added.

Wink seethed. "Those greedy barefoot maggots didn't even try to help me save Hatch! All they wanted was Spirit Slayer."

Echo cleared her throat. "Well, you know, Wink, that sword would come in handy if we decided to help you rescue Hatch."

Wink gave the elf a suspicious look. "I'm sure it would, and if I showed you where the sword was, then you'd have absolutely no reason to help me rescue Hatch."

"Yeah, well, treachery works both ways," Ontar stated bluntly. "Hatch is a powerful wizard who has spent the past five years locked away in a dungeon. Now, that's a long time for anyone, and there's no telling how imprisonment might have affected him. Who's to say that if we released him, he wouldn't just use his powers to kill us before going on a rampage through the countryside?"

"Hmm, kind of like the last magic user we fought against, eh?" Echo hinted with just a bit of sarcasm in her voice.

"What magic user?" Wink's asked as her eyes darted to Echo. The elf and Ontar represented her last best chance at freeing Hatch, and if she couldn't convince them to aid her cause, then she doubted that anyone else would either.

"A necromancer called Narcos..." Echo began before telling the pixie about their previous encounter.

Mulling over this new information, Wink said, "It sounds like this Narcos practiced black magic, which is something that Hatch has never done or would ever even think of doing. It's not fair to lump all spell casters together just because you encountered one bad one."

Ontar relinquished his argument, but not before raising another one. "Alright, even if Hatch isn't evil, do you know where he's imprisoned?"

"Yes, I do," Wink said while crossing her arms. "He's locked away in a Sibeian fortress just north of the border with Lareder."

"Why would they hold him in a fortress so close to an enemy kingdom?" Ontar wondered.

"Probably to keep him as far away as possible from any supporters he might still have in Sibeia," Echo replied.

"Be that as it may, this fort will surely be defended by heavily armed soldiers, archers, and a white knight." Looking down at the pixie, Ontar asked, "What makes you think that we'd even stand a chance at rescuing this guy?"

Wink looked him straight in the eye. "Because anyone who breaks into a museum and kills its guards just to rescue a pixie isn't afraid to take some risks in order to get what they want."

Nodding in approval, Echo said, "You know, it might be kind of nice having a powerful wizard traveling with us, and if he can reveal the location of Spirit Slayer, then it could well prove worth our time. I say we go for it."

"What do you think, Onnie?" Wink asked while looking at him with endearing eyes.

Ontar shifted slightly beneath her gaze. "Alright, but if he tries to betray us, then I won't hesitate to kill him myself."

"Yay!" cheered Wink. "Let's hit the road right now! I don't want to waste any more time than we have to."

Standing up with a disturbed look on his face, Ontar donned his helmet, grabbed Wink, and plopped her on his shoulder. Echo followed suit, and together, the three of them left the tavern and headed for the stables.

⊰⊱⊰⊱⊰⊱

It was another busy morning as the party stepped out onto the streets of Miltus. Moving towards a stable connected to the Peaceful Repose, everyone prepared to depart when they stopped to hear an announcement from a nearby a city crier.

"Ohy yea! Ohy yea!" the boy shouted. "The city museum shall be closed for the next week. During this time, new positions will be made available for all those who are interested…"

"News travels fast," noted Ontar.

"All the more reason for us to get going," said Echo.

Entering the stable, Ontar, Echo, and Wink scrunched up their noses at the foul smell of manure. Shooing away the flies that buzzed about their heads, they located a busy groom who used a pitchfork to spread some hay across the filthy floor and asked him to fetch their horses. Their steeds were quickly retrieved from some nearby stalls, and Wink slid into the hood of Ontar's cloak as he and Echo mounted up.

Maneuvering their animals through the busy city streets, Ontar and Echo were forced to ride at a slow trot until they reached Miltus's northern gate. The guards at this exit warily watched the travelers as they approached but did nothing to impede their departure. Passing from cobblestone streets onto a broad dirt road, the group surveyed a vast expanse of grasslands that spread before them.

It was a magnificent day, and an inexplicable sense of freedom washed over Ontar and Echo. Clutching tightly to the reins of their mounts, they lightly kicked the flanks of their horses and sent them galloping towards destinations unknown.

Crossing the Helsh Plains of Lareder required two days of steady riding. Traffic along the road outside of Miltus had been quite heavy at first, but as the party traveled further into the countryside, things lightened up. In truth, it wasn't long before the scenery surrounding the road became nothing more than large swaths of tall prairie grass dotted by the occasional farm.

The sun was high in the clear blue sky, and its increasing warmth was an early indication that summer would soon be upon them. Echo slowed her horse's pace to let Ontar know she was ready for lunch. Bringing their animals to a halt along the side of the road, the travelers dismounted and dug trail rations out of their backpacks. Peering out of Ontar's hood, Wink asked the big warrior if he could set her on some recently trodden grass close to where everyone would be eating. Once this was done, the companions all sat down facing each other and consumed a small portion of their meals. A slight breeze kept everyone cool while the constant drone of insects could clearly be heard in the background.

Finishing her meal ahead of the others, Echo decided to draw out her wooden flute and play an upbeat tune until Ontar and Wink were done with their lunch. The lively melody seemed to put Wink into a cheery mood, and she applauded when the song eventually reached its end.

"Wow! That was fantastic," the pixie exclaimed to Echo. "I haven't heard that song in ages. Who taught it to you?"

"My mother," Echo replied with a hint of sadness. "She always said that music was an easy way to entertain the human children I watched. They usually came with their parents to conduct trade in my hometown of Thramahas."

"Did it work?" Wink asked.

"For the most part," Echo said, grinning mischievously at Ontar. "Although, naughty little boys like Ontar preferred to smack the other kids with sticks over listening to the music I played for them."

"You knew Onnie as a child?" Wink asked with delight.

"Don't sound so surprised," Ontar added, having just finished taking a swig from his water skin. "My father owned a tavern in the small town of Kinnerba, which sits right on the border of the Illamine and Coronas. Every now and then, he'd take me to Thramahas to hire elvish musicians to perform for our patrons. As it turns out, one of those early trips led to my first encounter with Echo."

Pondering this new bit of information, Wink gave Echo a sly look from beneath the brim of her hat. "So, what did you do when Onnie was being bad?"

Echo thought for a moment. "I probably spanked him."

Wink shivered a little when Echo said that. "Ooh, what was it like to spank that little bottom of his?"

Quirking an eyebrow, Echo noticed this conversation was heading in an odd direction. "I don't know. Soft, wiggly, I really didn't pay all that much attention."

Ontar inadvertently tensed at being referred to as soft. No warrior worth his mettle would dare to let such a comment pass, and he wasn't about to be the first. "Well, I'll have you know, I've firmed up quite a bit since then," he said while stretching slightly to accentuate his broad powerful chest.

"Oh, I'm sure you have," Wink noted with a devious grin. "I bet your butt was rock hard by the time you got to be an adult."

Picking up on the not-so-subtle innuendo, Ontar decided it was time to change the subject. "So…Wink, where did you grow up?"

"Deep in the elvish part of Illamine Forest," she replied with a little disappointment at the new topic.

"Huh, must have been quite an adventure for you to eventually meet up with the Mage Lord of Sibeia," Ontar remarked in a manner that invited further explanation.

Wink shrugged. "Not really. My people just swiped him from one of the elves slave plantations when he was a baby."

"What in the world are you talking about?" Echo said, unable to keep the shock from her voice. "*My* people would never even dream on enslaving another intelligent race. Plus, humans aren't allowed that far into our territory."

Wink snorted. "Well, they are, and your people have used human slaves to work their lands for about as far back as the Age of Chaos.

Echo ardently wanted to argue this accusation, but elvish history stretched back for countless centuries, and she honestly didn't know enough about it to really make a valid point. So, instead, she decided to focus on her people's current beliefs.

"For as long as I've lived, no *wood elf* has ever condoned slavery. My people take great pride in hunting the wild animals of the forest and growing vegetables in our gardens. If any of my kind were to even consider supporting slavery, it would have to be the *high elves*."

Wink rolled her eyes. "Either way, we still kidnapped a human baby from an *elvish* slave plantation and raised it as our own. That's why finding Hatch is so important to me. In a lot of ways, he's kind of like my son."

Ontar found that sentiment a little touching. "So, if you and Hatch were both born and raised in the Illamine, how did the two of you wind up in Sibeia?"

A sad expression crossed Wink's face. "We were banished. You see, when my people take a baby, we replace it with a shape shifting creature called a changeling so the parents don't miss the one they lost. When the changeling reaches adolescence, it returns to us, and we send the human we stole on its way, and the process starts all over again."

"Why?" Echo wondered.

"Because we can give the human children a better life than their parents," Wink explained. "And in return, the children help us with tasks we are too little to accomplish on our own."

Giving her a curious look, Ontar asked, "So, how did the two of you get banished?"

Wink let out a sigh. "Hatch was my little boy no matter how old he got, and I didn't want him to leave when the changeling got back. So, we killed it on its way back home. Unfortunately, my people found out and banished us saying we couldn't come back until we brought them a new changeling. Turns out, they're a lot harder to find than I thought, and our hunt for a new one led us to Sibeia."

Ontar and gave the pixie a dumbfounded look. "You willingly went to Sibeia!?"

Confounded by his question, Wink said, "What? You act like Sibeia's some sort of all-powerful monster or something. Don't tell me you're scared of going there just because they humiliated your homeland's armies on the battlefield."

"They did not humiliate my homeland!" Ontar growled. "In fact, if it weren't for reinforcements from Coronas, then Lareder wouldn't even *be* here today."

Echo was far more subdued on this issue. Few races outside of the Illamine knew just how horribly crushed the elvish military had become in the aftermath of its war with Sibeia or how long the recovery would take. Echo could still remember some of the tragic tales her father had told her about that time, and she prayed such events would never again come to pass.

Thankfully, Wink was oblivious to Echo's darkening mood and continued talking to Ontar, "Good. If your kinsmen weren't scared of dealing with Sibeia, then you shouldn't be either. Now, I've told you how Hatch and I began our travels. Why don't you two tell me how you began yours?"

Ontar looked away. "I don't want to talk about it."

"Please Onnie." Wink pleaded. "The more we know about each other the easier it will be to work together."

"Ontar and I left out homes under heartbreaking circumstances." Echo said as she stared out across the horizon."

Approaching the elf Wink put a hand on her foot and asked. "Why, what happened?"

Echo sighed. "It seems like so long ago. At the time, I was living with my parents in our hometown of Thramahas..."

Interlude

PART ONE

Echo slowly opened her eyes to look out of the meditation room's sole window. It was dark outside, with only the slightest trace of a breeze to sway the window's eloquent green curtains. Sitting cross-legged on a decorative red pillow, Echo felt relaxed in the familiar surroundings. The meditation room was a circular wooden space with a small curving stairway that descended along one wall. The round pillow she sat on was located in the center of the room beneath a small iron chandelier. Directly behind her was a gray stone chimney, which led to the fireplace below. The chimney was a little bit blocky compared to the rest of the room, but it did allow for a full-length mirror to hang from it.

Equally-spaced around the room were three beautifully crafted wardrobes (one for each member of Echo's family). This type of expert craftsmanship was common among her people and could often be seen on their doors, framework, and windowsills. Echo's own wardrobe had a leather armor dummy positioned next to it, with a bunch of equipment at its base. She often donned this gear when training with Searce, but at her current stage in life, Echo started to doubt whether it would ever serve any real purpose.

Situated next to the wardrobe that Echo's mother used was a privacy screen that had images of leafy tree branches and small forest animals painted on it. The top of the screen was torn in several spots thanks to the sharp claws of the family's pet owl, Hootie, who decided to perch himself on top of one of the screens many folds while staring down at Echo with his creepy yellow eyes. Echo hated that owl and could never understand why her father insisted on keeping it around.

Stretching as she stood, Echo walked over to her pile of equipment and put on both her cloak and weapon belt. Digging through her backpack on the floor, she pulled out a small piece of jerky and a wooden flute, which she tucked into her belt. Making her way towards the stairs, Echo saw Hootie leap from his perch and fly over to the top of the steps, where he landed in front of her and spread out his wings while hooting loudly.

Echo was sorely tempted to kick the stupid bird across the room but decided against it. Instead, she took the jerky in her hand and threw it near the owl's talons. Pressing his wings against his sides, Hootie bent down to pick up the dried meat in his beak before shuffling off to one side to let Echo pass.

"Spoiled, overgrown, pest," Echo grumbled as she went down the stairs.

Descending towards the house's main level, Echo almost tripped over a tangled mess of tree branches that covered the living room floor. Littered about all over the place these slender branches were carelessly piled around a chair by the window where her mother sat. Working near a candlelit table, Echo's mom was stripping away the branch's bark with a knife so they could be woven into baskets. A few already completed baskets rested on the table next to some cups and plates filled with food.

As Echo approached, her mother said, "Wait a minute, young lady. There's no breakfast until you go knock down that imp's nest of the branch below our house."

"Can't Dad do it?" Echo complained.

Echo's mother shook her head. "I asked *you* to do it three days ago. Now, if you don't want the little monsters to rob us blind, then you'll do as I asked."

"Dammit," Echo grumbled as she stomped back upstairs. Grabbing her bow and an arrow, she dashed down the steps and went outside onto a railed wooden platform with a couple of rope bridges connected to it. Like most of the homes in Thramahas, Echo and her parents lived in a rounded house with a shingled roof high among the branches of an ancient tree. The tree itself was covered in flowering vines whose pleasant aroma filled the night air.

Leaning over the railing, Echo quickly found the nest her mother was talking about. Made out of mud, branches, and bark, it held an assortment of odd little objects the imp had already gathered. Aiming her bow, Echo fired on the nest and knocked it to the ground. She was about to head back inside when an angry voice exclaimed, "My treasures! What did you do to my treasures!?"

Looking back at the branch she had just fired upon; Echo saw what appeared to be a scrawny red-skinned creature standing there with two stubby horns that protruded from its brow next to a pair of large pointed ears. The imp was one of the many fey folk who inhabited Illamine Forest, and judging by the expression on his fanged face, the two-foot monster wasn't pleased by her actions. Spreading some thin leathery wings that sprouted from his back, the imp angrily whipped its long arrow like tail in her direction.

Unimpressed, Echo replied, "Those *treasures* were stolen and used to lure children away from their homes so that you can either extort their parents or sell them into slavery."

Figit did not deny her accusation. "There are humans who would pay good money for a little elf girl to play with."

"If I ever see you with one of our children, I'll kill you myself!" Echo warned.

A sinister smile crossed Figit's face. "You elves act like you're lords of the forest, but your time is coming to an end, and I, for one, will delight in watching you fall." Spreading his wings, he then leapt off the branch and flew through the trees until he was out of sight.

Not taking his threat seriously, Echo entered her home and tossed the bow she had used onto the sprawling pile of branches. She then grabbed a plate and some chopsticks before telling her mom what had happened. Afterwards, she took the food and went about her usual routine.

Using her chopsticks, Echo ate from the plate of sliced apples and honey roasted walnuts while effortlessly making her way across the rope bridge in front of her. The bridge led to an adjoining tree with a platform attached to it. This platform, however, had only the tree's trunk at its center and was connected by three other bridges. A spiral staircase located near one of these bridges circled around the tree and led to the forest floor. Echo took the stairs without paying much attention, and upon reaching the bottom, she stepped out and casually nodded to a couple of late-night shoppers.

The town's market was built beneath its citizens homes with many of the merchant stalls located directly below the houses in which they lived. Making her way to her father's stall, Echo knew that business would be light this late in the evening, which was probably why her dad felt confident enough to put her in charge while he went to go meditate. Approaching his stall with a smile, she saw him help a traveling merchant load a bunch of baskets onto a mule-drawn cart before it took off down the road. Setting her plate and utensils on the stall, she asked, "How'd we do?"

"Let's just say that we made enough to have a little fun later," Ranix replied with a grin.

Echo smiled. Life always seemed a little bit easier when her father made a good sale, but then she remembered her plans and said, "Dad, you've got to get your meditation in! I'm meeting with Favin soon and *really* can't afford to get stuck here waiting on customers."

Ranix held his hands up in a mock surrender. "Alright, I'm going. Just don't burn down the stall while I'm gone," he joked before picking up her plate and heading off for home.

Echo could tell it was going to be a good day.

A few hours later, Echo was getting antsy as she saw the sky start to brighten with dawns early light. Business had been slow, and she desperately wanted to make her date this morning. Looking through the growing crowd of people, she saw her father heading towards the stall and gave him a quick wave. When he waved back, she took off through the forest in a hectic search for her beloved.

Coming to a stop before an old familiar tree, she looked up to see Favin sitting on one of its upper branches. Taking a moment to admire his masculine silhouette as the wind blew through his short auburn hair, Favin could usually be found wearing brown pants and boots with a tight white shirt that emphasized his gorgeous physique. Perfectly balanced on a sturdy branch while resting against the tree's thick trunk, he casually strummed a lute that's strap was wrapped around his shoulder.

Reaching out to grab a slender branch, Echo climbed up the tree to meet him. Alerted by the sound of rustling leaves, Favin looked down and called out, "Hey, there you are! I've been waiting up here so long that I think I'm starting to gather moss."

"Oh, really? Well, that would explain what you've been using to fill the space between your ears," Echo replied. Pulling herself up to a branch slightly below the one he sat on, Echo placed her hands on Favin's leg and tilted her head back. As she did, he leaned over and gave her a long deep kiss. Afterwards, they held each and gazed out onto the horizon. Within minutes, the sky was awash with the sun's first golden rays of light that heralded the arrival of the dawn.

For a long time, Echo and Favin just watched in silence as the forest's lush green canopy sprung to life with the birth of a new day. Reveling in nature's glory, the two were completely caught off guard when a soft feminine voice called out from below, "Excuse me, are you two going to spend all day up there?"

Looking down, Echo saw an elf with long sandy-colored hair, which was tied in a braid that hung down her left shoulder, and Echo realized it was Cora. Dressed in a pale green shirt with a long brown skirt, Cora and Echo had been best friends ever since her mother had paired them up as children to go collect branches in the forest.

"Sorry, Cora, we'll be right down," Echo shouted as she and Favin climbed down to meet her. Waiting patiently, Cora took a step back from the tree to keep from being hit by the flurry of dew drops that preceded them.

Once everyone was on the ground, they traveled through the forest to find their favorite rehearsal spot. As they did, Favin asked, "So, which musical masterpiece should we attempt today?"

"How about "Shilder's Remorse,"" replied Cora. "I've always liked that song, and its melody is really touching."

Echo shook her head. "No, it's too nice a day to play something like that. What about an upbeat tune?"

Favin thought for a moment. "You know, let's try something that's a little of both. What would you say to "Seasons of Growth?""

"Oh, that is a pretty song," Cora said with a smile.

Echo agreed, "Yeah, I like it. Nice thinking, hun."

Favin chuckled. "Thanks...the moss was my inspiration."

Echo and Favin both laughed while Cora gave them a peculiar look. Arriving at a small glade, the trio came upon a large gray rock used as their rehearsal spot. Climbing up to a flat spot near the top of the rock, Echo sat down and pulled out her flute. Leaning next to the familiar stone, Favin tightened the strings of his lute while Cora stood nearby. Waiting for some imagined cue, Echo and Favin both started playing their instruments a few beats before Cora sang. While far from being professional minstrels, the three merrily performed together simply out of the joy of each other's company.

This particular practice session lasted for quite some time and didn't come to an end until Cora's little brother, Grik, burst through the trees and interrupted them. "Cora! Mom says you need to come home and finish your chores." Echo knew Grik was basically a good kid, he just had a lousy sense of timing. In many ways, he reminded her of a younger version of Favin.

"Ugh...why can't you help her with the chores?" Cora grumbled.

"This is my chore!" Grik explained with a devious grin. "I'm out here looking for you."

Favin waved his hands in a calming motion. "It's alright, Cora. I have to get going anyways."

"Why's that?" Echo asked.

"Velen Jolarie plans to address the town this afternoon, and he wants every guard present to display our strength," Favin replied.

"What for?" inquired Echo.

"I don't know," Favin said with a shrug, "but I think it has something to do with a drop in trade. The point is that we've all got things to do, and we can't neglect our duties any longer."

"I suppose," Echo said with a frown. Slipping her flute back into her belt, she casually accompanied her friends back into town.

❖❖❖

Echo's conversation with Favin had gotten her curious about what the velen was planning. Anything that required him to address the town with a full contingent of guards had to be serious so, obviously, she wanted to find out what it was. Fortunately, she knew someone who probably had a pretty good idea about what was going on.

Opening the door to her aunt's treetop home, Echo entered the modest dwelling to find Searce reclining in a chair with her feet up on the dining table. Strikingly beautiful even by elvish standards, Searce had long, wavy brown hair and dark mysterious eyes. Dressed in relatively plain clothing, she wore a violet shirt with blue pants and brown leather armor that matched her boots. A weapon belt was always fastened around her waist in case she should ever wish to draw her sword.

Drinking tea from a blue porcelain cup, Searce sat her beverage down on the table next to the diagram of a lock. This diagram happened to be located beneath an actual lock, which sat in the middle of the table. Sliding her feet onto the floor, Searce looked at Echo and said, "Good morning, Squeaker. I was wondering when you'd make an appearance."

Pulling up a chair, Echo sat down and asked, "What's that?"

"That," Searce explained, "is your project for the next few hours. It's basically a standard chest lock. Your task will be to figure out how it works, what tools you would use to pick it, and where it might contain the trigger for a trap."

"Wonderful," Echo said with a sigh as she leaned back in her chair and stared at one of the many large maps that were nailed to the surrounding walls. These maps had been cobbled together during Searce's countless years of adventuring through the Rashben Region and reminded Echo she didn't even know she had an aunt until her early adolescence when her father suddenly had to explain the appearance of a long-lost sister on his doorstep.

Searce had taken a great interest in Echo from the moment they first met. She even helped her build a relationship with Favin (after rejecting him along with most of the town's other suitors). Grateful for what her aunt had done, Echo decided to become her protégé and learn the ways of a dabbler. This led to her development in exciting skills like fighting and magic, along with more mundane practices such as lock picking.

Giving the lock a reluctant look, Echo thought of a good diversion and asked, "Hey, Searce, do you to know why the velen is planning an address this afternoon?"

Searce traced her finger around the rim of her cup. "It probably has something to do with the sudden halt in trade relations with Kinnerba."

"Do you think the humans are plotting something?" Echo asked with concern.

"I don't know?" admitted Searce. "But it does concern me that we haven't heard anything from our border rangers."

Echo shrugged. "The rangers usually stay out in the wilderness unless something is wrong."

Searce tapped the table with her finger. "That's exactly my point. Trade ceases with Kinnerba, and not a single ranger has shown up to report on it."

"Should we be worried?" Echo asked.

"I think we'll get the answer to that question when we hear the velen's address," Searce said as she took another sip from her cup.

❖ ❖ ❖

A few hours later, Echo and her aunt heard the horns that signaled a town meeting was about to take place. Leaving Searce's home, the two made their way to a nearby rope bridge that overlooked the velen's hall. The hall was a round, dome-like building on the forest floor with long oval windows and a stained-glass roof. The front of this wooden building, however, was dominated by a large flat wall with a simple stage attached to it. Centered along the wall was a prominent double door that had two life-sized stone statues of elvish warriors holding swords on either side of it. A little behind these statues were two great tapestries that depicted an apple tree beneath a cloudy blue sky. Which was, of course, was the emblem of the Illamine.

As the great doors opened, Velen Jolarie emerged to take center stage. Dressed in regal garments, the velen wore an elegant green sash across one shoulder, with colorful autumn leaves stitched into it. Slightly behind him was a white-robed cleric of Talana known as Teryl, and a serious-looking warrior with long brown hair called Jayvoe. Jayvoe was captain of the guard (which was apparent by the gold studded leather armor he wore). He also used a legendary long bow with a golden drawstring known as the Bow of Unyielding. Together, these three individuals were the most prominent elves in Thramahas.

Addressing the crowd that had gathered near the stage, Velen Jolarie spoke.

"Greetings, my friends. We are gathered here today to discuss a threat to the prosperity of our town. As many of you may know, trade relations with the human settlement of Kinnerba have suddenly ceased. Seeking answers to this drastic development, I sent an official inquiry to the kingdom of Coronas but received no reply.

"Taking the initiative, I then decided to have our border rangers investigate the area around Kinnerba. Sadly, it grieves me to tell you that not one of them has returned from this task. Now, as you all know, Kinnerba is only a couple days' travel from Thramahas, and any threats that have emerged there could easily endanger our lives as well.

"That is why I have decided to ask Captain Jayvoe to lead a company of guards on a mission to Kinnerba so that we may learn what has happened to the humans there and, if necessary, *crush* whatever enemies lurk on our country's border."

Stepping forward on cue, Jayvoe shouted, "Company… assemble!"

Echo watched as four lines of leather-clad guards gathered on either side of the velen's hall and marched forward to form ranks at the front of the stage. As the crowd stepped back to allow their protectors through, Echo spotted Favin moving in step with his comrades and waved at him. Flashing her a quick smile and a wink, Favin immediately adopted a sterner expression as he fell into place next to the other guards.

Spreading his arms, Velen Jolarie spoke once more. "Citizens of Thramahas, these brave elves stand before you today ready to lay down their lives for our safety. Let us honor them with our applause and remember them in our prayers for the road ahead will most surely be a difficult one."

Almost at once, the crowd started clapping as a feeling of pride washed over them. Looking down at the masses from her spot on the rope bridge, Searce asked, "So, Squeaker, what do you think?"

Echo's gaze was fixed on her beloved. "I don't know. I'm glad the velen's taking steps to keep our enemies from crossing the border but, at the same time, this is Favin's first real mission for the Illamine, and I'm worried that something might happen to him."

"Would you like to accompany them?" Searce asked, knowing full well that her niece would relish the opportunity.

The question surprised Echo. "What do you mean? I'm not a guard, and Jayvoe would never let me just tag along on something like this."

Searce gave her a sly smile. "I wouldn't worry about Jayvoe. The velen and I go way back, and I'm sure that if I asked him nicely, he would be more than happy to authorize your coming along. Besides, don't you think that it's about time to put some of that training and equipment I've given you to use?"

Echo was practically giddy at the notion of traveling with Favin on such an important mission. "Oh, Searce, you know I couldn't ask for anything more."

Listening to the two stupid elves mindlessly chatter away, Figit sat huddled on a nearby tree branch with a couple other imps. The velen's address had gone exactly as he had hoped, and soon, his plans would be complete. Leaning close to one of his companions, he whispered, "The trap is set, but we have to hurry back to Kinnerba. Lydon and his men need to cross the border and get into hiding before the elves arrive." Giggling maliciously, the three imps spread their wings and quickly flew off into the forest.

Ontar stretched beneath the blanket of his nice warm bed. Last night's drunken romp with Vye had been rather intense, and he had to admit there was nothing quite like having sex with an experienced partner. Turning to his side, he opened his eyes to see the lady in question happened to be absent when he awoke. This wasn't entirely unexpected since Vye was widely regarded as Fort Hasborne's pony. At some point, everybody got a ride, and last night happened to be his turn. The fact the serving wench was known for loving and leaving her men didn't really bother him… that is until he realized that all his clothes were gone!

Afraid of being robbed, Ontar got out of bed and searched his room for any other missing goods. Strangely, everything seemed to be in place right down to his weapon belt and coin pouch. So, if money and equipment didn't attract his would-be thief, then it was probably a prank of some sort. Unfortunately, Ontar wasn't laughing.

Grabbing the blanket off his bed and wrapping it around his waist, Ontar left his room and entered onto the main floor of a tavern that he had called home for the past five years. The Drunken Soldier was appropriately named given that it was located within the walls of a Coronasian fortress. Stepping into the dining hall, Ontar was relieved to see there were only a couple of patrons milling about, and that most of them were servants who worked at the keep. The military crowd usually didn't show up here until later in the evening.

Glancing around the hall, Ontar spotted Vye sweeping up a pile of crumbs and dirt near the buildings entrance. Alerted to his presence by stares from the other patrons, she looked up and smiled. "Hey, sweetie. So, did you have a good time last night?"

Sauntering up to her as casually as possible while wearing a blanket around his waist, Ontar said. "Last night was spectacular, and I think we could have enjoyed another romp this morning if you hadn't taken off with my clothes."

Vye leaned against her broom. "Oh, sorry about that. Gerig offered to take me out to dinner later if I gave him your laundry."

Ontar bristled! Gerig was a self-righteous prick who tormented him from the moment he arrived at Fort Hasborne. Apparently, he didn't like the fact Ontar was getting combat training without actually joining the army. So, stupid little pranks like this were concocted to make his life difficult, and he'd just about had enough of them!

Trying to stay calm, Ontar leaned close to Vye and asked, "Did you happen to see *where* he took my clothes?"

Vye thought for a moment. "I think I saw him heading over towards the flagpole."

Moving past her and out the tavern's door, Ontar stepped into Fort Hasborne's courtyard and saw the towering spiked logs that formed the fortress's walls and keep. It was a beautiful spring morning with only a couple of white clouds marring an otherwise bright blue sky. Looking towards the center of the courtyard, Ontar saw a tall wooden pole with a dark red flag that had the emblem of a lion's head with a flaming mane on it. This proud symbol of Coronas flapped wildly in the breeze, and above it was a large cloth bundle that had been attached to the top of the pole. Ontar guessed that his clothes were in there, and he hurriedly made his way towards it.

Unfortunately, he didn't get too far before he spotted four soldiers coming towards him while chuckling to themselves. Wearing their standard chain armor and surcoats, the only equipment these men lacked were their helmets and aventails. Ontar immediately spotted Gerig amongst them. A cruel man with greasy brown hair and a sneer on his lips, Gerig saw Ontar approach and said, "Look at that, boys. You sleep with whores long enough, and pretty soon, you start to dress like them."

"You son of a bitch!" Ontar growled as he clenched his fists and prepared to smash the other man's face in. However, just as he got within striking range, one of Gerig's cronies decided to step on the long blanket that haphazardly hung from around his waist. Stopped in his tracks, Ontar hastily grabbed onto the blanket and tried to preserve what little dignity he still had.

Snickering, Gerig said, "Careful, Ontar. Otherwise, the other girls might start to think you're easy."

Laughing loudly, Gerig and the soldiers pushed past him and made their way towards the keep. Giving them a dark stare, Ontar refastened his blanket before trying to vent his anger by shaking the bundle off the flagpole.

"Here try these," came a familiar voice from behind. Turning around, Ontar saw a scruffy soldier with short brown hair and stubble who held three small stones in his left hand. Yorus was Ontar's younger cousin, and the two had often played together as children. As an adult, Yorus decided to enlist in the army, and he even helped Ontar get his job at the Drunken Soldier. Deep down, Ontar suspected that Yorus wanted him to join the military as well, but with men like Gerig running around, he had some deep reservations about doing so.

"Thanks," Ontar grumbled as he took two stones and threw one at the bundle. It missed. "That bastard did it to me again."

Yorus gave a knowing nod. "He's just trying to provoke you."

"Well, it's working," Ontar growled as he missed with the second stone.

"Even so, you can't afford to lose your temper," Yorus warned. "The quickest way to get thrown out of here is if Sir Brovine learns you were pummeling his men." Taking the last stone in his right hand, Yorus threw it at the bundle and succeeded in knocking it off the flagpole. "There. Now, get dressed and go have some breakfast. I got Sergeant Raglak to spar with you this afternoon."

Ontar picked up the bundle and dusted it off. "Great! Is there any chance he wields a morning star?"

Yorus shook his head. "Nope. It looks like you two will be training with two-handed swords."

Ontar let out a sigh. While grateful for the chance to get in some training, he was always a little disappointed when he couldn't use the weapon he was most experienced with. "Ah well, I suppose any trainings better than none."

"That's the spirit," Yorus said as he clapped his hand on Ontar's shoulder and walked back with him towards the tavern.

❧❧❧

Ontar's light gray cloak fluttered around his legs as he stepped back from his opponent. Equipped in clothes and gear far more appropriate than what he was wearing this morning, he now wore a chain shirt with an iron helmet and had a normal shield strapped to his backpack. Holding a two-handed sword in front of him, Ontar squared off against Sergeant Raglak on the training grounds at the side of the keep. A few soldiers stood nearby and watched with interest as he raised his weapon and bravely charged the sergeant.

Adopting a defensive stance, the scraggly gray-haired sergeant parried the attack with the center of his sword then tilted his blade in a motion that brought its edge within a hair of Ontar's neck! Stepping back and lowering his weapon, the sergeant frowned and said, "Do you see what happened there? You brought your blade too far in on the attack. Ontar, you have to remember you're using a two-handed sword now, and its length is one of your greatest assets. Never let an enemy get any closer to you than you have to."

Ontar heeded the instruction with a nod. Two-handed weapons were always a bit tricky for him but learning how to master them was all part of the fun. Readying himself, he loosened his shoulders and said, "I'll keep that in mind. Shall we go again?"

Sergeant Raglak waved his left hand dismissively. "Nah, I think we've done enough playing around. Why don't you pull out that morning star of yours, and we'll get into something a little more serious."

Ontar could hardly contain his grin as he set aside the two-handed sword to draw forth his morning star and shield. Eager to begin the next match, he almost didn't notice when the gate to Fort Hasborne was pulled open to allow a plainly-dressed man on horseback into the courtyard. Dismounting when he reached the keep, the man talked with a couple of concerned soldiers, who took his horse before leading him into the building. Puzzled by the stranger, Ontar couldn't help but wonder what sort of business could possibly have brought him here.

❧ ❧ ❧

It was late into the afternoon before Ontar would get an answer to that question. By this time, his sparring match had been concluded and his weapons and armor were put away so he could take up the more mundane task of mucking out the Drunken Soldier's stables. Ontar hated this job, and it was one he'd been forced to do ever since he was a child. The smell of horse manure always made him gag, and to compensate, he learned how to hold his breath for extended periods of time.

Shooing flies away, Ontar noticed the stranger's horse (which he'd seen earlier) was now resting in one of the stalls. *Perhaps I'll get a chance to learn some more about this man from the tavern's staff once I've finished here,* he thought. Leaning over with his shovel to scoop up yet another steaming pile of crap, Ontar was caught off guard when Yorus suddenly appeared at the entrance of the stable. His eyes were red, and there was a pained expression on his face. "Ontar, I need to talk with you in private. It's urgent."

Hesitantly setting down his shovel, Ontar said, "Alright, follow me." Leading his cousin out of the stable, Ontar entered the tavern and headed towards his room. As he did, he noticed the man he saw earlier was seated at a table and eating a hefty meal.

Opening the door to his room, Ontar stepped inside and stood by the bed. Staring at his cousin, he asked, "Yorus, what's going on?"

Yorus closed the door behind him and took a deep breath. "Ontar, the man you saw in the tavern just now was a lumberjack from Shroka."

Ontar nodded in acknowledgement. Shroka was a village near his hometown of Kinnerba. Merchants from there would often spend the night at his family's tavern when coming off the trade route to the Illamine.

Yorus's voice wavered. "According to him, Kinnerba has been sacked, and all of its residents are dead."

"What…no!" Ontar exclaimed as his legs went weak, and he sat on the bed. Bracing himself with his hands on his knees, he said, "No, how could this happen? Who would do something like that?"

Yorus leaned over and rested a hand on Ontar's shoulder. "According to Sir Brovine, there is a bandit named Lydon, whose men have been raiding villages along the border and hiding in elvish lands to avoid capture."

"Why aren't the elves doing anything!?" Ontar demanded.

Letting out a sigh, Yorus replied, "Lydon hasn't attacked the elves directly, and they refuse to believe that a human could just pass in and out of their realm undetected."

Ontar could barely contain his sorrow. "So, what are we going to do now?"

"Sir Brovine is dispatching a patrol to investigate and determine where the bandits will attack next."

Ontar looked his cousin straight in the eyes. "Yorus, I have to be on that patrol."

A tear streamed down Yorus's cheek. "I've already made the request for both of us, and with any luck, we *will* find the bastards who did this."

"Thank you," Ontar said.

Squeezing Ontar's shoulder, Yorus stood up and quietly exited the room.

Ontar couldn't believe what he had just heard. His whole family was gone! Never again would he be able to taste his mother's home cooked meals or go fishing with his father down by the riverbank. Nor would he be able to give his little sister a big hug after coming home from a long journey. The indescribable feeling of loss that consumed him was overwhelming. Unable to hold back his grief any longer, Ontar buried his face in his hands and wept.

⊰⊱⊰⊱⊰⊱

"Are you nervous?" Favin asked Echo as they traveled with a company of guards down a dirt road through the forest.

"Of what?" Echo inquired as she squirmed within her leather armor. She and Favin both had exactly same equipment but, for some reason, hers felt heavy and binding while he, on the other hand, seemed to strut around as comfortable as ever.

Favin appeared to be irritated by the question. "Of traveling to a foreign land to fight against some fearsome unknown enemy."

Echo snorted. "Favin, I think you're being a little dramatic. Both of us have been to Kinnerba before, and anything that comes at us will also have to deal with just about every single guard in Thramahas."

"Well, just to be on the safe side, you should probably stay close to me," Favin warned. "Remember that Coronas is a violent realm which conquered the prosperous lands along our border to become the kingdom it is today. When they eventually grew bold enough to attack us directly, we taught them a lesson they'd never forget, but as a result, the humans continue to hold a lingering grudge."

Echo couldn't help but smile over the concern in his voice and was about to comment on it when someone up ahead called the company to a halt. Listening intently, she heard the sound of rushing water coming from close by, and knew they were near the river which formed the border between Coronas and the Illamine.

Speaking in a cautious tone, a scout came up to Jayvoe and pointed to the ground they stood on. "Hey, Captain, look at this. The earth around here is all soft and level, and the road practically blends right into it. It's almost as if someone is intentionally trying to smooth out the surrounding area."

Kneeling to study the earth, Jayvoe frowned. "There's magic at work here, and something is definitely trying to cover its tracks. I want weapons out and bows at ready. We'll move amongst the trees until we reach the river. Is that understood?"

The guards nodded in agreement as Echo and Favin drew their swords and left the road to sneak through the forest. It wasn't long before the company reached the banks of the Cherenon River and spotted a gray stone bridge that led into the human lands. On the bridge's far side was an old square watch tower that had a small stable connected to it. If Echo remembered right, the tower was Kinnerba's only real fortification, which wasn't really all that surprising given the size of the town.

Waiting for orders, Echo and Favin watched as Jayvoe sent his scout across the bridge. Moments later, Echo gasped as a flock of crows from the other side took off into the sky.

Leaning close to one of her pointed ears, Favin whispered, "Are you alright?"

Echo blushed. "Yeah, the stupid birds just startled me."

Seconds later, the scout appeared on the far side of the bridge and signaled for the others to come. Forming ranks, the company cautiously crossed the bridge to enter Kinnerba. As they did, a slight breeze carried a foul stench to Echo's nostrils...the stench of death.

Stepping onto human soil and moving past the watch tower, Echo saw a town whose buildings lined both sides of the main road. A tavern and a stone shrine marked the town's most notable structures while several small houses and shops comprised the remainder of this settlement. It all would have been rather ordinary were it not for a sight that chilled both Echo and her fellow companions to the bone.

Bodies…everywhere.

Echo looked as the corpses of men, women, and children were seen strewn about and rotting in the sun. It had been forty years since the last person had died in Thramahas, and when they did, the entire community gathered together to mourn their passing. Here, however, an entire town had been massacred! And there wasn't a single person left to weep for the dead. Echo trembled upon seeing this horror, and Favin sheathed his sword so he could put an arm around her shoulders and comfort her.

A cold expression crossed Jayvoe's face as he ordered his guards to search the town and surrounding forest. Favin and Echo had been given the task of exploring the watch tower. It would be a gruesome duty from the moment they began. Many of those who died had desperately sought the tower's protection, and the nearby corpse of a chain-clad guard indicated its poor defenders had doubtlessly tried to help them.

Entering the attached stable, Echo tried not to gag at the stench. Shooing away flies, she and Favin spotted the mutilated corpse of a second guard crushed beneath the body of his dead horse. *He didn't even have a chance to find help,* Echo thought before leaving the stable to explore the rest of the tower.

Stepping onto the cold gray stone of the towers first floor, Echo saw a large square room with stairs along the wall leading up to the buildings next level. The chamber had obviously been ransacked with its desk and dining table carelessly turned over.

A cauldron could be seen resting on its side by the fireplace near a couple of empty stools. If there was anything of value in this room, it surely must have already been taken.

Climbing up the stairs to the second floor, Echo and Favin came upon a room with three beds, a couple of empty weapon racks, and some stripped armor dummies. Echo shook her head. If the beds were any indication, then Kinnerba was probably only protected by three modestly equipped guards. Hardly a force capable of stopping any real threat. Continuing on to the top of the tower, Echo found this last room to be pretty bare, with only a small table and two stools located across from a wall lined with slitted windows and a few pairs of shackles. Looking out one of these windows, Favin saw Jayvoe standing near the center of town.

"Company…assemble!" called the captain.

Heeding his command, Favin and Echo left the tower to join the other guards as they crowded around Jayvoe.

Surveying those who had gathered, Jayvoe proclaimed in a loud voice, "A tragedy has befallen this town, and its dead deserve the respect they once had in life. Gather the bodies of those who have fallen and bring them here so that we may build them a funeral pyre."

Obeying his orders without question, Echo, Favin, and the other guards all proceeded to collect the corpses they found along with any other burnable material they could pile up in the center of town. Once this was done, Jayvoe approached the pyre with a burning torch in his hand.

"Kardok has claimed the souls of those who once lived within this town. Now, let Mirsha return their bodies to the soil so the land may be renewed."

With that said, Jayvoe took his torch and tossed it onto the pyre. Within minutes, its flames had consumed the bodies of Kinnerba's inhabitants. In a moment of solidarity, Echo and

Favin joined hands with the other guards who had gathered and formed a circle around the blaze. Staring into the burning inferno, the elves sang a song of mourning for those unfortunate innocents who had tragically perished.

It wasn't long after the song's conclusion that a scout called out, "Riders…approaching fast!"

Drawing his bow, Jayvoe looked to the others and commanded, "Conceal yourselves."

As the other guards scattered, Favin looked at Jayvoe and asked, "What about you?"

"I will see who we're up against," Jayvoe said as he nocked an arrow.

Ontar spurred his horse forward until it matched pace with his cousin's mount. The two were part of a six-man patrol riding west along a dirt road through Illamine Forest. Having pushed their animals hard over the past couple of days, the patrol was currently moving at a canter until they reached Kinnerba. Clearly bothered by the loss of his family, Ontar said, "Tell me, Yorus, what do you know about Lydon?"

Yorus tried to recall what little he knew. "They say he's one of our countrymen, and that he was part of several different bandit groups before starting one of his own. Some people believe he's won the trust of the fey folk by purchasing the children they steal and selling them to slavers."

"But how would I find him in a fight?" Ontar demanded.

"Look for a man with a blood red beard who uses two short swords in battle," Yorus replied. "Just be careful if you face him. He kills for a living and has a lot more combat experience than you."

Ontar felt his muscles tense. "It doesn't matter. Every man I kill in battle will only make me stronger. So, when I finally do face that son of a bitch, he will die realizing *no one* can stand against me!"

"Dammit, Ontar, get back in formation!" Gerig snarled from up ahead. "Just because Sir Brovine took pity on you doesn't mean I have to."

Ontar's grip tightened on the reins of his horse. Gerig's idea of a *formation* was to have him riding about as far back from the rest of the soldiers as possible. Ontar had nearly exploded when he learned the pompous little shit was put in command of the patrol. Unfortunately, he was there more as courtesy than anything else, which meant he didn't have any right to complain about Gerig's leadership. Reluctantly following orders, Ontar slowed his horse and fell into step behind Yorus.

Perturbed by the company he kept, Ontar tried to take comfort in the familiar surroundings that indicated he was close to home. Growing up in this part of the forest, he recognized almost every tree, rock, and shrub the patrol came across. In the past, these landmarks would have put him in pleasant mood before a homecoming, but now, they only served to increase his heartache. A part of Ontar deeply wished that he wasn't going to Kinnerba so that he could preserve the memories from his childhood. However, the need to know what happened there took precedence, and he was determined to find some answers.

Rounding a bend in the road, Ontar smelled smoke coming from up ahead. Gerig obviously caught the scent as well and ordered his men to follow him as he galloped towards Kinnerba. Within moments, the patrol had passed through the tree line and entered into the town of Ontar's birth. It was an odd sensation for Ontar to see the place that he once called home without the people who used to reside in it. What was even more peculiar, though, was that a large funeral pyre had been erected in the center of town with a single, long-haired elf standing next to it. The elf carried a fancy loaded bow and looked at the patrol as if he were expecting them.

Echo and Favin watched Jayvoe face the patrol from a slitted window at the top of the watch tower. Having their bows armed and ready, a single word from their captain would bring a hail of arrows upon the unsuspecting humans. Watching with nervous excitement, Echo saw the patrols leader trot up to Jayvoe on his horse.

"Hey...hey! What are you doing?" Gerig asked as he gazed between the elf and the funeral pyre.

"Paying homage to those who have passed before their time," Jayvoe replied calmly.

Gerig didn't really care for poetic nonsense. "Oh, really, because to me it looks like you're desecrating our dead."

Jayvoe was genuinely shocked at the accusation. "Not at all. I can assure you that my intentions are truly honorable. I am Jayvoe. Captain of the guard in Thramahas, and I've been sent here to investigate the tragic loss of life you see before you."

Gerig snorted. "Huh, well, I'm Corporal Gerig Arben. A ranking soldier of Coronas whose duty is to keep elves like you from prancing across our border."

"I see," Jayvoe replied coldly. He didn't appreciate the tone this *inferior* was taking with him. "However, the loss of life here is of concern to both our people, and I think that we can all benefit from helping each other in this matter."

"Somehow, I doubt that," Gerig said. "For all I know, your people were the ones who actually raided this town, and they left you behind to try and hide any evidence of their involvement."

"What! How dare you accuse me of such a disgusting act," Jayvoe snapped.

"Oh, don't bother getting all high and mighty," Gerig retorted. "I'm giving you one chance to flee from here while you still can."

Jayvoe's jaw clenched. "Is that a threat?"

Gerig was losing his temper. "Yes, you stupid *twig*. Now, get your ass back across that bridge before I kick it there."

Glaring at this insolent fool, Jayvoe said, "Try it."

Gerig was not about to let this challenge go unmet and immediately drew his sword. Ontar saw Yorus and the other soldiers follow suit but hesitated in joining them. As far as he was concerned, Gerig had provoked this fight, and he refused to participate in it unless absolutely necessary.

Watching the humans draw their swords, Jayvoe raised his Bow of Unyielding and fired a warning shot.

This *warning shot* completely took the patrol by surprise as Jayvoe's arrow passed straight through one of Gerig's legs, raked a long bloody cut along the side of Yorus's horse, and pierced the chest of Ontar's mount before emerging from its rump to continue its lethal path through the forest. One side of the patrol immediately fell into disarray as Gerig howled in pain while Yorus's horse reared up and threw its rider from the saddle. Ontar's animal didn't even accomplish that much as it simply collapsed to the ground dead.

Struggling to get off his slain mount, Ontar looked around and suddenly realized there were elves everywhere! Stepping out from behind trees, emerging from vacant buildings, and looking down on him from their rooftops, these silent warriors clearly had the upper hand in this situation. Reacting either out of fear or pain, Gerig ordered the patrol into a hasty retreat that sent them galloping back along the road. Unable to comply, Ontar watched helplessly as Yorus's wounded horse ran past him. Holding completely still, he cautiously waited to see what the elves would do.

"Should we kill them?" shouted an elf from a nearby rooftop.

Jayvoe raised his hand in a halting gesture. "No, let the inferiors flee for now. Perhaps when they return, it will be with someone who *isn't* a complete idiot."

"What should we do with those two?" asked an elf who stood by a tree and pointed to Ontar and Yorus.

Giving them a cursory glance Jayvoe said, "Bring them to the tower for questioning."

❧ ❧ ❧

Apprehended by elves, Ontar and Yorus were taken to the top floor of the stone watch tower where Ontar used to train with local guards as an adolescent. Shackled with arms up along a wall next to his cousin, Ontar saw the elves remove his backpack, shield, and weapon belt, which were tossed onto a small table across from him. There were two elves already in this chamber when Ontar and Yorus arrived, and they were selected for guard duty as the others left the tower.

Favin paced the floor in front of the prisoners and studied them closely. Echo, on the other hand, pulled up a stool and began rummaging through their equipment. It would be nightfall before any of them would choose to speak. Ontar gazed at the female elf for quite some time. Somehow, he felt like he recognized her but, at the moment, he couldn't put a name to the face.

Favin did *not* like the way Ontar looked at Echo. Lighting one of the torch-lit sconces, he asked, "What are you staring at, human?"

"He's probably just watching as you thieving elves rob us blind," Yorus blurted out.

"Silence, inferior!" Favin snapped. "My people are not thieves."

"Speak for yourself," Echo said as she took the coin pouch off Yorus's weapon belt and tossed it onto the stool next to her. "Here, Favin. Why don't you take this pouch and buy me something pretty when we get back to Thramahas?"

Yorus snickered, and Favin gave him a dirty look. However, before words could be exchanged, Ontar glanced at Echo and said, "I know you. Your name is Echo, isn't it?"

Initially, Echo hadn't bothered to pay much attention to the humans, but when one of them addressed her by name, she couldn't help but answer, "Yes…yes, it is. Have we met?"

Ontar nodded. "When I was a child, you watched over me while my father conducted business in Thramahas. Back then, they called me Onnie, but now I'm known as Ontar."

Standing up slowly, Echo approached Ontar and examined his features. Humans aged so terribly quick it was almost impossible to recognize them before they reached maturity, but there was something in Ontar's demeanor that reminded her of a little boy she used to tend to not so very long ago.

"Oh, yeah, I think I remember you. You used to have family around here, if I'm not mistaken."

Ontar winced at the comment as the anguish in his heart was still fresh. "Yes…I did."

Favin folded his arms. "Hmm. I didn't realize you were from this area. Perhaps then, you might know what happened to the residents of this town?"

Yorus gave him a surprised look. "Didn't you see the bandits who did this?"

Shaking her head, Echo said, "No. Everyone was already dead when we arrived. All we did was lay their bodies to rest."

"So, Lydon must have already fled across the border," Ontar stated with melancholy dismay.

"May I assume Lydon is the leader of the bandits who attacked this town?" came a voice from the stairs that caught everyone's attention. Entering the top of the tower, Jayvoe gave a stern, yet curious, look at his prisoners.

Ontar nodded. "Yes. We believe he's hiding on your half of the border even as we speak."

Echo shook her head. "No, that's not possible. We would have already run into him if he tried to do that."

"Not if he had help," Yorus argued.

"There are no traitors among my people," Favin snapped.

Ontar started to get a little annoyed with Favin. "What about the fey folk?"

Growing concerned, Echo asked, "You don't think the imps are involved, do you?"

"It might explain how they would be able to avoid detection by our rangers," Jayvoe mused.

"We have to get back to Thramahas!" Echo exclaimed. "Our families and homes are vulnerable while we're here."

Yorus frowned when he heard this. "I'm afraid it won't be that easy. Gerig thinks that your people attacked Kinnerba, and there's a good chance that Sir Brovine will send a contingent of troops to retaliate. If you abandon the town now, then there will be nothing to keep my kingdom from attacking whatever the bandits haven't already destroyed in Thramahas."

"*If* there are bandits in Thramahas," Favin argued. "These humans have offered no proof that anyone has crossed the border or are working with the imps. For all we know, they could be trying to lure our troops away from their defensive positions so that either the bandits or their soldiers can attack us from behind."

Echo personally didn't think the humans were lying. "Favin, I love you, but if you're wrong, then Thramahas could be in real danger."

"And if I'm right, then *we* could be putting ourselves in danger," Favin countered.

Jayvoe didn't like the uncertainty of the situation but knew he needed to act. "I think the best course of action would be to divide our forces. Favin, I want you to lead half of the guards back to Thramahas and ensure that it's protected from bandits. I will stay here with the other half to make sure that Coronas doesn't try to invade our lands."

"And the prisoners?" Favin asked.

Jayvoe pointed to Yorus and said, "He will stay as proof that we did not come here to kill all of the humans." Pointing to Ontar, he added, "That one will go with you to Thramahas. The velen can question him about any links there might be between the bandits and the imps."

Feeling honored to serve in a leadership position, Favin gave Jayvoe a respectful bow. "I'll make sure my guards are ready to leave at dawn."

Ontar exchanged an uncertain look with Yorus. By dividing their forces, the elves risked not having the strength to fend off either bandits or soldiers, and while soldiers could be negotiated with, the bandits wouldn't hesitate to cut down a weaker opponent. A situation that didn't bode well for whoever they decided to target first.

Two days later, Ontar found himself struggling to keep up with the brisk pace set by his captors. The elves' strange meditation practices allowed them to get by with only minimal rest, which meant they would push him to keep going from sunup to sundown, and well into the night. Adding to Ontar's discomfort were the ropes, which bound his hands behind his back and made sleep extremely difficult on his already exhausting journey.

Trudging along a dark dirt road through the forest, Ontar guessed that it was getting close to midnight and prayed they were near their destination. Tasked with watching over him, Echo carried a torch to light his way while Favin led the other guards towards their destination. Feeling pity for the human, she asked, "Does traveling this road bring back memories of your childhood?"

Ontar nodded. "Yes. My father always felt your people were such talented musicians. We even tried to sing their songs, but usually, our efforts ended in nothing more than laughter as we could never remember the lyrics."

"Your father was a good man," Echo added. "I remember the first time we met was when he came to Thramahas and saw me trying to rescue child who had climbed up a tree and was too afraid to get down. The child had panicked and refused all my attempts at help. Eventually, I got frustrated, threw a rock at the boy and caught him when he fell. Amused by the way I handled the situation, your father asked if I would watch you while he conducted his business. When I asked why, he said that sometimes reasoning with a child doesn't work, and when that happens, you have to be willing to throw a rock."

Smiling sadly, Ontar said, "He always was a good judge of character. I just can't believe the gods would let someone so kind be killed by someone so cruel."

For a brief moment, Echo saw the little boy she used to care for and wished she could comfort him. "Thramahas is just up ahead. Once we arrive, I'll make sure the velen treats you with respect while you're in his custody."

"Thank you," Ontar replied. He was about to say something further when the company of guards noticed a scout running back along the road towards them. Panting as he came to a stop, the scout looked to Favin and said, "You must hurry! Thramahas is burning!"

"I want bows and blades out NOW!" Favin ordered.

Moving swiftly, Echo joined half of the guards in pulling out their bows and loading them while Favin drew forth his sword and shield to fight with the other half. Prodded forward by the elves at his side, Ontar went along with his captors as Favin ordered the elves to, "MOVE!"

It wasn't long before everyone heard the faint sounds of crackling wood mixed with the cries of battle. The scent of smoke hung heavy in the air and as the company reached the end of the road where they stopped just outside the perimeter of Thramahas… and saw the town was burning!

Echo stood wide-eyed as she witnessed the homes of her friends and neighbors alight with searing hot flames that spread to the very trees they rested in. Those who lived in these homes could be seen running across rope bridges or jumping off platforms in a tragic attempt at escaping a fiery demise. Sadly, thing's on the ground weren't any safer. Watching in horror, she saw the burnt-out husk of a blackened house collapse onto a merchant stall where a terrified family had been hiding, killing them instantly.

Basking in the chaos of this moment was a host of wicked humans armed with a variety of deadly weapons and armor. Looting stalls, attacking innocents, and taking prisoners, these black-hearted bandits moved about the forest floor like blood-thirsty wolves eager to pounce on their helpless prey.

Favin refused to let these monsters destroy everything he held dear. Pointing his sword, he shouted, "Archers! Fire on any bandit who tries to reach our homes. As for the rest of you…ATTACK!" Watching his fellow guards charge towards the bandits' ranks, Favin turned to Echo and said, "Stay here…stay safe…I will come back for you." Not waiting for her to respond, he surged forth into the fray and swung his sword at the nearest bandit he could find.

Arrows whizzed past Echo's head as she watched her true love go. During their time together, Favin had always appeared to be kind and gentle person. To see him attacking an enemy that came from nowhere seemed almost surreal…but that enemy was not alone. As Favin fought against one particularly vicious foe, she spotted a second bandit armed with a war hammer coming to aid his companion.

Moving on instinct, Echo pulled out her bow and drew back an arrow. Never before had she taken the life of another intelligent being, yet when faced with a man who was attempting to kill her beloved, she didn't even hesitate to take aim and fire upon him. The bandit stumbled and fell as the arrow pierced his chest and punctured his heart. Favin barely noticed. Killing his opponent with unbridled fury, he rallied the guards at his side and charged deeper into the frenzied inferno of Thramahas.

The elves have made their move, Ontar thought as he witnessed the carnage around him. *Now, it's the bandits' turn.* Sure enough, an imposing bandit with long red hair and a beard had gathered his own archers near a merchant's stall within firing range of where the guards were positioned. Matching the description of the man who killed his family, Ontar saw Lydon was dressed in a tattered brown cloak that scarcely went past his shoulder blades and wore a crimson headband. His sleeveless tan shirt was barely visible beneath some chain armor that came to a stop just above his green pants and black boots. Clutching a short sword in each hand, he pointed one of the blades towards the bow-wielding guards and instructed his men to, "Fire!"

Seeing Echo was about to get struck by the barrage, Ontar slammed into her side, causing both of them to fall to the ground. The bold act saved their lives as the surrounding guards soon had their bodies riddled with arrows. Terrified by the sudden deaths of those around her, Echo said, "I have to find Favin!"

Shouldering her bow, she drew forth her sword and shield and told Ontar to, "Turn around." Ontar obediently did so and was rewarded with Echo's blade slicing the ropes that bound him. Free to meet her gaze, Ontar stared at Echo as she said, "Your life is your own. Do as you wish."

Watching as Echo went to join her suitor in battle, Ontar saw the devastation being wrought upon the elves and remembered what these bastards had done back at Kinnerba. Thinking of the family he'd never see again, he felt an unbridled rage wash over him, and clenching his fists, he grabbed a sword from one of the dead guards and followed her into the battle!

Catching sight of a leather clad bandit with a cloth sack looting a nearby merchant stall, Ontar lunged forward ready to strike. Seeing him approach, the bandit kicked over the stall to slow his advance as he grabbed a spear and thrust it outwards. Sidestepping the attack, Ontar felt the spear's head scrape across his chain armor just below the collar. Ready for a counterstrike, Ontar swung his sword and slashed the bandit's right hand, leaving him to wield his weapon with the left one. Distracted by the painful blow, the bandit died while switching his battle stance as Ontar plunged his sword deep into the man's side.

Watching his foe die caused Ontar to shudder. This was real! There were no trainers to mediate the fight or practice restraint to prevent serious injury. It was kill or be killed, and for all Ontar knew, he might actually die this night. The thought was sobering, but when compared to those who had already perished at the hands of these bloodthirsty bastards, he knew that any sacrifice on his part would be a small one. Ready to exact his vengeance on behalf of those who had fallen, Ontar raised his weapon and sought out his next opponent!

Elsewhere in the town, Echo found herself gazing through the anarchy about her while desperately looking for Favin. Calling his name over and over again, she frantically strained to hear his voice. Unfortunately, the first sound to reach her ears was the scream of a young boy who stood on the platform of his family's treetop home. The platforms rope bridges had been cut to prevent invaders from crossing, but a bandit with a short bow had fired a flaming arrow from the ground below and successfully hit one of the house's side walls. Taking action, the boy's father pulled him inside the house before emerging with a bucket full of water. As the distraught parent attempted to extinguish the blaze, the murderous bandit reloaded his bow and took aim at the easy target.

"No!" Echo shouted as she made a mad dash towards the bandit. Whether this was an act of bravery or stupidity, she couldn't be sure, but she *did* manage to get his attention as he quickly whirled about and fired on her. Relying on her keen reflexes, Echo raised her shield to block the arrow at the last possible moment. To her credit, she actually succeeded in intercepting the attack, but at such close range, the arrow still managed to pierce her shield and imbed itself in her forearm. Faltering from the explosion of pain, she recoiled from her attacker.

Taking the initiative, the bandit dropped his bow and drew a dagger from his boot. Holding the weapon blade down, he charged at Echo while attempting to stab her. Spotting his mistake the moment he made it, Echo swung her sword at the bandit and used its superior length to cut the man's weapon arm off at the elbow. Howling in agony, the bandit was killed by Echo's follow up attack.

Stepping away from her opponent's body, Echo attempted to remove the arrow from her arm. To accomplish this, she first had to snap the shaft by smashing it with the hilt of her sword. Gritting her teeth as she performed this excruciating task, she then sheathed her weapon so she could try to slowly slide her shield off the broken arrow.

Distracted by this procedure, Echo almost didn't hear the sound of a bandit rider in scale armor galloping towards her on his fearsome steed. Leaping out of the way, Echo avoided being trampled only to fall prey to the bandit's hidden net as he cast it over her. Jerking the drawstring, the bandit managed to capture his prey and drag her along the ground behind his mount.

Witnessing what just happened, Ontar ran across the bandit's blind side and intercepted him just as he was about to ride past. Swinging his sword, Ontar chopped off the bandit's leg in one smooth motion. Releasing his net and falling from his horse, the bandit hit the ground hard. Rendered immobile, the warrior could do little aside from raising his arms defensively as Ontar ended his wretched life.

Going over to release Echo from the net, Ontar stopped when he caught sight of the man responsible for all this devastation. Having just killed one of the few elvish guards brave enough to fight him, Lydon met Ontar's gaze and held his blood-soaked swords at ready. Clutching his own blade in two hands, Ontar felt an explosive fury consume him as he let out the most menacing battle cry he could muster. Filled with an uncontrollable rage, he surged towards Lydon and prepared to hack him into pieces!

It would have been hard for Lydon to miss Ontar's charge, and he could appreciate how engrossed his opponent was in the battle, but the warrior was clearly irrational, which would make him sloppy. The second Ontar came within striking range, he made a clumsy swing with his sword that possessed far more force than skill. Nimbly dodging the attack, Lydon let Ontar's momentum work against him as he used one of his blades to cut a nasty gash along the warrior's shoulder. As Ontar stumbled past him, Lydon spun around and used his other sword to make a wicked slice across his enemy's back.

Unable to see what was happening, Echo struggled to free herself from the net that had entangled her. Initially, she thought Ontar had come to her aid but, for some reason, he decided to abandon her at the last minute. Coping with a painful arrow wound, she pulled herself out of the net, then let go of her shield so she could tug the projectile free from her arm. Thankfully, the arrow wasn't embedded too deep, and it was actually removed when she jerked off the shield. With blood pouring from her injured forearm, Echo stood up and moved over to rip a piece of cloth off a dead bandit's cloak.

Once her arm was wrapped, Echo retrieved her shield. As she did, she saw three heavily-armed bandits running towards her. *Shit!* she thought. Preoccupied with caring for her wounds, she now found the bandits were practically on top of her. Prepared to meet a grisly end, Echo stood before her killers…and watched as everything suddenly went black.

Ontar gritted his teeth as one of Lydon's swords nicked the base of his chin. The bandit leader was a skilled fighter who effortlessly defended himself against Ontar's attacks. Wishing he had his morning star, Ontar reeled backwards while trying his best to guard against his enemy's short swords. Ready to face another bout of punishment, Ontar was surprised when a strange darkness came out of nowhere and consumed everything around him.

"Squeaker, where are you?" came a voice from the darkness.

A feeling of hope rose within Echo as she realized that her aunt was calling for her. "I'm over here!" she shouted.

"Stay right there, and I'll find you," Searce said as her voice grew closer.

Cursing the mystical darkness that encompassed him, Ontar backed away from Lydon out of fear that he'd be attacked while blinded. Overhearing the exchange between Echo and her aunt, he stumbled their direction and hoped they wouldn't think he was an enemy.

Lydon fumed over the abrupt end to the battle. Jerking his head upwards, he shouted, "Figit! Get your ass down here NOW!"

Echo tensed as she felt someone touch her shoulder. "Searce, is that you?"

"No, it's me," said Ontar. "Who's Searce?"

"Her aunt," replied a feminine voice just in front of him. "Who are you?" Ontar cocked his head curiously in that direction. There was something in this mysterious woman's tone undeniably alluring to him.

"A human named Ontar." Echo explained. "Don't worry he's with me."

Trying to let their eyes to adjust to the blackness around them, the trio were shocked when a small sphere of bright yellow light unexpectedly flashed into existence just off to their left. Hovering in the center of this sphere was a small winged creature that slowly seemed to be descending towards the ground.

"Ugh…not again," groaned Searce.

"What's that?" Ontar asked as he saw several more spheres light up nearby.

"Imps," Searce answered with a sneer. "They're using their magic to counter my spell."

Echo watched the imps fly low to the ground. As they did, the bandits' shadowy silhouettes moved once more. "We have to get out of here!"

"Take my hands," Searce said as she stepped close to Ontar and Echo. Ontar felt a tingle race up his arm as he took Searce's hand in his. Her touch was soft yet firm with smooth long nails that eloquently slipped between his fingers. It was silly, but for some reason Ontar felt like he could follow this unseen elf just about anywhere.

Together, the three crept through the darkness. All about them they heard the screams of innocents accompanied by the bandit's malicious shouts. Echo's imagination whirled to new heights with each tortured cry. *Please, Favin, please be alright,* she thought as a tear rolled down her cheek. Before long, the mystic darkness gave way to reveal a more natural forest setting. Looking back Echo saw a large black dome from whence they came, and above it were the burning homes of Thramahas.

At last, Ontar thought as he finally had a chance to gaze upon his rescuer. Turning to his left, he couldn't help but gape at the unquestioned beauty that held his hand. Searce could only be described of as a goddess in elvish form, and his palms sweated just from touching her. Noticing his tension, she glanced over at him and quirked an eyebrow. Ontar was in awe as the distant firelight from the burning homes cast her perfect features into deep, sensual shadows. Thanking the gods that it was too dark for her to see his face heat, Ontar abruptly let go of her hand and stood completely still as if frozen.

Oblivious to Ontar's reaction, Echo asked in a quivering voice, "What do we do now?"

Searce gave a sad little sigh. "There's nothing more we can do here. I think that we'll have to spend tonight in the forest and return to Thramahas in the morning. The bandits should be gone by then."

Nodding in silent agreement, the three set off through the woods with heavy hearts while trying hard not to look back at the chaos they left behind.

Interlude

PART TWO

Echo hugged her knees as she sat beneath the branches of an old maple tree and talked with Searce. Her aunt sat cross-legged as she calmly told Echo about how the bandits and imps had caught Thramahas completely by surprise when they started their raid. Clearly outnumbered, Searce had utilized her talents to help as many people as she possibly could to escape from the onslaught, but her single greatest regret was that no matter how hard she tried, she still wasn't able to reach Echo's parents in the midst of all the chaos.

Remembering how terrible it had been for her and Ontar to try and fight against the bandits, Echo tried to reassure Searce that everything that could have been done probably was. Looking over at her new human ally, Echo saw Ontar pull his cloak tightly around himself as he squirmed in his sleep. The brawny warrior had tried to join in their conversation earlier that evening but fatigue had finally caught up with him.

Wondering what he dreamt about, Echo wished that the horrors she had encountered earlier in the evening were just some sort of nightmare that would vanish with the coming dawn... but deep down, she knew they wouldn't. As the sun rose over Illamine Forest, Echo felt her heart ache as she painfully longed to have Favin by her side once more.

The sun had its effect on Ontar, too, as he awoke with a start after experiencing a number of bad dreams throughout the night. Plagued by images of his battle with Lydon, he could still remember the hatred he felt towards the bandit leader who killed his family. Sitting up hastily, he looked around while trying to get his bearings.

Echo sat beneath a tree with a forlorn expression on her face as her eyes rose to meet his. Her suitor had disappeared during last night's battle, and Ontar suspected that he had perished during the onslaught. Next to her was Searce, who looked absolutely radiant in the early morning light, and the way she sat practically begged him to lay her down on the forest floor and make sweet passionate love to her.

Trying hard to resist that particular urge, Ontar cleared his throat and asked, "Have you two been waiting long?"

"Not really," Echo replied. "We weren't planning on returning to Thramahas until first light."

"I see," Ontar said as he stood up. Walking over to Searce, he offered her his hand. "Then I think we should get going." Much to his delight, she took his hand and pulled herself up.

Releasing her grip and waiting for Echo to join them, Searce added, "Very well but remember, the place we're returning to has been ravaged by bandits. Try not to let the sorrow of others consume you or you'll be haunted by it for the rest of your days."

It was a short trip back to the outskirts of Thramahas. Mentally preparing herself for the worst, Echo trudged along quietly until she heard the mournful cries of her people reverberating throughout the forest. Swallowing hard, she looked past the trees and into the town itself when she first caught sight of all those who had suffered the bandits' wrath. Body after body could be seen scattered throughout the town and kneeling next to them were the tormented survivors who wailed at the loss of those they cared about.

Casting her eyes away from the terrible loss of life, Echo saw the burnt-out stalls and collapsed homes that now dominated much of Thramahas. Their smoldering ruins filled the air with a smoky smell that conflicted with the natural aroma of the tree's flowering vines. In a strange way, it was as if nature itself hadn't quite decided on whether or not embrace life or death in this instance.

Searce put a hand on Echo's shoulder. "I know it's horrible, Squeaker, and I wouldn't blame you if you wanted to return the forest for a while." Echo didn't budge, and Searce dropped her arm. "I'm going to try and arrange an audience with the velen to see what can be done. Ontar, I suggest that you stay out of sight until I return. I have a feeling the people here wouldn't welcome the presence of a human right now."

Ontar couldn't fault the wisdom of her advice. "I'll stay hidden until you need me."

"Alright, I'll be back soon," Searce said as she gave Echo a lingering look before heading into town.

Waiting until her aunt was out of sight, Echo slowly entered Thramahas. As she did, Ontar asked, "Hey, where are you going?"

"I have to find him," she replied ominously without looking back.

Ontar knew who Echo searched for and hoped that when she found him, she'd be strong enough to handle the grief that followed.

Echo tried not to tremble as she walked among those who suffered. To her left, a pair of adolescent boys tried to stay strong as they stood over the forms of their lifeless parents. To her right, an exhausted merchant picked through the charred remnants of his empty stall trying in vain to salvage what little remained of his life's work. A little past him was a young mother who sat on her knees and wept as she held a bloodstained cloth over the right side of her young child's face.

Echo felt the tears trickling down her cheeks as she thought over and over again. *Please…please, don't be here.* And then she saw him. Favin lay dead on the ground, with a sword still in his hand, and a gruesome cut across his throat.

"Oh…no…no, no!" Echo sobbed as she fell upon his chest. *What am I going to do?* she asked herself. *How can I live in a world without you?* Grief and an emptiness in her heart filled Echo with unbearable remorse. Lost without her soul mate, she wept over his body until there were simply no more tears to shed, and even then, she still couldn't bear to let him go.

Not far away, Ontar sat crouched with his sword by a tree at the edge of Thramahas. Looking out over a sea of butchered elves, he found that he couldn't stop thinking about the events that took place last night. These people didn't deserve to die the way they did, and when he saw what the bandits had done, it made him think of his parents and sister. From this moment on, elves and humans were united against a common enemy. One way or another, Lydon would die for what he did. Ontar only prayed that *he* would be the one responsible for his death.

Noticing that a crow had landed nearby to peck at some of the bodies, Ontar picked up a pebble and threw it at the damn bird. Cawing as it took flight, Ontar didn't realize that his actions caught the eye of a white-robed cleric who was using his powers to heal the leg of an injured elf. Standing up, Teryl spotted Ontar and stared at him for quite some time. Ontar knew that encountering a spell caster at this distance was a dangerous position to be in, but he didn't know if it was better to attack or flee? Moving slowly, Teryl shook his head and raised his hands submissively as he advanced towards Ontar.

"It's not every day that a bandit would drive away the scavengers from his kill."

"I'm no bandit," Ontar asserted.

Teryl nodded in agreement. "I know...I can see the sorrow in your soul."

Relaxing a little, Ontar said, "Somehow, I doubt your kindred would feel the same way."

"Perhaps," Teryl agreed as he lowered his hands. "But, unless I am mistaken, I would say that you have fought against the bandits on our behalf. Am I correct?"

"You are," Ontar replied.

"Then the least I can do is show you our gratitude. Come, I will take you to see the velen so that he can provide you with safe refuge while you are here."

Huh. Ontar started to like this elf. He only hoped that this *velen* he spoke of would be equally understanding.

⬦⬦⬦

Lost to the world around her, Echo was exhausted by the grief she felt and didn't want to move from where she rested next to Favin, but soon, she felt a small hand touch her arm and gently pull her attention back to the land of the living.

Angry that someone would interrupt her mourning, Echo turned and saw Grik standing next to her. His eyes were red from crying, and his face was filled with fear. Lost in her own sorrow, she snapped at him, "Go away, Grik!"

Grik recoiled slightly at the harshness of her words, but standing his ground, he quietly said, "I-I can't. Cora's missing, and I don't know where she is. Please, Echo, I'm really scared right now. Can you help me find her?"

Living or dead, Echo was *not* in the mood for granting favors, but when she glanced over at Grik's tragic expression, she knew she couldn't just leave him to look for his sister by himself. Cora would never forgive her for something like that...provided she was still alive. So, giving Favin one last lingering glance Echo kissed the first two fingers on her left hand and placed them on his lips. She then wiped away some tears and said to Grik, "Alright, you go home and see if she shows up there. I'll search around town for any sign of her."

A sad smile crossed Grik's face. "Thank you," he uttered before running off.

Standing up slowly, Echo said a quiet goodbye to Favin before continuing her journey through town. Trudging past the dead in search of her friend, she was overwhelmed by the cries of those around her. Unable to locate Cora amongst either the living or the dead, she quietly hoped there was still a chance Grik's sister would be alright.

Taking solace in that thought Echo headed for home. Drained by the sheer misery of the people she encountered, Echo longed for a sanctuary where she could distance herself from the outside world in the hopes of gathering her thoughts and taking in everything that had happened. Arriving at the tree whose spiral staircase would lead her up to the town's rope bridges, Echo remembered that many of these walkways had been dropped to prevent the bandits from reaching the homes of average citizens. Looking up to see if the bridge to her family's tree was still intact, Echo was shocked to find that both the bridge and her house were gone! Tracing a soot-laden path down the trunk of the battered tree, Echo saw the blackened remnants of her once cherished home lying in a decimated heap over what had previously been her father's stall.

"Mom...Dad," she uttered quietly. A heavy feeling of guilt washed over Echo as she realized her parents' fate. Up until this point, she had been completely focused on Favin, in part because she never imagined that something like this *could* ever happen to her parents. From little on, she had assumed they would always be there for her. After all, her people could live forever, and her folks were not the type to enter dangerous situations. Even now as her vision misted over, Echo could not believe they were truly gone.

Praying for some kind of miracle, she ran towards the remains of her house but jerked herself to a sudden stop when a feathery blur darted in front of her. Initially thinking that it was an imp, Echo reached for her sword only to stop herself when she saw that it was Hootie spreading his wings and hooting loudly in an all too familiar fashion.

"Dammit, Hootie, get out of the way!" Echo shrieked as tried to kick the stupid owl. Hootie barely dodged the attack and quickly took off into the air. Shouting in frustration, Echo cried. How could the gods spare such a worthless little creature like Hootie when the people she loved the most were slaughtered?

Stumbling forward with bleary eyes, Echo almost didn't notice that someone was coming up on her right. It was Searce, and judging by her tears, Echo knew that her parents had not survived.

"Oh, Squeaker, I'm so sorry."

Echo couldn't take it anymore. Spreading her arms, she and Searce held each other and wept over the mutual sense of pain and loss that tore upon their very souls.

❦ ❦ ❦

It seemed like a long time had passed before Echo and Searce made their way towards the velen's hall. Part of that time had been spent looking for Ontar and Cora, but a chance encounter with Teryl revealed that the warrior at least had been brought into the velen's home. Impressed that he was viewed as a guest instead of a prisoner, Echo wondered how Ontar managed to convince the cleric that he wasn't just another bloodthirsty bandit.

Arriving with Searce at the velen's hall, Echo noticed that aside from a few broken windows and some scorch marks, the building was still pretty much intact. The reason for this became apparent when she and Searce stepped onto the stage in front of the entry and discovered that it was covered in gory bandit remains. Searching for the cause of their demise, Echo noticed the statues on either side of the hall's double doors now carried swords that were stained a dark crimson.

Filled with disgust, Echo said, "I can't believe the velen would keep Thramahas's best protectors for himself instead of sending them out to fight against the bandits who ravaged our town."

Searce could understand Echo's feelings but offered a counterpoint, "I wouldn't judge him too harshly on that one. Remember that, if this hall was destroyed, there would be no place for the Thramahas's survivors to go find help during their hour of need."

Echo hadn't considered that, and the more she thought about it, the more she realized the velen was now responsible for taking care of the many victimized people desperately in need. A daunting task given the levels of death and destruction she'd witnessed.

Approaching the hall's main entrance, Searce pounded on the large double doors and waited for a response.

A meek feminine voice on the other side of the door asked, "Who's there?"

Speaking loudly, Searce said, "It is Searce Karashenmahagensea and my niece Echo."

"One moment, please," the voice responded as the sound of a dragging crossbar could be heard from inside. Seconds later, a nervous servant opened one of the doors and said, "Please, follow me."

Echo noticed the servant slid the crossbar back into place after she and Searce had entered the building. Following their guide down a long corridor, Echo glanced at the beautifully woven carpet she walked on and remembered just how pleasant the hall's surroundings really were. Intricate golden sconces with colorful stained-glass covers provided illumination for elaborate murals crafted out of wood and tremendous paintings that were painstakingly produced by elvish masters.

Smirking, Echo remembered all the different times she had broken into this building. Searce had encouraged her to do it on multiple occasions to increase her burglary skills, and as long as she didn't actually take anything, the velen usually forgave her. Echo's parents, on the other hand, were far less lenient. Biting her lip, she found herself actually longing to hear one of their disapproving lectures just one more time.

Coming to a stop next to a door that might as well have been a work of art, the servant knocked softly and turned the knob so she could peek her head inside. After a few quiet words, she opened the door to the base of what appeared to be a pie-shaped room. Peering into the chamber, Echo saw an outward diagonal wall off to her left that had a roaring fireplace at its center. To her right was a similar wall with a beautifully designed desk that rested in front of an intricate tapestry. At the room's far end was a long arcing window that had two tall standing shrubs on each side of it. The windows elegant curtains were closed, and Echo could see a small amount of broken glass lying on the floor.

In the center of the chamber, beneath a small crystal chandelier, was a circular carpet with four regal looking chairs evenly spaced around it. Sitting in one of these chairs was Ontar, while Velen Jolarie sat in another. Both warrior and noble seemed to focus their attention on Searce's arrival, with the velen saying, "Ah, Searce, I'm glad that you and Echo have finally come to join us. Please, take a seat. We have much to discuss."

Ontar couldn't help but leer at Searce as she sat down. He had *never* wanted to be a piece of furniture more in his entire life, and judging Velen Jolarie's reaction, he was not alone. When the two first met, the velen could barely restrain his fury at having a *human* in his presence during the wake of a bandit attack. Thankfully, Teryl was able to reason with him, and the elvish noble proved to be far more fair-minded than Ontar had initially hoped. Together, they discussed the bandits' activities in Coronas and the incident surrounding the attack on Gerig's patrol.

Once everyone was situated, Velen Jolarie began by saying, "As you all know, the bandit attacks both here and in Coronas have caused a terrible amount of damage to our countries. These brigands have killed without mercy or respect for our territorial sovereignty. So, as ruler of Thramahas, I have decided to recall our remaining guards and request that a contingent of troops be sent from the nearest city to deal with these fiends once and for all."

Looking between Ontar and Echo, he said, "Echo, I will be providing you and Ontar with horses to speed your passage to Kinnerba. Once there, I want you to deliver the withdrawal notice to Jayvoe and ensure Ontar isn't attacked by any of our people. Ontar, I humbly ask that you deliver a message to your superiors at Fort Hasborne, which will state the Illamine did not in any way violate Coronas's borders or attack its settlements."

"Why stop there?" Searce asked.

"What do you mean?" inquired the velen.

Searce elaborated, "Coronas has suffered at the bandits' hands almost as badly as we have. Why not ask them to join us in wiping them out?"

Velen Jolarie frowned. "That would require me to allow armed human soldiers to enter our territory. Considering there are already bandits wreaking havoc in this area, I think the arrival of any more unwanted foreigners would probably cause the people to riot."

"I doubt it," Searce said. "Besides, you have to take into consideration how long it will take for a city to rally enough troops together to defeat the bandits. Don't forget there's still a score of unprotected villages nearby extremely vulnerable to attack. Do you really want to risk those people's lives just to have our enemies killed by local soldiers?"

"No, I suppose not," Velen Jolarie admitted grudgingly.

Echo shuddered at the thought of having the tragedy that befell Thramahas spreading to other communities. Facing the velen, she asked, "Well, why don't you just continue with your original plan of sending the guards out to fight the bandits once they've been recalled from Kinnerba?"

Velen Jolarie shook his head sadly. "Because, after last night's raid, I feel that between the bandit's superior numbers, and their being aided by the imps, that our forces are no longer strong enough to handle them on their own."

"Which is why we should try to form an alliance with Coronas," Searce argued. "Ontar, how long do you think it would take for your kingdom's troops to rendezvous here in Thramahas?"

Ontar scowled. "Depending on what Gerig's told Sir Brovine, there could be a full brigade of soldiers marching towards the border even as we speak."

"You see," Searce added, "one way or another, you're going to have to deal with Coronas. Now, we can either face them down as enemies, or we could enlist their aid in defeating the bandits who caused this problem in the first place."

Taking a moment to ponder the conversation's direction, Velen Jolarie sighed and gave a resigned smile. "Ugh, Searce. I never could say no to you." Standing up and moving towards his desk, he added, "Echo, Ontar, I am going to compose a letter for both Jayvoe and Sir Brovine respectively to address what we've discussed here today. If the two of you would be good enough to deliver these messages, then I believe there is an excellent chance that we can eliminate the bandits and restore peace to our lands…provided, of course, that you're up to the challenge?"

Ontar felt the pride well up within him. For the first time in his life, he was asked to take responsibility for something far greater than himself. Nodding with a serious expression on his face, he replied, "It would be an honor to act for the benefit of both our people."

"I agree with Ontar," Echo said hesitantly. She knew that it was important to help her people, but by the same token, she also didn't want to surrender all her time for nothing. "However, I noticed earlier on that you said we'd be provided with horses to speed our journey. Would we be allowed to keep these animals once our quest was over?"

Sitting at his desk and pulling a quill from a nearby inkwell, the velen replied, "Yes, I think between the horses and Ontar's request for his cousin's freedom that your compensation has been settled."

Echo leaned back in her chair and grinned slightly at the deal she'd struck. In no time at all, Velen Jolarie finished his letters and sealed them with a wax insignia. Handing them over to Ontar and Echo, the two quietly joined Searce in exiting the hall. As they stepped out onto the waiting stage, Echo turned to her aunt and asked, "Hey, Searce, what are you going to do while Ontar and I are delivering our messages?"

Searce gave her niece a dark look. "*I am going to go find the bastards who killed my brother.*"

❖❖❖

Ontar and Echo swiftly raced through Illamine Forest on the back of their newly-acquired steeds. Eager to be back among his own people, Ontar couldn't stop thinking about the letter he was to deliver to Sir Brovine, and whether or not the knight would choose to aid the elves of Thramahas. Echo, on the other hand, was worried about how the guards at Kinnerba would handle the news of a bandit attack on their homes and families.

The sun had just dipped below the trees when Ontar and Echo brought their horses to a stop along the waters of the Cherenon River. Standing on the far side of the bridge leading into Kinnerba were two elvish guards with bows armed and ready.

Looking over at Echo, one of them called out, "Who goes there?"

Echo dismounted from her horse and signaled for Ontar to do the same. "It's Echo Karashenmahagensea, and I bring an urgent letter for Jayvoe from the velen."

"What about him?" asked the second guard.

"He's with me," Echo replied, hoping that her answer would be sufficient.

Eyeing them carefully for a moment, the first guard said, "You'll find Jayvoe at the tavern with everyone else."

"Including my cousin?" Ontar asked.

The guard shook his head. "Don't be stupid. He's still locked in the tower."

Echo ignored Ontar's scowl and thanked the guards as they guided their horses across the bridge and into town.

A part of Ontar couldn't believe that he was returning to his former home. The tavern was a two-story building with an attached stable and a hanging sign above the door that resembled a tombstone with the profile of a lion's head on it. The sign was symbolic for his family's name, and as Ontar led Echo into the stable to tether their horses, they heard a chorus of masculine singing coming from the building's dining hall. It was a song of battle and glory sung by elves who had not yet learned their homes had been destroyed.

Regretting what was to come, Ontar pulled his sword out from the horse's saddle and urged Echo to stay close as they entered the front of the tavern and saw that it was packed with elvish guards. Silencing their song on the approach of newcomers, the guards whispered to each other with surprised curiosity. Ontar felt a stirring in his heart as he stood in the dining hall. The elves had cleaned up any damage caused by the bandits, and he knew that his parents would have been thrilled with the number of patrons in their establishment…if only they were still alive to see it.

Echo spotted Jayvoe sitting alone at a small circular table sipping a mug of ale by the fireplace. Heading his direction with Ontar at her side, she approached the captain and met his cold hard gaze. Pulling the letter from one of the pouches on her belt, she nervously said, "Captain Jayvoe, I have been sent by Velen Jolarie to officially deliver this letter to you."

Leery of her formality, Jayvoe took the letter, broke the seal, and read it. Watching his expression, Echo saw the guard captain's eyes widen as his face went pale. Seconds later, his fists clenched and crinkled the sides of the letter. Looking up at Echo, she could see the silent fury raging within him.

"Is everything in this letter true?" he asked in an icy tone.

Echo tried not to fidget beneath his gaze. "I'm afraid so."

Jayvoe turned his attention towards Ontar and said, "I assume you will be leaving here as soon as possible."

Ontar nodded. "Yes, I just need you to free my cousin so that we may gather a few items before we go."

"Very well," Jayvoe replied before looking at a nearby guard. "Free the prisoner and return their possessions to them immediately."

"Sir?" the guard began, but a glare from his captain quickly silenced him.

Ontar kept a straight face as his backpack, shield, and weapon belt were returned to him. Secretly overjoyed at having his equipment back, he casually set aside the sword he'd been using in favor of his much more familiar morning star.

Bowing slightly to the guard, Captain Ontar said. "Thank you, milord. I shall finish my business quickly and be on my way."

Ignoring the human, Jayvoe cast his gaze at the fire next to him. Turning around, Ontar left the table and made his way towards a small hallway at the back of the tavern. As he departed, a guard standing next to Echo tugged on the sleeve of her shirt and whispered, "Echo, what happened in Thramahas?"

Nervous about answering that question, Echo glanced over at Jayvoe to see what she should do? His response was a simple nod as he closed his eyes.

Ontar opened the door to his old room and examined it. Memories of his childhood briefly came to mind as he looked over its simple furnishings and sighed. It seemed like forever since he had lived here, and anything that he did have of value went with him to Fort Hasborne ages ago. Closing the door, he then stepped across the hall and peered into his sister's room. Kearsta never could keep her room clean as colorful clothes were scattered across the floor next to an unmade bed. A couple of small wooden toys could be seen on her nightstand near a book used for drawing and practicing her letters.

Leaving his sister's mess behind, Ontar came to a battered door at the end of the hall leading to his parent's room. Entering this once private sanctum, Ontar saw the chamber had been ransacked by bandits, with broken furniture and dried blood splayed across the floor. Feeling a knot form in the pit of his stomach, Ontar gazed over the destruction and tried to imagine his family's final moments.

Focusing on a large bed with a shredded mattress in the center of the room, Ontar was sure that his parents had tried to use it to block the door from oncoming bandits. Unfortunately, it looked like the intruders had successfully managed to barge into the room before the bed was in place. Trying not to think of what happened next, Ontar spotted a small ragdoll at the base of what had once been a wardrobe. The doll had been a farewell gift to his little sister to keep her company after he left home. His mother said she never went to bed without it. Kneeling to pick up the once treasured possession, he realized that Kearsta must have died when the bandits discovered her hiding place.

Holding the doll a moment before slipping it into his backpack, Ontar felt like his heart had been ripped out and torn asunder. Standing up in a grief-invoked daze, he left his parents' room and numbly made his way back towards the dining hall. Oblivious to what was going on around him, Ontar didn't even notice the hostile environment he was about to step into.

Echo had already spoken with several guards about the attack on Thramahas and what had happened to their loved ones when Ontar made his appearance. Seething with rage, one of the guards saw her distracted companion and shouted, "Damn you, inferior! My wife is dead because of your kind."

Ontar looked over at the elf with surprise as the guard suddenly drew his sword. Seeking to prevent bloodshed, Echo stepped in front of him and raised her arms. "Wait! This human fought *for* our people not *against* them."

Pointing his sword at her, the guard growled, "Get out of the way!"

Before Echo had a chance to act, a mug of ale crashed into the guard's foot, spilling its contents everywhere. Looking in the direction it came from, Echo saw Jayvoe standing at his table with an angry expression on his face.

"That's enough!" he snapped. "No one under my command will *ever* stoop to their level," he said in reference to Ontar's race. "Is that understood?"

The guard immediately sheathed his sword. "Yes, sir."

Jayvoe sternly turned towards Ontar. "I suggest you leave now."

Outnumbered by a host of angry elves, Ontar couldn't agree more. Ignoring the hatred in their eyes, he quickly passed through their ranks and exited the tavern.

Echo was appalled by what just happened. Ontar had lost just as much as anyone else here, and *still*, he fought for their families when the bandits attacked. To see him treated so terribly was unforgivable.

"You should all be ashamed of yourselves," she scolded. "That man saved my life while trying to protect the ones you love from harm, and if any of you has someone to come back home to, it will be because of *him*!"

Unable to stomach the guard's presence any longer, Echo exited the tavern to a rapidly darkening sky and sought out Ontar at the stables. Finding him there with Yorus, the two seemed eager leave Kinnerba as soon as possible. She called out to him, "Ontar, wait!"

Holding the reins of his animal, Ontar asked, "Is something wrong?"

"Please, don't judge my people harshly," Echo pleaded. "The attack on Thramahas has fueled their anger. It will take time for me to help them distinguish between the good humans and the bad."

"Your people aren't the only ones who have suffered the bandits' wrath," Ontar noted.

Echo nodded and said, "I know, and to speed your journey, I'd like to lend your cousin my horse."

Yorus's eyes widened in surprise. "That's quite generous."

"Just make sure to tell Sir Brovine the elves are not your enemies," Echo pleaded.

Glad that he wouldn't have to share a horse, Yorus replied, "You have my word."

Three days later, Ontar and Yorus were close to reaching their next destination. Passing the tree line, the two came upon the towering spiked logs that made up Fort Hasborne's walls and gate. Bringing their horses to a halt, they were immediately recognized by two chain-clad guards moving among the gate's battlements. Shouting orders to men on the ground, the gate was pulled open to reveal a courtyard filled with soldiers, cavalry, and archers all formed up into various ranks and going through different training exercises. Ontar had never seen so much activity happening at the same time, which led him to wonder what was going on?

The answer to that question came about when he saw Gerig riding up to the gate on horseback and shout, "Well, look who's come crawling back. So, did the two of you manage to escape, or did the elves realize it wasn't worth the effort to keep you?"

"At least the elves aren't cowards who abandon their men," Ontar retorted.

Gerig scoffed when he heard this. "There's no way that a joke like you would ever be considered one of *my* men."

"But *I* was," Yorus said sternly. "And we've got a message for Sir Brovine from the ruler of Thramahas. So, shut your damn mouth and get out of our way!"

Gerig was a little nervous about what might be said to the knight. "If you think I'm going to stand back and let the two of you fill Sir Brovine's head with elvish bullshit, then you are sorely mistaken."

Now, it was Ontar's turn to scoff. "You just want to cover your ass."

"My word carries more weight than yours ever will," Gerig retorted. "Now, let's hurry up and get inside. I have better things to do then waste my day with the likes of you."

Flicking the reins of their mounts, the three men had their horses canter up towards the keep. Arriving at the building's main entrance, they all dismounted and handed their steeds over to some nearby soldiers. Walking with a slight limp, Gerig led Ontar and Yorus into the keep, which possessed a plain yet functional layout. The narrow corridors had wooden walls with torch-lit sconces attached to them. Soldiers and servants passed by at random intervals as they climbed up a flight of stairs and onto the second level.

Going down a long hallway, the trio came to a stop in front of a large door with two halberd-wielding guards stationed on either side of it. One of these guards sternly said, "State your business," to which Gerig calmly replied, "I am Corporal Gerig Arben here to address a new development in the situation regarding the elves."

Nodding once, the guard cracked open the door next to him and relayed the information to someone inside, who Ontar presumed was Sir Brovine. After a moment, the guard opened the door the rest of the way and said, "Proceed."

Stepping into the knight's office with Gerig and Yorus at his sides, Ontar noted the room was fairly small but official looking.

To his left was a window that overlooked the training grounds outside. On the right was a large map of the lands surrounding Fort Hasborne, while a tapestry depicting Coronas's coat of arms hung along the far wall. In front of this tapestry was a large desk that had a visored helmet with a red plume resting on it.

Sitting behind this desk was Sir Brovine. A middle-aged knight with long black hair and a moustache the man wore a surcoat and cape that barely stretched over his full suit of armor. Ontar had always been impressed by the knight's armament and hoped that one day he'd be able to purchase something just like it. The only ornamentation Sir Brovine possessed was a simple gold bracelet with a large round ruby set into it worn around his left wrist. Everybody had heard rumors about the mysterious Phoenix Shield, but few had actually seen it in use.

Greeting the three in a semi-formal tone, Sir Brovine said, "Corporal, I see that you've recovered the men who were lost during your patrol."

Speaking quickly, Gerig said, "Yes, milord. The elves were clearly incapable of holding even our least experienced men captive for very long."

Yorus was *not* going to let Gerig continue his false narrative against the elves. "We didn't escape, milord. The elves set us free as a gesture of goodwill."

"Why would they do that?" Sir Brovine inquired.

"Because they don't want us to punish them for attacking one of our towns," Gerig stated.

Yorus glared at Gerig and said, "You never even saw them attack Kinnerba."

"Just because I didn't see them doesn't mean it didn't happen," Gerig said through clenched teeth.

"It did happen," Ontar agreed as he drew forth a letter from his belt pouch. He handed it over to Sir Brovine. "However, if you read this, you will see that it was *bandits* who sacked Kinnerba. Bandits who are now rampaging through the elvish countryside."

Sir Brovine frowned. "And the elves are asking for our help in this matter?

"Yes, milord," Ontar replied with as much urgency as he could muster.

Breaking the letter's seal, Sir Brovine quietly read its contents. When he finished, he asked, "Can you attest to everything written here?"

"I attest on the on souls of my family who all died when these bandits attacked my home," Ontar vowed.

Gerig slowly shook his head. "The loss of one of our border towns is a terrible tragedy, but one that need not be repeated."

Ontar did not like where this was going. Unfortunately, Sir Brovine seemed intrigued. "What do you mean by that, Corporal?"

Clearing his throat, Gerig said, "The bandits have crossed from our kingdom and into the Illamine. If we send our forces into elvish territory, then there's a chance they could be ambushed by the very people we've come to help."

"The elves don't have the troops to do something like that," Yorus argued. "They already divided their numbers in half to protect Thramahas, and the ones who stayed to protect the town are now dead. Those who remain would be of little threat if we sent a full contingent of soldiers to the border."

"At the moment, that may be true," Gerig argued. "But once enough of our soldiers have died against these bandits, then who's to say the elves won't turn against us?"

"So, what would you suggest?" asked Sir Brovine.

"I think that we should retake Kinnerba and position out troops defensively along the border. That way, we can protect Coronas without putting our soldiers into a dangerous situation," Gerig answered.

"What about the elves!?" Ontar exclaimed.

Gerig shrugged. "The Illamine is a big place. I'm pretty sure that, if necessary, the elves will be able to handle things on their own.

Sir Brovine considered the debate for a moment while crossing his gauntleted hands and resting his elbows on the desk. Looking at Gerig, he said, "I can see the merit in your argument, but I don't agree with it. The bandits attacked *our* settlements long before they attacked the elves, and there is no honor in letting someone else kill an enemy that should have been laid to rest by our hands. If the elves are willing to humble themselves by asking for our assistance, then I say they shall have it. With Rightin's blessing, we shall rid our lands of this mutual enemy and strengthen the ties between our two realms."

Ontar gave a little sigh of relief over the knight's decision and quietly prayed the war god would be with them in the battle ahead.

❧ ❧ ❧

Ontar was glad to get on the road once more. Riding horseback through Illamine Forest with Yorus and an entire brigade of Coronasian troops, he felt confident they could end the bandit's threat once and for all. Thankfully, the soldiers had pretty much been mobilized before he and his cousin had even arrived at Fort Hasborne (although, originally, for an entirely different reason.)

When the brigade finally did move out, Ontar and Yorus found themselves at the rear of a cavalry unit that cantered closely around Sir Brovine. Behind them were the infantry and archer units who marched along at a steady pace and formed the remainder of their company.

Leaning close to Yorus from his saddle, Ontar muttered, "Kinnerba is just up ahead, and after that is the Illamine. How do you think Jayvoe will handle having so many humans in elvish territory?"

Yorus shrugged. "If Jayvoe respects the chain of command, then his feelings about us really won't matter. The ruler of Thramahas asked for our help, and Sir Brovine has decided to grant it. However, I do think that his lordship should keep our troops close together. It might prevent any unexpected *accidents* from occurring."

As Yorus finished his thought, he and Ontar heard the sound of another rider approaching them.

"My, my, Ontar. You certainly seem to be excited about getting back to elvish lands," Gerig taunted as he brought his horse near. "I suppose an elvish whore is the only one who'd take pity on you after being rejected by human ones."

Ontar was about to answer the jibe, but Yorus beat him to it. "At least Ontar's willing to look for a woman. Tell me, Gerig, when was the last time someone was willing to laugh at your limp little worm?"

"You bastard!" Gerig snarled as he reached for his sword.

"That's enough!" shouted someone from behind them. Looking back, they saw Sergeant Raglak marching nearby while giving Gerig the evil eye. "Gerig, if you don't want me reporting this incident to your commanding officer, then I suggest you leave. NOW!"

"This isn't over," Gerig said through gritted teeth as he kicked his horse forward.

"Thanks," Ontar said to the sergeant. "Gerig is the one person who really knows how to get under my skin."

Sergeant Raglak smiled. "Well, we are coming up to your hometown here, so maybe we can tether that ass to a tree and forget about him."

At that observation, the trees gradually parted way to reveal Kinnerba to the steadily advancing brigade. Ontar glanced about the deserted town uneasily as he half-expected to see either another funeral pyre or a host of angry elves ready to ambush them. Thankfully, this fear proved to be unfounded, but at the same time, it also left him with a feeling of emptiness. It was as if the last vestiges of his once happy youth were now forever gone.

Sir Brovine sat on top of a heavily armored warhorse with the visor of his helmet up so that he could talk to one of his scouts by the watch tower. At the conclusion of their conversation, he called for Commander Talgin and Gerig to speak with him. Addressing the commander first, he said, "Commander Talgin, it appears the elves have retreated back across the border. For the remainder of today, I'm going to have the brigade make camp in Kinnerba. Tomorrow, I plan on marching into the Illamine. While we're gone, I want you and your archers stationed here to defend against any possible incursion on our territory."

The commander frowned. "Milord, don't you want any of my men to accompany you on your journey?"

Sir Brovine shook his head. "The elves are renowned for their marksmanship, and I think your archers would be more effective here then gallivanting about on their side of the forest." Turning to Gerig, he said, "Corporal, I want you to lead a handful of infantry and cavalry in reinforcing Commander Talgin's position."

Ontar grinned as he saw Gerig's face drop. Normally, being given even a minor command position would be seen as an honor to someone of Gerig's rank, but to be given that position *instead* of being allowed to participate in the upcoming battle was a huge slap in the face.

Glowering over his new orders, Gerig sullenly replied, "Yes... yes, milord."

Guiding his horse towards the back of the unit, Sir Brovine came to a stop before Ontar and Yorus. "You two have had previous contact with the elves and most likely wouldn't be killed on sight. Would you be willing to serve as my advance riders into elvish lands and herald our coming to the velen?"

Swelling with pride, Yorus replied, "It would be an honor."

"We'll leave as soon as you're ready," Ontar added while he reveled in having a much more important role than Gerig in the events to come.

Figit flew through the forest as fast as his wings could carry him. Dodging trees and ducking branches, he raced towards the bandit's camp with information that he knew Lydon would find intriguing. The humans had proven to be a useful ally in crushing his people's enemies, which was why he tried so hard to conceal them now.

Flying into a rough clearing, Figit entered the bandit's camp and saw the settlement was basically a collection of tan-colored tents scattered between the trees. A large bonfire continually burned at the camp's center while humans equipped with various weapons and armor freely moved about the area. A few horse-drawn wagons were located near the bonfire that contained the spoils of the bandits pillaging. Preferring to keep their treasures close together, Figit noticed the bandits had also captured at least a dozen wood elves who, ironically, were chained around the very trees they claimed to cherish. Coming to a landing in front of Lydon's tent, Figit pulled open the flap and stepped inside the makeshift dwelling.

"Get out!" Lydon snapped as he threw back the brown fur blanket of his crudely made bed and looked down at the shivering naked elf beneath him. Cora had cried the entire time he was on top of her, and now all she wanted to do was to curl up in a corner somewhere and die. Unconcerned with the trauma he'd inflicted, Lydon got up and reached for his pants. Catching sight of Figit, he irritably asked, "What do you want?"

Watching the humiliated elf quietly scramble for her clothing, Figit said, "I bring terrible news. My spies have spotted a heavily armed force of Coronasian soldiers entering the Illamine! They're headed straight for Thramahas, and the elves aren't doing a thing to stop them."

Lydon pulled up his pants, then went for his weapon belt. "Took 'em long enough," he muttered absently. "Gather the men by the wagons. I'll speak with them there."

"As you wish," Figit replied before exiting the tent.

Lydon donned the rest of his gear then looked over at Cora. She had just finished getting dressed when he stomped up to her and grabbed the nervous elf by her braid. Cora whimpered as Lydon jerked her head down near his waist. Dragging her out of the tent, he saw a fellow bandit nearby and said, "Take her."

Once Cora had been passed off, Lydon made his way towards the wagons where Figit had gathered the majority of his men. Climbing onto the back of the first wagon he found, Lydon looked down at those assembled and said.

"Alright, boys, listen up. The elves have teamed up with Coronas in an attempt to take us down. Now, we all knew this fight was coming, and the stakes are going to be high. They're going to have greater numbers, nastier equipment, and an unquestioned thirst for revenge. If we try to run, they will hunt us down and rip us limb from limb, but if we fight them (and win), then we will have *at least* a month of easy pillaging from the villages around here."

Lydon took a moment to let what he just said to sink in. Several hushed conversations erupted among the bandits, and one of them finally got up the nerve to ask, "How are we going to fight against a force like that?"

Expecting this question, Lydon explained, "Divide and conquer. Remember that these are elven lands, and soldiers from Coronas don't have a whole lot of authority here. All we have to do is crush the elvish half of their forces, then fall back to camp. The Coronasians won't pursue us through foreign territory, and we'll be able to get back to looting and killing whenever we want."

Feeling a little more confident in their leader, the bandits muttered their general approval. After a few seconds, an experienced warrior said, "Sounds like a challenge. So, what have you got for details?"

Lydon smiled as he sat on one of the wagons crates. "First off, we're going to have to coordinate our attack with the imps. Figit, I want you to get as many of your kin here as possible. Once that's done..."

Yorus struggled to keep up with Ontar as they rode through the forest towards Thramahas. The sun had just set, and they were trying desperately to reach their destination before the light was gone altogether. Seeing a break in the trees, they were about to enter the town when two arrows shot in front of their mounts, causing the horses to rear up and almost throw their riders. Looking up to the trees, Yorus saw two elves with bows glaring down at them. "Damn it, you nearly killed us!" he exclaimed.

"That's the idea," the guard snapped.

Sliding out from behind the tree the guard stood on, Echo said, "Ontar...Yorus...I knew you'd bring my horse back. What word do you have from Sir Brovine?"

"He's advancing across the border to fight the bandits even as we speak," Ontar replied.

"I have a letter for the velen stating our intentions," Yorus added.

Reaching out to take the reins of their animals, Echo said, "I'll stable your horses while you two go meet with him. Ontar, I believe you know the way."

"I do," Ontar said as he dismounted with his cousin.

Entering the town, Ontar found that it was far more peaceful than when he last left. The bodies of the dead had all been disposed of, the interconnecting rope bridges had been raised to their former spots, and many elves could now be seen going about their normal business under the watchful eyes of some *very* edgy guards. Having never been to an elvish town before, Yorus noted that, in spite of obvious clean up, there were still trees with blackened platforms resting in their branches and debris from several demolished merchant stalls remained scattered across the forest floor.

Bidding farewell to Echo, the three quickly went about their various tasks. Finishing her duty first, Echo went to wait for them outside the velen's hall where she was soon joined by Searce. Her aunt had returned to Thramahas at roughly the same time she and the guards did, with information on the bandit's whereabouts. Together with Jayvoe, she and the velen had come up with a strategy for defeating their enemies, but it would require the humans help to do it.

Emerging from the building with a tired look on his face, Ontar said, "The velen has a specific time that he wants Sir Brovine's men to arrive tomorrow. Yorus and I are supposed to go relay that message to them after we get some sleep. Lodging was made available for us here at the hall, and while Yorus has already gone to bed, I just wanted to let you know what was going on first."

Searce gave Ontar a good hard look and noticed that he didn't have the Coronasian surcoat that his cousin possessed. "You're not a soldier, are you?"

Ontar shook his head. "No, I work at a tavern in the fortress where troops are based."

"Why didn't you enlist?" Echo wondered.

Finding the question to be a little odd, Ontar replied, "Because I want to follow my own path in life instead of someone else's orders."

Searce smiled when she heard this. "Good. Of course, the risk in being your own man is that you don't always have someone to watch your back when things go bad. However, you also get to choose the company you keep."

"I don't quite understand the point you're trying to make," Ontar said hesitantly.

"You will," Searce assured him while exchanging a look with Echo. "But first, how would you like to join Echo and I for a homecooked meal back at my place. I can't imagine eating rations for the past two days has been very satisfying for you."

She cooks! Ontar thought. *By the gods, she's perfect!* Hungry from a hard day's travel, he casually replied, "Yeah, sure."

Beckoning with her finger, Searce replied, "Great. Follow us."

Enthusiastically following the elves to a tree covered in flowering vines, Ontar made his way up a spiral staircase that encircled its trunk and onto a platform connected by rope bridges. From there, it was a quick trip to Searce's home where she offered Ontar a seat at a candle lit dining table. Pulling up a chair, Ontar noticed that elvish homes were far smaller than human ones, but they were also crafted with an artistic detail that no human peasant could ever hope to match. As for personal touches, Searce decided to decorate her walls with large maps that depicted various places throughout the Rashben Region.

As his hostess started cooking, Ontar asked, "So, were you able to locate the bandit's camp?"

Searce pulled some ingredients out of a cupboard. "Let's just say that when it's time to strike, we'll know exactly where to hit them."

Sitting down next to him, Echo said, "The upcoming battle with the bandits should be a fierce one, but what will you do once it's over?"

Ontar shrugged. "I don't know. I think it would be too painful to return to Fort Hasborne after all that's happened. Maybe I'll just roam the kingdom for a while."

"You could," Searce conceded, "but you might also want to try something with a little more purpose."

"Like what?" Ontar inquired.

Echo started to get excited. "Have you ever heard of the Bloody Side thieves' guild?" Ontar shook his head, causing Echo's shoulders to droop a little. "It's an elite organization that trains some of the best thieves the world has ever known, and it just so happens they have a guildhall in Coronas!"

Ontar gave Echo an odd look. "And you want me to help you join their ranks?"

"Yes!" Echo exclaimed. "Searce's already a member, and with your help, I could be one, too!"

Shaking his head, Ontar said, "I don't think I could do that. One thing the bandits have taught me is there are already too many ruthless bastards out there who prey on the innocent. The last thing I want to do is help to create another one."

Slamming her hands on the table, Echo stood up and said, "How dare you assume the Bloody Side is anything like the monsters that killed our families!"

"Sit down, Squeaker!" Searce demanded as she brought them two wooden plates of food along with a couple cups of hot tea. "In truth, the world is full of people who do more harm than good but joining the Bloody Side will allow you to spot, avoid, or even manipulate them as you see fit." Gazing sadly out the window, she added, "Maybe if I had bothered to keep up my ties with them, I could have prevented this tragedy."

Seeing the pain in her aunt's eyes, Echo reluctantly did as she was told.

Struck by just how sad and vulnerable Searce looked Ontar longed to comfort her, but somehow could only manage to say that, "Coronas is a big place, and while I don't condone your plans, I would still be willing to accompany you to your destination."

Offering him a sad smile, Searce said, "That's all we could ask for."

Ready to try the local cuisine, Ontar gazed down at the food suspiciously. It looked like some venison had been cooked and cut into cubes set next to a small cup of dark red sauce. Next to the cup were sliced celery stalks, with a pasty yellow substance spread along their grooves.

Taking some chopsticks from the side of her plate, Echo picked up a piece of meat, dipped it in the sauce, and ate it. Ontar grabbed the utensils and tried to manipulate them in a similar fashion but wound up knocking a piece of celery onto the floor. Afraid of making an ass out of himself in front of Searce, he took one of the chopsticks and stabbed it into the meat before eating it.

"What are you, a barbarian?" Echo asked as she observed his poor table manners.

Searce grinned at his efforts. "It's alright, Ontar. You can treat it like finger food if you like.

Echo snorted in disgust, but Ontar took solace in Searce's understanding. After their meal, Echo went up to the meditation room while Searce did dishes and Ontar returned to the velen's hall.

By the time morning had come, Ontar and Yorus were gone while Echo shared a light breakfast with her aunt. The sun had just risen above the forest's canopy when the sound of horns could be heard blaring off in the distance.

"Come on, there's going to be a town meeting," Searce said as she motioned for Echo to follow her.

Leaving Searce's house, the two walked along a rope bridge overlooking the velen's hall. There were guards everywhere, and several of them walked the bridges armed with bows. Looking down at the hall's stage Echo saw Velen Jolarie standing at its front with Jayvoe and Teryl on either side of him.

Speaking to an unsettled crowd the velen said:

"Greetings my friends. When last we spoke our hearts were filled with mourning over the loss of those who were killed by bandits. The pain which we all felt will never go away, yet as a testament to the strength of our people we were able to lay our dead to rest and begin the task of restoring all that had been destroyed by our enemies. I am proud of everyone who has participated in this undertaking, even though I know that it is not enough.

The men who ravaged our homes are still out there and standing in a pool of tears and blood, we prayed to Shareen for vengeance against those who tried to slaughter us. In her mercy, the goddess has answered our prayers by first returning our protectors to us, and then by granting us an ally that will wipe these cursed bandits from our lands forever! Behold, the unlikely saviors of our realm."

On this cue, the horns were blown once more, and the rear of the crowd slowly parted to reveal Sir Brovine riding on horseback at the head of a brigade of Coronasian troops.

Trotting with their mounts amongst the other cavalry riders were Ontar and Yorus, who saw the guards of Thramahas take up positions along the rope bridges and at the front of the velen's hall. *If only they were there when we needed them,* Ontar thought.

Riding up to the main stage Sir Brovine dismounted and made his way towards the velen. Passing by a whole host of angry elven guards the knight fearlessly stepped onto the stage and approached Velen Jolarie. Bowing before the noble, Sir Brovine then turned to face the crowd.

"People of Thramahas, the suffering you have felt at the hands of the bandits is no longer yours to bear alone. My kingdom has also had to endure the plight of these vile fiends, and today, we say *no more*! Whether among humans or elves, the protection of innocents is a value we all share, and I will not rest until those who challenge this belief are completely and utterly put to the sword!"

A loud cheer erupted amongst those gathered, and as confidence returned to the elves of Thramahas, both Ontar and Echo wondered what the battle ahead would hold for them?

Three days later, Ontar and his cousin found themselves marching through a rugged part of Illamine Forest with a combined force of elvish and Coronasian troops. Unable to march in lines due to the wooded terrain, the troops were bunched together in small groups of three to four people. At the head of this newly-formed brigade were Searce and Echo, who acted as scouts as they led a half-dozen newly-arrived elvish rangers towards the bandits' camp. Behind them was Sir Brovine and his cavalry riders who drove their horses slowly over the uneven ground. At the rear was the infantry and archer units who marched in segments divided by race. Jayvoe was in command of these troops, and he made sure *nobody* got out of line.

Stepping over a partially exposed tree root, Yorus said, "I can't believe my first battle will be against my own kind in elvish lands."

Ontar's eyes narrowed. "It doesn't matter where the battle is fought as long as it ends with Lydon's death."

"You'll get no argument on that one," Yorus stated. "However, I could sure use a drink once this is all over with. Any chance we could quench our thirst while passing through Kinnerba?"

Thinking a moment, Ontar said, "The bandits and elves damn near drank the tavern dry while they were there. However, I do think my dad kept a couple bottles of the good stuff hidden just in case there was a special occasion."

"Then I say we drink a toast to both his memory and all those who suffered at the bandits' hands," Yorus proclaimed.

Ontar couldn't help but smirk. "I'd like that."

Crouched behind some trees a short distance away from the advancing troops was Lydon and his cadre of bandits. Clutching a short sword in each hand, he looked to a nearby tree and saw Figit lurking among its branches. It took only a moment for the imp's hand gestures to signal that their enemies were in position. Ready for battle, Lydon signaled back to begin the attack.

Echo saw one of the rangers she traveled with raise her hand in a halting motion quickly repeated among the rest of the brigade. Clutching shields and drawing weapons, everyone watched the rangers intently as they crouched low to the ground. Knowledgeable in the ways of nature, these elves heard the startled scampering of woodland animals who had thought they were safe standing next to a bunch of inanimate humans. Looking up ahead of her, Echo saw ten leather clad bandits armed with short bows step out from the behind the trees and take aim.

"Take cover!" Searce shouted as the bandits fired their bows.

Dodging behind some trees with Searce and the other rangers, Echo noticed the bandits were actually targeting Sir Brovine's cavalry unit instead of them. Whizzing through the air these arrows struck both man and horse alike. Utilizing his Phoenix Shield, Sir Brovine caused a transparent circle of orangish energy to appear at his left side seconds before the arrow struck it. A burst of flame incinerated the arrow where it had made contact, leaving the brave knight completely unscathed.

Ontar and Yorus saw the bandits attack on the cavalry riders and looked to Jayvoe for orders. Grabbing his legendary bow, Jayvoe immediately commanded the archers next to him to, "Return fire!" The speed and skill invoked by these elves in their counterattack was truly devastating as a volley of arrows rained down on the bandit archers. Out of the ten men who had engaged in the attack, only four remained. These lingering bandits quickly turned around and fled deeper into the forest.

Sir Brovine surveyed the wounded riders with anger. Lowering his helmet's visor, he pointed his sword at the fleeing bandits and shouted, "Charge!" Galloping past Searce's rangers, the cavalry was easily able to overtake their fleeing enemies and cut them down in their tracks.

Figit shook his head as the last of the bandit archers died. The stupid humans never stood a chance, but they had fulfilled their purpose, and that was all that really mattered. Sitting among the tree branches with a horde of his fellow imps, he gave a high-pitched battle cry before descending on the cavalry below.

Watching the imps swarm around him and his men, Sir Brovine cursed himself for having fallen into such an obvious trap. Swinging his sword over and over again, he and the other cavalry riders tried desperately to kill the imps, but the nasty little monsters proved to be both quick and evasive.

Weaving in-between the frustrated riders, Figit skillfully used his tail to lash the flank of an increasingly frightened horse. Laughing with delight, he wondered how long it would take for the humans to realize his people never intended to face them in direct combat. Their goal was simply to keep the horses scared so the cavalry was out of commission.

Searce saw the chaos up ahead and knew she needed to act quickly. Looking back at Jayvoe while referencing her rangers, she said, "We'll help the cavalry." Raising her arm in a beckoning motion, she urged Echo and the others to, "Come on," as she led them towards the imps.

❦ ❦ ❦

Lydon smiled. The imps had managed to lure both the cavalry *and* the rangers into his trap. With those two units out of the way, he now had the men necessary to face what remained of the brigade with a decent chance of accomplishing their objective. Standing with blades at the ready, he shouted, "Attack!"

Ontar heard the bandits' war cries as they surged towards the brigade ready for battle. Spinning his morning star while raising his shield he expected the first of these bastards to come for him at any minute...but they didn't. Instead, they decided to bear down on the wood elves in some new unforeseen strategy.

Realizing the massive number of bandits charging their position, Jayvoe loaded his Bow of Unyielding and ordered his archers to, "Fire!" Letting loose his projectile, Jayvoe watched as the arrow passed through the throat of one bandit, the shoulder of the man behind him, rip off the ear of a third bandit, and finally exit the skull of one last enemy at the rear. The other archers proved to be almost as effective with their shots, and the first wave of bandits fell before their volley.

Unfortunately, a second wave was right behind the first, and it was eager for blood. Ontar saw three of them charging towards Jayvoe and the two guards he had at his sides. As the elvish captain reloaded his bow, two of the bandits cut down the guard on his left. The guard on the right managed to slay the bandit who came after him, but he was still only able to engage one of the two men who went after Jayvoe.

Recognizing the importance of the elvish leader, Ontar sprinted towards the distracted bandit as Jayvoe dodged his spear. Moving behind the man, Ontar landed an attack that broke bones and sent his enemy crashing to the forest floor. This action did not go unnoticed by the bandit who had just killed Jayvoe's remaining guard. Swinging his mace, he was about to attack Ontar's side when Yorus barged in front of him and parried the blow. This gave Jayvoe the time he needed to reload his bow and fire an arrow that easily ended the bandit's life.

Sergeant Raglak saw the elves take the brunt of the bandit's onslaught as he stood by his fellow soldiers. Raising his two-handed sword, he exclaimed, "Come on, men, we didn't come all this way so the elves could fight our battles for us." Charging into the fray with the infantry right behind him, he shouted, "For Coronas!"

The clash of weapons reverberated across Illamine Forest as Echo joined Searce and the rangers in aiding Sir Brovine's cavalry. Assessing the situation, Searce saw the riders struggling to control their mounts while simultaneously being beset by imps.

Issuing an order to those next to her, she said, "Get your bows ready and stay close."

Following her aunt's command, Echo readied her longbow as Searce cast a spell. Focusing on two riders who could barely control their horses, Searce caused five of the imps who harassed them to suddenly vanish. Figuring that her aunt had magically killed the imps, Echo was surprised to see that three of them abruptly reappeared when they collided with an equal number of their attacking brethren.

Echo's jaw dropped. She had never even considered using an invisibility spell for offensive purposes. However, its effectiveness could not be denied as the imps smacked into each other and fell to the ground. From there, the cavalry took over by bringing their horses' heavy hooves down on the bewildered creatures. Searce repeated her spell over and over again, causing chaos among the imps. A few of them caught on to what she was doing, but any who tried to attack her met a swift end as Echo and the rangers let loose their arrows.

Figit swooped under a cavalry rider's sword only to see one of his own people dart in front of him as they flew upwards. Dodging the idiot, he followed him above the din of battle and over to a high tree branch. Landing near the top of the tree, Figit angrily asked the imp, "What do you think you're doing?"

"I don't know!" the imp shrieked. "It's crazy down there!"

Looking down at the battle, Figit saw his people were fluttering about in a panic as some of them magically disappeared while others fell to human swords. This was *not* how things were supposed to go, and none of Lydon's plans could change that. Snarling in fury, Figit gave a sharp, loud whistle.

"Fly away!" he commanded before leaping off the tree branch. The humans had won this battle, and if Figit wanted to minimize his people's losses, then they would have to flee…for now.

Sir Brovine saw an imp accidentally explode as it flew too close to his shield. Cleaving another of the little monsters in half with his sword, he watched as they soared above his head and into the canopy. Aware of the magic used to defeat his enemies, the knight looked out from atop his horse and spotted Searce flanked by elven rangers. Raising his blade in a brief salute, he then called out to his men. "To me...rally to me!" Pointing his sword back at the brigade, he kicked his horse into a charge and led the cavalry straight towards the bandits.

Ontar breathed heavily as he killed another enemy with a blow from his morning star. Searching for a new opponent, his heart sunk when he saw that Yorus and Lydon were locked in combat! Lydon snickered as one of his swords caused a bloody wound to appear across Yorus's right leg. Attempting to counter, Yorus swung his sword at him, but Lydon parried the attack with his left blade, and then ran him through with his right one! Withdrawing his weapon from the stunned soldier, Lydon granted Yorus a quick death by easily beheading him with the short sword in his left hand.

"Yorus..." the name came out as a whisper as Ontar watched his cousin die. *This can't be happening,* he thought. How many loved ones would have to perish before this nightmare came to an end? Why were the people in *his* family the ones who had to bear the brunt of the bandits' savage wrath? Who could do something so awful to so many who truly didn't deserve it? These thoughts swirled through Ontar's head until they coalesced into one single answer...*him!*

Clutching his morning star, Ontar wanted nothing more than to smash Lydon's brains into a sticky pile of goo! Unfortunately, just as he moved against the bandit leader, the sound of pounding of hooves stopped him in his tracks. Sir Brovine had led his cavalry back into the fray, causing Ontar to lose sight of his enemy somewhere amongst the thundering horses.

Finding himself overwhelmed, Lydon parried the blade of a Coronasian soldier with his left short sword while he used the right one to stab an elven archer in the gut. As the elf died, Lydon ducked the soldier's blade and sliced at the man's knees. The soldier went down hard, and Lydon killed him with his next attack.

Noticing that Coronas now had cavalry bearing down on his men, Lydon knew the battle was lost. *Damn you, Figit!* he cursed as he scrutinized this new development. The elves had been nearly finished by his men, but he still needed time to escape. With cavalry running around, that part of the plan would now come with a whole lot of casualties. Unfortunately, he had no other choice. Making a break for it, Lydon shouted, "Retreat!"

Those words were like music to Sir Brovine's ears. Sidling up to his cavalry captain, he said, "Take your men up ahead and cut off their escape. I'll have the infantry mop up any stragglers."

Echo felt her heart racing as she stealthily followed Searce and the other rangers into the bandits' camp. It was an evil place, sparsely guarded by a handful of shifty-eyed warriors. Moving to eliminate these men, Searce divided up her unit so they could all attack at once. Echo was charged with killing a bandit next to the trees where they chained their prisoners.

With sword and shield drawn, she snuck behind the bandit and was about to make her attack when an excited voice exclaimed, "Echo…Echo over here!"

Echo looked over to her right and noticed that Cora was chained up with the other prisoners. Relieved to see that her friend was still alive, Echo could only curse when she realized the bandit she'd been stalking had been alerted to her presence.

Wearing a slightly battered breastplate, the bandit grasped his heavy war mattock with both hands and shouted, "Intruders!"

Other cries immediately followed as the camp erupted into chaos. Echo swung her sword at the bandit, but he easily parried the attack. He then countered by swinging his war mattock at her. Bringing up her shield, Echo blocked the blow, but the weight of his weapon pushed her back and caused her to stumble. Advancing towards her, the bandit struck again and, this time, cut the leather protecting her upper right arm.

Cora was horrified at the danger she had put Echo in and immediately tried to help. Pulling against her restraints, she lifted up her feet and kicked the bandit square in the side. Watching her enemy knocked off balance, Echo took her sword and made a deep slice into his pelvis. The bandit fell quickly from the wound, and upon his death, she searched for keys to free the prisoners.

Lydon's headband darkened with sweat as he ran towards camp. Weaving through the forest, he had almost been spotted twice by cavalry as they cut his comrades to ribbons. Reaching the outskirts of their encampment, Lydon had hoped to gather the men who were left behind on guard duty and make a run for it. However, the moment he passed the first tent, he heard the sounds of combat and saw that his guards were under attack by elves!

Racing towards the horse-drawn wagons, he found himself joined by a dozen other bandits who had managed to escape the cavalry. Climbing onto a wagon, Lydon turned around and gave orders to the men trickling in.

"Dilb, I want drivers for these wagons NOW! Egav, I'm going to need you and anyone you can find to cover our escape. We'll rendezvous at—"

Lydon didn't get a chance to finish his orders as an arrow from nowhere burst through the center of a tree, shredded the middle of a tent, and destroyed the side rail of his wagon. Startled by the sudden jolt from behind, the horse whinnied and took off into the forest, causing Lydon to fall over and be carried from his men in their time of need.

Watching their fearless leader unwittingly depart, the bandits looked to see where the arrow had come from and saw Jayvoe emerge from the forest with an entire brigade of Coronasian troops at his side. Reloading his bow, the wood elf looked at the remaining bandits and said, "Surrender or die."

Taking his threat seriously, the bandits all dropped their weapons and raised their hands.

❧❧❧

A few hours later, the captured bandits were surrounded by soldiers who sent them marching towards Coronas. Sitting atop his horse, Sir Brovine saw the elves take down their enemy's camp and said to Jayvoe, "You have a beautiful country here. It was an honor to fight by your side to defend it."

Jayvoe was in no mood for flattery. "Next time, keep the filth on your side of the border."

Sighing, the knight shook his head before riding off to join the rest of his men.

Echo wrapped Cora in a blanket after her friend had finished her meal. Raiding the bandits' supplies, she and Searce made sure all their former prisoners had the strength they needed to make the trip back home. After hearing from Cora about the cruelties they endured, Echo felt that for many of them the food would be of small comfort.

Standing up, Echo searched her surroundings until she found Ontar kneeling by the body of his cousin. With his face red and eyes moist, he looked up at her and asked, "Have they found Lydon?"

Echo shook her head. "No. They're interrogating the bandits who were captured, but chances are, he's simply abandoned them."

Standing up, Ontar angrily said, "You have to help me find him. He killed Yorus before my very eyes, and I *swear* that he will die for it!"

"I'm afraid that won't be possible," Searce said as she approached Ontar and Echo. "Humans are forbidden from intruding any further into the Illamine, and Velen Jolarie expects you to return with Sir Brovine to Coronas."

"Are you saying that Lydon is just going to be allowed to escape!?" Ontar raged.

Searce shook her head. "No. I will personally be hunting him down, and when I find him, I will send word to the Bloody Side so that you and Echo can end his life yourselves. All I ask in return is that you help her join the guild so she can continue to advance in her training."

"Swear to me that you won't just kill him on sight!" Ontar demanded.

"I swear on the souls of my brother and his wife," Searce replied.

Satisfied by her oath, Ontar said, "Very well. I will stay by Echo's side until Lydon is found."

Searce confirmed his vow by simply saying, "I promise you will have your revenge."

"After that, Ontar and I left the Illamine, and with his help, I did succeed in joining the Bloody Side. We've been on the road ever since," Echo said as she finished her story.

Having spent much of the afternoon lost in each other's tales the party sat quietly in the Helsh Plains and reflected on what they learned.

Saddened by the story Wink said, "I can't believe it took such a horrible tragedy to bring you two together."

"It was a long time ago," Ontar explained. "What happened then has made us stronger and helped us to persevere through the difficult times in our lives."

Wink cocked her head thoughtfully, "Have you heard anything from Searce since the incident?"

Echo gave a little smile. "She sends word when she can, but as far as we know, she's still hunting Lydon."

Clearly relieved to hear that Ontar and Echo had a purely professional relationship Wink said, "Well, let's get going. We've spent far too long frolicking in the grass as it is."

Standing up slowly and putting on his helmet, Ontar grabbed the pixie and placed her on his shoulder. "I don't frolic," he said sternly.

Echo ignored the two. Rising to her feet, she gathered the horses and mounted up. When Ontar and Wink had done the same, she decided to take the lead and immediately sent her animal galloping down the road before them.

Chapter Six

good ride helped the party forget about past traumas, and shortly after breakfast on the proceeding day, they caught their first glimpse of the magnificent towering tree line that made up Illamine Forest. Slowing their horses to enter these verdant woods, the companions embraced a feeling of calm that washed over them as they passed into familiar territory. Everyone present knew this sense of peace was somewhat misplaced since none of them had actually been in this part of the forest, but they didn't care.

In truth, the bulk of these enormous woodlands rested in elvish territory (hence the country's namesake), but nature seldom acknowledges the arbitrary borders of *civilized* races, and Illamine Forest had spread its vast bounty into four human realms as well. Trotting beneath the broad green canopy of ancient seasonal trees, the party relished the cool shade that nature provided after dealing with the bright hot sun on the Helsh Plains. Watchful for any roots along the road their horses might trip over the travelers once again picked up their pace.

It was another two days of riding along the dirt road before the group eventually came to a stop. This was a pleasant time when the companions listened to the steady rhythm of their mounts by day and laughed to stories and music by the campfire at night. Setting out in the morning to begin a new day's travel, the party brought their horses to a halt when they came across a gray, four story, square stone watch tower with dark green moss growing along its sides all the way up to its parapets. A small stable was connected to the tower, which seemed to have a fair amount of usage based on the well-trodden ground about it.

The tower was positioned at the right side of the road that came to an end at the foot of a long wooden bridge. The bridge spanned a beautiful, clear blue river that cut through the forest and made crossing it by any other means highly unlikely.

Standing next to the bridge was a brown bearded guard from Lareder. Casually leaning against his spear, he wore a light green and blue surcoat with a crest at its center that depicted an upward pointed sword in front of a golden bell. "Morning," he called out. "It's a fine day to be out for a ride."

"It is at that," Echo said with a smile. "So, are you the caretaker of this bridge?"

The guard nodded casually. "Eh, more or less. Officially, I maintain the border between Lareder and Sibeia, however, most of the time, I just warn people about the dangers beyond the Kaegis River."

"What sort of dangers?" Echo asked while shifting in her saddle.

The guard elaborated, "You see, the forest on the other side of this bridge is home to two rival tribes of ogres and tiki. Now, the tiki are a fairly peaceful lot who serve an ancient idol sworn to protect these lands even though their creators are long since dead. Treat them fairly, and they'll do the same to you."

"And the ogres?" Echo asked with a bit more concern.

Hesitating a moment, the guard replied, "The ogres are a savage bunch of killers, and if you see one, just ride away as fast as you can. If you keep up a good pace, then you'll find the road leads right to a Sibeian fort. From there on out, you should be pretty safe."

Upon hearing word of the fortress, Wink stood up excitedly in the hood of Ontar's cloak and whispered beneath his helmet, "Hatch is in that fort! I can't believe we're so close."

"I just hope he's still sane," Ontar murmured before Wink punched him in the shoulder.

Echo looked down at the guard from her steed. "Thanks for the warning," she said.

"Don't mention it. I'm just doing my duty," the guard said with a hint of pride as he headed back towards the tower.

As he left, Echo tilted her head towards Ontar in a beckoning motion before the two set their horses cantering across the bridge. A slight breeze tussled their animal's manes while the sounds of rushing water and hooves pounding on wooden planks filled the air. Reaching the bridge's other side without incident, the party found a dirt road continuing through the forest and decided to speed their horses past this dangerous patch of woods in lieu of contacting some of the previously mentioned creatures.

The horses raced along the road for almost an hour before a loud, inhuman bellow emanating through the trees caused them to rear and halt in their tracks. There was something dangerous in these woods, and a score of wild birds chirped loudly before taking flight from some nearby branches.

Having difficulty controlling their animals, Ontar and Echo dismounted their skittish steeds and struggled to pull them forward by the reins.

Peeking out from Ontar's hood, Wink nervously asked the warrior, "What is it?"

Dropping his free hand down by his morning star, Ontar looked about cautiously. "I don't know, but I have a feeling we're about to find out."

The forest seemed unnaturally still as with each passing step; the party drew closer to a creature whose deep bellowing cries were now accompanied by tormented moans to assail their ears. Echo's mind raced at what this possible new threat might be. Was it an ogre, a tiki, or something else entirely different lurking amongst the trees? Either way, she could tell the cries were isolated and seemed to grow louder as she and her companions approached. This was good because whatever creature was up ahead it obviously didn't know they were coming. *Perhaps I'll be able to sneak around and ambush it,* she thought.

Echo extended the reins of her horse to Ontar. "Here, take these. I'm going to slip into the forest and see what we're up against."

"Right," Ontar responded as he took hold of the animal.

"I'm coming, too!" Wink squeaked as she popped out of Ontar's hood. Gingerly sliding down the side of his cloak, she gracefully landed on the dirt road next to Echo, who was a little bit apprehensive about having such a noisy little pixie accompany her in first place.

"Do you think you can keep quiet and out of sight?"

Wink snickered. "Are you kidding? That monster will probably spot, kill, and eat you *way* before it would ever take notice of someone like me."

As pleasant a thought as that might be, Echo had to concede that Wink's size did give her a certain advantage in this area. "Alright, come on," she said as she drew forth her sword and shield. Moving silently off the dirt road, Echo entered the forest with Wink stealthily sprinting behind her.

Their trek was not a long one, and they didn't have to stray far from Ontar's location. Following the sounds of anguished moaning, the two spies knew they were close to their target when they caught a whiff of the creature's foul stench and peered through the trees to see what it was.

The sight that greeted them was that of a large menacing ogre who sat on the ground with his legs spread out right in the middle of the road. A slovenly brute, the ogre's skin resembled that of a human's except for being covered by random scars and scratches. Virtually naked, the ogre wore a brown loin cloth barely visible beneath his round bloated belly. Fleshy arms and legs were surprisingly muscular while the ogre's hairless head had two small eyes, a runny nose, and a slightly oversized jaw with two tiny tusks sticking upwards.

Considered by most races to be a deadly monster, this particular ogre was far more pathetic than either Echo or Wink had initially expected. Its hideous howls were not meant to terrify enemies but, instead, seemed to indicate the foul brute was actually crying. Closer scrutiny soon revealed the ogre had tears streaming down its dirty face, which it futilely tried to wipe away before once again bellowing loudly.

"Not exactly as fierce as its reputation lets on now is it?" Echo observed quietly.

"Aw…he looks so sad," Wink said with a long face. "We should see what's wrong."

"Are you crazy!" Echo exclaimed. "If we even get near that thing, he'll rip our arms off and stick them down our throats."

"That will only happen if we scare him," Wink replied.

Echo's jaw dropped. *"Scare Him!* What's to stop him from scaring us? Besides, why would you even want to talk to him in the first place?"

Wink was already starting to come up with a plan. "The ogre probably lives around here, and if we find out what's wrong with him, then he might turn around and help us rescue Hatch."

"Or he could pound us into little puddles of goo," Echo noted skeptically.

"Well, it won't hurt to try," Wink declared as she faced the ogre's direction.

"What are you going to do?" Echo asked.

Wink smiled. "Just work a little magic. After all, who do you think inspired Hatch in the first place?" Closing her eyes, she then spoke the words to cast a simple spell. Interested in seeing where this was going, Echo noticed that after Wink's incantation her mouth and lips continued to move normally, but her voice now sounded like it was right next to the ogre.

Speaking in an overly-exaggerated spooky tone, Wink said, "Eeeeevil ogre, I am the *SPIRIT* of the forest. Why do you weep this day?"

The ogre stopped his blubbering and curiously looked about the trees with tear filled eyes.

"Oh, for cripe's sakes," Echo muttered as she kicked a bit of dirt at the pixie. Wink turned around irritably as Echo asked, "Do you really think he's going to help us after you just got done calling him evil?"

"Well, what am I supposed to call him? Fat and ugly?" Wink replied.

The comment was meant for Echo, but her spell made the insult carry to the surprised ogre's ears. Looking down at his rotund gut, the ogre rubbed his belly and sighed. "Hmmm... spirits angry today," he said to himself.

Echo lowered her sword and shook her head at her companion's foolishness. Wink merely winced and shrugged before turning her attention back to the ogre.

"Myyyy apologies, dear ogre. Please...tell me what troubles you."

"Oh, me so sad," the ogre shouted as he wiped a line of snot along his forearm. "Me spend *really* long time finding special black and white kitty deep in forest to give to Chiefs Number One Daughter, but when me give it to her, she say it stinks! So, me punch her in the nose. Then everyone throw Bub out of tribe!" Finishing his short yet tragic tale, the ogre once again wailed loudly.

Well, that explains the odor, Echo thought. Personally, she believed that if Bub was stupid enough to give the chieftain's daughter a skunk as a gift, then maybe he deserved to be exiled. This whole conversation seemed to be a waste of time, and she was about to say as much to Wink when the pixie started talking again.

"Beeee at peace, oh mighty ogre. Your tale of woe has touched my heart, and I have decided to help you win back the one you love."

What!? Echo thought with a mixture of shock and rage. She almost stepped on the little rat just to shut her up but decided against it when curiosity got the better of her.

"I will send threeeeee noble heroes to help you in your plight. A valiant warrior, an adorable pixie, and a crabby elf," Wink said as she stuck her tongue out at Echo. "They will help you with your beloved, but in exchange, you must promise that your tribe will assist them in a noble quest of their own."

Bub nodded his head rapidly. "Oh, yes. Me promise that once Chiefs Number One Daughter likes Bub again, everyone will help heroes."

Wink smiled brightly at his pledge. "Very welllll. Wait where you are, and the heroes shall emerge shortly."

Bub stood up jubilantly. "Thank you, forest spirit! Me wait right here for heroes."

⬦⬦⬦

Ontar's tone was flat. "We're going to do what now?"

Echo could only imagine the look on the warrior's face as she smoothly reclaimed the reins of her horse.

Wink continued explaining, "We're going to aid the ogre so that his tribe will help us rescue Hatch."

"And how are we going to do that?" Ontar asked as he removed his helmet and held it under his arm.

"I don't know. We'll just have to ask him," Wink replied with a bit of frustration.

"For that matter, what's to stop the ogres from killing us once we help them," Echo added.

"Because Bub promised they wouldn't, and if you can't trust an ogre's promise, then who can you trust?" Wink said naively.

Ontar gave Echo a skeptical look. "Alright, this is what we'll do. While Wink's got the ogre distracted, Echo will sneak up behind him and attempt a back attack. When he turns to face her, I'll—"

"We're NOT killing the damn ogre!" Wink shouted. "Now, listen. An attack on the Sibeian fort by Bub's tribe is the best possible distraction I can think of while we sneak in and rescue Hatch. Sure, there's a chance they'll rip us limb from limb, but if everything goes right, we could have some powerful new friends on our side and a mighty wizard who will travel with us until the end of his days. So, quit being such chickens and COME ON!"

Not waiting for a response, Wink turned around and marched down the road.

Watching her go, Ontar muttered, "I suppose if we did have to fight the ogre, a frontal attack would be a better challenge." Tugging on the reins of his horse, he guided the animal to follow Wink.

Echo grumbled to herself. "I don't know who's the bigger fool here. Her for going, him for following, or me for coming along." Pulling her own mount forward, she fell into step behind the others.

◆◆◆◆◆◆

Moments later, the party watched as a foul-smelling barefoot ogre came bounding up the road towards them. "Noble heroes! Noble heroes! Bub wait long time for you." Ontar's eyes widened upon realizing that he only came up to the behemoth's armpit, and he gaped as it staggered to a stop in front of him. The horses whinnied and reared at the sight of the brute. "And you bring horses! Mmmm…me like horses. Thems good eatins," Bub proclaimed loudly as he reached out to touch one.

Terrified by the ogre coming at them, one horse nearly stomped on Ontar's foot with its hoof, then pulled its reins free as it ran into the woods. Nearly being trampled by the animal, Echo was forced to release her own mount while dodging out of the way, and she watched as it took off a different direction.

"Damnit!" the elf exclaimed as she pointed at the ogre. "Look what you did!"

Bub's lower lip pouted, and he stood still. "Crabby elf let go of horse. Not Bub."

"I am not a crabby elf," Echo said as Wink snickered below her. "My name is Echo, this is Ontar, and that's Wink," she finished while gesturing to her other companions.

Wink looked up, smiled, waved, and said, "Hi there."

Crouching on his knees, Bub examined the pixie with a big grin of his own. "Ooh, you sound just like forest spirit. Now me know you good friend."

Eager to keep the ogre from thinking too hard about that statement, Ontar quickly spoke up, "So, Bub, the forest spirit said that you'd help us on our quest if we assisted you with your mate. Is there anything we can do to get you back in her good graces?"

Standing up, with his head hung low, Bub sadly replied, "Me have to give really good gift. Something whole tribe would like."

"Such as?" Echo asked while wondering what in the world a whole tribe of ogres could possibly like.

Bub's expression brightened. "Two-headed squawker!"

Wink giggled at the silly sounding name, and Ontar cocked his head. "What's that?"

"Big orange bird with two heads. Very good eatins," Bub explained.

Figures, Echo thought. "So, where do we find one of these birds?"

Bub's eyes narrowed and his voice turned gruff. "Tiki have one, but they no share."

"Why not?" Wink inquired.

Scowling at the question, Bub replied, "They hide best tasting animals in village. Make me want to smash them!"

"Well, we'll just have to show them the error of their ways now, won't we?" Echo said as a sinister smile touched her lips.

Ontar highly doubted diplomacy was what Echo had in mind. "Would you be able to take us to the tiki village?" he asked Bub.

"Oh, yes, Bub know way," the big ogre replied as he swung his arm in a following gesture and sauntered off the road and into the forest.

"Wait a minute! I'm not going anywhere until I get my horse back," Echo insisted.

"That could be dangerous," Wink warned. "We should forget about the horses and stay close to Bub."

"No way!" Echo replied as she stood up. "Those are some perfectly fine animals, and we can still get plenty use out of them."

Admitting to the animal's value, Ontar scooped Wink up onto his shoulder and said, "There's nothing wrong with taking a moment to look for the horses. Wink and I will look for our horse over there." Pointing in a different direction, he continued, "Echo, I think your horse went that way. Bub, you wait here until we get back."

Echo drew her sword and shield. "Sounds like a plan," she said confidently.

Wink turned towards the ogre and gave him a warning. "Don't leave this spot, Bub, or the forest spirit will get very mad at you."

"Me wait right here," Bub replied while standing rigidly.

Traversing the forest's uneven floor, Echo felt lost amongst its towering trees. Staring at the ground, she knew she had no real idea what she was doing. Searce had spent more time training her on how to stalk someone through a dark alley than on how to spot an animal's tracks. All she could really do is hope that something would happen to cause her horse to reveal itself. As luck would have it, she managed to hear the sound of a dried twig snapping and quickly advanced towards its position.

Peeking behind the trunk of a large tree, Echo let out a startled yelp at the sight that greeted her. Standing at roughly rib height was a barefooted tiki dressed in little more than a loincloth held up by a crude weapon belt. Being somewhat mannish in appearance, the tiki had brown skin with arms and legs that were covered in elaborate red tattoos. Drawn to the little person's most defining feature, Echo saw the tiki wore a long rectangular wooden mask that obscured its face and neck. Colorfully-painted, the mask had big white teeth lined by red lips, which were cut into the shape of a grimace. Blue and green coloring around the eyes definitely stood out from the line of orange flowers and yellow feathers carved above its brow.

Reacting to the elf's appearance with surprise, the tiki defensively raised a weapon, which resembled a wooden oar with a stubby handle and a big notch along the sides of its paddle. Pointing its kotiate at her, the tiki looked up and said, "Aagh! Don't scare me like that, you crazy elf. For a second there I thought you were an ogre."

Echo cautiously lowered her blade. Obviously, the tiki didn't know she was currently traveling with an ogre since he probably would have attacked her on sight. Thinking quickly, she realized that this could be an opportune time for her to find the tiki village and apprehend Bub's bird without raising too much suspicion. She only hoped the others weren't far away in case things turned nasty.

Smiling broadly, she nodded to the tiki and said, "Forgive me. My name is Echo, and your mask made me think that you were some sort of monster."

"I suppose I am rather intimidating," the tiki replied as he lowered his weapon. "Well, just to let you know, my name is Tavah, and I'm curious as to why an elf like you would be stumbling about this part of the forest?"

Echo racked her brain for a moment trying to come up with a believable story. After a brief pause, she stated, "You can call me Echo, and I'm a hunter who's out looking for game when I heard that this area had some vicious boars which I could test my skills against."

If Tavah had thought that Echo was lying, he certainly didn't show it. "Yes, it's true that we do have some fierce boars around here. However, it's the ogres in these lands you should really worry about."

"Ogres!" Echo exclaimed in mock surprise. "Hmmm…I don't think I could handle one of those. Damn, I wish I had my horse here. Then I could flee this place without worry of being attacked."

Tavah sympathized. "Well, I can tell you that I've patrolled these woods all morning and have yet to come across a lone horse. Unfortunately, I do think that you'd be in great danger traversing this stretch of forest by yourself. Why don't you accompany me back to my village? From there, I can arrange safe passage back to elvish territory for you.

Echo appreciated the tiki's compassion and felt a little guilty about lying to him. Were her circumstances different, she would have truly preferred to deal with Tavah over Bub. Sadly, a tribe of ogres would be far more useful against a Sibeian fortress than anything a tiki could produce. So, she decided to stick with her original plans.

Extending a friendly hand towards the trusting tiki, Echo said, "Thank you so much for your kindness."

Taking her hand in his, Tavah looked up at her and replied, "It would be my pleasure."

Wink frowned as she crouched down by the tracks on the forest floor.

"What's wrong?" Ontar asked, noticing her expression.

"The hoofprints I found are surrounded by boar tracks. I have a feeling that our horse is being hunted," she remarked while standing up and pacing the area.

Shaking his head, Ontar bent down by Wink and opened his gauntleted hand while saying, "Come on, let's head back. We don't need to waste any more time looking for a lost horse when we can just as easily get about on foot."

Wink shrugged and climbed into the big warrior's hand. Lifting her up onto his shoulder, Ontar turned around and headed back to where they had left Bub. Nearing the spot where the big ogre sat, Ontar was about to call out to his odd ally when an enraged cry from up ahead caused him to draw his morning star and shield. Dashing through the trees as Wink slipped into his hood, Ontar approached Bub's location and saw the ogre stood with three darts lodged in different parts of his body.

Facing the irate ogre, a short distance away, was a tiki with a slender wooden blowpipe in his hand. Taunting Bub with laughter, the tiki loaded his weapon with another dart that had been tucked into his loincloth. The ogre was not amused and charged him at a wobbling sluggish pace, which indicated that he'd been poisoned. Looking to further wear his opponent down, the tiki ran through the forest with Bub roaring behind him in hot pursuit.

Ontar tried running after the two, but his heavy armor made it difficult. Stopping to catch his breath, he doubted he could ever gain on the bitter adversaries when, suddenly, he heard orders being shouted on either side of him. Looking about, he saw two more tiki armed with blowpipes trying to take aim at their distant foe.

Thankfully, the warriors were targeting Bub instead of him, and Ontar realized the tiki's initial attack was simply a diversion to set the poor ogre up for an ambush. At which point, all they would have to do is keep their distance and fill him full of darts until he was rendered immobile…unless, of course, Ontar decided to stop them.

Spinning his morning star, Ontar sprinted towards the tiki on his right just after he had finished blowing a dart. Alerted to the warrior's presence by the clamor of his armor, the tiki turned to face his enemy and threw his empty weapon the moment Ontar came into striking range.

The blowpipe bounced off Ontar's tower shield, leaving the tiki defenseless before him. Ontar then sent his morning star crashing into his foes mask causing it to shatter as he died. Surprised by what happened next, Ontar watched with fascination as the tiki's body turned into a pile of clay dust.

Unable to relish his victory, Ontar overheard a battle cry from behind him and spun around to see the second tiki had drawn his kotiate in addition to the blowpipe. Utilizing both weapons at once, the tiki blew a dart at Ontar's gauntlet, causing his hand to sting despite its protection and forcing him to pull back his morning star. This action allowed the tiki to close in and slam his foe's armored stomach with the flat of his kotiate. Recoiling from the strike, Ontar spun his weapon in front of him to keep the little tiki at bay.

Prepared to make a second strike at his adversary, the tiki heard an odd screaming sound and turned just in time to see his companion, who had been chased by the ogre, fly into him at a lethal speed. Dying on the spot, both tiki's burst into clay dust while Ontar turned to see Bub standing by a tree, breathing heavily with a dart in his chest and two more in his back.

"Bub back hurt," the ogre said as he brushed the dart out of his chest.

Ontar withdrew his morning star and shield, then reached towards his hood to pick up Wink. The pixie saw his open gauntlet and climbed into it. As he set her on the ground, Ontar said, "Wink, we should have run into Echo by now. See if you can spot any tracks around here that might have been hers. I'm going to take a moment to go help Bub."

"No problem," Wink replied as she ran about the battle ground searching for anything that seemed out of place.

Ontar walked up to Bub and spoke to the ogre respectfully, "Why don't you turn around, and I'll get those darts out of your back."

A hint of a smile formed on Bub's lips as he turned to display his massive back, the ogre then crouched down so Ontar could remove the projectiles.

Ontar couldn't help but admire the ogre. Bub had fearlessly fought against the tiki's with companions that he had known for less than a day. He envied the ogre's ability to trust a group of total strangers when a far more intelligent race would have undoubtedly questioned their motives. Pulling out the darts from Bub's back, Ontar let him know that it was okay to stand.

The ogre was just about to express his appreciation when Wink called out, "Onnie, I think I've found Echo's tracks, but it looks like she's traveling with a tiki."

Ontar didn't like the sound of that. Either Echo was a prisoner, or she had something else up her sleeve. Unfortunately, the only way to find out which was to follow her tracks and see where they led. Hopefully, whatever happened she still managed to keep her wits about her.

Echo struggled to find landmarks during a rapid trek through the forest as Tavah guided her to his village. The tiki moved with nimble confidence over terrain unfamiliar to her. She was just about to suggest they stop when the trees gave way to a narrow clearing where a long wall had been erected. Built with a line of branches that were intermittently attached to big sturdy logs, Echo and Tavah followed the wall until they reached a carved wooden gateway whose sides resembled four painted tiki standing on top of each other. A similar tiki mask could be seen at the gates gabled top, which was connected by some flat outstretched arms. Manning the village's gate were two armed guards, one of whom asked, "Tavah! How did you get such a pretty elf to follow you home?"

"Can't you tell? She's obviously drawn to my masculine body," Tavah boasted in a claim that prompted a snicker from Echo.

"Well, we both know she isn't attracted to your face," stated the second guard. "Tavah's so ugly he could make an onion cry."

Putting his hands on his hips, Tavah retorted, "Oh, please, Bital, your face is so bad that when you go to the river for a drink the water changes course."

Bital heard the other guard laugh and exclaimed, "You think I'm hideous! Well, in case you didn't realize it, most people around here would prefer talking to your ass simply because it's the easiest part of you to look at."

Chuckling at the exchange, Echo interrupted the tiki by saying, "There's no way you guys can really be that ugly."

"Sure, there is," Tavah argued. "Why do you think we all wear masks?" Unable to answer that question, Echo saw Tavah gesture to her. "Follow me. I'll take you to see Moai."

Entering the village, Echo walked into a settlement dotted by wooden huts with a single open door and window positioned beneath a small veranda. The huts roofs were made of tree bark and their front resembled the upper part of the gate she had just passed through. Giving her some curious looks, the tiki whispered questions to each other about the elf's arrival.

Largely ignoring their stares, Echo passed one of the many wooden tiki statues that dotted the area and noticed the village had several different animals walking freely between them. Deer, foxes, and some young-looking boars all sauntered past the tiki without any concern. Mildly interested in the different creature's appearance, Echo's attention was piqued when she heard a strange multiple squawking sound off to her left. Taking a quick glance, she saw an orange, two-headed bird with yellow beaks and small wings pecking at the ground. This peculiar beast would have been large enough for her to ride on if she had only been given a saddle.

Wondering how she was going to capture the weird bird, Echo's eyes widened as she and Tavah came to a stop near the center of the village. Looming over them (and every other hut in the village) was a gray, thirteen-foot monolithic statue, whose oversized head had a heavy brow complemented by its long nose and ears. Looking at her with empty shadowed eyes, the Moai kept its sharp angular arms pressed against a heavy torso that lacked any sign of legs, while slender hands with long fingers appeared to be covered in a thick brown clay.

The clay itself had been part of four small mounds, which had been dumped at the idol's sides. Fashioned from these mounds in front of the Moai were six mannish figures destined to become tiki. Noticing that three small holes made up the figures eyes and mouth, Echo looked at Tavah and thought, *No wonder they all wear masks.*

Kneeling before Moai and tugging on Echo's pants until she did the same thing, Tavah said, "Oh, great and powerful Moai, I have brought an elvish hunter named Echo to see you. She lost her mount in the forest, and I was hoping that we could guide her safely home."

"Greetings, my elvish friend," Moai said in a deep, booming voice. "As one whose people care deeply about the forest I welcome you to our village."

Displaying the proper reverence, Echo replied, "It is an honor to be in your presence."

"So, tell me, little elf, how did a hunter like you find yourself so far from your own lands?" Moai inquired.

Echo lied, "The game my people hunt is all so very common. My goal was to find something unique that I could bring back to them."

"Ah, but a great prize comes with a great risk," Moai warned. "I assume that Tavah has told you about the ogres. Many tiki have lost their lives against those savages. I'd hate to think you would share their fate."

Echo sighed solemnly. "I can see why you would want me to end my hunt. With ogres lurking about, it would be far too risky for me to continue my pursuit of wild game…although, I have to admit that one of the tamed creatures here has caught my eye."

"Would that creature happen to be the didex?" Moai guessed.

Echo liked the tiki and their talking idol. She really didn't want to steal their bird if she could help it. *Perhaps I could strike a deal with them,* she thought. "The bird is like nothing I've ever seen before, and it would be a glorious prize for my people if I could return with it. Would you consider a trade for the creature?"

Moai shook his enormous head. "I'm sorry, but in order to give my tiki life, I have to sacrifice the animals in their keeping, and that includes the didex."

"Why don't you just replace the bird with a different creature?" Echo asked.

"Because one didex offers the same magical properties as two regular animals," Moai explained. "And the less killing of nature's children we can do, the better."

Echo barely disguised her disappointment. It looked like things were about to get a lot more complicated. "Of course. Forgive me for mentioning it."

At that moment, Bital ran up to the group and exclaimed, "Forgive me, oh glorious master, but three of our warriors have been killed! It looks like an ogre was behind their deaths, and from where their remains were spread, we're guessing the monster is perilously close to our village."

Tavah punched the ground when he heard this. "The bastards grow bolder with each passing day. Please, master, allow me to assemble a war party to hunt it down. We mustn't let the ogre get close enough to attack our home."

"Very well," Moai replied. "But be watchful of casualties. Your lives are just as important as anyone else's. So, try not to waste them." Standing up, Tavah and Bital immediately went to gather their warriors.

Echo kept herself impassive during the conversation, but deep down, her mind raced. It wasn't difficult to discern that her companions had tracked her down and were probably waiting outside the village at this very moment! If she was going to do something, it would have to be quick before the war party discovered them. Rising in front of the idol, Echo said, "This sounds like trouble. I think I'll go help Tavah against this new threat before anyone else gets hurt."

"If you wish," Moai grumbled, "but should the ogre prove to be more dangerous than…"

Echo had already turned her back on the big statue and was now making her way towards the war party. Initially claiming to join them, she followed the tiki out of their village gate and into the forest. However, once amongst the trees, she found it easy to slip away from the warriors and seek out her companions.

Wink crouched low as she ran along the wall of the tiki village. Being small enough not to attract much attention, she had been sent by Ontar and Bub to scout around in search of Echo. Seeing the elf following their war party into the woods, she pursued them until Echo broke away from the group, which prompted her to call out. "Echo, over here."

Echo's pointed ears easily heard Wink's cry, and she located her with little difficulty. "Where's Ontar and Bub?" she asked quietly.

"Not far from the village," Wink replied while jerking her head towards the wall. "Did you find the bird?"

Crouching down close to the pixie, Echo whispered, "Yes, it's just wandering around the center of the village. Our only problem will be getting ahold of it undetected."

Wink thought for a moment, then smiled. "Who says it has to be undetected? If you can get me past the wall, I can use a spell that will drive the bird out into the forest. All the rest of you would need to do is take care of any guards at the gate."

Picking up the pixie as she stood, Echo said, "I think we can handle that. At least for a little bit." Sneaking back over to an obscure portion of the wall, Echo kicked in one of its branches until it made a hole large enough for Wink to slip through. Afterwards, the pixie told Echo where Ontar and Bub were hiding before the two quietly parted ways.

Keeping along the village's wall and away from the huts where the tiki dwelled, Wink took a moment to marvel at the massive Moai they served until she spotted the didex and positioned herself to be directly across from the tiki's gate. Chuckling wickedly to herself, she uttered an incantation that no animal would ever be able to withstand. Suddenly, a gut-wrenching odor filled the air so vile it nearly caused Wink to choke on her own handiwork. The animals reacted almost immediately to the stench, with the boars squealing loudly and the deer violently shaking their heads. The didex's beaks both opened to emit an ear-piercing shriek, which sent the other beasts fleeing past the startled tiki and to-wards the gate.

Alarmed by the stampede heading their way, Bital and an-other guard took turned around and did their utmost to block the exit. Unfortunately, this did not end well for them as an arrow and bolt struck the back of their heads and reduced them to piles of clay dust. Putting away his crossbow in favor of a morning star and shield, Ontar saw Echo reload her bow and said, "Bub and I will get the bird. You go find Wink."

Fading into the woods near the village's wall, Echo said, "I'll look for you after I get her."

Unconcerned by the elf's departure, Bub saw the animals charging through the tiki's gate and let loose a mighty roar when the didex came into view. Charging up to the frightened animal, he spread his arms and effortlessly slammed the bird's two heads together. The beast collapsed to the ground in a heap, and Bub grabbed one of its talons before dragging it off into the forest.

❦❦❦

Ontar and Bub ran hard through the woods, weaving in-between trees and ducking beneath low hanging branches. Everyone knew the farther they could get from the tiki village, the safer they would be. The only thing slowing them down was Bub struggling to drag the didex behind him.

For a brief moment, there was a slight hope the tikis would not pursue them, but then a dart slammed into Bub's stomach, causing him to howl in pain. Cursing their misfortune, Ontar heard a dart *ping* off his shoulder plate as he realized they had stumbled into the tiki war party. Watching four more darts stick into Bub (while three bounced off his armor), Ontar watched the woozy ogre fall limply to the ground. Seeking to stop any further darts from flying, Ontar surged towards the enemies who fired at them.

Feeling safe in numbers, two tiki with blowpipes fired on Ontar the moment he came into view while a third who held a kotiate prepared to engage him in combat. Ignoring the darts, Ontar used his morning star's superior length to wrap its chain around the tiki's wrist and hurl him into a tree. The death blow that followed frightened one of the tiki, who dropped his blowpipe and drew a kotiate only to be killed before he had a chance to use it. The last tiki had also drawn a weapon and struck one of Ontar's knees from behind, following the defeat of his friend.

Dropping before his smaller adversary, Ontar raised his shield in defense as the tiki attacked him. Thankfully, an arrow from somewhere in the woods killed the tiki and gave Ontar a reprieve from his attackers.

Unaware of what had happened to his fellow warriors, Tavah looked on with joy as the dart filled ogre laid prone on the ground. Ordering five other tiki to join him as he pulled out his kotiate, the group advanced upon their enemy and the groaning didex at his feet. Prepared to kill his foe, Tavah was caught off guard when Bub kicked the bird into him in an act that sent both rolling across the ground. Enraged, the other tiki beat Bub repeatedly with their weapons.

Thinking that victory was close at hand as he struggled to get up, Tavah gasped in shock when Echo fired an arrow that killed one of his warriors! This was followed by Ontar limping slightly into view while whirling his morning star and telling the tiki they should. "Prepare to die!" It was a clever distraction that allowed Bub to grab a tiki by the leg, pull him to the ground, and rip his head off!

Afraid that he no longer had the numbers to fight such formidable foes, Tavah shouted, "Retreat!" as he fled with his brethren into the forest. Watching them go, Echo feared their response should they ever cross paths again.

Popping up out of the hood on Echo's cloak, Wink said, "We need to get out of here. Come on, Bub, let's go!"

"Me no go!" Bub said after a couple of grunts. "Too tingly."

"Those darts must have been poisoned like the others" Ontar observed. "We'll have to stand guard until he recovers."

Watching the trees suspiciously, Echo said, "Let's just hope the tiki don't try anything while we wait."

Thankfully, the next few hours passed without incident. Bub quickly recovered from the poison after the darts were removed, and with his prized didex in tow, the party headed out once more.

Chapter Seven

O ntar quietly cursed as a horde of insects swarmed about his head. Evening had fallen on Illamine Forest, and after tending to their wounds and dining on rations, the party found they were once again following Bub towards some unfamiliar (and probably dangerous) location. Blessed with poor night vision, Ontar was forced to carry a torch in one hand and his helmet under an opposing arm while they traveled. Wink slept quietly in the hood of his cloak as he struggled to keep his footing on the rugged terrain.

Not that any of his companions enjoyed the hike all that much. Although, Echo certainly seemed to be having the easiest time of it. The wood elf was in her element and was only bothered by the slower pace of those she traveled with. Bub, on the other hand, grunted and groaned continually as he took the lead while still dragging the didex behind him. Ontar noticed that one of the pathetic creature's heads would let out a tormented squawk from time to time while the second one hadn't shown any signs of life since being pummeled by the ogre earlier that day.

Tired of roaming the woods, Ontar asked, "Bub, how much further is it before we can rest?"

Bub stopped lugging the didex and panted slightly. "We close now. You watch."

Ontar was about to ask a follow up question when Echo raised her left hand in a cautionary gesture and had her right one fall towards the hilt of her sword. "Shhh, someone's coming."

"What's going on?" Wink asked groggily as she crawled out of Ontar's hood and onto his shoulder.

"Could be trouble," Ontar said as he held his torch out defensively.

Emerging from the trees in front of them was an ogre whose size and features closely resembled that of Bub. The only difference between the two was that this new arrival had a long scar running over his left eye, and the tusk beneath it was missing.

Looking suspiciously at the group, the ogre said, "Bub, why you come back to tribe? We no like you anymore."

This simple question caused a pained look to cross Bub's face. "Uge, me so sorry. Bub make it better by bringing two-headed squawker to Chiefs Number One Daughter."

Uge pointed a finger at Ontar and Echo and asked, "Who they?"

Bub smiled proudly. "Them's me little helpers. They let Bub take squawker from tiki."

Ontar and Echo glanced at each other a little bewildered by Bub's description. Ontar hadn't been called a *little helper* since he was a boy filling the snack bowls at his parent's tavern, and for Echo, it had been even longer.

Uge obviously wasn't impressed with either of them. "Tiki's gone now. We eat helpers, then bring squawker back to chief."

Ontar instinctively wanted to drop his torch and grab a weapon, but when he saw that Echo had stayed her hand, he decided to do the same.

"No!" stated Bub. "Great forest spirit send them to help Bub. We no make spirit angry."

Uge crossed his arms and studied the group for a moment. He then lowered one hand while beckoning with the other. "Okay, we go to tribe now." Everyone breathed a sigh of relief as Uge walked over to the didex, grabbed it's one free talon, and helped Bub pull it along.

Following behind the ogres, Ontar felt Wink lean close to his ear and say, "Gee, Onnie, you should feel *really* special having such a *great spirit* sitting on your shoulder."

"Uh-huh," Ontar replied with a smirk. "Well, oh wondrous spirit, I'd watch your ass before that bug over there decides to bite it."

"Where!?" Wink exclaimed as she flailed her arms about trying to shoo away the insects. Ontar chuckled, and Wink quickly realized he was teasing. "Meanie," she retorted in mock anger as she punched him in the arm.

The trek to the ogre's home was not a long one, and there were now marker's in the forest to clearly identify their tribe's territory. Ontar almost missed one as he followed behind Bub and Uge. Then a slight gasp from Wink alerted him to a tall tree branch sticking out of the ground with an animal's skull on top of it. Looking around, Ontar noticed more of these crude posts scattered randomly about the woods.

Echo suspected the ogres would try to do something to scare intruders away from their lands and wasn't terribly surprised by the skull posts. What did catch her off guard though was when a slight breeze carried a powerful stench from the ogre's perceived destination to assail her nostrils. Scrunching up her nose at the putrid odor, she noticed Ontar and Wink had similar disgusted expressions on their faces. *Gods, why does everything with ogres have to stink!* she thought.

Keeping a close eye on Bub and Uge, the party finally emerged from the forest onto a wide piece of open land the ogres called home. With her vision no longer obscured by the forest's canopy, Echo looked up into the starry sky and saw the large full moon had changed its color from orange to a dark red. It was an omen that summer had officially begun on Calatan. Echo knew that warmer days were now ahead, but the red moon also had a more sinister connotation. This is because it was a commonly held belief that those of evil intent gained in strength at this time of year.

While Echo's attention was drawn skyward, Ontar decided to focus on what was in front of him. Gazing upon the ogres' stomping grounds, Ontar saw the party's arrival immediately drew a crowd of the savage brutes. The huge ogres unabashedly stared down at Ontar and Echo as they moved among their ranks. A few of them even tried to touch the tormented didex, but Bub slapped their hands when they got too close.

The ogres lived in squalid conditions. Skull posts stood near random piles of rotten meat and excrement while the decaying remnants of animal bones were scattered about the ground. A few ogres stood guard by a huge central bonfire that flared brightly as the party cautiously passed by it.

A short distance from the fire was a hill with an old dead tree at its top that served as the ogre's home. The tree's branches had been stripped away ages ago while its long-exposed roots framed a dark cave situated at the hills base. Peeking out from this shadowy fissure was a handful of pudgy ogre children who curiously tried to watch and see what had garnered their parent's attention.

Aware of the hungry eyes that were upon them, Ontar and Echo stayed close to Bub as he and Uge came to a stop before three powerful-looking ogres. There sitting on a large tree stump surrounded by skulls was the mighty ogre chief. A commanding figure to behold, the chief sat with one hand resting on his knee while the other clutched the butt of an enormous wooden club whose blood red stains could be seen even by firelight. Wearing a necklace made of sharp animal teeth, the chief emphasized his importance with an elaborate headdress comprised of sprawling deer antlers.

Standing with his arms crossed to the chief's right was a mean-looking ogre that had a brown fur cloak draped over his broad shoulders. The cloaks hood was actually made of the upper half of a bear's head, and its toothy snout slightly shaded the ogre's stern gaze.

To the left of the chief was a female ogre everyone assumed to be his daughter. Looking at Bub with excitement in her eyes, she wore a tattered fur dress slung over one shoulder. The Chiefs Number One Daughter had greasy auburn hair pulled back into a high ponytail. Her nose was still discolored and swollen from where Bub had struck it. Thrilled by the sight of her lost love, she came towards him while saying, "Bub, you back!"

However, before she could approach him, the chief grabbed her arm and glared at Bub with narrow eyes. "Bub! Me no want you, tribe no want you, daughter no want you. Why you here?"

Falling to his hands and knees, tears came to Bub's eyes as he replied, "Oh, me so sorry. Me never mean to hurt Chiefs Number One Daughter. That why Bub bring two-headed squawker, so she forgive him."

"Bub bring good gift," the Chiefs Number One Daughter said. "Me forgive him; you forgive him. We eat bird."

Unfortunately, the cloaked ogre was a little more skeptical. "Who they?" he asked in a gruff tone.

"Them's me little helpers," replied Bub. "Great forest spirit send them to fight tikis with Bub."

"What spirit?" the chief asked with interest.

Bub proceeded to tell the chief about how he met the party and their struggles with the tikis. The tale seemed to captivate the surrounding ogres, and as he finished, Bub stood up, feeling a little more confident in the eyes of his people.

Leaning back on his stump, the chief furrowed his brow and asked his daughter, "What you think?"

Stepping forward, the Chiefs Number One Daughter said, "Bub, Uge, show me squawker."

The two ogres obediently stepped aside to allow a better view of the didex. The poor birds one surviving head let out a long miserable cry as the ogress approached it. Shutting its beak with her powerful hands, the Chiefs Number One Daughter placed a big bare foot along the bird's collar and pulled hard. The didex's wings shuddered violently for a moment before the ogress successfully ripped its head off! Holding the bird's cranium in her hand, the Chiefs Number One Daughter opened its beak and tore off the upper half of its skull, exposing the brains within. Pulling out the didex's brain, she tossed it in her mouth and threw away head.

Witnessing such a horrific display, Wink leaned next to Ontar and said, "I think I'm going to be sick." before placing a hand over her mouth.

Swallowing the tasty treat, the Chiefs Number One Daughter came up to Bub and said, "Oh, Bub, me so glad you home."

A resounding cheer came from the other ogres as Bub and the Chiefs Number One Daughter moved to embrace each other and kissed passionately. At first, Ontar was relieved the couple was able to patch things up …but then he saw the Chiefs Number One Daughter grab Bub's loin cloth and forcefully jerk it down to expose his bare body. Furrowing his brow, Ontar cocked his head and asked Wink. "Why in the world did she? Ugh!"

Bending down by her knees, Bub grabbed the ogress's dress in his big sweaty hands and pulled it up over her head. The ogre's roared with delight as the couple stood naked before the tribe. Pawing at each other like wild animals, Bub and the Chiefs Number One Daughter slammed their bloated bodies together and fell to the ground in carnal pleasure.

Echo tried hard to look anywhere far away from the couple. Unfortunately, all she managed to accomplish was briefly meeting the gaze of the cloaked ogre who stood near the chief. Clearly unhappy with the intimate display that had enticed his comrades, the ogre grumbled, "Bub have small cock," before he turned around and pushed his way through the crowd.

Overhearing the ogre's comment and seeing the curious look on Echo's face, Uge leaned down by the elf and said, "Gorg just jealous. Bub have good sex now." Echo knew jealousy could be a dangerous trait for anyone to possess, and she decided to keep a close eye on Gorg while in the ogre's presence.

Ontar stared in horrid fascination as Bub and the Chiefs Number One Daughter rolled around on the ground. It was like watching someone getting publicly tortured. He knew he should look away, but he just couldn't. Their moans reminded him of a pig and a donkey going at it. Which is probably why he was a little surprised when Wink caressed his ear and seductively whispered, "Kind of puts you in the mood now, doesn't it?"

At that moment, Ontar doubted if he would ever again be able to have an erection. Looking over at Wink, all he could say was, "Not even if Clowani herself spread her legs before me," referencing the love goddess. Wink's shoulders slumped a little bit as she stared at the ground, pouting.

Thankfully, after a noisy climax, both Bub and his beloved went silent. Realizing the show was over, the ogres decided that it was now time to devour the dead didex. Unsure of what to do next, the party inconspicuously went to warm themselves by the fire.

Feeling a little out of place, the group waited until, eventually, the ogre chief approached them. Smiling broadly, the towering chief clutched a partially eaten didex leg in one hand. "Forest spirit send you to make daughter happy. You help Bub do this. You good people."

"Good enough that you'd help us rescue my friend from the human fortress?" Wink asked optimistically.

The chief frowned and shook his head. "Humans no fight fair. Hide behind stone walls and shoot arrows at us. We no go there. Attack when they in forest instead."

"But Bub said you'd help us!" Wink exclaimed.

"Me chief, not Bub," the ogre stated.

Thinking of a way to convince the chieftain, Echo said, "Are you sure you want to break Bub's promise to the forest spirit? I've heard that bad things happen to those who make her angry."

The chief shifted a bit nervously. "What things?"

"All your food will turn to dust in your mouth," Echo warned.

"You start pissing blood," Ontar added.

"And your daughter will never bear children!" Wink concluded.

Going slack-jawed at the horrible fate that awaited him, the chief hastily said, "Me no make forest spirit mad. Tomorrow, we fight!"

Those were the words the party had longed to hear, and having gained the ogre's trust, they now felt confident they could successfully plan Hatch's rescue.

❖❖❖

Echo smiled as she heard a bird's chirping melody and opened her eyes to see a robin perched on a tree branch off to her right. Stretching, she carefully stood up on one of the tree's thick limbs that she'd been sitting on during the night and let go of the branch that had assisted her with balance in favor grasping a higher one. One of meditations many blessings was that it would hold her body in whatever position she wanted while engaging in it. This meant that Echo could climb a tree and recuperate over the night without any risk of falling from it. It also kept her safe from possible ground-based predators…such as ogres.

Watching the robin fly away as she moved, Echo slowly climbed to the highest point she could on the tree and calmly looked around. Dawn approached fast, and it wouldn't be long before the ogres below awoke to start their day. Echo thought it was interesting that only the chief and high-ranking members of the tribe got to sleep in the cave with their children. The remaining ogres slept outside by the fire or leaned against a sturdy tree. Ontar and Wink both chose the latter of those options, preferring to nap out of sight in case a random ogre wanted a midnight snack.

Feeling a sense of inner peace wash over her, Echo looked towards the sky just as the suns first golden rays of light crossed the horizon. It was both a serene and sad moment for her. Echo's suitor, Favin, had made it a tradition that every morning they would get up to watch the sun rise together. For over thirty years, Echo embraced this ritual with a passion, and it wasn't until Favin's death that she stopped adhering to it rigidly. Still, she did engage in the practice from time to time…and when she did, her heart ached that he wasn't there to hold her hand and share in the joy that comes with being young and in love. Instead, Echo found she now had to contend with life's harsh realities.

Unsure of how long she had stared at the sun, Echo realized there was noise and activity coming from the ogres below and figured that it was time for her to go check it out. Grabbing her backpack and shield from a split in the tree, Echo climbed down from her high perch and reached the ground to see an irritated ogre glaring back at her. A quick glance showed that she'd shaken some dew drops down from the leaves above to give the hulking brute an unwanted shower. Preferring not to provoke him further, Echo decided to quickly scurry off and find her companions.

Her first stop was over to the smoldering bonfire, where she saw Bub sitting cross-legged and eating some poorly-cooked meat with a few of his brethren. Sitting on his knee in a similar fashion was Wink. Gnawing on a piece of meat, she looked like a little green bug next to the enormous ogre.

"Huh, I'm surprised there was anything left of the bird after last night?" Echo said while approaching them.

Bub spoke while chewing on his meat, "This no squawker. We find horses in forest to eat." The other ogres grumbled in agreement.

Echo cocked an eyebrow. "Did these horses have saddles and look like the ones Ontar and I were riding yesterday?" she demanded.

Bub thought for a moment. "Yup."

Echo threw her hands up in frustration. "Errr...Bub, you just ate our horses!"

Wink looked up from her meal and smiled. "Mmmm...me like horses. Them's good eatins," she said.

Echo shot her a nasty look, then turned to go find Ontar. *Someday, I'm just going to feed that pixie to the wolves,* she thought.

Ontar stood at a spot alongside the ogre's hill. Stacked in front of him were two piles. One consisted of small boulders, while the other was stacked with short thick logs. A little to his left, she saw that Uge and another ogre were pulling branches off a good-sized tree that had obviously been uprooted earlier that day.

"Preparing for the attack?" she asked as she stood next to him.

"Yeah," replied Ontar in a distracted tone. "The piles are going to be ammunition for the ogres, and Uge is making them a battering ram."

"Hmm. Think any of your experiences at Fort Hasborne will help us now?" Echo wondered aloud.

"Perhaps," Ontar conceded. "The big problem the ogres will face is having to deal with archers. If they can use these boulders to destroy the battlements above the gate, then it should reduce the number of positions they can be attacked from."

Echo was impressed. "Do you think they could actually take the fort?"

"No," Ontar said plainly. "They lack the numbers and organization to handle a disciplined military unit. That's why it will be important for you to find Hatch and get out of there as quickly as possible."

Echo was about to say something further when Wink came running up to them. "Onnie, Echo, the chief's forming a war party, and we're supposed to meet Bub by the fire pit." Even as Wink informed them of this new development, they saw that a few ogres headed in that direction. Not wishing to be left out, Ontar scooped up Wink, and the three of them went to go find Bub.

Joining the cadre of assembled ogres, Ontar saw their chief had his club slung over one shoulder while he selected the strongest of his warriors to form the war party. Bub, Gorg, and Uge were among the ten menacing ogres chosen to assault the fort. In a telling sign of her apprehension, the Chiefs Number One Daughter stood quietly by her father and tightly clasped her hands together when Bub was chosen to fight.

Standing before his warriors, the chief spoke loudly and said, "Forest spirit send little helpers to crush tiki and make daughter happy. We thank spirit by *smashing* humans hiding in fort!" A booming cheer went up from all the ogres assembled, and the chief waited for quiet before continuing. "Bub, you please whole tribe last night. Today, you lead them in battle."

"No!" shouted Gorg. "Me better fighter then Bub. So, *me* lead war party. Not him!"

Bub's face twisted with anger, and he clenched his fists while turning towards Gorg.

Mirroring Bub's expression, the chief's eyes narrowed as he spoke, "Gorg, me chief, not you! Bub lead war party. *Obey* or *die!*" Emphasizing his point, the chief slammed his imposing club into the open palm of his left hand.

Gorg made a fist and gazed straight into his chieftain's eyes. The air was tense, and everyone present wondered if the two would come to blows. Then, after a long moment, Gorg growled audibly and looked away. The other ogres relaxed a little bit, and the chief continued speaking.

"War party smash humans *together.* Now, go!"

Following the chief's orders, the war party had gathered their assault equipment and were excitedly trudging through the forest towards the Sibeian fort. Surrounded by ogres, Ontar couldn't help but feel a little conflicted by his current actions. Ogres were supposed to be vile, savage monsters whose brutality was unquestioned. Yet, here they were assisting him in an attack on a *human* fortress. Not that Ontar had any love for Sibeians, but it was just a little strange for him to side with those who would attack his own kind.

If there was anything that could put his mind at ease, it would have to be that Bub was a fairly competent leader. Following Ontar's advice, the ogre agreed to travel to the fort via the rugged forest instead of along the road where they could have been easily spotted. Bub also arranged to have his ogres destroy the battlements above the gate during their initial onslaught, much to Ontar's relief.

In fact, the only concern Ontar had about the raid was if Gorg would follow orders. The ogre spent much of his time grumbling to himself while helping Uge carry the battering ram. Echo seemed to share in Ontar's apprehension and kept a vigilant eye on the suspicious ogre during their long march.

It was close to noon when Bub brought his warriors to a stop. Catching Ontar and Echo's attention, the ogre pointed past the tree line to a high wall of dull gray stone and said, "Fort up ahead. We attack when you ready."

Ontar looked at Echo and asked, "Do you think you can reach one of the fort's side walls without being spotted?"

Echo smiled. "Easily. I sincerely doubt the Sibeians are looking for a lone elvish infiltrator, and once the attack begins, I shouldn't have any problems finding Hatch."

"Great. Let's go!" chimed Wink as she slid down Ontar's cloak and walked towards Echo.

Ontar clearly saw the look of trepidation on Echo's face and decided to speak up, "Wink, you can't go with Echo. We need you here."

"What for?" Wink protested. "Echo doesn't even know what Hatch looks like."

Echo rushed to reassure her. "Trust me, I'll find him."

Kneeling, Ontar tried to comfort the pixie. "Wink, we need a lookout to tell us when Echo both enters and escapes the fort. Otherwise, the ogres might launch their attack too soon and needlessly waste their lives."

Bub overheard that last bit and pointed a scolding finger at the pixie. "You no waste Bub's life," he said gruffly.

Wink sulked a little bit. "Alright, I'll do it your way." Looking up at Echo, she earnestly said, "Hatch is a chubby old man with a gray moustache who's bald on top but has shoulder-length hair at the sides."

Echo nodded once. "Got it. Ontar, could you get the rope and grapple from my backpack?"

"Sure," Ontar replied as he stepped behind Echo and pulled the requested objects from her pack.

Holding the rope in her hand, Echo looked down at Wink. "I'll be approaching the fortress along its far east wall near the tower. Don't signal the attack before I get there."

"I'll remember, just be careful okay," Wink pleaded.

"I promise," Echo assured her as she moved away from the party and stealthily advanced towards the fort.

As Echo departed, Bub watched Ontar pick up Wink and place her on a low tree branch. The pixie then proceeded to scale the tree using its rough bark as handholds. Distracted by Wink's climb, Bub almost didn't see Gorg stomping up to him.

"Bub, you wait too long. Me break down gate and lead attack. You stay behind and throw rocks."

Bub was not about to let Gorg take charge. "Gorg, we attack when me say so! You listen to Bub or we throw rocks at you!"

Looking around, Gorg could see a number of ogres in the war party lifting their boulders towards him. Giving Bub the evil eye, he growled slightly, then headed back towards the battering ram.

Ontar was impressed by the strength of Bub's will. Donning his helmet and readying a crossbow, he knew the ogres would fight well this day.

Wink stood on a high tree branch and squinted as she watched Echo's progress. The wood elf had been difficult to spot among the thick foliage, but once she passed from beneath the tree line, Wink found she could easily track her movements. Crossing the clearing as quickly as possible, Echo pressed herself against the fortress's wall and crept along its face until she reached her position. Wink held her breath as two soldiers casually strolled the parapets directly above where Echo lurked. The soldiers wore armor similar to that of other guards and covered it with white surcoats that had the Sibeian emblem of an elaborate golden knot centered on their chests. Thankfully, they were completely engrossed in conversation and didn't even notice Echo as she subtly arrived at her destination.

Focusing her attention downward, Wink shouted, "Hey, Bub, Echo's at the wall!"

Bub knew what he had to do and turned to address his fellow ogres, "Time to fight. Remember, rocks first, then ram."

The other ogres grunted in agreement, and Bub shot a challenging look at Gorg. His rival met the gaze but chose to say nothing. Scooping two boulders up under his arms, Bub turned towards the fort and shouted, "Attack!"

Bilk and Chav milled about the battlements above Fort Vakid's tall wooden gate. The two soldiers squinted while chatting with each other under the noonday sun, both looking forward to grabbing a little lunch once they were off duty…that is until they heard several deep, bellowing roars coming from forest. Peering over the wall, they watched as ten hulking ogres surged into the open carrying boulders, logs, and what looked to be a crude battering ram!

Turning towards the gate tower in front of him, Bilk shouted, "Ogre attack! Sound the alarm!" It was the last order the soldier would ever give.

Chav watched in horror as the ogres threw a volley of boulders straight through the air and into the battlements around him. "Gods!" he shouted as one of these boulders slammed right into Bilk. The blow killed his friend instantly and knocked the poor man's body straight into the courtyard below.

The gate trembled beneath the ogre's onslaught, and Chav crouched low to make for a more difficult target. Realizing he was a dead man if he stayed where he was, Chav decided to make a mad dash for a nearby tower in front of him. Heart pounding in his ears, Chav was only a few paces from the tower when a boulder slammed into the wall on his left side, causing both the parapets and a chunk of the walkway to crumble before him.

Chav cursed his misfortune and stood with his back to the undamaged right side of the wall. Sliding his feet along what had become a narrow ledge, the soldier knew that if he could just get past this point, he would be able to make it to the tower. Staring out at his menacing enemies, Chav saw that four ogres carrying a crude battering ram now charged towards the gate. The sight distracted him for only a moment, but in that moment, a surprise crossbow bolt suddenly pierced his thigh. Screaming first in pain, then in horror, Chav lost his balance and fell from the battlements towards the unforgiving ground below.

❖❖❖

Echo listened intently with her pointed ears as she discerned the events that transpired around her. The ogre's battle cry, frenzied shouts from humans, and the sound of stone collapsing into rubble were all clear indicators the attack was well underway. Taking advantage of this sudden burst of chaos was exactly what Echo intended to do to begin her daring rescue.

Gripping her rope near its upper half, Echo spun the grapple until she was sure that enough momentum had been built. She then released it and watched as the rope shot up alongside of the fortress's wall and eagerly waited for the telltale clang of the grapple reaching its target. When that happened, Echo tugged on the rope until it was taught, then began the entirely too slow process of scaling the wall. Praying she wouldn't be spotted by a passing soldier, Echo attempted to make the climb as quickly as possible.

Sir Debren swallowed his last bit of ale and put the cup down next to an empty plate. Sitting at a long wooden table with three of his fellow officers, the white knight had short gray hair and a moustache. Like most knights, he wore a full suit of armor beneath his surcoat and had a long white cape fastened by two golden clasps, which were connected with a strand of matching chain. Always well-armed, Sir Debren had a brown leather weapon belt secured about his waist that held an old broadsword in a scabbard, which currently scraped along the chair where he sat.

The mood in the dining hall had been a relaxed one until the assembled men all heard the thundering crash of stone collapsing from outside. This was followed by a sudden ringing from the shrine's bell tower. Sir Debren and his dining companions immediately stood up and made their way towards the hall's exit. There were only two reasons for the shrines bell to ring, and the white knight knew for a fact there were no services scheduled for today.

Throwing open the dining hall's doors, Sir Debren saw a panicky gatekeeper skidding to a halt in the long corridor before him. Raising his hand in a hasty salute, the man said, "Sir Debren, we're under attack! Ogres have descended on the south gate and destroyed the battlements. Two of our men are dead."

News of an ogre attack was not unheard of to Sir Debren, and he'd encountered situations like this before. The only thing the gatekeeper said that really caught him off guard was they had destroyed the battlements. Normally, ogres would just focus on breaking down the gate. Unfortunately, this new strategy of theirs would limit the effectiveness of his archers but, in reality, it did little more than that.

"How many?" he asked.

"Ten, milord," replied the gatekeeper. "Four working a battering ram and six throwing projectiles."

"That will be all," Sir Debren said to the gatekeeper as he and his entourage proceeded down the corridor. As he walked, the white knight began giving orders, "Commander Meras, I want every archer we can muster up on the gate towers. Have your men train their bows on the ogres using the battering ram. Captain Acrit, I noticed there are some wooden beams resting near the workshop. Rally our infantry and have them use those beams to reinforce the gate. Captain Nolcha, I want two lines of cavalry armed with lances behind the soldiers. Acrit, if the ogres break down the gate, I'll need you and your men to fall back and regroup at the entrance to the keep. Nolcha's horsemen should give you the cover you need to make an orderly withdrawal."

The entourage had reached the end of the corridor and were about to split down separate hallways. As they divided, Captain Nolcha asked, "Milord, where will you be stationed?"

"I'll be at the top of the southwest gate tower with Commander Meras," Sir Debren replied with a grim smile. "Perhaps I can whip up a little magic that will put this matter to an end sooner as opposed to later."

✦✦✦✦✦

Echo grunted as she pulled herself up over the wall and onto the battlements. Crouching behind one of the parapets, she slid her backpack down on one shoulder and stowed her rope and grapple. The sound of soldiers scrambling across the fortress's courtyard towards the south gate was a good indication she hadn't been spotted, and she intended to keep it that way. Closing her eyes and concentrating, Echo cast a spell that shrouded her body in shadow.

Feeling more confident in her ability to stay hidden, Echo drew her sword and shield and made her way to the nearest tower. Reaching her objective with little difficulty, Echo was relieved to see the towers door was unlocked. Slipping inside the round stone structure, she looked to its curving walls and saw a winding stairway going down. The tower was dark, and with the addition of her shadow spell, Echo appeared almost completely invisible. The only light she had to deal with came from the narrow arrow slits above the stairs. Peeking through one of these slits, Echo surveyed the nearby keep.

Easily the fortress's most dominant building, the keep's main entrance was filled with soldiers passing through its large double doors. Echo knew that even with her spell, she'd never be able to enter the building that way. So, she kept her eyes peeled for a second entrance. It didn't take long for her to spot a plain-clothed man with a sack slung over his shoulder racing across the courtyard and coming to a stop at a small wooden door on the side of the building. Smiling to herself, Echo saw the door open and watched as the man slipped through the slave's entrance...she had found her way in.

Descending the tower's steps, Echo reached a door at its base and slowly cracked it open. The keep was directly in front of her. Unfortunately, the courtyard was crawling with people who would probably notice a living shade moving amongst them. Echo knew that if she was going to reach the keep, she would have to blend in with the shadows around her. She just needed one big enough to sneak behind.

That was when she spotted several horsemen armed with lances heading from the stables towards the gate. Their mounts cast a small shadowy bridge behind them that Echo could use to help her reach the keep. All that it would require was a little bit of speed, timing, and luck.

Holding her breath, Echo waited for the riders to pass. Listening to the beat of their horses' hooves, she watched as the cavalry passed her position before bolting from the towers darkened doorway. Running at an angle to stay with the horses' shadows for as long as possible, Echo crossed the courtyard at a fevered pace and slammed herself against the keep's wall, desperately hoping that no one had noticed her.

Taking shallow breaths, Echo saw the riders continued their journey towards the gate. Not wishing to attract their attention, Echo slowly scooted along the wall until she came to the servant's entrance. Grabbing the door handle, she was pleased to see the entry wasn't locked as she stealthily slipped inside the building.

Ontar watched the ogres struggle as he loaded his crossbow. Initially, their attack had gone very well, and Gorg's team of warriors managed to inflict some heavy damage to the fortress's gate before the archers arrived. Sadly, once archers gathered at the top of the gate towers, they unleashed a relentless hail of death on the poor ogres who worked the battering ram.

One of these ogres died early in the counterattack. Shortly afterwards, a second ogre stumbled away from the battering ram, clearly delirious. His body bristled with arrows while crimson blood oozed from the multiple wounds he had received. Staggering on for a little bit, the ogre drew heavy fire from the archers above until he finally groaned and collapsed to the ground dead.

Bub and his fellow warriors attempted to avenge their fallen comrades by hurling logs at the archers. A couple of these projectiles managed to reach their targets, but most of them crashed uselessly against the towers stone walls. Then came the moment Ontar had been dreading...the ogres were out of ammunition.

Relentless in the defense of their fortress, the Sibeians let loose a deadly volley of arrows that struck deep against the assembled ogres. Bub groaned in pain as arrows penetrated both his thick left leg and right shoulder. The ogre next to him had an arrow pierce his unprotected forehead. It took a moment for the ogre to recognize the deathblow as his eyes crossed to stare at the arrow in his skull. Alas, a slight trickle of blood signaled the ogre's end, and he quickly fell over dead.

Ontar finished loading his crossbow, then looked at Bub to see what the ogre would do. Would he continue to fight against such overwhelming odds? Or would he cut his losses and order a retreat while he still could?

The answer came when Bub defiantly raised his fist and shouted, "More rocks!" With that simple statement, the ogres at his side charged the gate and grabbed the large chunks of rubble, which were scattered about from the destroyed battlements. Throwing the rocks at the gate, Ontar saw small holes now appear in the heavily-battered wood. Caught up in the battle frenzy,

Gorg tried to stick his hand through one of the new holes in an eager attempt to grab the gate's crossbar. However, the ogre rapidly withdrew his arm when he received a nasty cut from a defending soldier on the other side.

Ontar couldn't tell if it was bravery or battle frenzy that drove the ogres. Either way, they continued to press their attack and buy Echo some much-needed time. Knowing he couldn't let the ogres take all the credit for this day's battle, Ontar raised his crossbow and took aim at an unsuspecting archer.

Sir Debren stood on top of a high stone tower surrounded by archers. He watched as the ogres hoarded around Fort Vakid's heavily-battered gate, eager to destroy the defenders on the other side. Ready for battle, his men stood resolute before the oncoming threat. A threat the white knight hoped he still had time to turn away.

Gazing down at the ogres, Sir Debren focused his consciousness on touching a hidden power that lay deep within his soul. It was an ability only mentalists possessed and was a key requirement for any man who desired to become a white knight. Grasping at this power, which was a part of his very being, Sir Debren felt its amazing magic grace his mind with an unmatched clarity.

Thinking of a spell that would aid him against the ogres, Sir Debren wordlessly formed the magic into something he could use. All of a sudden, he heard the ogre's thoughts. Passionate, savage, jealous, hurt, and angry, the ogres were consumed with slaughtering those who caused them pain (even if they were the ones who initiated the conflict). Scanning their primitive thoughts, Sir Debren searched for a leader, knowing that if he could find the one who led them in battle, then perhaps he could also find a way to end their attack without any further loss of life.

◆◇◆◇◆◇

Echo almost choked on the heavy scent of lye as she entered a short narrow hall illuminated by torch-lit sconces. On either side of her were two open doorway's that led to rooms obviously used by local servants. To her left was a laundry room where the powerful aroma originated from. Here, sacks of clothing were piled near wooden tubs with washboards in them and a couple of wringers. On her right was a sewing room that had a spinning wheel surrounded by stools with sewing kits and pincushions on them. Hearing voices from up ahead, Echo kept close to the wall and slowly bypassed the two rooms.

Coming to a stop before an intersecting corridor, Echo almost jumped as the plain-clothed man she saw earlier busily passed in front of where she stood. Echo knew the keep was full of people actively moving about, and if she didn't want to risk detection, then she would have to find Hatch quickly.

Rationalizing where the wizard might be located, Echo felt certain that he was probably locked up in a dungeon located at the base of the keep. She also figured that most dungeons were accessed at the rear of a building to make escape through its main entrance more difficult. Since a dungeon wasn't normally considered the highlight of any military structure, Echo doubted that it would have an elaborate staircase leading to it. Instead, either a small guarded staircase, or an extension on the stairs within one of the keep's corner towers might lead down to her destination.

Following her instincts, Echo quietly slipped into the main corridor and moved towards the back of the keep. Sure enough, after dodging a few distracted slaves, she spotted a long hallway that led to a wooden door with a small barred window in it. The door was located at one of the keep's corner towers and standing on either side of it were two spear-wielding guards who chatted anxiously about the activity outside.

Defeating these guards was crucial to rescuing Hatch, and Echo would have to dispatch them swiftly to prevent the entire keep from learning of her presence. Gripping her sword, Echo raced down the hallway ready to strike. The guard who was her target saw a shadowy figure rapidly coming towards him and barely got out the word, "What," before she ran him through.

The violence of Echo's attack canceled out her shadow spell, and the guard next to her shouted, "Intruder," before taking his spear in both hands and thrusting it at her. Echo was prepared for this and deflected his blow with her shield. She then withdrew her bloody blade from her initial target and focused on the remaining guard. Capitalizing on her natural agility, Echo swung her sword straight at the man's head.

Raising his weapon, the guard successfully parried her attack. He then slashed at her with the tip of his spear and was rewarded with a shallow cut that pierced her leather armor just below her breasts.

Echo winced at the pain but took advantage of the guard's wider swing to bring her own sword to bear across the back of his left arm. Rending a nasty wound that sliced through the guard's chain armor, Echo watched as the man let go of his spear with his left hand.

Tightening the muscles in his one good arm, the guard attempted a flimsy attack that Echo easily dodged. Deciding to end the battle, Echo took her blade and stabbed it straight between the man's eyes. He dropped to the ground dead just as she removed her weapon.

Sheathing her sword, Echo scoured the guard's bodies until she found a set of keys on a metal ring. Sliding the ring around her wrist, Echo took what coins she found on the first guard and slid them into her pouch. Thinking of Hatch, she proceeded to remove the second guards weapon belt altogether and fastened it around her waist above the one she already wore.

Looking around to see if anyone was watching, Echo went to the tower door and tried a couple keys in the lock until it clicked open. A winding staircase descended before her, and Echo dragged one of the dead guards over to the door and pushed him down the stairs. She then grabbed the second guard and pulled him through the door before shutting it behind her.

Heaving her load onto the tower steps, Echo crinkled her nose at the unpleasant smell of body odor and excrement. It was darker in the tower than it had been in the proceeding hallway, and Echo was about to drop the dead guard when she saw a dim light at the base of the steps and heard an older man's voice say, "What in the world?" The man obviously saw the first guard's body, and Echo would have to silence him quickly before he raised the alarm. Pushing the corpse down the stairs, Echo heard the man yelp in surprise as she drew her sword.

Bounding down the steps after the deceased guard, Echo came face to face with a fat, plain-clothed, man with little hair who held a candlestick in one hand and a quivering short sword in the other. Echo swung her blade straight across the jailor's rotund belly and watched as blood spurted from the lethal wound. Dropping his sword, the human let out a piti-ful groan as he died. Bending over his body, Echo wiped her blade on his shirt, then sheathed her sword before swiping another key ring from his weapon belt. After that, she claimed his coin pouch and emptied its contents into the one on her second belt.

Picking up the jailor's candlestick, Echo held the light high so she could survey the room. To her left was a simple wooden desk covered in papers that had a large cabinet with cubby holes behind it. The walls to her front and right had locked wooden doors with small barred windows in them.

Approaching the door to her right, Echo peered through its window and saw a small torture chamber with a rack and whipping post in it. This meant the door in front of her led to the dungeon itself. The nasty odor wafting from that door should have tipped her off on where she should have tried first, but wishful thinking led her to the torture chamber instead. Now, left with no other options, Echo took her keys and unlocked the entrance to the dungeon.

Sir Debren smirked as he looked down at the invading ogres. *I found you,* the white knight thought as he stared directly at Bub. Scanning the other ogres' minds, Sir Debren learned that this particular monster was their leader...a leader who would now order his warriors to retreat from battle. Casting a second spell, the white knight easily took control of Bub's feeble mind and quietly mouthed the words, "Run Away!"

Gorg seethed with fury as he saw another warrior cut down by arrows. The cowardly humans hid behind their walls and archers, but no longer! Grunting a command, he and his fellow ogres slammed their battering ram into the fortress's gate and watched it splinter and break before them.

Captain Acrit saw the ogres break through the gate and gave them a steely look. He and his men had done everything they could to hold back the enemy, but sadly, as the wooden beams used to reinforce the gate snapped in two, the old soldier knew that this battle was over. Giving the order he sincerely wished he didn't have to give, he shouted, "Fall back, men! Fall back!" Heeding his own command, he hastily retreated towards the keep.

Giving a triumphant victory cry, Gorg stepped through the gate and saw the puny humans scatter before him. Now, he would smash them to pieces for their spinelessness. Reaching out to strike one of the fleeing soldiers, Gorg pulled back his hand when he heard a strangely calm voice behind him say, *"Run Away."*

"No!" shouted Gorg as he turned around to see who had given the order.

Bub greeted his outraged look with empty eyes and a blank expression on his face. The other ogres glanced at each other in confusion, then back at Bub. Once again, Bub called out, "Run Away!" and this time, he turned around and fled from the gate.

"Stay here!" commanded Gorg. He was determined not to lose this fight.

The other warriors, though, didn't agree. Uge was the first to act. Hesitantly stepping away from Gorg he retreated from the gate, and then ran after Bub. The remaining three ogres decided to follow suit, and Gorg quickly realized that he was now all alone. Debating whether to make a heroic last stand, Gorg looked about the courtyard to see what he was up against.

Captain Nolcha sat atop his horse and watched the ogres flee. He didn't understand why they decided to abandon the fight, although he highly suspected that Sir Debren had something to do with it. In any case, there was only one ogre left at the gate, and he assumed that a simple show of force would be able to drive him off. Clearing his throat, he shouted in a strong clear voice. "Cavalry, present arms!"

Gorg watched as two lines of disciplined horsemen pointed their lances directly at him! The ogre clenched his bloody fists in frustration. He could never face so many opponents on his own and hated Bub for taking away his warriors. Angry, he knew that if he couldn't kill the humans, then at least he would survive long enough to tell the chief of Bub's failure to lead them in battle. Making a disgruntled noise, Gorg turned and fled from the gate.

Witnessing the last ogre's departure, Captain Nolcha mulled the notion of ordering a charge on the retreating invaders. Unfortunately, Sir Debren hadn't given him any express orders to do so, and he couldn't be positive there weren't additional ogres waiting to ambush his forces in the woods. So, in the end, he decided it would be better to hold his position and commanded his men to stand down.

Ontar had a sinking feeling in the pit of his stomach as he watched the ogres retreat from the fort under a barrage of arrows. Personally, he was a little surprised to see their withdrawal after they had successfully managed to break down the gate, but then again, he couldn't fault them for running when clearly outnumbered by Sibeian soldiers. Looking up at the tree next to him, he asked Wink, "Have you seen any sign of Echo or Hatch yet?"

"No!" she replied with concern in her voice.

Wonderful, Ontar thought. Time was running out, and if Echo didn't find the old wizard quickly, then she might wind up joining him in the dungeon. Grumbling as he loaded his crossbow,

Ontar took aim at one of the tower archers. All he could do now was try to create a distraction for their enemies.

✦✦ ✦✦ ✦✦

Commander Meras stood atop the gate tower and jerked his head in the direction of an agonizing cry to see that one of his archers had been hit by a crossbow bolt in the shoulder. Irate at the incompetence his men displayed in front of Sir Debren, he angrily called out, "Who fired that shot?"

The response came from an archer standing near the tower's parapets. "It wasn't us, sir. There's someone helping the ogres from the forest."

Sir Debren approached his position. "Where?" asked the white knight.

"There, milord," the archer said while pointing out towards Illamine Forest.

Staring into the woods, Sir Debren spotted a warrior clad in a full suit of armor that brandished a crossbow and dodged his men's arrows by using a tree as cover. *Of course,* the white knight thought. The ogre's strategy of destroying the battlements was probably cooked up by this elusive ally, but for what purpose?

Suddenly, Sir Debren's eyes widened in understanding, and he turned towards Fort Vakid's courtyard, looking for Captain Acrit. Catching sight of the officer, he cast a spell that let him telepathically communicate with the man.

Captain Acrit! Get your men to the dungeon now! I think someone's trying to free the prisoner.

The mental command from nowhere startled Captain Acrit, but he recognized Sir Debren's voice and the urgency that came with it. Addressing the soldiers next to him, he said, "Everyone inside. We've got an intruder in the dungeon." With those words, the large wooden doors to the keep were thrown open, and Captain Acrit led his men to face the unknown trespasser.

Unaware of what was going on above, Echo held a candlestick in front of her as she entered the dungeon. Its light helped her to see a large dismal chamber, with chains attached to the walls and rats skittering across the floor. A trace amount of natural light passed through this foreboding place from a few small barred windows located at the top of the dungeon's far right wall. Otherwise, a lit sconce on a column in the center of the room was the only additional illumination provided.

Chained to the walls were two scrawny men with long beards who regarded Echo with surprise as she looked around. The shackles around their wrists indicated they were prisoners, and when they saw her, both stood up and pleaded for their release. Echo ignored them for the most part. Hatch was too important to be imprisoned with common criminals, and for all she knew, the two men yelping at her could have actually been locked up for legitimate reasons.

Scanning the walls, Echo saw another door with a small barred window in it at the far side of the dungeon. Switching the candlestick to her shield hand, Echo moved to unlock the door with one of the jailor's keys. Behind it, she saw a long corridor stretching before her, lined with locked doors on either side. Smiling at having discovered the private cells, Echo entered the corridor and locked the dungeon's door behind her.

Going from cell to cell, Echo peered through one small window after another until she came to a stop at one with a small wooden bed attached by chains to the wall. Within these confines, sunlight from a high barred window fell upon the figure of an elderly man sitting on the bed next to a crude chamber pot.

If the man was Hatch, though, he was far from the chubby individual Wink had portrayed. Slender, with a full bushy beard and long fingernails, the prisoner wore little besides a tattered brown tunic and ragtag shoes. In fact, the only thing that made him stand out from the criminals in the dungeon was that he wore a thick iron collar around his neck that had three glowing green gems and a small lock plate embedded in it.

Stepping close to the barred window, Echo asked, "Are you Hatch?"

The old man looked up at Echo with sad yet curious eyes. "Yes, who are you?" he inquired in a hushed, fluttering voice.

Echo sorted through the jailor's keys, trying different ones on the cell door's lock. "My name's Echo. Wink sent me to get you out of here."

"Wink…after all this time. I can't believe it," Hatch exclaimed as he stood up.

"Uh-huh. She's waiting with a companion of mine just outside the fort," Echo said as she found the right key and unlocked the door.

Just as she was about to open the cell, Echo heard numerous voices and clanking armor that heralded the arrival of Sibeian soldiers entering the dungeon. The prisoners she had ignored earlier now betrayed her position with vindictive joy. As her pursuers reached the door to the private cells, Echo slipped into Hatch's prison and closed the door behind her and locked it.

Once inside the cell, Echo dropped her candlestick, put away her shield, and removed the second belt from around her waist, tossing it to Hatch. "Here, take this," she said while approaching the spell caster. Echo then flipped through the jailor's key ring trying to find one that would fit Hatch's collar. "I hope you have a spell that can handle a horde of angry soldiers," she said dryly.

"Get this collar off me, and I'll show you what I can really do," replied Hatch as he fastened his newly-acquired belt.

Captain Acrit and his men reached Hatch's cell and peered through the barred window to see a leather clad elf removing the wizard's collar. "Open the door," he muttered to one of his men before addressing the elf inside. "You there, step away from the prisoner," he ordered.

Echo heard her heart pounding in her chest as Hatch cast a spell while the soldiers attempted to unlock door. Deep down, Echo wondered if the old man would complete his casting in time. If he didn't, would the soldiers she now faced take her prisoner, or would they simply kill her on the spot? As the cell door opened, Echo inhaled sharply in anticipation. Then a rush of air surrounded her, and she was forced to blink back tears from her eyes.

Once the air settled, Echo found herself squinting beneath the afternoon sun. Hatch had a similar expression on his face, and the two looked around, trying to get their bearings. It took Echo only a moment to realize they were now on a dirt road in Illamine Forest, facing the fortress' northern gate. Grabbing Hatch's hand, she quickly pulled him off the road and into the trees for cover. "What just happened?" she asked with a bewildered look on her face.

"Teleportation," Hatch explained. "It's a type of magic that allows me to travel to a fixed location I've been to before."

Shaking her head in disbelief, Echo said, "Come on. We have to get out of here."

Hatch resisted. "No, if we flee now, the soldiers will hunt us down like dogs."

"Well, what are we supposed to do then?" Echo asked, a little exasperated.

Hatch pulled his hand free then focused on the fort. "Watch," he replied in a serious tone. Echo saw a look of dark determination cross the old man's face as he moved his arms and began casting a spell so great she could actually *feel* him drawing in power from the world around them.

Sir Debren led the archers at his side through the courtyard and up to where Captain Nolcha waited with his cavalry. "Any word yet from Captain Acrit?" he asked.

Captain Nolcha looked down at the knight from atop his horse. "No, milord, but he only entered the keep a short time ago."

Clearly bothered by this news, Sir Debren considered giving further orders when a wispy gray cloud began to rapidly rise from the very ground they were standing on. Eyes widening in fear and recognition, Sir Debren commanded, "Evacuate the fort!"

"But, sir, the ogres?" Captain Nolcha exclaimed. The white knight ignored him and made his way towards the broken gate when his features were completely shrouded by the haze. Watching the cloud rise towards his mount's head, Captain Nolcha shouted, "Flee for your lives," before kicking his horse's flanks and leading his fellow cavalry riders out through the gate.

Sir Debren heard the horses pass by and wished that he could have gotten the alert out earlier. The cloud's poisonous vapors seemed to fill his lungs with fluid and made breathing difficult. Laboring to reach the now-obscured gate, Sir Debren felt what could only be described of as an electrical charge crackling in the air around him. Realizing that he had to escape before it was too late, the white knight cast a spell that enhanced his speed to the point where he became nothing but a blur that zipped through the gate. Clearing the deadly cloud, Sir Debren caught his breath outside the fort's walls and went to rendezvous with Captain Nolcha.

❦ ❦ ❦

Wink almost fell off her branch when she saw the sudden rustling of tree leaves on the far side of the fort. To the untrained eye, this wouldn't be much of a phenomenon, but to a pixie who had spent decades living with magic users, the sudden displacement of air was a clear indication that a teleportation spell had been cast. Looking down at Ontar, she shouted, "Onnie, I'm pretty sure that Hatch and Echo have just escaped!"

Praise the gods, Ontar thought as he finished loading his crossbow. Things had gotten intense once the Sibeian archers had started targeting him, and the tree he had his back against was beginning to look like a pincushion. Fortunately, they could now seize their chance to get the heck out of there. Glancing up at Wink, he asked, "Where are they?"

Wink was climbing down the tree about as fast as her little arms and legs could move. "It looks like they're on the far side of the fort." Briefly stopping in her descent, Wink noticed a peculiar haze started to shroud the stronghold and said, "Uh-oh. I think Hatch just unleashed his death cloud. He must *really* be angry right now."

Ontar watched in awe as a sinister gray cloud rose from the ground near the fort and completely enveloped the structure. Raising his gauntleted hand to catch Wink as she gracefully jumped into it, he said, "Dammit, I knew something like this was going to happen. Your wizard's going to kill us all!" Ignoring the pixies protests, Ontar tossed her into the hood of his cloak and readied his crossbow before charging off into the forest.

"Onnie…no…wait!" Wink cried as she bounced around the warrior's hood. Fear welled up inside of her as she realized Ontar might actually try to kill Hatch! She had to keep that from happening and immediately cast a spell.

Echo watched in fascination as Hatch's cloud covered the fortress. Afraid that it might be poisonous, she was actually glad to see that some of the Sibeian cavalry riders made it out alive. She was about to ask Hatch how long he intended to continue his spell when the horrible sound of thunder abruptly reached her pointed ears. Instinctively, her breath quickened as Echo saw a flash of lightning come from several places within the cloud.

All of a sudden, Echo felt like a child. Cold, wet, and scared, the flash of lightning pierced her very soul as the memories of falling and enduring enormous pain washed over her. Letting out a stifled cry, Echo dropped to her knees while throwing her arms up over her head. Hatch didn't even notice her reaction. Lost in concentration on his spell, he was completely engrossed in seeing the lightning strike Fort Vakid again and again.

Ontar saw the lightning and knew that Echo would be incapacitated by it. Dashing through the forest, he successfully found the old wizard standing near the form of his terrified companion. Coming to an abrupt stop, Ontar raised his crossbow and took aim. He was about to put an end to this menacing spell caster when Wink's high squeaky voice boomed from all around them.

"STOP!" she pleaded.

Ontar was a shocked by how loud her voice had come across and stayed his hand from the crossbow's trigger. Hatch, too, had heard the magically enhanced cry, and turned to face Ontar as he slowly became aware of his surroundings.

Wink popped out of Ontar's hood and climbed onto his shoulder. "Hatch, it's me Wink."

Hatch stared in wonder at the pixie for a moment, then shook his head in recognition. "Wink...I never thought I'd see you again."

Wink slid down Ontar's cloak and onto the forest floor. She then walked towards him. "You silly old man. I took care of you as a baby. What made you think I'd stop taking care of you now?"

Hatch chuckled, then knelt by the pixie. "I guess I just thought that everyone had forgotten about me."

"Fat chance." Wink snorted. "I even recruited Onnie and Echo here to save you," she replied with a smile.

Hatch looked over at the two would-be heroes. Ontar had lowered his crossbow when he saw Hatch's death cloud starting to dissipate. He was now crouched by Echo to see if she was alright. The elf initially had a peculiar reaction to Hatch's spell, but now she seemed to be regaining her composure.

Removing his helmet, Ontar helped Echo to her feet while addressing the party. "The names Ontar, and while Hatch's spell has bought us some time, if we don't get out of here now, the Sibeians will surely find us."

Hatch picked up Wink and set her on his shoulder. "Where are we going?"

"North," Echo replied.

"But that will take us deeper into Sibeia," Hatch noted.

Echo gave Ontar a wry grin. "Which is exactly why the search parties won't be looking for us there."

Chapter Eight

"Hatch, you need to slow down or you'll choke," Wink warned as she stood next to the hungry wizard.

Sitting on the ground with his back against a tree, Hatch coughed as he finished his third bundle of trail rations. "Oh, forgive me. This is the first meal I've had in five years that doesn't center on hard tack and gruel."

"Here, take this," Ontar said as he offered Hatch his water skin. The group had pushed themselves hard during their trek through Illamine Forest and didn't stop until evening had cloaked the trees in darkness. Building a fire not far from the road, Ontar kept his eyes peeled for any sort of search party from Fort Vakid. Thankfully, it appeared they had evaded capture for the time being. Not that Echo was much help in keeping their location a secret. Overjoyed by their successful escape, the elf sat cross-legged by the fire and played a lively tune on her flute. Waiting until she finished the song, Ontar scolded her. "You need to stop that. There's no telling who will hear your song and try to hunt us down."

"The fire has already given away our position, and no amount of music is going to change that," Echo argued. "Besides, I'm in far too good a mood to care. I just rescued a wizard who's far more powerful and important than anyone Searce has ever saved. All I need now is to get my hands on Spirit Slayer and my place within the Bloody Side will be secure."

Finishing his water, Hatch cocked his head and gave Echo an odd look. "The Bloody side? Aren't they a thieves' guild?"

"One of the biggest and best there are," Echo claimed with pride.

Hatch glanced at Wink and asked, "What have you gotten me into?"

"Nothing you can't handle..." Wink began as she, Ontar, and Echo got Hatch caught up on the events that led to his freedom. Taking it all in, the old wizard said, "My goodness, you've certainly gone to great lengths to find this sword, and while my rescue may have been incidental, I am still grateful that you freed me from that terrible dungeon."

"You wouldn't happen to be grateful enough to help us retrieve the blade now, would you?" Echo asked in an almost expectant tone."

Hatch nodded. "Of course. I only hope that Wink actually knows where the sword is kept."

"Hatch!" Wink exclaimed.

Echo's eyes quickly narrowed. "What do you mean?"

Shrugging off the question, Hatch replied, "It's just that I've never even heard of Spirit Slayer before today."

Ontar didn't like the sound of this. "Wink, you do know where the sword is kept, don't you?"

"Well, not exactly..." Wink began.

"You lied to us!" Echo exclaimed.

Wink rapidly shook her head. "No, not really. You see, after Hatch got captured, Thove and I took up the task of rescuing him. My job was to find where Hatch was imprisoned while Thove was supposed to get Spirit Slayer so that we could bribe the guards to help him escape."

"Who's Thove?" Ontar wondered.

"He's my son," Hatch replied after a long sigh. Glaring at Wink, he then said, "You shouldn't have gotten him involved in this. He still has a family to care for."

"It was his idea!" Wink protested.

Stuffing her flute back into her pack, Echo angrily said, "I don't care whose idea it was. You promised me a sword, and by the gods, I'm going to get it! Now, where can we find Thove?"

"He lives in the village of Habed," Hatch replied. "And while it's a few days travel from here, I'd be happy to serve as your guide throughout the journey."

"You damn well better," Echo grumbled.

Wink looked up at Ontar and pleaded, "Please, don't be mad at me, Onnie. Lying was the only thing I could think of to get people to help me."

Ontar frowned when he heard this. "It's hard to trust someone when the first thing they say to you is a lie, but I do understand why you did it. Just promise me you'll be honest with us from now on."

Running up to hug his armored knee, Wink said, "I swear that I'll be true to you from now on."

"Well, I'm glad that's settled," Hatch added after a big yawn. "Now, if you'll all excuse me, I plan on spending my first night of freedom sleeping under the stars."

Sharing his sentiment, the party decided to join him and turn in for the evening.

⊹⊹ ⊹⊹ ⊹⊹

Waking up early the next morning, the party returned to the dirt road they'd been traveling on and continued their journey deeper into Sibeia. Agitated by Wink's earlier deception, Ontar almost didn't notice when the ancient trees of Illamine Forest gave way to the vast flowing prairie grass of the Wistwind Plains. A warm summer's day quickly caused Ontar to miss the shade of the forest, and seeking a distraction from the heat, he gave Hatch a quick look before saying, "So, you have a son named Thove. Is he a wizard like you?"

Wink let out an amused snort from Ontar's shoulder while Hatch replied, "Not hardly. Thove decided to follow in the footsteps of my former friend, Dolsch, who served as a mentor to the boy. In many ways, he was like a second father to him. That all changed though when Alean got him to testify against me during my trial."

"Who's Alean?" Ontar asked.

Answering in a disgusted tone, Wink replied, "*Lady* …Alean is a black-hearted bitch who consumes men's souls and leaves their bodies to be mourned over by their families."

"In other words, she's my ex-wife," Hatch said grimly. "Although I do think Wink's description of her is far more accurate."

"Of course, it is!" Wink huffed. "The old gold-digger practically divorced Hatch and married the golden lord all at the same time."

Wink's mentioning of his ex-wife seemed to bother Hatch, and he decided to steer the conversation in a different direction.

"Well, as far as I'm concerned, they can have each other. I've had my fill of their lot, and now I'm free to pursue a new path in life."

Interested in Hatch's family dynamic, Echo asked, "So, why did Thove side with you over his mother?"

"Thove never wanted the noble life that Lady Alean tried to shove down his throat," Wink replied. "That's why he married a peasant girl and settled down to raise a family."

Echo quirked an eyebrow. "Doesn't sound like the type of life that Lady Alean could really relate to."

"*I*, on the other hand, have always encouraged my son to forge his own destiny. The choices he's made are his alone, and I will always respect and support him for that," Hatch said with a hint of parental pride.

"Hmm," Ontar uttered quietly. *His* parents had never completely understood why he chose the life he did and used to constantly question him on it. For a brief second, he wondered what it would have been like to have Hatch for a father. Then he remembered that Thove had started a family of his own and asked, "When Thove settled down, did he have any children?"

Hatch's shoulders slumped. "Yes, their names are Kit and Aniata, and to this very day, I regret not spending more time with them when I had the chance."

Wink gave the wizard a sympathetic smile. "Don't be sad, Hatch. Now that we're free, we can go see them as much as you'd like." Looking over at Ontar, she added that. "Aniata is the younger of the two. We used to have a lot of fun playing together before I was imprisoned." Returning her attention to Hatch, she gazed at the old man and said, "I hope she still remembers me."

"I'm sure she will," Hatch replied reassuringly before turning back to the group. "Kit, on the other hand, is closer to your age and has decided to follow in her father's footsteps of becoming a skilled ranger. From what I've been told, she's easily been able to excel at her training."

"Huh. Think she'll take a cue from her dad and marry a farm boy?" Ontar asked while subtly trying to figure out if Kit was available.

"No," Hatch replied bluntly. "Kit is far too young to be settling down yet, and if any sweaty muscle-bound fool ever tried to take advantage of her innocence, I would be forced to incinerate him with one of my spells."

"Oh," Ontar muttered as he took the hint.

Intrigued by Hatch's past, Echo frowned slightly when she heard the steady rhythm of a horses' hooves pounding on the ground behind her. Looking back, she saw a rider driving his horse hard along the road and casually called out, "Rider," before she and her fellow companions instinctively stepped aside to let the horseman pass.

Hatch squinted as the rider approached and noticed the man wore a white Sibeian surcoat. Guessing that he had been sent from Fort Vakid, the wizard clenched his left hand into a fist and cast a spell.

Ontar was next to notice the rider's colors as his mount shot past the group at a breakneck speed. Dropping his helmet, he fumbled for his crossbow, but knew there was little chance of getting it ready in time. Conversely, Echo didn't even bother going for a weapon, preferring instead to see what Hatch would do.

Finishing his spell, Hatch opened his hand to reveal a slightly rounded flame twice the size of the palm it hovered over. The magic fire crackled with an intense heat as a wispy trace of smoke could be seen rising from its top. The rider had already covered a good distance since passing the party, and Hatch took quick aim with his spell before throwing it. The firebolt shot from Hatch's hand with amazing velocity and hit the horseman square in the back.

Crying out in surprise and pain, the rider fell from his mount, which veered off the road and gallop into a field. Ontar and Echo were impressed with how quickly Hatch had dispatched the horseman, and this admiration turned into awe when the wizard uttered a single spell word, then actually *leapt* the entire distance between the party and the downed rider.

Picking up his helmet, Ontar turned to Wink and exclaimed, "Whoa! What else can he do?"

The pixie smiled. "Trust me, you don't want to know."

Landing next to the wounded rider, Hatch took the prone man's dagger and killed him with it. By the time Ontar, Echo, and Wink had reached the rider's body, Hatch had already claimed anything of value and had gone into the field to find the man's horse. Guiding his new mount back to the road, Hatch stopped before the group and withdrew an opened letter that had been tucked into his belt and handed it over to Ontar. "Take a look. The letter was sent from Sir Debren of Fort Vakid to Magistrate Blustal who rules the city of Ranig."

Ontar held the letter and read it while Wink and Echo peeked over his shoulder. The message clearly stated that Hatch had escaped imprisonment and managed to instigate a deadly attack on the fort. Ontar himself was vaguely mentioned as a fully armored warrior who brandished a crossbow and assisted in orchestrating Hatch's flight.

Echo made a frustrated sound and stepped away from Ontar. "I can't believe this. *I'm* the one who risked my neck trying to reach the forts dungeon. How come Ontar got all the credit for the escape?"

Hatch wagged his finger. "Ah-ah, if you read a little closer the letter says Ontar may have also had accomplices."

"Besides, Hatch's death cloud probably killed anyone *you* came into contact with," Wink added.

Ontar didn't care who got credit for the escape. Turning to Hatch, he said, "The important thing is we've intercepted the rider. How much time do you think we have before Sir Debren realizes what's happened?"

"Could be days, could be weeks. Magistrate Blustal has never really cared for the white knights, and while he would have alerted the city guards had he received this letter, the courtesy of sending a timely response is probably considered beneath him," Hatch replied while exaggerating a dismissive wave.

"Seems like there's some bitterness between Sibeia's authorities," Ontar observed.

Hatch nodded. "The six lords have always tried to emphasize the importance of the factions they represent. In this case, resentment between those loyal to the market and warrior lords will come to benefit us."

"So, let's not waste that benefit and get the heck out of here," Wink griped.

Everyone agreed and waited patiently for Hatch to mount his new horse before heading out.

❧❧❧

It was a cool evening by the time the party had reached a lone roadside tavern known as the Misty Mug. In many ways, the three-story building resembled the Peaceful Repose in Miltus. The only difference was that its main level had a couple of widows with shutters on them instead of a large stained-glass one, and the hanging sign above the door depicted a mug with a cloud surrounding its top.

A full dark red moon was struggling to share the sky with some clouds that were trying to obscure it. Hatch dismounted his tired steed and said, "I'll tend to the stabling of my horse. You three go on ahead." Offering little argument Ontar, Echo, and Wink slipped into the tavern.

Entering the noisy building, the party was surprised to see that almost every table in the dining hall was packed with boisterous warriors clad in everything from leather to plate armor. Swapping stories over plates of hot food and spilled drinks the men had an atmosphere of merriment about them. This gaiety didn't necessarily extend to the serving wenches who exhaustedly refilled cups while putting up with leering eyes and pinched bottoms.

"Ugh...we're never going to find a table in here," Ontar complained.

"What about that one?" Wink asked as she pointed to a round wooden table occupied by only a single person.

Ontar and Echo glanced at where Wink pointed and blinked in disbelief at the man who sat there. Easily as big and muscular as Ontar, the man was an imposing figure with black skin and long hair pulled back into thinly-braided strands behind an elaborate beaded headband with a gold medallion at its center. His demeanor seemed to be both strong and assured as he was dressed in foreign garments that included a red shúkà, which was fastened by a leather belt around his waist. His other adornments were a layered, beaded necklace of multiple colors, a couple of wooden bracelets around his wrists, and sandals. Subtly displaying that he was a warrior, the man had a gold headed spear propped next to the table with a matching shield whose sun emblem covered a backpack resting on the floor.

"Krudkur," Ontar said with a hint of reverence in the name.

"Who's Krudkur?" Wink asked.

Echo explained, "A while back, I was in a fierce competition for admittance into the Bloody Side thieves' guild. Now, the cheating for this competition was expected to be rampant, so the guild hired Krudkur to minimize the amount of outside interference."

Ontar frowned at the memory. "I was one of the outsiders who happened to be helping Echo during the competition. Krudkur hunted me, and all the other outsiders, like some damn ravenous wolf."

Wink sized up the man. "He doesn't look that tough. I'm surprised you didn't challenge him to a duel."

"That would have been playing to his strengths," Ontar replied. "Krudkur is a champion coliseum fighter back in his native land, and the only foreigner to have ever won the Chapskin Empire's imperial games. If I had squared off against him then neither of us would have been able to stop the other outsiders from attacking Echo."

Wink shrugged. "Well, the competition's over now. So, why don't we all go over and have a couple of drinks with him?"

"Fat chance," Ontar snicker as he plucked the pixie off his shoulder and dropped her onto Echo's. "If you two want to visit with that butcher then go ahead. I'll be over here at the bar."

"Suit yourself," Echo said as Ontar departed.

Sitting at a stool next to the bar, Ontar waited for the tavern keeper to notice him, while he sat there, a man on his right spoke up, "Smart move staying away from the likes of him," he said in reference to Krudkur.

Ontar looked over at the man and saw that he was a warrior with a butch haircut and a long scar going down his left arm. Scale armor covered his torso, and a battle ax was strapped to his back. A half-empty tankard of ale rested on the bar in front of him.

"Why do you say that?" Ontar asked the stranger.

"Because he's not like the rest of us here. My names Bulak, and I lead one of the mercenary bands in these parts. We've tried recruiting him before but didn't have much luck. Lately, my boys have been hearing nasty rumors that he's gone and attacked one of our rivals while they were out on a job."

"And what job might that be?" asked a hushed, fluttering voice Ontar knew belonged to Hatch.

Bulak gave the scruffy old wizard an odd look, but Ontar quickly explained, "He's with me."

Continuing, the mercenary said, "Most of the guys here have been hired for seasonal protection by the local villages."

"Protection from what?" Ontar asked.

"Big…man-sized bugs called maazhat, which pop out of the ground this time of year to raid the nearby farms for food," Bulak replied before taking a drink from his tankard.

Hatch grew concerned. "Have any of the villagers been hurt yet during these raids?"

Bulak finished his drink and snickered. "Not while they're payin' us."

Ontar could see Hatch's relief in that answer and knew the spell caster feared for his family's safety. Seeking greater information on this possible threat, he decided to ask Bulak to go into detail on his previous battles against the maazhat.

Echo could understand Ontar's wariness about dealing with Krudkur, but she wasn't about to let a personal grudge keep her from finding out why such a formidable warrior was staying at this overcrowded tavern.

Approaching his table, she nodded to the big man. "Greetings, Krudkur. It's been a while since we've last met."

Krudkur looked her over with his deep brown eyes. "Indeed, it has," he replied in a slow, deep voice punctuated by a heavy accent.

In contrast, Wink sounded like a squeaky little mouse when she spoke. "I've never seen a human like you before. So, where in the world do you come from?"

Considering the question a moment, Krudkur replied, "I hail from the jungle kingdom of Magunda in the Eshada Region."

Echo pulled out a stool from his table and sat down. "I think a better question might be *what* in the world are you doing here?"

Krudkur grinned, but before he could answer, a serving wench approached the group and took their dinner orders. After she left, Krudkur set his hands on the table, leaned in a little bit, and crossed his fingers.

"I've been hired by the ruling magistrate to purge a colony of large insects known as maazhat from this land."

Huh. A good example of a Sibeian noble hiring outside help instead of relying on his own soldiers, Echo thought.

Wink cocked her head and asked, "Well, why aren't you drinking with the other warriors then?"

Krudkur's expression turned grim. "Our objectives are quite different. The mercenaries were hired only to protect the surrounding villages from harm. *I,* on the other hand, am here to eliminate the problem once and for all."

"Which I bet puts you at odds with the men here since your task would be to rob them of a regular income," Echo surmised.

"Perhaps," Krudkur conceded. "But at the moment, there is no one alive who would dare object to my presence."

Echo caught the drift of what the deadly warrior was saying, and while she doubted there would be much profit in squashing a bunch of bugs, she had to admit that his task was a noble one.

Getting acquainted with their new dining companions, the party talked and relaxed well into the evening before getting a room for the night. The next morning, they greeted some of these same people at breakfast prior to continuing their journey. Shortly afterwards, Krudkur and the mercenaries left the tavern as well to complete their own various missions.

The sudden exodus of travelers caused life at the Misty Mug to get rather quiet for the people who worked there. This relative calm lasted only until the end of the day when an odd pair of men entered the tavern and sat down to request some dinner. Having left his nightmare and its cart to mill about the plains until he needed them, Narcos had ordered a meal for both himself and Marcain. Seeing the young lord's eyes were bloodshot, he asked, "What's the matter with you? You've had nothing to do but sleep in the cart during our travels and you still look exhausted."

Setting his elbows on the table, Marcain put his face in his hands and said, "I can't sleep. Every time I close my eyes, I have visions of people and places that I've never even seen before."

"Those visions are from Eragosh, and you should be happy to have them," Narcos explained. "His spirit is the only reason I've bothered to keep you alive at all."

"But why are we searching for this hidden city in the first place?" Marcain complained. "You've already proven your power over the dead. Isn't that enough?"

Narcos slowly shook his head. "No. Although, I used to think it was. I even had my minions conquer an entire village, which I then ruled over like a king. Confident in my power, I was shocked when a local lord led his troops into battle against my zombies. Aided by a cleric of Talana, the soldiers used her holy magic to crush my forces and send me fleeing back to the Order of Kardok for safety. It was a harsh lesson that made me recognize my limits as a magic user and try to figure out a way to surpass them."

Briefly appearing with their meals, a serving wench set down plates of chopped liver with a wedge of cheese and two tankards of ale. Drinking deeply of his beverage to help tolerate his dining companion, Marcain asked, "What could possibly be stronger than an undead yet still willingly accept you as their master?"

"Demons," Narcos replied.

Marcain gave Narcos an odd look. "What is a demon, and why do you want one?"

Narcos didn't hesitate with his response. "Demons are vicious monsters summoned from a plane of existence that is vastly more horrific than our own. While some are capable of destroying entire worlds, most are just savage, simple-minded killers."

"So, you want these demons to replace your undead in conquering your enemies," Marcain assumed.

"No," Narcos asserted. "Demons are treacherous and difficult to control with magic. In fact, it would take most of my power just to have one do my bidding. Which is why I had to choose my next slave carefully."

Marcain didn't like the sound of this. "And who did you pick?"

Taking a bite of liver, Narcos replied, "A weak little smoke demon named Zattermox. You see, during my research into these foul beings, I learned the ancient Ha-Ress Empire had once fought a war against them and the hidden city of Uch-na-Mach was the site of a major battle. Zattermox was a scavenger who stole enchanted relics from fallen foes for his masters to use during the war.

They say, that when Eragosh's army drove the demons from Uch-na-Mach, Zattermox was sealed away by one of his own stolen artifacts until his masters could return to release him. Unable to find where the demon was located amongst the ruins,

Eragosh destroyed the city's underground entrances and left it lost for all time."

Finishing his cheese, Marcain said, "Do you seriously think Zattermox possessed any artifacts strong enough to turn you into an almighty conqueror?"

"The demons and the Ha-Ress used artifacts of devastating power against each other during the war," Narcos claimed. "If I could possess even one of them, then it would be more than enough to crush the puny kingdoms which exist today."

"Your quest for power will cost you your life," Marcain warned after finishing his drink. "And if I had any say in the matter, I wouldn't hesitate to kill you myself."

Narcos sneered at the comment. "You turned your back on power, *milord*, and now you shall forever be forced to serve those who seek it."

Giving the necromancer an indignant look, Marcain waited for him to finish his food before they got a room for the night.

Narcos and Marcain awoke the next morning and ate an early breakfast before returning to the spot where they had left the nightmare and its cart. Tired from another evening of bad dreams, Marcain hoped to catch a breeze during their travels to help stave off the sun's punishing heat. Watching as Narcos climbed into the back of the cart, he asked, "What are you doing?"

Narcos responded with a single word, *"Eragosh."*

Shuddering slightly, Marcain's expression suddenly went blank as his posture drastically improved. Speaking in a voice that did not belong to his descendant, Eragosh asked, *"Master, what is your will?"*

"Take me to the entrance of Uch-na-Mach," Narcos demanded.

Climbing into the cart driver's seat, Eragosh flicked the reins and sent the nightmare galloping back down the road. Moving at a feverish pace, things proceeded smoothly until about noon when Eragosh abruptly drove the cart off the road and into the grassy plains. Jostled by the sudden change, Narcos clung to the sides of the cart for fear of being bounced out of it. The rough ride seemed to last forever, and when it finally came to a stop, the sight that greeted him proved to be quite interesting.

Looking out across the plains, Narcos saw a large pond with a couple of trees growing along its edge. Suspecting that this was some sort of watering hole, he saw that a small herd of cattle had gathered here to get something to drink. While not entirely unusual for such creatures, the fact that every cow in the herd was now dead and littering the ground appealed to the necromancer's dark nature.

The monsters that slaughtered these animals appeared to be dark red insectoids roughly the size of a man. These slender, mantis-like creatures had long antenna's sprouting from the top of their heads just above two black compound eyes dwarfed by their sharp, oversized mandibles. Four spindly legs protruded from their stout abdomen, while two slender arms ended in small clawed hands that emerged from their thorax. Armed with a makeshift sickle in each hand, the monster had actually made the weapons from the scavenged mandibles of its fallen brethren and put them to good use.

Engaged in combat against the maazhat was Bulak and his band of mercenaries. Swinging his mighty battle ax, he fearlessly led his men in what would soon by an obvious victory over their enemies. However, there appeared to be casualties on both sides of the conflict, and the mercenaries would only have six men left who survived the encounter.

Unsure of what was going on, Narcos said, "Eragosh, why have you brought me here?"

"This is the entrance to Uch-na-Mach." Eragosh replied.

"Where?" Narcos asked.

Eragosh pointed to the pond. *"There."*

"Of course," Narcos muttered to himself. "What better way to conceal the entrance than to submerge it under a pool of water. Is there a hidden door or something we should look for?"

Shaking his head, Eragosh replied, *"No, the entrance is buried at the bottom of the pond."*

"I suppose we'll have to dig it up then," Narcos mused. "Can you kill the men who are fighting by the pond?"

Eragosh nodded. *"Yes."*

"Then do so," Narcos commanded.

Getting down off the cart, Eragosh strolled up to the nightmare and drew forth the sword under its saddle. He then advanced towards the mercenaries.

"Hey, Bulak, who's that?" one of the mercenaries asked as he pointed his sword at Eragosh.

Gazing out across the plains, Bulak saw not only the man coming his way, but also noticed Narcos and the nightmare were behind him. "I don't know. However, it looks like he serves a wizard whose horse has a flaming mane. Get ready to rush him if things go bad." Waiting for his men to line up at his sides, Bulak then called out, "Hey! I don't know who you are, but if you don't want me to chop your damn head off, you'll stop right there and tell me what you want!"

Eragosh kept moving.

"That's what I thought," Bulak grumbled before telling his men to, "Kill him!"

Seeing the mercenaries were already tired from fighting the maazhat, Eragosh greeted their charge with one of his own.

Getting out the first strike, he made a diagonal slash across one of the men's chest, splitting his leather armor and causing him to drop to the ground in pain.

Avenging his wounded comrade, a mercenary armed with a spinning morning star and shield, wrapped the chain of his weapon around Eragosh's sword and held it in place while two of his sword-wielding companions attacked him from the sides. Utilizing a surprise attack unique to someone in his position, Eragosh had the upper half of his ghostly form shoot out from Marcain's left hip and raked the stomach of an approaching mercenary, causing him to drop to the ground in pain with severe frostbite along his gut. The move startled his other attackers, allowing Eragosh to stab the morning star-wielding mercenary in the heart and subsequently freeing his blade. He then dodged a halfhearted attack from the mercenary on his right before slitting the man's throat in a retaliatory strike.

Gawking at the ghost, which slipped back into Marcain's body, Bulak saw that he now only had one man left to fight alongside him! Afraid the wizard would use his magic to kill them even if they did beat his champion, he decided to make a break for it by shouting, "Scatter!" while running in the opposite direction of his comrade. Chasing down the mercenary closest to him, Eragosh easily cut him down with an attack from behind. Unfortunately, this allowed Bulak to put some distance between them.

"Coward." Narcos sneered as he unhitched the nightmare from his cart. Galloping after the pathetic mercenary, it didn't take long for the undead horse to catch up with its prey.

Bulak heard the nightmare coming up behind him and knew that he could never outrun such a beast. Refusing to cower in front of a damn horse, he spun around and swung his battle ax with enough force to lodge it into the base of the nightmare's neck. Much to his horror, the attack did nothing to stop the nightmare's momentum as it knocked Bulak over before trampling him to death. After which, it simply returned to its master.

Pulling the battle ax from his mount before allowing it to fall to the ground, Narcos saw that Eragosh stood off in the distance waiting for instructions. "Kill the wounded, then be silent until I have need you." A simple nod was Eragosh's only response before he set about his task with ruthless efficiency.

Awakening as if from a trance, Marcain gasped when he found himself standing over a dead mercenary with his blade covered in blood. Having never killed a man before, he was shocked to see someone lying dead from wounds he didn't even remember inflicting. "By the gods…what have I done?"

"Don't flatter yourself," Narcos uttered in disdain. "Eragosh was the one who killed these men. He just had to use your body to do it."

"Why?" Marcain wondered.

"The entrance to Uch-na-Mach lies within that pond, and I need some undead to dig it out," Narcos explained.

Seeing the maazhat bodies scattered amongst the dead, Marcain asked, "Wouldn't these creatures have been enough?"

Narcos shrugged. "The more hands I have to do a job, the quicker it will be done. Now, quit pestering me with your questions. I have work to do."

Raising his arms, Narcos uttered a dark incantation that spread across the bodies of man and maazhat alike. Nervously backing away from the zombies as they rose, Marcain watched as one by one they shambled into the pond's rippling water. Looking out from one of the nearby trees, he sadly suspected that whatever secrets the pond held within it would soon be revealed.

Unaware of how close their enemies actually were, the party had finally arrived at the village of Habed and decided to stop at the local mercantile so that Hatch could get himself cleaned up before visiting his family. Pulling out one of several fishing poles sitting in a barrel, Ontar gazed at it fondly and remembered when he and his father would sit on the banks of the Cherenon River and spend the whole day trying to catch something to eat. Neither of them was much of a fisherman and, most of the time, they came home empty handed, but for Ontar, that really didn't matter. It was spending time with his dad that really counted. Smiling at the recollection, he slipped the pole back into its barrel and went to look at something else.

Milling about the main level of a wooden two-story shop, the group was happy the store's owner had let Hatch use his back room to change into the clothes that he had eagerly purchased from him. The store itself was clean and simple. A few standing shelves filled with miscellaneous objects were placed near ones that were mounted to the wall. Sacks of seed and grain occupied random spots on the floor while wagon wheels, scythes, and different types of coiled up roped were all hung from pegs on the wall.

Wink was thoroughly bored. Hatch had set her on a wall shelf before leaving to try on clothes. The annoyed pixie sat down on a bundle of candles and swiped thimbles from a nearby stack so she could chuck them into an empty cauldron below her. The noisy *clang* from each successful throw clearly began to get on people's nerves.

Echo, for one, was sorely tempted to grab a thimble and throw it at Wink's head. Before the pixie's irritating game, she and Ontar had been having a nice time looking through a store that carried objects that didn't necessarily pertain to their adventurous lifestyle. Of course, they still bought rations and replenished their supply of projectiles, but now she was content to just relax and admire the shop's limited supply of baskets. This was primarily due to the fact that Echo's parents had been merchants who wove and sold such baskets for a living. So, seeing some of the simple containers stacked in a corner brought back pleasant memories of home. However, her reminiscing came to an end, though when she heard the floorboards by the front counter creak, and glanced over in that direction to see a much cleaner looking Hatch emerge from the back room.

"So, what do you think?" Hatch asked as he stood before his fellow companions.

Echo had to admit the old wizard certainly looked far better than when she first encountered him. Hatch had shaved his beard and meticulously groomed his mustache and nails. The tattered tunic she had found him in was replaced by a tan shirt, black pants, and a brown cloak. He still wore the weapon belt she had given him, which happened to match well with the new leather shoes he currently wore. Purchasing additional equipment to handle a life of travel, Hatch now had a backpack slung over his shoulders and held a simple wooden quarterstaff in his right hand.

Wink leaned back on her bundle of candles and tried to suppress a snicker. "Alean would have had a heart attack if she ever saw you dressed like that."

Hatch grinned. "Then maybe I should have tried it on year's ago."

"Well, it looks like you have everything you need," Ontar said to Hatch as he picked up Wink and placed her on his shoulder. "I think it's time to have a family reunion."

"I have to admit I'm a little nervous," Hatch confessed. "I haven't seen them in years, and when they didn't come to my trial, I initially assumed they were ashamed of me."

Wink gave him a disgusted look. "The only reason they didn't attend your trial was that Lady Alean assigned guards to keep them away. She wanted you to feel like shit for humiliating her and tried to give the impression the entire family had abandoned you."

"And it worked," Hatch admitted. "I never felt more alone in my life then when I was thrown in the dungeon with no one I could even say goodbye to."

Scowling when she heard this, Echo said, "Lady Alean is an ice-cold bitch. Ontar and I would give anything to say goodbye to the loved ones we've lost, and for her to take that from you is just plain cruel."

"But now, you've got a second chance," Wink said. "So, let's go and show them you can't keep a good man down."

Exiting the mercantile and collecting their horse, the party found that Habed was a sleepy little community with a handful of houses situated along the road while several others were scattered about the adjoining fields. A few of the locals stopped to chat about the new arrivals outside a stone shrine dedicated to the goddess Mirsha, but the buildings cleric soon shooed them away after scolding them for gossiping. Keeping his eyes peeled, Hatch spotted a small dirt path that split from the road and subsequently led everyone down it. Passing through lush farmland, the party found themselves coming upon a one-story house surrounded by a waist-high picket fence, which was covered in sprawling ivy vines.

Barely having a chance to survey their destination, Ontar and Echo were surprised to see the fences gate was suddenly flung open to reveal a girl with bright blue eyes looking out at them.

The child seemed to be between the ages of ten and twelve and had long blonde hair pulled back into a ponytail. Clothed in a high-quality garment, the girl wore a puffed shoulder pink dress with a lacy white collar, belt, and shoes. A beautiful sapphire brooch pinned beneath the collar gave a clear indication that this child was more than some mere peasant.

Giving a wide smile, the girl spread her arms and cried out, "Grandpa," before she raced down the path towards the party.

Grinning from ear to ear, Hatch brought his horse to a halt and spread his arms as he exclaimed, "Aniata," before his granddaughter ran up to give him a big hug.

"Hey, don't forget about me!" exclaimed Wink as Ontar took the pixie off his shoulder and held her in his hand.

"Wink, you're here, too!" Aniata squealed as she moved to grab the pixie.

Ontar found the whole scene to be rather touching. For him, it brought back memories of coming home from Fort Hasborne and having his kid sister greet him in almost the exact same manner. Smiling sadly, a part of him wished he had one last chance to feel her loving embrace. Lost in thought, he almost didn't notice the slender middle-aged woman standing at the open gate. A motherly figure, the woman had brown hair pulled back in a bun and wore a long maroon skirt with a tan shirt beneath her white apron. Trembling as she saw the party, the woman gasped and fell to the ground weeping.

"Mom!" Aniata shouted as she (and inadvertently, Wink) raced to where the poor woman had fallen.

Ontar and Echo shot each other a questioning look while Hatch followed behind his granddaughter. Joining the ring of those concerned was a sweaty man whose dirty clothes indicated that he obviously had been working in the garden. Tall and slender, he had long brown hair and a beard. Wiping his hands on a well-worn shirt, the man had tan pants with patches sewn in at the knees and brown leather boots. Sprinting towards the woman, he knelt beside her and put a comforting arm around her shoulder.

"There, there, milady. It will be alright," he said in soothing tones.

Coming up beside the others, Ontar and Echo saw the woman look up at them with tears in her eyes. "I'm sorry. I didn't mean to make such a display. I must appear to be an absolute lunatic." The woman rose and used her apron to wipe away some tears. "My names Saren Malay. This is my daughter Aniata and our slave Drub," she explained while gesturing to the bearded man who stood up beside her.

Hatch looked at her with concern in his eyes. "Saren, what's wrong?"

"Oh, Hatch, Thove and Kit are gone. They left just the other day to find an ancient sword they thought they could offer up in exchange for your freedom," Saren said with a sigh.

The mere mention of Spirit Slayer instantly piqued Echo's interest, and she listened intently to see if Saren would say anything more about the relic.

"Figures." Wink snorted. "Thove always did have the worst sense of timing."

"Where did they go?" Hatch asked while looking deep into her eyes.

Saren briefly bit her lower lip. "To the maazhat colony."

Everyone present knew the danger of going to such a place, and Ontar instinctively asked, "How do we get there?"

Saren looked at the big warrior a little surprised. "I'm sorry, but who are you?"

Ontar blushed at his over-eagerness, and Hatch cleared his throat. "Of course, forgive me. Saren, this is Ontar and Echo.

With Wink's help, they were the ones who rescued me from imprisonment."

Saren studied the two. "I had prayed to Talana the goddess would shine her light upon our home and find a way to heal our family. I only wish she had sent the two of you to accomplish this task a little bit earlier."

Making a dismissive gesture, Saren continued on, "Please, join my family for dinner. It's the least I can do to show my gratitude for freeing Thove's father." Turning to Drub and Aniata, she gave out instructions, "Drub, please take Hatch's horse to the stable and fetch some wood for the fire. Aniata, I need you to pick a few rabbits from the hutch and bring them to me in the kitchen." Addressing the others, Saren said, "Dinner will take a little time to prepare but, please, feel free to enjoy the comforts of my home."

Aniata looked down at the pixie in her hands. "Come on, Wink. Let's try to find some fat ones."

"I bet I'll spot the biggest one before you do," Wink taunted as the two ran off through the garden and behind the house.

Saren beckoned for the others to follow her as they passed through the ivy shrouded gate and into the garden. Echo was immediately taken aback by the size and beauty of what she saw. The garden was filled with the sweet scent of flowers, which she admired while traversing a thin gravel path that led from the gate to the house. On either side of the path were short juniper hedges that divided the garden between food and floral plants. To her left, cabbage, turnips, and watermelons were all placed beneath the watchful shadow of a scarecrow. On her right, violets, lilies, and daffodils all grew peacefully around a big plum tree.

Moving past the garden's natural beauty, the party came up to a house far more luxurious than any average peasant dwelling.

Built with wooden framework and green walls, the house had a shingled roof with two stone chimneys. A small stable was attached to the buildings left side, while windows with open shutters had flower boxes at their base filled with colorful daisies.

Entering the structure, Saren asked Ontar, Echo, and Hatch to have a seat by the fireplace while she went to make dinner. Removing backpacks, helmets, and shields, Ontar and Echo sat down on a cozy-looking couch close to a window. Hatch preferred to sit on one of the two soft chairs that faced them.

The house was exceptionally clean, with sturdy decorative rugs set out at key spots along the wooden floor while simple, yet homey, curtains framed every window. Decorated with a nature theme in mind, a large set of deer antlers could be seen mounted to the wall above the fireplace. Hatch sat politely, but his attention seemed to be drawn to a small bookcase located just behind the chair he rested in.

"You have a beautiful home," Echo called out to Saren as she banged pots and pans around in the kitchen.

"Thank you," came a slightly distracted reply from their host.

Ontar looked around and observed, "Ranger's must make a pretty good living to reside in a place like this."

"Well, I'm sure it helps that Thove's parents were one of the rulers of this country," Echo pointed out.

Ontar agreed with that assessment, then watched as Aniata and Wink burst into the house, swung through the kitchen, and headed towards where everyone sat. Aniata held the pixie in her left hand, which she drew close to her and said.

"Hey, Wink, I still have your house in my room. Do you want to go see it?"

"Sure," Wink exclaimed.

"Wait a minute," Ontar blurted. "Your house? Are you saying that you used to live here?"

"Of course," Wink replied. "You don't think I wasted my life studying magic and playing politics with Hatch now, do you? When Thove was born, I spent my time helping to raise him into the man he is today, and when he married Saren, I tagged along to make sure their kids grew up happy and healthy."

Echo thought about what Wink had said for a moment, then asked, "So, when did you start living with Hatch again?"

An awkward silence briefly filled the room before Wink answered, "It was around the time that he and Lady Alean got a divorce."

Aniata knew that this was an uncomfortable subject for those present. Looking down at Wink, she said, "Come on, Wink, let's go," before she spirited the pixie off to their new destination.

Sensing the need to switch topics, Echo saw Drub bringing an armload of firewood into the kitchen and asked Hatch, "How can you condone Thove having a slave when you yourself were born among them?"

Hatch leaned back in his chair. "First off, it was Alean's idea to give them the slave…not mine. Secondly, I think that Drub's presence here has been a real asset to this household. Thove's duties as a ranger can take him away from home for days to even weeks at a time, and there are certain tasks that Saren just can't do here on her own."

"Which is why she has two daughters to aid her," Echo argued.

Hatch didn't want to discuss this topic any further and was relieved when Drub approached the dining table with plates and silverware. "So, tell me, Drub, do you know what possessed my son to find the maazhat colony now?"

Making sure the table was properly set, Drub replied, "My master thought the best time to enter the colony was while most of them were out raiding farms across the countryside."

"How did Thove manage to find the colony in the first place?" Ontar asked.

"Well, it wasn't easy…" Drub began as he told the party about the dangers involved in Thove and Kit's attempts to track the maazhat. This conversation lasted until Saren announced that dinner was served.

Saren's meal was an absolutely delicious dish of roasted rabbit served with salad and a loaf of sliced bread. A pot of tea was drunk in good quantity, while plum pudding was served for dessert. Dinner conversation around the dining table centered on Thove's outrage at his mother's infidelity and the family's grief at Hatch and Wink's imprisonment. The discussion turned interesting when Saren revealed that Thove had vowed to find a way to rescue his father from imprisonment by either trading his freedom for Spirit Slayer, or selling the blade and using the money to bribe the guards. Receiving tips from some of Hatch's former friends, Thove spent a great deal of time researching several different artifacts before he learned of the powerful sword held deep below ground in the ancient city of Uch-na-Mach.

Eager to help her father, Kit believed they could reach the subterranean city by traversing the maazhat colony. Scouring the land, Kit and her father found the colony then set out to recover the sword.

"And now they're gone, risking their lives without even realizing their goal has already been accomplished," Saren said as she used a napkin to wipe away a tear from her eye.

Evening had descended on the home, with Drub lighting candles and stoking the fire to provide illumination. He even managed to collect and wash the dishes without disrupting dinner conversation.

Hatch shook his head. "Did Thove leave any notes on the colonies location or additional information on the ancient city?"

Saren nodded. "They're in the bookcase. You're free to look at them if you'd like. However, it's getting late, and Aniata and I need to get to bed."

"But I'm not tired," Aniata protested.

"Shhh…don't complain," whispered Wink. "After everyone's asleep, we can stay up late and tell ghost stories."

"Don't even think about it," Saren scolded. "Besides, Aniata, you're sleeping in my room tonight so that one of our guests can rest in yours."

"What!" Aniata whined.

Echo held up her hand. "You don't need to do that, Saren. I can get by without a bed for the night."

Saren crinkled her brow. "Well…if you're sure."

"Great!" chimed Aniata as she picked up Wink. "Goodnight, Mom." Moving over to Hatch, she kissed him on the cheek. "Goodnight, Grandpa." Turning to Ontar and Echo, she said, "It was nice to meet you," before scurrying off to her room while whispering to Wink in a conspiratorial tone.

Saren gave the two a suspicious look prior to standing up and addressing the rest of her guests. "Hatch, the guest room has been kept just as you remember it. Ontar, you're welcome to stay in Kit's room during her absence and, Echo, please feel free to make yourself comfortable. I'll see you all in the morning."

Everyone bid Saren a goodnight and watched as she departed. Standing up, Ontar, Echo, and Hatch all headed back towards the couch and chairs by the fireplace.

Scooping up his equipment, Ontar said, "Well, there's a soft warm bed waiting for me, and I wholeheartedly intend to use it. Wake me if you must. Otherwise, I'll see you two in the morning."

Hatch nodded absentmindedly as he picked out some thick tomes from the bookcase and sat in a chair near the fireplace.

Echo watched Ontar head to bed, then searched the bookcase for some rolled up parchments. Finding what she was looking for, Echo curled up on the couch and spread one of Kit's large maps before her.

It was late into the evening before Echo ended her studies. Aside from Drub offering beverages before he went to bed, she and Hatch had worked uninterrupted throughout much of the night. Echo couldn't help but admire Kit's mapping technique. The ranger had found where the maazhat colony was located by keeping a record of the villages they attacked and estimating how far a raiding party could travel while carrying large amounts of pillaged food. After that, it only took a couple months of scouting the open plains before she found the entrance to their lair.

Setting aside the map, Echo glanced over in Hatch's direction and saw he fought the urge to nod off while reading from a thick book that rested on his lap. Standing up, she moved over to Hatch's chair and knelt by one of its arms.

"Hatch, you need to get some sleep. Tomorrow, we're all going to go find your son and granddaughter, but to be successful, we'll need to have your mind sharp and spells at ready."

Hatch peered at Echo through bloodshot eyes. "This shouldn't have happened. A father is supposed to take care of his son, not the other way around. Why would Thove risk his life *and* Kit's just to save a pathetic old man like me?"

"Love," Echo said simply. "In spite all of your faults, Thove and Kit still love you a great deal. If they didn't, then I doubt they'd be fighting so hard on your behalf."

"Hmm. I suppose there's some truth to that. Although, I seriously doubt that love is the reason you're helping me with my family," Hatch noted.

Echo shrugged. "I'll admit I'm more interested in finding the sword Thove was looking for, but I don't see why we can't help each other out since our goals are intertwined."

Hatch stared down at the floor and sighed. "I don't think I could ever forgive myself if Thove or Kit got hurt while acting on my behalf."

"Then don't let their actions be for nothing. Tonight, you need to get some sleep so that tomorrow you can effectively use your magic to protect them," Echo prodded.

"You're right," Hatch admitted as he grabbed his staff from the side of the chair and used it to stand himself upright. "I only hope that nothing terrible has befallen them."

Echo rose next to Hatch and reassuringly set her hand on his bony shoulder. "We'll make sure that doesn't happen."

Chapter Nine

Ontar smiled as he heard the soothing sounds of Echo's flute while she played her instrument beneath a big plum tree out in the garden. It was a beautiful morning, and the house overflowed with the pleasant aromas of fresh flowers and savory food. Kit's bed was inordinately comfortable, which made getting out of it all the more difficult. Ontar had experienced a little trouble falling asleep last night with Wink and Aniata giggling in the room next to his, but once things quieted down, he quickly entered into a deep slumber. However, once morning came, the girls' insidious plan was quickly revealed.

Sneaking out to the plum tree while Aniata watched from the kitchen window, Wink made sure to stay directly behind Echo while she was preoccupied with her music. Whispering a spell that couldn't be heard over the sound of the flute, Wink then touched the tree upon its conclusion and instantly caused every plum on it to fall off at exactly the same time. Pelted by fruit, Echo heard the pixie's sinister laughter as she ran back to the house and angrily called out, "Wink!"

At the sound, Ontar sat up and shifted over to the side of the bed so that he could grab his boots and begin the well-rehearsed practice of donning his equipment for the day. Kit's room was simply furnished with a wardrobe, a nightstand, and a chest at the foot of her bed. As Ontar made the bed, he noticed a couple of the room's unique features. The first being a book placed on the nightstand that had the bronze symbol of a seed with a worm wrapped around it on the cover. Paging through the book, he saw that it contained prayers and spells devoted to Mirsha the goddess of nature. The second object he noticed was a small box like wooden maze that had been set in one of the room's four corners. A little hole had been cut into the maze's exterior wall to make for a simple entrance, while an oversized pin cushion located at its center was covered in crumbs. Ontar decided he'd have to ask Kit about the peculiar object once he has a chance to meet her.

Thinking of Kit reminded Ontar of his upcoming plans for the day. So, he decided to leave her room and set his backpack, shield, and helmet on the couch by the fireplace. Turning towards the dining room, he saw Saren setting the table for breakfast. "Good morning, Saren," he said cheerfully as he headed towards the table. "Might I ask what delicious meal you've prepared for us today?"

"Actually, I'm not the cook this morning," Saren corrected. "The girls got up early to make something special for you."

Ontar pulled out a chair and sat at the table. "Well, from what I've heard outside, it sounds like breakfast wasn't the only thing on their mind."

Saren nodded and looked back towards the kitchen. "I swear, Wink just brings out the worst in Aniata. Hopefully, the food will help make up for all the mischief they caused."

"Somehow, I doubt it," Echo grumbled as she opened the door to the house while holding Wink by the back of her dress.

Flailing wildly until Echo sat her on the table, Wink said, "You wouldn't know good food if it fell on your big empty head… which, by the way, it did!"

Saren shook her head and cried out, "Aniata, the table's set. Are you coming?"

"Yes!" came a slightly rushed reply. Moments later, Aniata exited the kitchen carrying a platter stacked high with waffles. Setting the platter on the table, Aniata took Ontar's plate and slid the top waffle onto it. Ontar noticed the waffle squares had blueberries in them, and he grabbed a fork eager to take a bite.

"Wait!" Wink cried as she stared at Ontar intently. "Don't you notice anything special about the waffle?"

Ontar examined the waffle closely. *Dammit, why do girls always have to pull some sort of cutesy crap when it comes to a man's meal,* he thought. It took over a minute before Ontar saw what Wink was hinting at.

"Oh, the berries are shaped like a heart," he muttered before digging into the dish.

Wink smiled broadly, then looked back at Aniata. "See, I told you. Onnie likes *my* cooking the best."

"*Your* cooking? Last I checked, you couldn't even lift a pan by yourself, let alone use it," Echo pointed out.

Wink scowled at the remark. "At least I don't eat waffles with spit on them."

"I don't…" Echo stopped herself when she saw Aniata slide a waffle onto her plate. "Forget it. I'm not hungry."

"Well, let's make sure Ontar's not the only one who gets something to eat," Saren added as she went to find Hatch in the guest room.

Greeting his companions with tired, bloodshot eyes, Hatch yawned, sat at the table, and said, "Ah there's nothing like a home cooked meal, and we better enjoy it while we can because I have a feeling that we've got a very busy day ahead of us."

❦ ❦ ❦

It wasn't long after breakfast the party decided to say goodbye to Saren and Aniata so they could go pursue their missing loved ones. Having carefully studied Kit's map, Echo took the lead in guiding her companions off the main road and away from Habed. Crossing into open farmland, the group soon found themselves trudging through the tall prairie grass of the Wistwind Plains.

Hatch was not in a good mood. There were insects buzzing and flittering about everywhere he went, and as the hot summer sun continued to ascend above the horizon, he knew that travel was going to be particularly unbearable. Stopping in his tracks, he said, "Enough! I refuse to bake in this unrelenting heat."

Ontar and Echo looked at each other, unsure of what he was driving at. Raising his arms, Hatch cast a spell that caused a strong cool breeze to suddenly blow across the desolate plains, creating a wave-like effect among the tall grasses as they slowly twisted back and forth in the wind. Delighted in the result of his magic, the party embraced this simple spell and noticed that it also stymied some of the insect activity around them.

"Much better," Ontar proclaimed as the party continued their trek. "So, does anyone here have an idea on what we're going to do once we find the maazhat colony?"

Hatch cleared his throat. "Exploring the colony should eventually lead us to the ruins of Uch-na-Mach, which is an ancient underground city once part of the mighty Ha-Ress Empire. From what I've read, an army of hideous demons had come from another realm to reduce much of Uch-na-Mach to rubble. However, that was a long time ago so, hopefully, we'll be able to find Thove and Kit safely there amongst its remains."

"Huh, I didn't know these lands used to be part of an empire," Ontar pondered.

"Most people don't," Hatch explained. "You see, many countries today like Sibeia and Lareder first rose to power during the current era. Even some of the older civilizations like the Illamine didn't officially establish themselves until sometime during the Age of Chaos. Now, from what I've read, the Ha-Ress Empire predates *both* of these time periods and is widely regarded to have been the singularly most powerful nation ever created. Uch-na-Mach itself is a testament to their glory since it was built underground specifically to house an army capable of rising to the surface, attacking an enemy by surprise, then dragging the bodies out of sight to make it appear as if an entire legion of troops had just vanished."

Wink poked her head out from the hood of Ontar's cloak and stretched. "And yet, like all the other countries you big races try to create, it still wound up becoming nothing more than dust in the wind."

Hatch wagged his finger. "I wouldn't cast aside the empire's contribution to our world so lightly. Thanks to their influence, we all now share a common language, religion, and currency."

Echo spotted a patch of wildflowers that Kit had used for a landmark and guided her companions towards their direction. "Well, if Uch-na-Mach was part of such an amazing empire, then

I bet they had some really powerful weapons to defend themselves with against the demons."

Nodding in agreement, Hatch elaborated, "Oh, they most certainly did, and among them, of course, was Spirit Slayer. Wielded by a mighty warrior, it was originally thought to have been lost after he perished at the hands of a demon overlord named Da Shō."

"Did Da Shō take the weapon after he killed its owner?" Echo asked.

A thoughtful expression crossed Hatch's face. "Yes, but he didn't use the blade for its original purpose. Instead, he hid it away from his enemies somewhere in the ruins until he could retrieve it later. After the Ha-Ress had defeated the demons, their soldiers destroyed the entrances to Uch-na-Mach and went off to fight other battles."

Wink groaned. "And Thove decided that a weapon which was discarded by *both* the demons *and* the Ha-Ress would be the perfect relic to try and buy your freedom." Shaking her head, she looked at Hatch. "Honestly, I thought we raised him better than that."

"Actually, if Thove had known where you were being held prisoner, then a sword of that age and power would be the perfect relic to bribe a jailor," Echo argued a bit testily.

Hatch scoffed. "My jailor was a cruel man who would never deserve such a blade."

Echo furrowed her brow. "Was he kind of a fat guy with little hair?"

"Yes, how did you know him?" Hatch asked.

"I killed him not long after I broke into Fort Vakid's dungeon," Echo explained.

"Oh, thank the gods," Hatch uttered. "He was a monster. Did you know…"

Hatch began telling tales of how the jailor tormented him during his imprisonment. The party listened intently to his plight while they continued on their journey to the maazhat colony.

✥✥✥

It was late in the afternoon, and Echo was getting a little worried she might have led her companions astray. Having traveled past even the most isolated of farms, she was now having difficulty finding a point of reference to gauge her distance among the wide-open prairie. Afraid she was going to have to backtrack, Echo was about to give up hope when she saw something peculiar off in the distance. Willing to accept any landmark at this point, she decided to push ahead and hope for the best.

Unaware of Echo's uncertainty, the party followed the wood elf until they, too, came to recognize the object she focused on. Increasing their pace, the group continued their advance until they reached what surely had to have been their destination. Casting its shadow over the barren plains was a towering mound of earth and sand that could be nothing else but the huge entrance to the maazhat colony. The mound's top seemed to dip inwards and scattered around its base were the dark red bodies of dead maazhat.

"What happened to them?" Echo asked as she peered over the corpses.

Ontar looked over the insectoids and replied, "These were soldiers killed in battle."

"How can you tell?" Echo asked.

"A mercenary Hatch and I met up with a while ago told us about their ranks through coloring," Ontar explained while examining the remains. "From what I can tell, they didn't all die at once, either. The dust on some their bodies is a lot thicker than others. My guess is that a couple of guards were killed early on while the rest were attacked when they went to see what happened."

Wink scratched her head. "Who would have the guts to just sit outside a maazhat colony and kill anything that poked its head out?"

"Krudkur!" Echo said in sudden realization.

Ontar stood up. "I should have known *he'd* be here. He was probably trying to whittle down their numbers before entering the colony itself."

"Now, just relax," Hatch said calmly. "Right now, this Krudkur person is fighting a common foe, and if we can benefit from his assistance, then that makes our objective all the easier to obtain."

"That doesn't mean I have to like it," Ontar grumbled as he donned his helmet.

Wasting little time, the party began their steep hike up the earthen mound. It was slow going at first, with loose sand slipping beneath their feet but, eventually, the group reached the top of the mound where they were able to get a panoramic view of the plains around them. Looking for an entrance, Ontar noticed the mound sloped sharply downward into a dark round hole at its center.

Trying to peer into the hole from where he stood, Ontar heard Wink mutter, "Be careful, Onnie, the ground here isn't very..."

Suddenly, the sand beneath Ontar's feet gave way, and both he and Wink let out a surprised yell before they slid uncontrollably towards the center of the mound!

"Ontar!" Echo exclaimed, followed by Hatch shouting, "Wink!" The two watched helplessly as they saw their companions fall through the mounds dark hole. Moving carefully, Echo and Hatch made their way down the slope and came to a stop at the hole's sandy edge.

"Ontar, are you okay?" Echo asked as she shouted into the darkness.

It took a couple seconds before he responded, "Yeah, we're fine. The drop's not that deep, so feel free to come on down."

Echo exchanged a hesitant look with Hatch, then sat down on the hole's edge and pushed herself off. Holding her breath in anticipation, she fell only a short distance before landing hard on her feet. Hatch followed behind her but seemed to float down at a much slower pace. Gently touching the ground, he did a quick scan of the area until he saw Ontar and Wink.

Standing in a circle of light that shone down from above, the party noticed they were now in an underground chamber whose walls and floor were made entirely out of packed earth. The temperature here was much cooler than on the surface, and there was a dark tunnel that gently sloped further beneath the earth.

Having survived an embarrassing fall with only a little damage to his pride, Ontar had set his tower shield next to his leg and slid his backpack down on one shoulder so that he could pull out a torch. Grabbing at some flint and steel, he was about to light the torch's tip when Hatch put a hand on his forearm and whispered, "It will make too much noise." Uttering a quick spell, Hatch passed his hand over the torch and watched as its head suddenly flared up.

"Nice," Ontar said as he handed Hatch the light and repositioned his equipment.

Eager to explore this subterranean world, Wink said, "That light will do nothing but call attention to us. I'll scout ahead and shout if something comes our way. Just be sure to follow me on my signal or I'll be caught in the dark by myself."

Reasoning that Wink's size would make her difficult to spot, the party let her take the lead down the sloping tunnel. It wasn't long before they heard a little whistle that indicated they should follow behind her. The party moved slowly as they descended down the long passage. Keenly aware of the angle they were traversing, everyone diligently watched their footing so as not to fall or risk knocking someone over. Ontar's torch cast long shadows on the surrounding walls, and the big warrior couldn't help but wonder how Wink could have gotten so far from the group without at least some form of light. The answer to this question came when he spotted a dim orange glow flickering at the base of the tunnel.

Echo knew there was something significant with this second light and listened intently for any noises coming from up ahead. Sure enough, she heard the gurgling roar of what could only be some sort of menacing beast. As the party progressed, the animalistic sounds grew louder and were accompanied by the occasional grunts and groans of what was probably a human opponent.

With each passing step, Ontar's visibility improved as he approached the new light source. Thankfully, the tunnel leveled out, and he saw a large hole at its end, with Wink crouched down along a side wall in front of it. The pixie was gazing through the hole into an area filled with activity. Irritated she didn't inform the group about what she was up to, Ontar moved behind her and asked, "Hey, why'd you just disappear like that?"

Wink pointed ahead of her and said, "Look."

Following her finger, the party peered through the hole and was shocked by what they saw. The subterranean space ahead of them was huge and appeared to be littered with the bodies of dark red maazhat. The area was lit by a small torch lying on the ground nearby. Its light barely displayed another tunnel located off on the far wall.

Dominating the deadly surroundings was a massive cave worm that reared back its smooth round head and let out a booming roar from its large circular mouth lined with long pointed teeth. The creature must have been over twenty feet in length with its colorless body revealing many shadowy organs. Covering the worm was a clear, acidic substance that hissed as it inched along the ground. While this acid was definitely potent, it wasn't quite strong enough to prevent the worm from receiving a multitude of nasty gashes scattered all over its body.

These gashes were brought about by the cave worm's primary opponent. Standing before this wretched monster with a spear in one hand and a shield in the other was Krudkur. Exhausted, the imposing warrior was covered in sweat and had a tired but determined look on his face. A few shallow cuts could be seen along his body, but they were nothing compared to the damage he'd dealt to the worm.

Unaware of the party's arrival, the cave worm made a re-gurgitating sound and spat a short stream of acid straight at Krudkur. Ready for this particular attack, he raised his mag-nificent shield to block the deadly acid as it hissed and steamed along its golden face. Unable to get away completely unscathed, Krudkur grunted as drops of the deadly substance burned his arms and legs. Enraged at the failure of its attack, the cave worm lunged towards the puny human, who promptly tried to dodge out of its way.

Ontar had seen enough. Discarding his torch, he and Echo both drew their weapons and moved to attack. Krudkur wasn't exactly an ally, but Ontar felt that no man deserved to face such a terrible beast on his own. Uttering a loud battle cry, he knew that with the number of wounds the creature had already sus-tained, it wouldn't survive long under the full force of a direct assault.

Moving with grace and speed, Echo was the first to attack, delivering a nasty cut deep into the cave worm's elongated side. In fact, the cut was too deep, and the acid that covered the worm's body splattered along the hilt of Echo's sword and burned her weapon hand. Dropping her blade, Echo instinctively tucked the injured appendage under her left arm.

Making sure that he didn't repeat his companion's mistake, Ontar kept his morning star at full length before he struck the cave worms' body. The blow should have been a devastating one, but the cave worm's rubbery hide caused his weapon to bounce off its intended target while inflicting little to no damage whatsoever.

The arrival of new opponents distracted the cave worm from its battle with Krudkur. Seeking to quickly dispose of the pests, the vile beast whipped its massive tail at the elf who had caused it pain. Ontar saw that Echo was preoccupied with her injury and moved to intercept the blow. Bracing himself behind his shield, Ontar was slammed by a heavy attack that nearly knocked him off his feet. Acid coating the cave worm's tail sizzled as it struck Ontar's shield and armor.

Hatch could see the difficulty his companions were having in fighting the cave worm and quickly cast a spell to aid them. Raising his left hand, he felt the ground beneath him tremble as a dozen, five-foot stone spikes rapidly erupted from the earth and impaled the beast in several spots along its lengthy body.

The cave worm gurgled in agony as the spikes pierced its hide and pinned it to a single location. Realizing the need for mobility, the cave worm intentionally endured the pain of slamming itself onto a few more spikes so that its head could touch the ground. Lying flat, the monstrous creature tried to roll off the sharp stones in a single tremendous motion.

Krudkur grinned viciously as he saw the cave worm's hideous round head landed just to the side of where he stood. Ready to finish the beast off, he took his spear and thrust it deeply into the creatures exposed cranium. The monster shook as his weapon easily sliced into its brain. Giving one last defeated gurgle, the cave worm went limp, slowly drooling acid from its now silent mouth.

Wink ran up to the tired warrior, who breathed heavy and wiped sweat from his brow. Gesturing to the bodies around them, she said, "Wow! I can't believe you took on both a cave worm and all these maazhat *by yourself!*"

Smiling slightly, Krudkur had come up with a novel idea on how to carry his discarded torch by skewering it on the end of his spear. "The maazhat used this creature to help make their tunnels. It had to be dealt with," he replied.

Echo flexed her fingers and examined her hand. The acid burn had hurt when she first received it, but Echo had always been a quick healer, and she now believed she could wield her sword once again. Looking over at Ontar, she saw him washing the hilt of her blade off with a waterskin she had given him. Once this was done, he picked up the weapon and handed it to her before replacing the waterskin in her backpack.

"So, how's your hand?" he asked casually.

Echo sheathed her sword. "I think I'll manage. How about you?"

"About the same," Ontar replied as he went to pick up his torch. Together with Hatch, the three decided to go over and talk with Krudkur. Unfortunately, Ontar started the conversation on a sour note. "Ah, Krudkur. From killing thieves to squashing bugs, you must be getting soft as time goes on."

"Not at all," Krudkur replied irritably. "I was merely searching beneath the earth for an opponent who *wouldn't* flee at the first sign of a danger."

Ontar clenched his jaw beneath his helmet and gave Krudkur an icy glare. Echo could tell that things might turn ugly if she didn't speak up so, addressing Krudkur, she said, "I know you probably haven't been down here for very long, but by any chance have you seen two rangers running about?"

Krudkur's expression turned thoughtful. "No, I haven't. Are they of any significance to you?"

"Yes," replied Hatch. "They're my son and granddaughter, and they searched for some underground ruins, thinking the maazhat colony would be the best way to reach them."

"Hmm. They would have had to have been most skilled to delve this deep into the colony undetected," Krudkur mused.

Wink snickered. "Yeah, Thove has a real knack for getting himself into trouble he can't always get out of."

Krudkur nodded. "Very well. We shall face the maazhat together until you find your missing comrades."

"Oh, this should be fun," Ontar grumbled as he made his way towards the exiting tunnel.

Once again, the party found themselves descending a steeply-angled passage. Wink reprised her role as scout (after receiving a lengthy lecture about keeping others apprised of her activities), and the group slowly navigated the uneven ground behind her. Ontar and Echo had never been this deep beneath the earth before, and both were wary of what they could encounter.

Just as the tunnel started to level out, Ontar saw Wink running towards him with a worried look on her face. Coming to a halt and signaling the others to follow suit, he looked down at her and asked, "What did you see?"

"There's a large cavern up ahead that's crawling with maazhat!" Wink exclaimed in dismay.

"What color were they?" Ontar asked afraid of what the answer might be.

"Dark red," Wink replied dismally.

Soldiers, Ontar thought. "This could be a difficult fight."

"Not necessarily," Hatch interjected. "I think I know a spell that might help us to even the odds."

"Well, feel free to use it," Ontar said as he stepped aside to let Hatch pass. Taking the lead, the old wizard curled his left hand into a fist and began an incantation as he advanced towards a circular opening at the base of the tunnel.

Ready to finish his spell, Hatch stepped in front of the opening and stared out into the large cavern that lay before him. Just as Wink had foretold, the cavern was filled with maazhat soldiers that each wielded two sickle-like weapons in their clawed hands. While battle hardened maazhat dominated much of the area's standing room, Hatch noticed that a quarter of the cavern's far right corner was occupied by a dark black chasm. Next to the chasm was another shadowy tunnel where the maazhat probably originated from.

Facing a horde of angry insectoids, Hatch completed his spell and opened his left hand to reveal a slightly rounded flame that resembled the firebolt he had cast earlier. The only difference was that Hatch held the flame until it grew to a size slightly larger than the spell caster's head. This action instantly attracted the maazhats' attention, and they immediately advanced towards him. Unafraid, Hatch tossed his fireball over the maazhats' heads and straight towards the center of the cavern. Upon reaching its destination, the lethal projectile exploded in a massive burst of fiery destruction that consumed his shocked enemies.

Stepping back from the cavern's entrance, the party squinted as a wave of light and heat briefly washed over them. Moving cautiously, the group peered back into the smoldering area to assess the spell's damage. Everywhere they looked, they saw the charred bodies of dead maazhat lying prone on the ground...or at least that's what they initially thought.

This notion changed when they heard the *crack* of a whip echoing loudly throughout the cavern. Following the noise's direction, the party saw that a fearsome black maazhat had emerged from the shadowy tunnel across from where they stood. Ontar remembered Bulak saying that any sizable maazhat raiding party was usually led by a dark-colored leader. Carrying a tan whip fashioned out of a large root, Ontar guessed that this particular maazhat was probably the one in charge.

Cracking its whip a second time, the leader began shouting to its soldiers in their strange clicking language. Much to everyone's amazement, many of the charred maazhat grabbed their weapons and slowly stood up. Apparently, while some of the insectoids had been killed by Hatch's fireball, the majority of them were protected from the flames by their hard exoskeletons.

"Hmm, I guess that spells more effective against human opponents," Hatch mused before Krudkur shoved him aside.

The seasoned warrior could tell the maazhat hadn't organized yet, and he certainly wasn't about to give them the chance to do so. Flinging his torch off the top of his spear and into the cavern, Krudkur made a mad dash for the leader. Unfortunately, one of the maazhat soldiers stepped in front of him with its sickles crossed defensively. Krudkur raised his shield and slammed straight into the soldier, trying in vain to knock it over.

The maazhat didn't budge. Bracing itself on four spindly legs the soldier effectively withstood Krudkur's assault. That is until the powerful human used his spear to jab at the maazhat's front legs. Falling onto Krudkur's shield, the soldier felt its nemesis push forward and slide under its abdomen. Then, in an amazing feat of strength, Krudkur flipped the maazhat over his shield and onto the ground behind him. Having successfully gotten past the first soldier, Krudkur scowled when he saw that more maazhat had arrived to take its place.

Following Krudkur's example, Ontar and Echo immediately entered into the fray. Picking an opponent, Ontar charged at a nearby maazhat with his morning star in full swing. Refusing to go down without a fight, the soldier raised his right sickle to parry the attack. Ontar's weapon shattered the sickle upon impact and left him in a strong position to defeat his enemy.

Undeterred, the maazhat used his left sickle to hook Ontar's tower shield and pull it down. Then utilizing its natural weapons, the soldier moved in close and spread its oversized mandibles in a vicious attempt to cut the warrior's head off!

Thinking quickly, Ontar stiffened his neck and brought his helmet to bear against the maazhat with a nasty head butt. Stumbling back, the soldier felt its skull crack as blood trickled down from the wound. Ontar felt a little bit wobbly, but he managed to regain his senses first. Spinning his morning star, he struck a lethal second blow to the maazhat along its upper thorax.

Not to be outdone by her human companions, Echo advanced upon a maazhat whose arms were spread in a battle stance. Capitalizing on her natural speed, she swung her sword in a wide arc towards the soldier's head. The attack should have been fatal, but at the last second, the maazhat's forelegs dropped, sparing it from death. Echo tried to adjust her swing to counter the maneuver but only managed to clip the top of the maazhat's head and sever one of its antennae.

Unfazed by the wound, the soldier used its hind legs to push itself forward and hooked its sickles behind the elf's thighs. Jerking its arms back, the maazhat's weapons sliced through Echo's leather greaves and gave her legs a wicked pair of shallow cuts.

Gritting her teeth in pain, Echo was afraid the maazhat might actually try to chop her legs off! In order to prevent this from happening, she took the hilt of her sword and slammed it into the soldiers exposed antenna stump. The maazhat shook his head violently as the stump slammed straight into its brain. Unable to stand, Echo ran the soldier through before collapsing to the ground.

Watching his comrades fight from within the cavern's entrance Hatch surveyed the battle and waited for his chance to strike. It didn't take long before he spotted a group maazhat who tried to surround his fellow companions in an attempt to overwhelm them. Casting a spell that would foil their attack, Hatch waved his left arm in front of him and watched as five of the ambushing soldiers collapsed to the ground in a deep slumber. Clutching his staff in both hands, Hatch then ran out to meet his unconscious foes and ensure they would never wake up.

Ontar was engrossed in the combat around him. It had been a long time since he faced such a tenacious enemy, and he was just about to square off against two maazhat at once when he suddenly felt the harsh snap of a whip that coiled about his left arm just above his shield. Swinging his morning star in a wide circle above his head to keep the other maazhat at bay, Ontar looked over his shoulder and saw the leader was the one who had ensnared him. Attempting to shake off the whip, Ontar noticed the fiendish weapon constricted around his arm and squeezed what had once been protective armor into his flesh.

Blocking a soldier's attack with his weapon, Krudkur noticed Ontar's shield arm going limp out of the corner of his eye and knew the whip was to blame. Choosing to aid his armored ally, he skillfully killed the maazhat he was fighting and found the torch that he had tossed into the chamber earlier. Whacking it upwards with the head of his spear, the torch struck the leader square between the eyes. The leader's whip immediately went limp, which allowed Ontar to resume the battle.

Echo felt the warm blood trickle down her legs as she laid with her back to the ground. If given a chance, she would have attempted to bandage her wounds were it not for a vindictive maazhat attacking her in this weakened state. Raising her shield while propping herself up with her weapon arm, Echo desperately attempted to block the repeated sickle attacks, knowing full well she was particularly vulnerable.

The soldier was about to come at her again with another series of blows when, out of nowhere, a huge green apple the size of a barstool suddenly popped into existence and hovered over Echo's body. Confused, the maazhat tried slicing at the apple only to find that its sickles passed right through the strange fruit.

Realizing that it was an illusion, Echo quickly repositioned herself so she could swing her blade and sever the maazhat's thorax from its abdomen. As her opponent went down and the apple disappeared, Echo got to her knees and searched the area for her hidden savior. She soon spotted Wink standing by the chasm, pointing excitedly off to her left.

Glancing in that direction, Echo gasped as she saw the leader's whip instantly wrap around her neck. Possessing a life of its own the deadly weapon immediately strangled her. Refusing to be beaten, Echo took her sword and started hacking at the whips end until she finally managed to cut it off. Coughing hard she watched as the unnerved leader slowly withdrew from her presence.

Hatch had done well in killing his enemies. The sleeping maazhat were completely defenseless as one after another he ended their lives. Approaching the last of his victims, Hatch raised his staff to strike an easy death blow when, out of nowhere, the supposedly sleeping soldier decided to reach out with its clawed hands and grab the bottom of his weapon. Caught completely off-guard, Hatch could only watch as the maazhat jerked his staff downward and cut it in two with its razor-sharp mandibles.

Dropping his now useless weapon, Hatch uttered a single spell word while the soldier retrieved its sickles. Lashing out at the wizard, the maazhat made an angry clicking sound when its weapons were deflected by some sort of invisible barrier. The soldier tried again and again to get past the barrier, but each attempt was met with failure. Hatch kept calm during this violent barrage knowing full well that, as long as he maintained his concentration, no physical attack could ever harm him. Unfortunately, the amount of additional focus required by his spell also prevented him from casting anything else that would be necessary in defeating his opponent.

Thankfully, Ontar came to the old man's aid, swinging his morning star in a successful back attack. The distracted maazhat was quickly killed, which gave Ontar and Hatch a chance to go and tend to Echo's wounds. Kneeling beside his injured companion, Ontar withdrew his weapon and tried to prop her up, telling Hatch to pull some bandages from his backpack.

While this was taking place, Krudkur had eliminated the last of the maazhat soldiers and proceeded to advance upon their leader. Facing his nemesis, the leader cracked its whip in a stinging strike that opened a bloody gash over Krudkur's left knee, causing him to stumble. Attempting to disarm the menacing fighter, the leader chose to lash its whip around Krudkur's right forearm.

Keeping hold of his spear while the whip constricted, Krudkur decided to use the maazhat's weapon against it by pulling his arm back and throwing the leader off balance. Not falling for

Krudkur's tactic, the leader let go of his whip and denied the warrior a chance to carry out his plan. Krudkur then smiled as the unarmed insectoid suddenly realized its mistake and desperately dove for one of its dead comrade's sickles. Refusing to give the foolish maazhat even a remote chance at survival, Krudkur tossed his deadly spear and watched it plunge into the leader's heart.

❖❖❖

Waiting until the last maazhat had perished, Wink cautiously surveyed her surroundings before running over to where Echo rested. Sliding some leather greaves back onto her now bandaged legs, Echo saw Wink coming and gave her a tired greeting. "Hey, thanks for your help in distracting that maazhat. I didn't even know you could use that sort of magic."

Wink grinned. "I've got all sorts of tricks to play on my enemies."

Offering his hand so that Echo could pull herself up, Ontar made sure the wood elf was steady on her feet before he released her. He then went to retrieve his torch while saying to Wink, "You don't happen to have a trick that would help us find Thove and Kit any faster now do you?"

"Not a trick necessarily, but I did find a grappling hook with a long rope attached to it at the edge of the chasm," Wink added excitedly.

"Can you show us where it is?" Hatch inquired.

"Sure, follow me," Wink said as she led the party over to the chasm.

Hatch spotted the grappling hook and knelt beside it. "This has to be Thove's, and if I were to venture a guess, I would say that Uch-na-Mach probably rests at the bottom of this chasm."

"Then you should go to him," came a heavily-accented voice from behind. Krudkur stood near the party with a bandaged leg and a torch back on top of his spear.

"But what about you?" Echo asked. The warrior's skill in combat had come in handy, and she hated the thought of losing the extra help."

Krudkur shook his head. "The bulk of the maazhat forces have been destroyed. My task now is to go and kill their queen, along with any who still remain to protect her. However, in thanks for your assistance, I shall stand guard by this grapple until you all have safely reached the chasm's floor."

"Fine by me," Ontar said as he moved towards the grapple.

"Wait," Hatch warned as he stood up. "I know an easier way to reach the chasm's floor."

"How?" Ontar asked suspiciously.

"Jump," Hatch replied. He uttered a spell word before Ontar had a chance to question him further. The old wizard then gestured towards the chasm. "There, the landing spell has been cast. All you have to do is jump off the chasm's edge, and you shall reach the ground unharmed."

Ontar's eyes widened in disbelief. "Are you kidding me?"

Wink climbed up Hatch's cloak and onto his shoulder. "Don't worry, Onnie, the spell's completely safe. I've had it cast on me at least a hundred times before."

Somehow, Ontar doubted that, but he figured that if he jumped close enough to the grapple, he could probably catch hold of the rope before anything really bad happened. "Eh, why not," he muttered to himself. So, shrugging and keeping a firm grip on his torch, Ontar took a deep breath and stepped off the edge of the chasm.

Echo immediately went to the chasm's edge to see if Ontar was alright. Much to her relief, there were no shouts of terror or sickening thuds coming from below. She merely watched as Ontar and his flickering torch slowly floated down into the darkness. Feeling a little more comfortable with Hatch's magic, she decided to have the landing spell cast upon her before hesitantly jumping in after Ontar.

Watching their companions' descent, Hatch and Wink turned to Krudkur. Bowing slightly, Hatch said, "I can't thank you enough for helping me to find my family."

Krudkur's expression was blank. "Our objectives briefly happened to coincide. Should that change in the future, do not expect to count me as one of your allies."

"I understand," Hatch said as he cast the landing spell on himself. Turning around, he and Wink jumped into the chasm.

"You don't think he'd ever try to hurt us, do you?" Wink asked from the hood of Hatch's cloak.

"I don't know?" Hatch replied solemnly.

Chapter Ten

"Kit...Kit, where are you?" Thove asked as he raised his torch to get a better view of the surrounding area. The ruins of Uch-na-Mach had been built across a vast subterranean chasm where the stone foundations of crumbling buildings were virtually all that remained of the society that once resided there. Strolling near a dried-out riverbed, which crossed the city's lower half, Thove saw a few small fragments of a dilapidated wall that still managed to line the settlement's perimeter. Suffering from the ravages of time much of the city's remains had been swallowed by the unyielding sides of the chasm's incrementally eroding rock. If given another thousand years or so, Thove believed that this place would probably disappear from the world altogether.

Spotting the light from Kit's torch near a long dark tunnel, Thove heard her call out. "Dad, I'm over here!"

"Kit, we've already explored that tunnel, and it's a dead end," Thove complained as he approached his daughter. An attractive young woman in her early twenties, with deep blue eyes, Kit had long blonde hair parted up the middle and curled slightly inwards at her shoulders. Possessing an average build for someone her age, she wore a dark green cloak over her light blue shirt tucked into a pair of tan pants.

Equipped to handle any of the possible dangers within these underground ruins, Kit protected herself with some brown leather armor that covered her torso and matched the weapon belt around her waist. Making sure she always had a way to defend herself, Thove insisted that Kit keep a dagger in her boots while she carried both a sword and quiver full of arrows in her weapon belt. The arrows were meant for a longbow, which was slung across her shoulder beneath a well-worn backpack.

Looking down at a little white mouse, which sat on its haunches and skittishly sniffed the air, Kit said, "Dad, there's something wrong. Every time I pass by this tunnel, Whiskers gets jumpy."

"Do you think the maazhat might have followed us?" Thove asked.

Kit always appreciated her father's faith in the instincts of animals. A middle-aged man with far too many worry lines on his face, Thove had short blond hair that partially covered his brown leather headband. Dressed in a light green shirt with a pair of blue pants, Thove's boots, armor, and other equipment were almost exactly like that of his daughters.

Afraid that his question was a valid one, Kit replied, "I don't know? Should we check?"

Thove shook his head. "If there is something in there then our torches will immediately give us away." Handing her his torch, he drew his sword and said, "I'll go ahead and call for help if there's trouble."

Watching him enter the tunnel, Kit glanced down at her pet mouse and said, "Whiskers, go hide. I'll come find you when it's safe."

The rodent immediately obeyed her command.

Moving silently along a tunnel that slanted upwards, Thove squinted as the light faded behind him. Reaching a point where he couldn't see anymore, he was about to turn back when his boot splashed a tiny trickle of water. *That's odd, there wasn't any water down here before?* he thought. Listening carefully, he soon heard an eerie scraping sound coming from the darkness up ahead. Suddenly, out of nowhere, the scraping sound turned into what could only be described as the crash of rushing water!

Turning around, Thove attempted to flee from the oncoming torrent only to find himself swept up in it. Losing his sword as he flailed beneath the water, Thove felt something smack against him as the current brought him back to the tunnel's entrance. Alarmed by all the water that splashed around her boots, Kit watched it ebb onto the floor of the ruins while scattering everything that had been caught in its wake. Raising her torches, she saw her dad lying on the ground next to the bodies of maazhat and men alike.

Coughing as he got onto his hands and knees, Thove was about to get up when a maazhat next to him reached out and dug a clawed hand into his ankle! Shocked to hear her father's cry of pain, Kit charged towards the maazhat and beat it with her two torches. With its exoskeleton already cracked in multiple places, Kit had little difficulty reaching the creature's innards and burning them until it stopped moving. Afterwards, she knelt and asked, "Dad, are you alright."

Thove grimaced as he touched his broken and bloody ankle. "I can't move my foot!"

Thinking of how she could help, Kit tensed when she saw that some of the zombies and maazhat started to get up! Tossing one of the torches, she slipped her free arm under Thove's and said, "We have to get out of here!" Pulling him up into a semi-standing position, Kit and her father fled from the increasingly active undead.

Narcos and Marcain made their way down the tunnel into Uch-na-Mach. Carrying a torch for his despised master, Marcain heard their boots splash through countless little puddles as they entered the ruined city. Finding that most of the nearby zombies had gotten up and now stood waiting to serve, Narcos noticed that both a smoldering torch and stray sword were scattered among the undead.

"We're not alone. Marcain take some zombies and search the center of the city for any signs of life. I'll have the maazhat with me as we make our way around the ruin's edge."

Unsure of what he'd uncover during his hunt, Marcain asked, "What should I do if I see someone?"

Narcos had little use for explorers and simply told Marcain to, "Kill them."

"As you wish," Marcain grumbled reluctantly while drawing forth his sword.

Watching the light fade as Marcain headed out, Narcos touched his temple and cast a spell that allowed him to see no matter how dark things got. He then began his own journey along the chasm's walls.

"Whiskers, is that you?" Kit asked as she heard the mouse squeaking by the corner of a stone foundation just tall enough for her to hide behind. Setting Thove down along the wall, she told the rodent, "Good job," while dropping her torch so she could reach into her father's backpack and get some bandages. Wrapping his leg, she said, "I don't understand. I could have sworn those bodies were dead when the water carried them in. How could that maazhat have attacked you?"

"Do you remember what Chairbis told you about the undead?" Thove asked.

Kit nodded. "Yes."

"Good, because that is exactly what we're up against, and why your grandfather insisted on making sure that we carried enchanted swords with us," Thove replied.

"But why are they here?" Kit wondered.

Wincing as she tied his bandage tight, Thove could only say, "I don't know?"

Adding to their conversation in his own little way, Whiskers' ears twitched, and he ran about Kit's feet while squeaking wildly. Drawing her sword, Kit said, "Something's coming!"

"Hand me your torch!" Thove instructed. "If they get behind the wall, then it will be the only thing I have to defend myself."

Kit did as she was asked, but then clutched the hilt of her sword with both hands and boldly proclaimed, "I won't let them hurt you!"

Listening to the sound of shuffling feet coming her way, Kit saw a zombie peek out from behind the foundation wall and raise its arms to attack her. Swinging her sword, she chopped off the zombie's head only to fall back as its hands tried to take a swipe at her. Leaning forward, Thove jabbed his torch into the zombie's leg and caused it to fall over. Kit then hacked at the fiend until it stopped moving.

"Well done," came a voice from behind the wall. "If I were able to, I would have loved to join you in slaughtering every last zombie in sight."

"Who's there!?" Kit asked as she headed towards the voice.

Seeing her shadow move in the torch light, Marcain quickly shouted, "Stay hidden! I don't want to fight you if I don't have to."

Holding her battle stance, Kit asked again, "Who are you?"

Letting out a sad sigh, Marcain responded by saying, "I am Lord Marcain D'Shad of Lareder, and I have been forced against my will to serve an evil necromancer named Narcos."

Kit scowled when she heard this. "Why?"

"Because Narcos seeks to unleash a demon called Zattermox that is sealed by a magic artifact somewhere within these ruins," Marcain explained.

"He must be talking about Spirit Slayer," Thove assumed.

Marcain nodded in understanding. "Ah, you two must have come here in search of the artifact itself."

"We have," Thove acknowledged. "But what will happen if this demon is freed?"

Marcain cringed at the thought. "Narcos claims that Zattermox will lead him to ancient relics of untold power."

"Do you think the demon will share his knowledge willingly?" Thove inquired.

Lowering his sword, Marcain said, "No, but Narcos can use his black magic to enslave Zattermox just like he used it on me."

Growing curious, Kit asked, "Why are you telling us this?"

"Because someone needs to stop him," Marcain urged. "And if you are unwilling to, then I pray that you'll find someone who can."

Unable to fight the necromancer herself, Kit said, "My father is hurt, and we need to get out of here."

"I understand," Marcain replied. "The city's center is full of zombies. If you flee opposite of where I'm standing, then you should be able to reach the ruin's edge while avoiding Narcos. However, you must tell me how you entered the ruins in the first place."

"Why?" Kit asked, one eyebrow raised.

Marcain's response was bitter. "Because Narcos knows you're here, and if I'm to tell him that you've already escaped, then I need to know how you did it."

"There's a hole at the top of the chasm, and we used a rope and grappling hook to get here," Kit replied.

Smiling when he heard this, Marcain said, "Good. I'll try to keep the zombies distracted while you make your escape. Just don't leave until after I'm out of sight."

"Thank you, milord," Thove said in appreciation. "I never expected to find a friendly voice in a place like this."

Turning to leave, Marcain replied, "All my life people have made sacrifices on my behalf. If I can return the favor in even a small way, then maybe those sacrifices will be worth it."

Ontar heard his cloak flutter as a cool draft buffeted him from the chasm below. It was dark in this foreboding environment, and if the light from his torch didn't touch upon the rope dangling next to him, then he'd swear that he was slowly floating down into a bottomless pit. The fact that he was floating at all was a little peculiar, but then again, as long as the spell held, he wasn't going to complain.

Seeking out his next destination, Ontar was relieved when his torch's flickering flame finally revealed the ancient city of Uch-na-Mach...or, in fairness, what was left of it. Eagerly awaiting his chance to have solid ground beneath him, Ontar thought that it might be best to wait for his companions to arrive before searching for Hatch's son and granddaughter. Thankfully, it didn't take long for everyone to gather together and discuss how best to proceed.

"We should try to find the city's castle," suggested Hatch. "Chances are, it would be the first place they'd head towards if they wanted to retrieve Spirit Slayer."

"Remember, though, they don't know we're down here," Ontar warned. "Let's make sure our presence is known so they don't try to ambush us."

Echo frowned at this idea. "Are you sure we should be calling attention to ourselves? What if there's something else lurking down here that might try to attack us?"

Ontar shrugged. "Don't worry. I'm sure that I can handle anything that comes our way."

"That's right!" Wink exclaimed as she sat on Hatch's shoulder and nudged him. "I just love it when my man takes charge." She then whistled a light-hearted song that really didn't fit their ominous environment.

Staying close to Ontar to maximize the use of his light, the party advanced through the ruins while keeping an eye out for the two rangers.

Echo grew antsy. From what she could tell, there was no sign of anyone or anything in this desolate place. Eager to reach the castle, she casually glanced at her surroundings and saw a little white mouse running along the foundation of a building she walked past. Watching the little creature go, she remarked, "Well, that's odd. I don't think I've ever seen vermin this far below ground before."

Hatch and Wink both spun her direction. "Where?" Hatch asked with far more interest than Echo expected."

"There," she said, pointing to the mouse.

Wink's face brightened as she caught a glimpse of the rodent. "Is that Nibbles!" she cried out enthusiastically before sliding down the side of Hatch's cloak. Sitting on its haunches the mouse stared at her as she approached and gave a little squeak.

"Huh?" Echo muttered as she shot Hatch a questioning look.

Hatch smirked. "Nibbles was Kit's pet mouse, and she's never gone anywhere without him."

Well, that explains the maze in her room, Ontar thought before saying, "So, if Nibbles is nearby, then so are Kit and Thove."

"Exactly," Hatch added in agreement.

Wink knelt by the mouse and frowned. "Hey, wait a minute Nibbles was brown, this little guy is all white."

"Maybe she got a new mouse," Ontar guessed. "It has been a while since you last saw each other."

"I suppose it's possible," Wink conceded. "Come on, Mr. Mouse, let's go find mama."

Squeaking loudly, the rodent skittered off in the direction of a large stone foundation with a set of crumbling steps attached to it. Wink followed in hot pursuit, with the rest of the party close behind her.

Echo saw their supposed guide climb to the top of the steps with Wink. Normally, this action wouldn't have been any cause for alarm, but as Wink ascended the stairs, Echo noticed that a dark figure with its sword drawn lurked in the shadows slightly to the left of the distracted pixie. *The mouse is just a lure!* Echo realized before calling out. "Wink, stop!"

Heeding her companion's command with surprising speed, Wink halted in her tracks and looked around for any possible threat.

Ontar could tell there was trouble by the tone in Echo's voice. Switching the torch to his left hand, he immediately reached for his morning star. Ready to draw forth his weapon and defeat whatever it was that hid from view, Ontar stayed his hand when the figure Echo had spotted cautiously stepped out into the light.

Shocked by the lovely vision that stood before him, Ontar saw Kit pointing her sword at the party while focusing her attention on the pixie next to her. "Wink, is that you?"

Wink smiled and waved. "Hi, Kit. So, who's your new mouse?"

"His name is Whiskers," Kit replied uncertainly as she lowered her sword. "What are you doing here?"

"We've come to bring you and your father home," Hatch stated boldly as he stepped in front of Ontar and Echo.

Kit's eyes widened in disbelief. "Grandpa!? I don't believe it?"

"Yes, my dear, and thanks to these two brave heroes, I have once again gained my freedom," Hatch said while gesturing to Ontar and Echo.

Ontar appreciated the hero comment, and with a free hand, removed his helmet so that he could flash Kit one of his most charming smiles. "Hello there, milady. My name is Ontar Liongrave, and it's a pleasure to finally meet you."

Echo nodded in agreement. "And I'm Echo Karashenmahagensea. I studied your map to find the maazhat colony and was really impressed by the amount of detail you put into it."

"Thanks," Kit replied, "but I wouldn't have even known what to look for without help from my father." This whole conversation was very surreal for Kit. All her life, she had heard that elves were a bunch of weak, snobby, tree-huggers. Now, she found herself not only being complimented by one, but one that happened to have rescued her grandfather from imprisonment.

"So, is Thove around here?" Wink asked with hands on her hips.

"I'm over here," came a man's voice from behind the stairs.

Wink climbed to the top of the crumbling steps with Whiskers and casually looked down. "Oh, there you are," she uttered before pressing her hat to her head and jumping out of sight. Thove then made a mild grunting sound that everyone assumed came from when she landed on him.

Kit sheathed her sword and went to retrieve Whiskers. If Wink and her grandfather both trusted Ontar and Echo, then she saw no reason to be wary of them. Beckoning the party to follow her, she led them behind the stairs and into the full view of her father.

Thove sat with his back to the steps and Wink was in his lap. A torch lying on the ground next to him revealed that his leg was bandaged tightly around the ankle.

Hatch was the first to react to the sight of his wounded son. "Thove, my boy, are you alright?"

"Yeah, Dad, I'll be okay, but there are far more wicked things down here than I ever imagined," Thove warned.

Quirking an eyebrow, Hatch asked, "Like what?"

This question prompted Thove and Kit to reveal what they learned from their encounter with Marcain and the undead. Amazed by what she heard, Echo said, "Lord Marcain is here? I wonder if Narcos needed him to find this place."

"And if he's a slave, then I'm sure he'll blame us," Ontar added.

Echo tensed when she heard this. "It's not our fault. We had no idea what he planned to do with Marcain, and even if we did know, we still failed to deliver him. The fact that he got himself captured doesn't have anything to do with us."

"I doubt he'll see it that way," Ontar retorted.

Trying to piece their conversation together, Kit prodded them a little. "How did the two of you meet Lord Marcain?" The question prompted Ontar and Echo to reveal their previous encounter with him.

When they had finished, Hatch said, "Whatever your past experience with Lord Marcain might have been, it doesn't change the fact that Thove is injured and has to get out of here." Looking at the rest of the party, he said, "Everybody, gather close, and I'll teleport us to safety."

Echo balked at the idea. "Whoa, wait a minute! Hatch, I'm glad you found your family, but I didn't come all this way just to go back empty handed."

"You want the sword, don't you?" Thove guessed.

"That's right," Echo declared.

Kit gave Echo an odd look. "Aren't you worried about Narcos and the undead?"

"Nah, she's too greedy," Wink quipped, prompting a scowl from Echo.

Thove took the pixies joke seriously. "Lord Marcain believed that Spirit Slayer was used to seal a demon called Zattermox. Are you really prepared to face such a threat if it's unleashed?"

"I can slay anything that's weak enough for Narcos to control," Ontar assured him.

"And if he can't, then Hatch will be there to aid us with his magic," Echo added. "After all, even freedom comes at a price."

"Yes," Hatch replied warily, "I suppose it does."

Ontar looked to Kit and asked, "Where can we find Spirit Slayer?"

Pointing them in the right direction, Kit said, "In a castle over there. Most of the building is buried in solid rock, but its entrance is still visible."

"Is the entrance guarded?" Ontar asked, leery of what he might find down here.

Kit shook her head. "Not when we first got here, but with Narcos present, I can't be sure."

"We should be able to handle a couple of zombies," Ontar muttered to himself.

Echo turned to Hatch with a serious look in her eyes. "I imagine you want to take Thove and Kit back home. How long will it take before you return?"

"It will be late when we arrive at Habed," Hatch explained. "I'll stay the night and return for you in the morning. That is, unless you want to come with us?"

Echo shook her head. "Ontar and I will stay here and make sure Narcos doesn't run off with *my* sword."

"We will?" Ontar asked with a slightly disappointed look on his face.

"Yes!" Echo asserted.

"As you wish," Hatch said as he stood by Thove and Wink, then beckoned for Kit to join them. Gathering her pet mouse, Kit huddled together with her family while Hatch began casting his teleportation spell.

Wink looked over at Ontar and waved. "Bye, Onnie. I'll see you soon."

Ontar didn't have a chance to give her a response. The moment Hatch finished his incantation, he and his loved ones vanished from the warrior's sight, causing a slight rush of air to fill the space they had once occupied.

Unbelievable, Narcos thought as he stood in a large stone chamber void of any signs of habitation. Having found the castle where Zattermox was supposedly sealed, the necromancer was thoroughly disappointed to discover the foyer's interior walls merged with the chasm's hard rock to block off any passage that might have led deeper into the building's interior. Frustrated by this turn of events, he left the foyer through a large archway and stepped out onto a broad flight of stairs covered by undead maazhat.

Looking out over the ruins of Uch-na-Mach, Narcos saw Marcain approach the steps with a cadre of zombies at his side. "Report," he said sternly.

Marcain secretly delighted in giving the necromancer bad news. "I'm afraid that whoever lurked in these ruins has fled upon our arrival. I found a rope dangling from a hole at the top of the chasm."

Glancing at the chasm's roof, Narcos saw Ontar's faint flickering torch light as he magically floated to the ground below. "It appears that our would-be explorers have returned with reinforcements."

Could they have gotten help already? Marcain thought. "What should we do?"

"You will guard the castle steps with these undead while I watch from the ruins to see what we're up against," Narcos instructed. "Say nothing of my presence."

Climbing the stairs, Marcain reluctantly replied, "As you command."

The light from Echo's torch burned steadily as she sat on the ground beside it and meditated. Pacing within the foundation of a ruined building, Ontar took over the watch while his companion recuperated. Both he and Echo had an interesting time while waiting for Hatch to return. This was because Narcos had gotten tired of waiting at the castle and sent out his zombies to scour the city for them. While dangerous as a group, the zombies were now scattered randomly about the ruins and easy to dispatch when they were encountered. In fact, Echo had brought down two of them while Ontar slept.

Patience does have its virtue, Ontar mused as he thought about whittling away at the necromancer's forces. Hearing the sound of footsteps shuffling his way, he raised his shield and spun his morning star. However, the zombie that came into view proved to be a little unnerving since it turned out to be Bulak! Remembering the mercenary as a man who disliked Krudkur and taught him about the maazhat, this pitiful figure was a pale shadow of his former self. Raising its arms to attack, the zombie's chest had been caved in beneath its scale armor, and a chunk of its skull was missing to reveal the brains inside.

Repulsed by what he saw, Ontar wrapped the chain of his weapon around Bulak's wrist and pulled him in to be bashed by his shield. The zombie quickly fell to the ground, where Ontar repeatedly struck at it until the wretched fiend had stopped moving. *Poor bastard,* Ontar thought. *Hopefully, you'll stay dead this time.*

"Another zombie?" Echo asked as she awoke from her meditation.

Ontar nodded. "Yeah, he was a mercenary I met back at the tavern. He and his buddies were hired to kill the maazhat, but it looks like Narcos got the drop on them."

Grabbing the torch as she stood up, Echo said, "His days as a mercenary were numbered. Krudkur was going to finish off the remaining maazhat once and for all, which would force the remaining mercenaries to find a different line of work."

"Yeah, but Narcos took away his ability to make that choice, and his life," Ontar argued. "Personally, I think he deserved better than that."

Suddenly, a blast of displaced air caused Echo's torch to flicker as Hatch reappeared before his companions. Looking down at the zombies on the ground, he said, "My goodness, I thought you were going to wait for my return before attacking the undead."

Handing him her torch so she could draw forth her sword and shield Echo replied, "We did, these three just got tired of waiting."

Ontar noticed Hatch was alone and asked, "Hey, where's Wink?"

Hatch shrugged. "She decided to stay back and spend some time with Thove and Kit."

"Oh well, if there's no more reason to stick around here, then I suggest that we all head towards the castle," Ontar declared as the trio embarked on their journey.

Walking at a brisk pace across the ruins of Uch-na-Mach, the party arrived at a broad flight of stairs that led up to a towering archway that served as the castle's entrance. Covering these stairs was a host of undead maazhat that seemed to gather around none other than Lord Marcain himself. Holding his sword in one hand and a torch in the other, the perpetually tired nobleman had seen the group approach and said in a nasty tone, "So, it looks like the dirty thieves have switched from kidnapping to grave robbery. May I assume that your new master here has come to steal an ancient sword from these ruins?"

Echo noticed that Marcain carried himself far more regally then Rolit and cursed herself for not seeing the peasant for who he really was. "Lord Marcain...Hatch is nothing like Narcos. In fact, you even helped his son and granddaughter escape when they were being hunted by zombies."

"Yet you *did* serve Narcos," Marcain pointed out.

Echo nodded. "Yes, but—"

Marcain interrupted her. "And you *did* kill my guardian before delivering a trusted friend into his clutches now, didn't you!"

Echo didn't like the noble's tone, but grudgingly replied with a simple, "Yes."

"Because of your actions, Rolit not only died but was also brought back to tell Narcos where my beloved and I were located!" Marcain fumed.

Echo tried to defend herself. "We didn't know he was going to do that."

"But it wouldn't have mattered if you did!" Marcain roared. "You intended on bringing me to that monster! While you may try to hide behind the incompetence of your failure, it doesn't change the fact that because of your actions, Narcos not only enslaved me, but he also killed the woman I loved AND our unborn child!"

"Incompetence!" Echo snarled. "Ontar and I were hired to do a job, and while we may have failed at our task, at least we tried, which is way more than you ever did!"

Marcain wasn't used to having a peasant talk back to him. "Excuse me!"

"You sent a soldier and a peasant to their death because you were too much of a coward to face us yourself," Echo argued. "If you had joined your guardian to fight us in battle, then maybe the two of you could have been victorious and gone on to live life as you saw fit."

"Not likely," Ontar snickered under his breath.

Echo continued to speak, "For that matter, if Ontar and I had killed you in battle, then we would have nothing to give Narcos. This means that your friend, lover, and unborn child would still be alive today were it not for your *selfish cowardice!*"

"How dare you insinuate that I killed Lomana!" Marcain raged.

"You can run from us all you like, but you can't run from the truth," Echo shot back.

Touching Ontar's shoulder plate, Hatch whispered, "Keep him talking while I cast a spell."

Ontar overheard the old man utter an incantation and tried to stall. "Marcain, you can still have vengeance for the ones you lost. Tell us where Narcos is so that we can end his life and give you back your freedom."

Infuriated by their conversation, Marcain couldn't have told them where Narcos was even if he wanted to. "Do you really think I would trust someone like you?"

"Marcain, I'm offering you a chance to get back at Narcos for what he's done," Ontar stated.

Pointing his sword at the warrior, Marcain said, "Narcos wouldn't have been able to do anything to me if it wasn't for you… and I will make you suffer for what you've done!"

Marcain's threat seemed genuine, but his rage-induced argument had distracted him long enough for Hatch to complete his spell. Suddenly, a tremor shook the stairs that Marcain and the undead maazhat stood on, followed by massive cracks that shot across the steps in all directions. Struggling to maintain his balance, Marcain let out a startled yelp as the entire stairway collapsed into rubble, sending a plume of dust into the air. Seeing that everyone on the stairs had fallen over, Hatch pointed to the mess while telling Ontar and Echo to, "Get them!"

Surging over the rubble, Ontar and Echo wasted no time in eliminating the prone undead. Surprised by what just happened, Marcain got to his hands and knees but coughed from all the dust he inhaled. Hacking away at a nearby maazhat, Echo heard the young noble and kicked a rock at his head while it was still close to the ground. Knocked out cold by a blow to the brow, Marcain could do nothing to stop the slaughter of the undead around him.

Ontar finished off his last foe, then came to stand over Marcain's unconscious figure. "Should we kill him?"

"No," Hatch replied as he slowly made his way over the rubble.

Echo frowned when she heard this. "Why not? If we let him live, he'll just try to come after us again."

"Not if we kill his master first," Hatch countered. "Marcain kept my son and granddaughter from being hunted by undead and indirectly provided us with information on Narcos's intentions. I say we show him mercy in the hopes that, after we kill Narcos, he will be able to let his vendetta against you go."

"We did contribute to his current situation," Ontar conceded. "And, personally, I don't like killing someone who can't fight back."

Echo rolled her eyes when she heard this. "The man blames us for ruining his life. I don't think sparing him now or killing Narcos will change his mind in the slightest."

"Be careful not to turn into a villain that's worse than the one we're already fighting," Hatch warned as he continued his climb towards the large archway.

"Say's the man who's been locked away in a dungeon for the past five years," Echo grumbled while following Ontar and Hatch through the castle's entrance.

Stepping into the foyer, Ontar's shoulders drooped when he saw that it was empty. "Huh, it looks like Narcos isn't here."

"And neither is the sword," Echo said.

Hatch raised his torch to get a clear view of both the chamber's natural and manmade walls. "I figured the sword wouldn't be here. If it was, then Thove and Kit would have found it by now."

"Which means Narcos is waiting for us to get it so that he can ambush us with undead when we exit the castle," Ontar assumed.

Hatch smirked when he heard this. "Too bad he doesn't realize that I can teleport us out of here the moment we have the blade."

"If we can find it," Ontar noted.

Echo was not going to be beaten. "Hatch, do you have a spell that can help us pass through this rock?"

Hatch held the torch close to his face. "I do, but it won't do us any good if we don't have a destination in mind."

"Leave that to me," Echo stated as she moved to the center of the chamber. Closing her eyes, she raised her sword close to her face and began an incantation that Searce had taught her years ago. As she completed her spell, a vision appeared in Echo's mind of a sword with an artistically crafted black hilt and a large ruby at its center thrust into a stone altar, which was covered in glowing white runes. Echo's magic easily allowed her to locate the object she searched for and be drawn to its presence. Opening her eyes, Echo took her sword and pointed it in front of her. "There. We'll find Spirit Slayer beyond that wall."

Following the weapon's direction, Hatch walked up to the targeted wall and proceeded to cast a spell of his own. Cracks soon erupted all over the wall before it collapsed into a pile of rubble that revealed a corridor beyond it.

"Now, we're getting somewhere," Echo cheered as she led her companions into the new passage.

Hmm. So this is what Hatch can do, Narcos thought as he stood amongst the castle's demolished stairs and saw they were littered with the bodies of dead maazhat. Hidden within the ruins, he had watched the battle outside the castle with great interest. Now, using his staff to help him get over the debris, Narcos came across Marcain's unconscious form and sneered at it in disgust. The young lord had never mentioned encountering Hatch's son and granddaughter. He also failed in defeating Ontar and Echo, even though the undead at his side had given him superior numbers. *I should have just summoned Eragosh,* he concluded before continuing up to the archway.

Entering the castle's foyer, Narcos saw where Hatch had destroyed a solid wall, and in the process, revealed a previously unreachable corridor. *And now, their use has come to an end,* Narcos decided before closing his eyes and casting a spell. Employing magic similar to what Echo had used to locate Spirit Slayer, the necromancer was able to learn there was a long dead entity that still resided in the castle, and that it could easily be roused to attack his enemies.

Uttering a second incantation, Narcos let his dark powers flow through the structure in a spell that would allow him to wake the dead. It was black magic at its finest. However, not being in direct sight of the undead meant Narcos wouldn't be able to control it. Unconcerned, he left the castle assuming that he would just have to post some zombies by its entrance to eliminate anything that tried to leave the building.

⁘ ⁘ ⁘

The air was cool and stagnant as the party continued their trek down the corridor. Ontar heard little aside from the echo of everybody's boots, and he wondered where this passage would take them. Passing by several empty rooms, the corridor ended at a narrow set of stairs that went deeper into the castle. Descending these steps, the party stopped and tensed when they heard what sounded like tortured screams of agony coming from up ahead.

Echo jumped up and held her sword at ready. "What was that?" she asked.

Ontar glanced in the direction of the sound while clutching his morning star. "It sounds like someone's in trouble, but in this place, I doubt that someone is human. Either way, going ahead is the only path available to us. So, we better be prepared for whatever's at the bottom of these stairs."

Echo and Hatch nodded in agreement and, together, the three of them continued past the steps and into a chamber that reminded her of the dungeon at Fort Vakid. The primary difference though was that most of these dungeon walls had been replaced by natural rock. It also lacked the vile smell that came from those unfortunate enough to be locked away in a place like this.

That wasn't to say this particular dungeon didn't have its own type of prisoner, and the party's attention immediately fell upon an ancient stone column in the center of the room. Hovering just a couple feet off the ground, with its back to the column, was the translucent figure of a haggard man whose body was illuminated by dull blue glow. The apparition wore little save a ghostly loincloth, and its arms were pulled above its head presumably by shackles that no longer existed.

Feeling pity for the tortured soul, the party cautiously advanced towards it, hoping to understand how it got to be in such a wretched state. Suddenly, the apparition looked up and uttered a bone-chilling yell. This action was followed by it arms dropping down and its hands covering its ears. Gritting its teeth, the apparition fell to its knees and tucked its head between its legs.

Transfixed, the party stared with morbid fascination as the curled up undead shook violently. As its shaking increased, the group noticed dozens of tiny black holes appear all over the apparition's body. Echo gasped as patches of the undead's translucent flesh were ripped from its tormented form and sucked in through these tiny holes. The apparition's figure soon became a gruesome display of exposed muscles and veins. This horrific act of torture appeared to have *killed* the spectral figure as its body stopped moving, and the screams came to an end…but that was also when the worms appeared. Wriggling up from the holes in the apparition's body, these ghostly worms flailed about wildly at first. Then they all lunged towards the party. As they did, the apparition's body stretched, and its hideous arms slowly reached out towards the group.

Echo breathed rapidly as the apparition floated towards her. What was she going to do? She didn't want to die or suffer like the undead had. Where could she go? The ghostly worms could follow her no matter where she ran, which meant she was helpless. No one could save her from this, and she knew the worms would burrow straight into her soul and consume it! Tears trickled down her cheeks as she realized that her very existence was about to come to an end.

Ontar's weapon arm trembled as he felt his own mortality slipping away. There was no way that he, or anyone else, could stand against the apparition. Glancing to his right, he saw Echo with tears in her eyes. Looking to his left, he saw that Hatch was extremely pale with a cold sweat covering his brow. They both knew the end was near and were horrified by it. Refusing to cower in his final moments, Ontar faced his enemy and awaited his fate.

It was at that moment Ontar saw a slight smile cross the apparition's lips. *It's a spell!* Ontar thought as he stared at the undead. Rage and understanding filling his head as he realized the apparition was using fear to defeat its enemies. Clutching his weapon tightly, Ontar spun his morning star and moved in to attack the vile specter. Echo and Hatch watched in total amazement as Ontar's weapon struck the undead's arm and caused it to briefly disappear.

Gliding back from Ontar, the apparition snarled at the warrior before swiping at him with its translucent hand. Ontar struck the appendage with his morning star, incurring further damage to the undead. Trying a different approach, the crafty apparition chose to sink into the ground in front of the party.

Ontar cast a hasty glance around the room as he tried to spot the undead. As he searched, the apparition rose from the floor behind Echo and Hatch and screamed bloody murder. Terrified, the two ran from the spectral menace and almost smacked straight into Ontar. Distracted by his companion's actions, Ontar didn't have a chance to defend himself when the apparition thrust its fingers through his shield and into the side of his chest. In a surprising twist, Ontar didn't feel pain where the wicked undead had initially touched him. Instead, his left arm exploded in agony from the remembered pain of when a banshee had touched him there.

Echo saw the blow Ontar had received and realized that he'd survive it. Overcoming her fear, she took her sword and slashed at the undead's leg. Howling at this fresh attack, the apparition shot up into the ceiling. As it departed, Hatch no longer felt the effects of its fear spell. Ashamed of having succumbed to the specter's black magic, Hatch prepared a spell of his own that would vindicate his earlier cowardice.

The battle was now becoming fierce, with the apparition zipping in and out of walls and trying to strike at the party whenever possible. Returning the favor, Ontar and Echo would constantly attack the specter whenever it passed by them. Attempting a difficult maneuver, the apparition popped out of the ground directly beneath where Ontar stood and phased right into his body. Ontar felt the wicked strike of a tiki's weapon slam against his knee in a remembered blow that sent him falling before the apparition.

Echo was powerless. She couldn't attack Ontar while the apparition passed through him, and the foul fiend had no problem grasping at her weapon arm even before her companion's body had hit the ground. Dropping her sword, she felt the burning sensation of a cave worms acid sear her right hand.

Taking joy in the suffering it had caused, the apparition grinned as the injured elf was forced to step away. This wicked pleasure would not last, though, for upon completing his spell,

Hatch opened his left hand to reveal three hovering firebolts that he simultaneously launched at his enemy. Crying out in fury, the apparition had a firebolt strike its right arm, torso, and head. The trio of attacks were simply more than the undead could endure, and it let out one last agonizing scream before vanishing from existence.

Hatch ran over to where Ontar was lying and tried to see if he was alright. Echo soon joined him after retrieving her sword. The apparition's defeat nullified the damage it had wrought, and even Ontar found himself recovering from its horrible effects.

"Ugh…I'm really starting to hate these evil spirits," the warrior grumbled as he got to his feet.

Echo shuddered. "I've never fought something so horrifying before."

Hatch nodded in agreement. "It is truly a tragedy when a man experiences suffering so great in life that his soul fears leaving the very dungeon it was once imprisoned."

"I only hope the gods spare me from ever having to endure such torture," Echo added uneasily as she turned to leave this awful place.

⋆⋆⋆

Continuing to explore the underground castle, Echo used her locate object spell reveal a rock wall that concealed the way to their objective. Using a now familiar spell to destroy the wall, Hatch revealed another long corridor that led to a small room that held the objective of their quest. Spirit Slayer appeared just as Echo had envisioned it, with the sword's blade thrust down into a small stone altar covered in glowing white runes.

"That's the sword we've been looking for?" Ontar said with a snicker. "What a waste of time."

Echo was immediately offended by the remark. "What do you mean by that?"

Ontar pointed at the weapon with his morning star. "Look, it's a two-handed sword. You couldn't lift that thing even if you wanted to."

"Well, it's not like I'm going to use it in a fight," Echo declared as she went to inspect the weapon. "This beautiful blade is meant to ensure my place next to Searce within the Bloody Side."

Hatch's features were shadowed by the torch he carried as he moved to examine the altar. "Before we draw this sword, I think we'd better take precautions against the demon that's sealed by it."

Echo quirked an eyebrow. "What did you have in mind?"

"I can summon a wall of fire to appear in front of the altar right after you draw the sword," Hatch explained. "Should the demon try to attack us, then it will be burnt by the flames and vulnerable to additional attacks by you and Ontar."

"What if the demon tries to wait out the spell instead?" Ontar wondered.

Hatch shrugged. "Then I will simply throw firebolts through the wall until I kill it that way."

Ontar's helmet lowered slightly in disappointment. "I hope it tries to go through the wall. I've never killed a demon before."

"Well, now you'll get your chance," Echo claimed as she withdrew her regular sword and shield so she could grab Spirit Slayer by the hilt. Feeling a strange tingling sensation run up her arms, she waited for Hatch to start casting his spell before she flexed her wiry muscles and pulled the ancient sword free in one smooth motion.

Spirit Slayer was a magnificent artifact to behold with a blade that had glowing blue runes inscribed along its center that led up to a luminous ruby embedded in its hilt. However, the gleam from those runes and gem quickly faded once the sword was taken from its resting place.

Hatch immediately noticed when the glowing runes on the altar also began to go dark. Finishing his spell the moment Echo backed away with her new blade, he caused a line of fire to circle around the altar just before a six-foot wall of flame rose up to contain whatever threat may come their way.

Oddly enough, the first indication that something sinister was about to happen came in the form of a nasty stench that filled the air with the scent of burning garbage. This foul odor was accompanied by a plume of smoke that erupted from the center of the altar and shrouded it in an unnatural cloud. A rasping voice from within the cloud joyfully declared, "At last, the seal is broken."

Watching as the cloud of smoke swirled above the altar, the party noticed its noxious fumes soon took on the solid form of a scrawny looking demon just over five feet tall, which sat crouched on the spot where Spirit Slayer had rested. Gazing at the group from its perch, the gray-skinned demon had dark red eyes with long, slitted pupils that dipped like valleys beneath its sinister brow. Two curved black horns protruded from the monster's forehead and were of a similar hue to the sharp nails present on its fingers and toes. A wicked grin spread across the demon's face to reveal its jagged yellow teeth.

Addressing the group, Zattermox made a simple observation, "Hmm. Two humans and an elf protected by a wall of fire. It appears my master has been defeated by the Ha-Ress after all."

Hatch was quick to correct him. "The Ha-Ress Empire and the demons they fought against have both disappeared from this world a long time ago."

Intrigued by the remark, Zattermox said, "Well, isn't that interesting. You see, I am known as Zattermox the Treasure Keeper, and with my master's demise, I have no reason not to share his treasure with you."

"Why would you do that?" Ontar asked.

"The three of you rescued me from countless ages of imprisonment," Zattermox explained. "The least I can do is reward you for my freedom."

Ontar snickered when he heard this. "We came for the sword. You're just something we have to kill in order to keep it."

"But why settle for one powerful artifact when I can offer you many?" Zattermox wondered.

Clearly interested, Echo asked, "What sort of artifacts?"

Zattermox grinned at her question. "For a beautiful elf like you, there is a mirror whose reflection will not only show you the person you want to be, but also give you the power to achieve that vision."

"I could finally get out of Searce's shadow?" Echo said to herself.

"I doubt it," Hatch retorted. "Whatever treasures Zattermox claims to possess were most likely lost through the centuries."

Zattermox wagged a finger at the wizard. "You don't know that for sure."

"No," Hatch admitted, "but I do know a man of dark intent seeks the very treasures you just offered to us. Treasures from another time that have no place in today's world."

Ontar agreed, "Echo, you have Spirit Slayer and will secure your place within the Bloody Side. I say we kill this piece of shit before Narcos gets ahold of him."

Clutching the ancient blade in both hands, Echo reluctantly nodded. "I suppose you're right."

"It's a shame you feel that way," Zattermox said as he slid off the altar and walked up to the flaming wall. "Because you see, smoke demons are immune to fire!" Lowering his head, Zattermox rushed unhindered through the wall in a vicious surprise attack! Startled by what he saw, Hatch made a feeble attempt at dodging out of the way just as one of the demon's horns cut into his left side while a shoulder also struck him in the gut. Groaning from the wounds, Hatch fell hard onto his knees.

Ready to help her injured companion, Echo swung Spirit Slayer at the demon only to have Zattermox turn into a cloud of smoke before making contact. Spreading his gaseous form to envelop all three of his enemies, Zattermox said, "You should have taken me up on my offer. I might have spared your lives if you had."

Coughing on the foul-smelling smoke that threatened to choke them to death, Ontar withdrew his morning star and shield so that he could grab Hatch and throw him over his shoulder. Picking up the wizard's torch, he told Echo that, "We'll die if we stay here!"

Echo's eyes stung, and she felt tears trickle down her cheeks. "I can't see!"

"Put the blade of your sword along corridor walls and RUN!" Ontar instructed.

Doing as she was told, Echo used Spirit Slayer to help her run from the wretched demon. Listening to the blade as it scraped against the wall, Ontar followed her as fast as he could go. Together, the party soon emerged from the smoke and found themselves back in the dungeon where they had defeated the apparition. Leaning against a wall to gasp for breath, Echo saw Zattermox's noxious cloud flow into the room and exclaimed, "He's just going to keep following us. Hatch, we need to escape!"

Hatch was still coughing when he told Ontar to, "Take me to the other side of the room."

Ontar raced to the far end of the chamber with Echo at his side. Setting Hatch down on the ground, they listened while he frantically cast a spell. Zattermox could be heard laughing as his cloud of smoke drew ever closer. Prepared to envelop them once again, the demon was surprised when Hatch finished his spell and caused the trio to vanish in a rush of displaced air.

Chapter Eleven

"Ugh..." Marcain groaned as he sat up amongst a pile of rubble and touched a bloody gash along his brow.

Filled with contempt for the man, Narcos stood just beyond the castle's ruined stairs and said, "Get up, you pathetic excuse for a lord."

Putting a hand to his head and applying pressure to the wound, Marcain asked, "Where are the three who attacked me?"

Narcos pointed with his staff to the castle's archway, which was now guarded by a cluster of zombies. "After brushing you aside like a fly, they went into the castle to do my work for me."

Finding his sword and sheathing it, Marcain tore his one good shirt sleeve and wrapped it around his head like a bandage. "I never saw *you* in the fight against them."

"I've already done my part," Narcos replied. "I've raised all the undead within that castle to sap their strength and reduce their numbers. If the demon hasn't killed those who remained, then the zombies at the entrance will finish them off."

Marcain grabbed his torch and slowly stood up, "So, now, we just wait for someone to exit the castle."

"*I* will wait," Narcos retorted. "*You*, on the other hand, failed to tell me about your earlier encounter with Hatch's family. So, now, silence will be met with silence."

"What do you mean?" Marcain wondered.

Narcos answered the question by simply saying, *"Eragosh."*

A slight tremble and an improved posture quickly signified that Marcain was no longer in control of his body. Asking a familiar question, Eragosh inquired, *"Master, what is your will?"*

"Watch and wait for the demon," Narcos commanded as his attention turned to the archway.

The two did not have to wait long. Smelling a vile odor in the air, Narcos looked to the castle's entrance and saw a cloud of smoke billow through its opening. The zombies on guard moaned as the cloud swirled around them but could do nothing to stop it from rising towards the top of the chasm. *Oh, no, you don't,* Narcos thought before telling Eragosh to "Stop the demon".

Eager to leave the ruins of Uch-na-Mach behind, Zattermox heard a deathly moan below him and saw Marcain drop to the ground unconscious just as a pale ghostly figure resembling a knight shot up through the air and passed through his gaseous form. A freezing pain tore into Zattermox and destroyed his concentration causing his body to return to a solid state. Letting out a startled shriek, he plummeted through the air and crashed hard onto the ground beneath him. The fall would have killed a human, but in Zattermox's case, it was merely a painful reminder of what a crafty enemy could do.

Waiting for "Marcain" to get up as Eragosh returned to his body, Narcos looked down at Zattermox's aching figure and said, "Behold, demon! I am Narcos, your new master."

Having spent most of his life groveling to demon overlords far more powerful than Narcos, Zattermox had little trouble adopting the role of a sniveling slave as he got onto his hands and knees while trying to look pitiful. "Oh, most glorious master. I humbly bow before your might."

"I have no interest in flattery, Zattermox, only your treasures," Narcos replied.   Zattermox cocked his head with interest. "Forgive me for asking, master, but I have been sealed away for countless ages. So, how do you know me?"

"I learned about you and your treasure while studying the ancient battle of Uch-na-Mach," Narcos explained.

"I see," Zattermox mused. "So, do you know of the people who broke the seal that imprisoned me then?"

"I do," Narcos replied before going into detail about his previous experiences with Ontar, Echo, and Hatch.

Listening intently, Zattermox stood up and told the necromancer about his own brief encounter with them. "...the three may have fled with Spirit Slayer, but the sword is virtually nothing when compared to the treasures held in Da Shō's Vault."

"I assume that Da Shō was your former master," Narcos guessed.

Zattermox nodded. "Da Shō was one of the many overlords who invaded the Ha-Ress Empire. My role during the war was to scour the battlefields of every major conflict and gather any enchanted artifacts I could find to place within his vault."

Something seemed odd to Narcos about this practice. "Why didn't Da Shō just redistribute the artifacts among his other minions?"

The question seemed to agitate Zattermox, but it didn't stop him from answering it. "Because Da Shō intended on using the artifacts as a bribe to gain sacred knowledge from the dragons of this world."

Intrigued, Narcos asked, "What sort of knowledge?"

"Da Shō wanted to find a way to be in the actual presence of different gods," Zattermox replied.

"Why?" Narcos wondered out loud. Everyone knew the gods and demons were sworn enemies. Demons constantly sought different means of preying on the gods' followers so they could weaken the divine barriers protecting this world from their unholy wrath.

"So that he could eliminate them!" Zattermox stated ominously.

"That's impossible," Narcos said with a derisive snort. "Didn't your former master know the gods are immortal?"

"Never confuse immortality with invulnerability," Zattermox warned. "Da Shō's Vault is filled with ancient relics powerful enough to bring down enemies both divine and mortal alike."

"Oh, really," Narcos said as he leaned against his staff. "And just what sort of relics are you referring to?"

Ah, he's finally taken the bait, Zattermox thought. "Well, master, I can think of one treasure within the vault that could enhance your already considerable powers to almost inconceivable levels." Pausing to build anticipation, Zattermox continued on after a slight wave from Narcos. "It is called the Crown of Darkness. Forged by demons long before they invaded this world, it is said that: *He who wears the Crown of Darkness is master of the dead.* I myself have seen the limitless power contained within the crown and trembled before its might. Of course, I would never dare to defy Da Shō's will by touching such a valuable treasure. Especially since, even in death, his presence can still be felt."

"So, it's just been sitting there. Even after all this time?" Narcos asked.

Zattermox lied. He really had no idea if the crown was still there, but if his plans were to succeed, then he would have to at least see if the vault still existed. "Yes, master, and I would be honored to show you to the vault's location if you're interested?"

"If the vault still exists, then where would I find it?" Narcos demanded.

Afraid of revealing too much and losing his value to the necromancer, Zattermox tried to be vague. "The vault is hidden somewhere within the Bone Fields of Gatoris."

Unfamiliar with the location, Narcos turned to his other companion and asked, "Eragosh, where would I find the vault today?"

Utilizing both ancient and current knowledge, Eragosh replied, *"In the Kingdom of Coronas is a place called Vakerdurn's Maze. That is where you'll find the vault."*

"Eragosh, hmm. I see you serve your master in death almost as well as you did in life," Zattermox noted.

"Too bad his descendant is practically useless without him," Narcos noted in regard to Marcain. "Either way, I see no reason to linger here any longer. Zattermox, I expect you to open the vault and identify what each relic inside can do."

Bowing to his new master, Zattermox humbly replied, "Your wish is my command."

Hatch squinted as he tried to look away from the bright sun overhead. His battle with the smoke demon Zattermox had left him with injuries that needed to be treated. So, when he teleported the party away from Uch-na-Mach, he decided the best place to reappear would be at the village shrine in Habed. Being a devout follower of the nature goddess Mirsha, the shrine's brown-robed cleric had him rest upon a nice soft flower bed in the back of the building while he magically healed Hatch's wounds. The combination of soft dirt and scented flowers were quite soothing to Hatch, who oddly didn't feel the summer heat as he took the time he needed to recuperate.

Being in a far better condition than Hatch was, Ontar and Echo had gone to Thove's house to tell his family what happened. While they were gone, the shrine's cleric kept him company by engaging in small talk. "It's funny that a father and son would use the same flower bed to recover from their injuries. If I didn't know any better, I'd say you were jealous he got hurt first."

"We've always been a competitive family," Hatch teased.

"Yes, but you must be careful," the cleric warned. "Thove can take these kinds of wounds. You, on the other hand, might not survive if you continue in this competition with him, and he has spent a great deal of time and energy trying to get you back into his life again."

Hatch quirked an eyebrow. "May I assume you won't tell the local authorities I'm here?"

The cleric smiled. "Of course not, milord. Your son is a good man who has always looked out for the village in times of trouble. If you wish to live out a quiet life with him, then no one here would stop you from doing so."

Except those years might not be all that peaceful if I let Zattermox roam the world unchecked, Hatch thought. However, when addressing the cleric, he said, "Peace can only last for so long, and with two stubborn men thrashing about her house, Saren might just have to kill one of us in order to maintain her sanity."

Chuckling when he heard this, the cleric saw some familiar faces walking down the road and said, "Well, I guess you'll find out now, won't you?"

Slowly sitting up, Hatch saw Thove had been completely healed by the cleric and led the party towards the shrine. Strolling next to him was Ontar, who had his helmet tucked under one arm while Wink sat casually on his shoulder. At the rear of the group was Echo, who still carried Spirit Slayer (blade down) in her hands. Going to greet them, the cleric chatted for a little bit, then retired to the shrine itself, giving Hatch privacy to talk with his companions.

Approaching his father, Thove said, "Hey, Dad, how are you holding up?"

"Quite well," Hatch replied. "Apparently, this flower bed works wonders no matter who's lying in it."

"See...I knew he'd be alright," Wink proclaimed.

Hatch gave his son a curious look. "Where are the girls?"

"They're all at home preparing a big celebratory feast," Thove replied as he extended a hand to help Hatch up. "Our family is whole again, and the people who rescued you have claimed the sword they sought. It's a winning situation for everyone."

"Yes," Hatch admitted. "However, I fear Narcos might be enjoying his victory as well."

"You think he and Zattermox might have joined forces following our escape," Ontar assumed.

Hatch nodded. "It wouldn't surprise me."

"So what?" Echo asked. "You yourself said Zattermox's treasures were probably lost to the passage of time."

"But I can't be sure," Hatch warned. "I think it would be better if we return to Uch-na-Mach and kill the demon so Narcos doesn't gain any more power than he already has."

Ontar frowned when he heard this. "How are we supposed to kill a demon who can turn into a cloud of smoke?"

Raising her newly-claimed sword, Echo deviously said, "We'll eliminate him in a sneak attack before he has a chance to change forms."

"Are you mad? There's *undead* down there!" Thove exclaimed.

"Yeah, but they're nothing we can't handle," Ontar claimed.

"Then why don't you and Echo go fight them?" Thove snapped. "Dad's done his part in helping you get Spirit Slayer."

Wink gave Thove a nasty look. "He wouldn't have even done that much if you had your way on the matter."

Echo gave the pixie a curious look. "What do you mean?"

"Thove didn't want Hatch to come back for you and Onnie after he teleported the rest of us out of the ruins," Wink explained.

"You backstabbing piece of shit!" Echo exclaimed as she glared at Thove.

Thove was quick to defend his actions. "I told Dad that releasing the demon was a bad idea, and I was right. Not only did he get hurt, but now there's a chance this Narcos person could use Zattermox to wreak havoc across the lands."

"It was a risk unleashing the demon," Ontar admitted. "But now, your father wants to make amends for what happened, and I think it's the right thing to do."

"And what if he gets killed? Or worse, turned into an undead," Thove argued. "I have spent the past five year's trying to secure his freedom—"

Interrupting him, Echo said, "*You* tried, but *we* succeeded. You have no right to deny my claim to Spirit Slayer any more than you have a right stop your father from killing Zattermox."

Hatch saw that his son was getting angry and tried to calm him down. "Thove, I appreciate all that you've done on my behalf, but I still have to be allowed to make my own decisions in life. Otherwise I've merely traded one dungeon for another."

"I can't believe you think that I actually want to be your jailor!?" Thove insinuated. Turning around he angrily stormed down the road back towards his house.

"Thove...wait!" Hatch pleaded.

Wink waved her hand and told Hatch to, "Let the baby have his tantrum. Hopefully, by the time we get back, Saren will have spanked some sense into him."

Hatch disagreed, "Thove is perfectly justified in being angry with my decisions. He just doesn't have the right to stop me from making them."

"Well, he's not the only one who's angry," Echo complained. "He tried to stop you from honoring your debt to us."

"But he didn't," Hatch argued. "And at the end of the day, it's only the final result that really matters. So, let's go find Narcos and stop his schemes before he has any chance at carrying them out."

Agreeing with him, the group gathered around the old wizard and waited for him to cast a spell that would teleport them back into the ruins of Uch-na-Mach.

❧❧❧

Unfortunately, the party found little sign of their enemies within the underground ruins. Narcos had left his zombie guards to randomly roam the city after his departure but slaying them did nothing to reveal their master's location. Eventually, the group located the tunnel he had used to reach Uch-na-Mach and followed it back up to a now empty pond in the middle of a vast plains flanked by a couple of trees.

Disgusted by all the dead cattle in the hot sun, Echo waved away the flies that covered the corpses and said, "Ugh...did Narcos really have to kill all these animals just to find the entrance to Uch-na-Mach?"

Kneeling to let Wink track their enemies, Ontar pointed to a variety of weapons on the ground and said, "Narcos didn't kill those cows. Judging by what I see here, I'd say they died during a battle between the mercenaries and the maazhat."

"And Narcos just used their corpses afterwards to serve his own purposes," Echo assumed. "So much for allowing the dead to rest in peace."

Having wandered a short distance from the rest of her companions, Wink stared at a patch of grass and said, "Damn, we're too late."

"What do you mean?" Hatch inquired.

"Narcos, Marcain, and Zattermox all walked through mud when they left the pond," Wink explained. "I was able to follow their tracks up to this spot, but then they disappeared. I thought they might have had horses waiting for them, but there's no sign of droppings or eaten grass."

"They're probably undead," Hatch assumed. "A normal horse would roam the plains unless it was tethered."

Echo shrugged when she heard this. "I guess all we can do then is hope that we cross path's when we bring Spirit Slayer back to Miltus."

"Provided they even went that direction," Ontar added. "In all honesty, we have absolutely no idea where they're even going or the trouble they'll cause when they get there."

Wiping sweat from his brow; Hatch turned thoughtful. "What if there was a way that we could actually get some answers to these questions?"

"What did you have in mind?" Ontar wondered.

Hatch was happy to elaborate. "In the Chapskin Empire is a legendary oracle who could possibly provide us with the knowledge we seek."

Echo gave the wizard a suspicious look. "What's the catch?"

"The catch is that, even on horseback, it would take half a year to reach him," Hatch replied. "Which means the only way we could accomplish our goal would be to steal a sky whale from the Mage Lord of Sibeia."

"Yea! We're going to get Orla back!" Wink squealed.

Echo wagged her finger and said, "Wait a minute. Hatch, I think you've got a double motive here."

Lifting his hands while shrugging, Hatch said, "I won't deny I'd enjoy getting some revenge against my successor, but it is *not* my primary motivation here."

"Well, I have absolutely no problem with revenge," Ontar stated firmly. "However, I would like to know what we'd be up against if we decided to do this."

"That's fair enough," Hatch conceded. "The manor on Orla's back is primarily defended by a handful of guards under the leadership of a white knight. There's also a ranger who guides the sky whale, and a cleric—"

"Chairbis would never try to hurt us," Wink interrupted.

Hatch shot the pixie an agitated look. "Even if that were true, it still wouldn't change the fact we would also have to contend with the mage lord himself."

"Do you think you could beat him?" Ontar asked.

Hatch nodded. "With your help, I believe so."

Frowning when she heard this, Echo clutched Spirit Slayer and said, "I don't know. I'd really rather get this sword back to the Bloody Side."

"Ah, but you're forgetting the benefits from this undertaking," Hatch argued. "Once we've taken over Orla, you'll all have complete access to her manor and be able to travel back to Miltus in far greater luxury than any of you could possibly imagine."

Building on Hatch's argument, Wink said, "Not to mention the fact that stealing a Sibeian sky whale would drastically improve your standing within the Bloody Side."

Echo's thoughts whirled with this new information. She desperately wanted to do *something* to stand out from her aunt.

Perhaps defeating the mage lord and swiping his sky whale would help to accomplish this goal.

Ontar, however, wasn't quite convinced. "This is the second time that we'd be going up against Sibeian authorities. Chances are, it could lead to some really nasty consequences later on."

Wink walked up to Ontar, folded her hands together, and looked up at him with her big brown eyes. "*Please*, Onnie! I'm too little to do this without you."

Ontar knew the pixie's plea was absolutely shameless. Yet, for some reason, he couldn't bear to turn her down. "Well, I have always wanted to challenge a white knight to battle."

Echo rolled her eyes at his flimsy reasoning. "Ugh, you're pathetic."

"Not at all," Hatch corrected. "As far as I'm concerned, both of you are absolutely essential to the success of this undertaking."

"There's someone else who's going to be essential to our plans as well," Wink added.

Hatch's mood darkened. "Yes, I'm afraid that if Orla's ranger sides with the mage lord, then we're going to need someone else to guide the sky whale on our behalf."

Wink nodded. "We know two rangers who might be up to the task, but since Thove has a family to care for, that means Kit is the only one available."

"Ugh...I'm not looking forward to that conversation," Hatch groaned. "Thove is already angry that I'm not going to be settling down with him. The thought of taking *his* daughter away might cause him to snap altogether."

Echo didn't like the thought of Thove or Hatch deciding Kit's fate. "Do you know if Kit would even *want* to go with us?"

"I don't?" Hatch admitted. "But I suppose we should at least give her the opportunity to choose for herself."

"How charitable of you," Echo quipped.

Clapping her hands to get their attention, Wink said, "Alright. Onnie, Echo, you two see if you can lure the fawn while Hatch and I will take on the buck!"

Ontar chuckled when he heard this. "I usually don't go after the weaker opponent, but in this case, I think you might be right."

"And don't you forget it," Wink replied with a giggle.

Gathering together, the party waited for Hatch to cast a spell that would teleport them back to his family's home.

❊ ❊ ❊

Spotting the party's sudden arrival, Aniata climbed down from the gardens big plum tree and went to greet them. "Grandpa… Wink…I knew you'd come back! Dad said we should just toss out all the food that we made for dinner, but Mom and Kit thought that you might still make it in time to eat, and they were right!"

Sitting atop Ontar's shoulder plate, Wink replied, "Of course, they were. Onnie's got two hollow legs and a big gut to fill, and only a home cooked meal can possibly make that happen."

Ontar tapped his stomach and said, "Hey, this is all muscle."

"Sure, it is, Onnie…sure it is," Wink teased.

Following Aniata into the Malay family's home, the party found Thove standing by the fireplace, with Kit at his side. Being a little more excited by their appearance than her father, Kit exclaimed, "You're back! Did you kill the demon?"

Hatch shook his head. "No, I'm afraid he escaped by the time we returned."

"Well, you did all you could," Thove said with a sigh of relief. "Looks like Narcos and Zattermox are someone else's problem now."

"And it's not like you came away empty handed," Kit added as she looked at Echo. "You can now claim Spirit Slayer as your own. Fetching a brown leather shoulder scabbard off the mantle, she then presented it to Echo. "Here. I thought you could use this. Dad had originally gotten it for when we found Spirit Slayer, but since the blade is yours now, I think that you'll probably get more use out of it."

Thove smiled and said, "Think of it as our way of saying thanks for bringing my father home."

Knowing her companion's plans, Echo felt a little sheepish in taking the gift. "Thank you. It'll be nice not having to drag this thing with me everywhere I go."

Enticed by the aroma of food in the air, Ontar saw Saren emerge from the kitchen with additional plates for the table and said, "Dinner smells delicious. When can we eat?"

"Just as soon as Drub returns from the mercantile with some fresh bottles of wine," Saren replied.

"Ugh…it might as well be forever," Aniata grumbled while pulling up a chair at the table.

"Not necessarily," Wink countered as Ontar set her down by the girl. "I think that it might be *just* enough time to have a little fun." Looking between Echo and Hatch, the pixie said, "Echo, strike up the music. Hatch, I think I'll need a dancing partner."

Taking the hint, Echo reached into her backpack and pulled out a wooden flute. Sitting down in a chair next to Hatch, she watched as the old wizard uttered an incantation that caused a translucent little blue man in golden clothing to suddenly materialize before them. Aniata's jaw dropped when she saw the figure was Wink's size and moved towards the pixie as if they were old friends.

Observing what was taking place, Echo saw that Wink and her partner were quietly facing each other. Lifting the flute to her lips, she played an upbeat tune that sparked a fast-paced dance between the two tiny people.

Careful not to touch her illusionary partner, Wink kicked, spun, and laughed to the sounds of music. Aniata was absolutely enthralled with the performance and giggled with delight when Kit set Whiskers on the table next to Wink. The poor mouse was absolutely terrified at having been put in such a situation and desperately searched for some means to reach the floor. Showing no remorse for the little rodent, Wink and her partner merrily chased Whiskers across the dinner table while performing ridiculously elaborate dance moves.

Ontar thought the whole production was a little bit silly for his tastes. Seeing that Thove had taken a chair near the fireplace, he decided to join the ranger by sitting down on the couch across from him and saying, "Hey, I noticed that you and Kit were able to get through the maazhat colony pretty much unscathed. Care to reveal how you were able to pull that off?"

"Well, it wasn't easy..." Thove began as he and Ontar shared stories of their prior exploits.

Time passed swiftly in the Malay house as lively entertainment and good conversation spanned well into the evening. Opening the wine Drub brought, Thove let his guests drink to their hearts content and encouraged them to relax and enjoy their meals. After dinner, Saren quietly called for attention.

"Excuse me, everyone. I just want to say that it's been a long time since we've been able to enjoy the company of so many friends and family, and I was hoping we could all join hands and offer up a little prayer to the goddess responsible for this joyous reunion."

"Go for it!" Wink shouted as she stood on the table and braced herself against a cup filled with wine. The pixie seemed a little bit tipsy, but she tried her best to compose herself.

Holding hands, everybody around the table silently bowed their heads. As they did, Saren spoke, "Merciful Talana, your guiding light has become a beacon to reunite our family and bring new friends into our midst. We are humbled by this blessing and pray that you find us worthy of it. May the bonds we forge in life always be kept so that our loved ones are never forgotten."

Once the prayer was finished, everyone released each other and focused on the remnants of their meal. Staring at her empty plate, Echo had a troubled expression on her face. Clearly bothered by something, she abruptly stood up and said, "Excuse me," before leaving both the table (and the house) altogether.

Seeing some concerned looks on the other's faces, Ontar stood up and quietly said, "I'll go after her," as he left the table in search of his missing companion.

It was dark outside the house, and a full red moon lit up the evening sky. Catching a glimpse of Echo off in the distance, Ontar left the surrounding garden and entered into a farmer's field. Coming up behind his troubled companion, he saw that Echo stared at fireflies, which flickered and flitted about the night air.

"Hey, are you alright?"

Continuing to look at the fireflies, Echo said, "I hate this."

"Hate what?" Ontar asked.

Echo sighed. "Feeling like I'm alone and there's no one left who cares about me."

Ontar shook his head. "Echo, that's not true."

Turning around to face her longtime companion, Echo stated, "I know that's not true, but it still feels like it. Ontar, our loved ones are gone! For the most part, I can accept that fact, but coming here with Hatch and Wink and watching them interact with their family…it just hurts knowing that we'll never be able to experience something like that again."

Ontar could see Echo's eyes misting up and felt the pain in her words. Approaching the anguished elf, he wrapped his muscular arms around her slim wiry body and held her close. Leaning next to one of her pointed ears, he softly whispered, "I miss them, too."

Kit stood near her homes ivy-covered fence and watched Ontar and Echo hold each other in a sorrow-filled embrace. Feeling pity for their troubled souls, she approached while trying to think of a way to distract them from their troubles.

"They're beautiful, aren't they," she stated in a cautiously cheerful voice.

Ontar and Echo released each other and gave her a questioning look.

Kit continued on, "The fireflies. I think they'd brighten half the sky if we just told them where to shine."

Welcoming the change in topic, Ontar said, "Yeah, it's just a shame that we can't ask them to shed a little light our way."

"Or maybe we can," Kit said with a smile.

Closing her eyes, she cast a quick spell, then raised her hands high above her head. Seemingly drawn by this strange gesture, a swarm of fireflies gathered in the air just above her fingers. Opening her eyes and spreading her arms Kit caused the flashing insects to swirl about her in a rapid clockwise direction. She then made a pushing motion with her arms and sent her flickering minions racing in a stream of light towards Ontar and Echo.

Mesmerized by the impromptu light show, the two stared with fascination as the fireflies barreled towards them. Waiting to see what would happen next, they watched as the stream of insects circled around them twice before shooting towards the sky. Moments later, the fireflies changed formation and shifted themselves into the image of a large spinning star.

Kit glanced over at Ontar and Echo and was pleased to see that her magic had taken their minds off their problems…if only for a while. The world was filled with so much hardship, and she thought that everybody needed a break now and then. Especially since such reprieves tended to be depressingly brief.

"That's quite impressive," Ontar admitted. "Have you ever tried to control anything larger than an insect or a mouse?"

Kit nodded. "I've had to lure stray cattle back to their farms from time to time."

"What about something like a sky whale?" Ontar asked.

"Are you talking about Orla?" Kit wondered.

"Yes," Ontar began before he and Echo told her about their plans to take control of Orla.

Listening nervously, Kit hesitated with her response. "So, you want me to help you kill the mage lord and steal his sky whale! I can't. If I got involved in something like this, the six lords would—"

"Do absolutely nothing," Echo stated while interrupting her.

Kit looked at her dumbfounded. "What?"

"Kit, your grandmother is married to the golden lord, which means you and your family won't suffer any repercussions for helping us," Echo asserted.

"But what about Grandpa, Wink, and the two of you?" Kit countered.

Ontar gave her a determined look. "Kit, we all believe crushing Narcos's threat to the lands is worth the risk. Will you join us?"

"I-I don't know," Kit mumbled. "I have to talk to my dad about it first."

Ontar and Echo exchanged curious looks and quietly wondered what her final decision might be.

"Are you *insane?*" Thove more or less asked his father. Sitting next to Saren at the dinner table, the three of them had gotten into a heated discussion on Hatch's plans for the future. "You just spent the past five years rotting in the six lords' dungeon, and now you want to turn around and provoke them!"

Hatch took a second to rub his eyes. "I'm not trying to provoke anyone, but I am worried about what will happen with this demon we released."

"Dad, it's a smoke demon. I'm pretty sure that it's not going to try and conquer the world," Thove said.

Arguing his point, Hatch said, "An overlord like Da Shō could have killed Zattermox on a whim. So, why did he choose to imprison him instead?"

"Who cares?" Thove countered. "The Ha-Ress Empire collapsed long after its battle with the demons, which means that any schemes or allies that Zattermox might have had at the time all died out ages ago."

Hatch tried to explain that, "Just because the world has changed doesn't mean that remnants from the past have suddenly disappeared. Narcos knows that both the demons and the Ha-Ress used powerful magic and relics to further their ambitions. Who's to say that he won't try to unearth one of these ancient evils to wreak untold havoc upon us?"

"Or Zattermox's relics have been scattered to the winds and forgotten, leaving a petty demon to serve his petty master until the end of his days," Thove added.

"Perhaps," Hatch agreed, "but the only way to know for sure is to take the mage lord's sky whale and seek out the Nung-Dow oracle."

Thove's temper flared. "That's bullshit! You're just using the demon as an excuse to get revenge on those who imprisoned you."

"Watch your tone!" Hatch snapped.

Saren patted her husband's hand. "Thove, you need to calm down."

Thove slammed his fist on the table and looked at Hatch. "No! For the past five years, Kit and I have done everything possible to set you free, and now that you've been rescued, the first thing you want to do is turn around and try something that will either get you captured again or killed!"

Hatch sighed. "I'm sorry, Son. I appreciate all that you and your family have done for me, but at the end of the day, I have to live my life by following my own conscience. If I can't do that, then I might as well just crawl back into the dungeon I've just escaped."

Frustrated, Thove took a drink from his cup and set it back on the table. "So, who are you going to get to navigate Orla once you've finished stealing her?" he asked in reference to the sky whale.

The question was phrased rather crudely, and Hatch braced himself for the reaction to his answer. "I think that Kit would be the ideal person to fulfill that role."

Shock washed over Thove and Saren, but Hatch could quickly see the rage building behind his son's eyes. "Over my dead body!" Thove shouted. "I can't stop you from destroying your life, but I'll be *damned* if I let you ruin hers!

"HEY!" Came Wink's high-pitched voice as she emerged from Aniata's room and stomped over to the dinner table. "Will you guy's SHUT UP! At this rate, Aniata and I will *never* get any sleep."

Saren quirked an eyebrow and looked down at the pixie. "I'm pretty sure I just heard the two of you talking about stealing treats from the kitchen after we finished our conversation here."

A guilty expression briefly crossed Wink's face. Waving her hand dismissively, she quickly said, "We're getting off topic. Thove, now that Kit is an adult, you have no right to dictate what she will or won't do with her life."

"I'm her father. That gives me *every* right," Thove argued.

Catching a glimpse of Kit, Ontar, and Echo out the window, Saren tried to quiet her husband by touching his arm, but he didn't notice.

Hatch, however, did and continued to press his argument. "Every parent has to let their child go at some point."

Thove wanted to stop that idea dead in its tracks. "Forget it. Kit isn't ready to face that kind of danger."

"What in the world are you talking about?" Wink snapped. "She was at your side when you snuck into the maazhat colony, *and* you watched her fight off a bunch of zombies after you got injured."

"Yes, but she wouldn't have been able to accomplish any of that if I wasn't there to guide her," Thove argued.

"So, you basically think that I won't be able to accomplish anything without you?" Kit asked as she entered the room with Ontar and Echo at her sides.

"Kit…" Thove stammered.

Leaning close to him, Saren whispered, "I tried to tell you."

Kit looked at her father with pain in her eyes. "Dad, what was the point in training me to handle myself if I'm never actually allowed to do it?"

Shaking his head in exasperation, Thove said, "Kit, you have no idea on the type of danger your grandfather wants to put you in."

"Excuse me, but we faced countless dangers when you were her age, and not once did Hatch ever try to stop you from doing them," Wink asserted.

Thove gave Hatch a dirty look. "Well, that just shows the kind of father he really was."

"Thove!" Saren scolded when she saw the hurt look in Hatch's eyes. "Now, that's enough."

Angry at how awful her father was being, Kit stepped forward and said, "Dad, I'm ready, and deep down, I think you know that, too."

Thove thrust his hands onto the table and pushed himself up. "I can't believe what I'm hearing! It's as if my entire family's gone absolutely mad. Saren, I'm going to bed. Hopefully, by tomorrow, the rest of you will realize just how foolish this entire undertaking really is."

Standing up to follow her husband, Saren briefly addressed the group, "I think it would be best if we *all* turned in for the night. Sleep well, and I'll see everyone in the morning."

Ontar waited until Thove and Saren had closed the door to their room before turning to Hatch with a question, "So, where are we supposed to find this sky whale?"

Bringing his voice down to a whisper, Hatch replied, "There's a religious festival that takes place in Ranig a few days from now. As mage lord, I never missed it, and I doubt that my successor will either."

"Then that is when we'll strike," Echo stated softly.

It was late into the night when Echo first heard the sound of rustling throughout the house. Sitting in a chair by the fireplace, she laid the book she was reading down on her lap and glanced about her surroundings. Ontar was wrapped in a blanket and sleeping on the couch across from her. Shifting uncomfortably, he had relinquished his stay in Kit's room so she could spend one more night in her own bed. Letting him sleep for the moment, Echo listened carefully for any additional noises and heard what sounded like someone rattling around in the kitchen.

Initially alarmed, Echo relaxed a little when she saw a lit candle on the dining room table, which revealed Kit holding a wooden bowl of table scraps in one hand and a blown-out match in the other. Setting the bowl down on the table, she then plucked her pet mouse off the floor and set him by the food. Whiskers immediately nibbled on the scraps, and Kit smiled as she watched him eat.

"Having a midnight snack?" Echo asked quietly.

Kit was startled by the question and gave Echo a surprised look. "Oh! I'm sorry. I didn't mean to wake you. I guess I'm not quite used to having so many guests over."

Echo gave her a dismissive wave. "I wasn't sleeping. Although, I have to say, it's a little peculiar that you'd choose to feed your pet at this late an hour."

"Is it that obvious?" Kit asked bashfully as she sat in the chair next to Echo. "Alright, I'll admit that I'm a little nervous about tomorrow. This is the first time that I've ever left home and done something dangerous without my father, and I really don't want to let anybody down."

Echo leaned forward in her chair. "Kit, you don't have to worry about anyone but yourself, and if you want to try and find a little independence in your life, then go for it."

"Thanks," Kit said halfheartedly. "I guess that you've probably been walking your own path for quite a while now."

"Trust me, you have no idea..." Echo began as she started to talk about some of her previous exploits. Their conversation lasted well into the evening but, eventually, Ontar stirred, and they both decided to turn in while they still could. Entering into a meditative posture, Echo's last thoughts were of how Kit would be a welcome addition to the party. Especially when facing the conflicts that were to come.

❖❖❖

An air of anticipation gripped the party as they prepared to depart from the Malay family's home. Saren made a light breakfast for everyone, which was quickly gobbled up before they gathered their equipment. Thove said little during the meal but subtly made sure that Kit and Hatch had all the equipment they needed afterwards. Assembling outside the front of the house, everybody was relieved to see that a cloudy sky and a strong breeze kept the summer's heat at bay.

Waiting for his family to bid them farewell, Hatch noticed that Drub guided a pair of horses out from the stable and towards them. Giving Kit a questioning look, he remarked, "Two horses?"

Kit nodded. "One of them is mine. I thought that we could all reach Ranig a little bit quicker if we just doubled up."

"I'm riding with Onnie!" Wink chirped as she sat on the warrior's shoulder.

"I will, too," Echo stated before Drub offered her the reins to their animal.

Wink scowled and slipped into Ontar's hood. "You know, Echo, two's company and three's a crowd."

"Oh, are you planning on staying behind?" Echo asked while holding the horse steady for Ontar to mount up.

"Not a chance," Wink replied as Ontar offered his hand to Echo so she could climb on.

Kit felt tears stream down her cheeks as she gave her mother a hug. "I'll miss you, Mom."

Pulling back from the embrace, Saren wiped her eyes with a handkerchief. "I hate goodbyes. Just promise me that you'll come back home as soon as you can."

"I promise," Kit said with a sad smile.

Next in line to get a hug was Aniata, who handed Whiskers over to her sister and said, "Don't be sad, Kit. As long as Whiskers is with you, you'll always have something that can cheer you up."

"That's very true," Kit said as she slipped the rodent into the hood of her cloak.

Last, but not least, was Thove. Giving Kit a quick squeeze, he said, "I'll miss you, kiddo. Now, remember your training and always stay close to your friends."

"I won't forget," Kit uttered as she tried not to choke on her words. Turning around, she went over to her horse and proceeded to mount it.

Ontar and Echo both found themselves personally touched by Kit's farewell to her family. For Ontar, it reminded him of how gut-wrenchingly difficult it had been to say goodbye to his parents and sister when he set off to begin his training at Fort Hasborne. Echo, on the other hand, looked back at saying goodbye to her parents with more guilt than anything else. Traveling with Favin and a cadre of guards to a nearby town she brushed off their fears and assured them that everything would be alright. More interested in spending time with her suitor, she never imagined the horrors that would take them from her life forever.

Oblivious to his companion's inner turmoil, Hatch followed Kit in saying goodbye to the family. When coming up to Thove, he couldn't ignore both the pain and sorrow he saw in his son's eyes. Thove slowly set a hand on his father's shoulder. "I still think you're a damn fool for doing this."

Hatch smiled. "Well, I guess there's no fool like an old fool."

Both men laughed, then hugged. When Hatch stepped back, Thove leaned next to his ear and whispered, "Take care of my little girl."

"Of course," Hatch replied as he patted his son's hand. He then went over by Kit, who helped him onto her horse. With everyone mounted, Drub opened the gate to the garden and held it there until the party was ready to depart.

"Goodbye, everybody!" Wink shouted as she waved her hat while the party spurred their horses towards the gardens exit and off towards their next destination.

❦ ❦ ❦

It was a long day's travel for the group as they left Habed and galloped along a lengthy stretch of dirt road leading to Ranig. Riding past both farmland and open prairie, the party's horses carried them through the Wistwind Plains with relative ease. Stopping only when necessary, it wasn't until the setting sun turned the clouds overhead a pretty shade of pink and violet that everyone decided to rest.

Once the party dismounted, Kit pulled their horses off the main road and led them over to a good grazing spot. As she did, Ontar began gathering some dried grass from nearby so they could start a fire. Meanwhile, the remainder of the group all seemed content plunging into their rations and water skins. Glancing over at Kit, Ontar asked, "So, how are you holding up?"

Kit stroked her horse's mane. "Pretty well. I usually enjoy being able to go on a nice long ride. It helps me to clear my head and take in how big and beautiful our world really is."

Ontar nodded in agreement. "Yeah, it is pretty peaceful out here. Although, I have to admit that I am going to miss your mother's cooking."

A fond look crossed Kit's face. "Me too, and I think I'm really going to miss not being able to join them for family dinner."

"I can sympathize with you on that one," Ontar said with a distant look in his eyes. Shaking it off, he took his bundle of grass and headed back towards the others.

Kit couldn't help but feel like something bad had happened in Ontar's past. His reaction to her comments just now, and that mournful embrace he gave Echo last night, all indicated that something tragic must have befallen the two. Driven by curiosity, she decided to broach the subject later that evening.

It was dark out as the party huddled around the fire. Conversation had been lighthearted up until this point when Kit looked over at Ontar and Echo and said, "Do you mind if I ask you two a question?"

Ontar exchanged glances with Echo before responding, "Sure, what's on your mind?"

"I was just wondering what was troubling you last night?" Kit asked in an unassuming manner.

Echo fidgeted. This was not an easy topic for her to talk about. "Oh, that. We were just remembering some tough times we had with our families."

Kit pressed the issue. "Did something happen to them?"

"Yeah, they died." Wink blurted out.

"Wink!" Hatch snapped. "It's not your place to reveal Ontar and Echo's struggles without their consent."

"But it's a really good story." Wink whined before turning to Ontar. "And a sad one."

Kit grew curious. "Why what happened?"

Raising his hands Hatch exclaimed. "Ugh, you're as bad as she is."

Echo shared a brief look with Ontar then said. "That's alright. I'd rather you hear the tale from us then get whatever warped version the pixie comes up with."

"Hey!" Wink grumbled indignantly.

"So where should we begin?" Ontar asked Echo as he stared distantly at the fire. Once again, the two were sharing their tragic tale, but it didn't bother them so much this time. Finding comfort in building a bond with their new companions the two longed for the sense of family that they had witnessed earlier and hoped that their trust would indeed bear fruit.

Chapter Twelve

The dwarves' echoing boots came to a halt as they reached the end of the cool gray cavern. Somber eyes diligently watched the shadows from beneath heavy brows as the bearded guardians stood ready for the first sign of danger. The entourage was composed of six warriors and one dignitary. While none of the travelers stood taller than a man's armpit, their gruff demeanor easily indicated they were individuals *not* to be trifled with.

Well-equipped to handle even the most fearsome of enemies, the dwarvish warriors wore chain armor that had broad iron shoulder plates, with small spikes set along their rims and center. Beautiful, thin silver circles surrounded these spikes and crossed over each other like ripples on the water. A similar design could be recognized on the dwarves' helmets, while a small iron crest in the center of their chest depicted a horned helmet with a battle ax and mace crossed beneath it in a clear symbol these warriors were soldiers of the Chapskin Empire. Fur capes hung from beneath the dwarves' shoulder plates, while any weapons they carried were well-hidden beneath their heavy woolen garments.

The guardians would have made for an imposing sight if not for the obnoxious braying coming from their over-packed donkeys. These poor creatures had carried their heavy loads for over a week and were unaccustomed to spending time underground. Their skittish behavior wore on the dwarves, who were more than happy to let the animals rest for a moment. The donkey's behavior was hardly unexpected. The only light available to them was a lantern held by the dignitary at the center of the group. Every new shadow it created was considered a possible threat by the frightened animals.

Ignoring the donkeys' behavior, Emissary Harshtone raised his lantern high to get a good look at what lay ahead of him. An old dwarf with a long gray beard and hair, he dressed in noble garments, which included a heavy black fur cloak, with a brown shirt decorated with several lines of vertical golden studs. A brown leather belt matched his boots but was fastened by an eloquently crafted golden buckle. The belt was a family heirloom and served its purpose well in holding up the old dwarf's black pants.

Gazing ahead to where the light fell, the dwarves saw a sign their journey was finally near an end. Before them was a broad stone stairway that ascended the mountain's interior. Flanking the stairs were two large stone statues that faced each other and resembled a pair of rearing dragons. Emissary Harshtone quickly noted the two statues didn't necessarily represent local dragons. Possessing an oriental appearance, their bodies were longer and more serpentine than other dragons, and they lacked the wings commonly associated with the beasts. Their arms and legs were also quite stubby, while their snouts were squared, with long whiskers dangling from the sides.

These particular statues had one claw extended towards the stairs, with a small bowl in it. Walking over to a nearby donkey, Emissary Harshtone opened the animal's sack and reached for a candle. Alarmed by the dwarf's sudden action, the donkey struggled and tried to back away, braying loudly before its handler managed to get it back under control. Taking hold of the candle, Emissary Harshtone broke it into two pieces and used his lantern to light the wicks. Afterwards, he tossed each piece of the candle into the dragons' bowls and watched in satisfaction as they lit up brightly like a torch.

Turning to face his fellow companions, the old dwarf smiled and asked, "All right, lads, who here wants to haul their asses up the stairs?" to chuckles from the travel weary group.

A brown-bearded dwarf approached the emissary and ventured a suggestion, "While the stairs are broad enough for us to travel up two at a time, I think it would be better if we just formed a line. The animals are easily spooked as it is, and cramming too many in a row will only make things more difficult."

Emissary Harshtone thought a moment. "Strongstrike has a good point, but if we go that route, someone will have to take the lead and carry the lantern. It'll be easier to guide the donkeys if they're following the light instead of having it behind them."

The other dwarves immediately volunteered for the job, but Strongstrike's voice carried over all of them. "I'll take the lead!" he exclaimed. Then hesitating for a moment, he asked, "But where will you stand, milord?"

Emissary Harshtone's shoulders sagged. "I'll take a position in the middle of the line," he replied irritably. "Just don't expect me to drag along one of those stubborn asses," the emissary stated as he motioned towards one of the donkeys. "I'm too old to be playing with ponies."

The dwarves quickly formed a line with Strongstrike at its head, carrying a lantern in one hand and pulling a donkey in the other. As he took his place among the others, Emissary Harshtone took one last look at the dragon statues. Try as he might, the old dwarf could never figure out why the humans held such reverence for the overgrown lizards. Dragons were greedy, selfish, arrogant, and always claimed the best caverns for themselves. As far as he was concerned, the world would be a far better place without them in it.

It was at this moment the emissary was distracted from his musings by the skittish braying of donkeys, which struggled noisily after their masters began the arduous task of pulling them up the long stairway. Every step the pack animals took seemed to take forever. To make matters worse, the dwarves did nothing but pull, curse, and complain the entire time. Emissary Harshtone could hardly blame them. The donkeys stank something fierce, and the poor dignitary stepped in their droppings at least twice during the trip.

Relief eventually came to the dwarves when they felt a slight breeze coming ahead of them. It didn't take long before visibility increased as a dim light appeared at the stairway's end and grew brighter with each passing step. The fading darkness seemed to calm the animals a little bit, and the dwarves took full advantage of the shift in mood by quickening their pace.

Before long, the tired travelers had reached the top of the stairs and saw before them a simple cave exit rimmed with stony, tooth-like points, and a beautiful blue sky beyond them. Stepping out into the light, the dwarves saw they were on one of the many rocky plateaus high in the Crimson Ranges. It was a sunny day, with a few lazy clouds hovering just above the mountains' peaks.

Contrary to their name, most of the surrounding ranges were gray in color, with a few being topped off with just a little bit of snow.

Having finally reached their destination, the dwarves gladly let their donkeys wander a little as they took in their surroundings. Pulling his cloak around himself, Emissary Harshtone looked back at the stairway he had just emerged from and snickered when he saw their entrance was actually the mouth of a large, stone oriental dragon head.

Turning his attention away from the stairs, Emissary Harshtone instead focused on the high stone wall that occupied much of the plateau. At the center of the wall was one of the most interesting gateways the dignitary had ever seen. Built with a subtle elegance, the gate had a unique roof covered in orange ceramic tiles and flared eaves. Supporting the roof were four dark red pillars placed on either side of a set of steps. Next to the outermost pillars were two bronze statues of what appeared to be fierce, sitting lions. The steps led up to a pair of large wooden double doors that had probably kept intruders out for ages.

Readying himself for the business at hand, Emissary Harshtone turned towards his fellow companions and called out, "Strongstrike! I think it's time we let out hosts know they've got company."

Following his lord's cue, Strongstrike walked towards one of the gateways outer pillars that, upon closer inspection, was revealed to have a small bell and rope attached to it. As he did so, the other dwarves rounded up their wayward donkeys and pulled them into lines near the emissary.

Strongstrike pulled on the rope several times, and the bell rang out for all to hear. Afterwards, he walked up the steps and waited by the large wooden doors. It took a little bit but, eventually, a small slot on one of the doors slid open to reveal a pair slanted brown eyes that looked down on the dwarf with curiosity.

"Who seeks the oracle?" asked a man on the other side of the door.

"I am Strongstrike, a protector of Emissary Harshtone who has journeyed across the Chapskin Empire to seek the wisdom of the Nung-Dow," the dwarf replied with formal courtesy.

"Ah, one moment, please," responded the man as he quickly closed the slot.

Several minutes passed as Strongstrike waited patiently by the gate. Then came a sound that reminded the dwarf of a crossbar being slid into a new position. Strongstrike instinctively withdrew from the gate and stood near his comrades. As he did so, the large wooden doors were pulled open, and several humans advanced cautiously across the gateway.

Easily recognized as monks, the Nung-Dow were far different from the empire's other human citizens. Calm, yet alert, these men all had tan skin, bald heads, and slanted brown eyes. Dressed in a similar fashion, the monks all wore orange tricivara robes with sandals. Their leader had blue prayer beads covering his left hand and approached the dwarves with three monks flanking him on either side. Recognizing the man, Emissary Harshtone strode before his own guards to address him.

Looking down at the old dwarf, the lead monk bowed slightly and said, "Emissary Harshtone, you honor us with your presence."

Glancing up at the monk, Emissary Harshtone snorted abruptly and replied, "Yesu, you wouldn't be honored by *my* presence unless I shit gold."

Not missing a beat, Yesu looked at the old dwarf and uttered, "Well, shall I fetch you a chamber pot?" Laughter quickly followed as the monks and dwarves casually mingled.

Clasping Yesu's hand and arm, Emissary Harshtone smiled and gestured back towards the donkeys. "Come on, man, let's head in. We've had a long journey, and I've brought dinner."

With help from the monks, the dwarves were easily able to guide their animals through the open gate. Entering into the courtyard of what appeared to be an expansive monastery, the travelers immediately noticed a large dark red building with wooden framework and a multi-tiered roof that resembled the gateway they had just passed through. A few smaller buildings of similar design could also be seen nearby. Emissary Harshtone could even see the Nung-Dow had managed to grow a couple of decent-sized trees in their courtyard. An impressive feat considering their rocky environment.

As they approached the main building, the entourage was beset by the temple's other residents. Children eagerly surged forward to greet the dwarves and see what was in their donkey's sacks. A mere step behind them were their mothers, who desperately tried to maintain discipline among the youngsters.

The Nung-Dow women all had features that resembled the men, except for their long black hair, which they wore styled up. Dressed in colorful outfits, the women wore pastel yukata's with beautiful floral prints, a dark red obi sash, and sandals. Their daughters wore similar clothing but were allowed to let their hair down. The boys all had short black hair and ran around in tan jinbei.

The dwarves had expected this type of greeting and began passing out pouches of marbles and chalk to the youngsters. Satisfied with their presents, the children were gathered up by their mothers who (after apologizing to the dwarves for their rambunctious nature) quickly shooed them away from the tired travelers. As the children departed, a handful of monks came forward to unpack the donkeys and lead them to the stables.

Relieved of their burden, the dwarves accompanied Yesu and his companions into the main building. Climbing up a small set of wooden stairs, the monks stopped on a covered porch with railings just outside the buildings entrance. Here, an old woman sat next to the main doorway with a small straw mat in front of her. Following a practiced routine, the monks removed their sandals and handed them to her so she could neatly arrange them on the mat.

When Emissary Harshtone approached the doorway, the old woman scowled but made no attempt to reach for the dwarves' boots. The Nung-Dow had learned a long time ago about the pungent aroma that emerged from a dwarf's foot and decided it would be easier for them to clean the floor than stomach their guest's foul stench. Smiling to himself, Emissary Harshtone quietly entered the monastery.

Following Yesu's lead, the dwarves and monks walked down a hallway with clean wooden floors, large windows, and small colorful lanterns hanging from the ceiling. Turning a corner, the group saw the monasteries interior walls were comprised almost entirely out of white paper panels. Turning down another hallway, Yesu brought the group to a halt as he pushed aside two sliding doors, which looked almost indistinguishable from the walls, and beckoned for his guests to follow him in.

Entering the dining hall, the dwarves saw a long wooden table with short legs set on top of a big straw mat. The room's panels were decorated with ink landscape paintings, while a wooden wall at the head of the table had a decorative scroll hanging from it and a small built-in platform at its base. Resting on the platform were some beautiful flowers and a porcelain vase with reeds that emitted the sweet smell of incense.

Standing at the head of the table, Yesu spread out his arms and said, "Welcome, my friends, to our table. Please, feel free to sit and relax. Dinner shall be served shortly."

Stomping up to a spot near his host, Emissary Harshtone looked down at the table and frowned. "Dammit, Yesu, I've been coming to this monastery for the past one hundred years, and *not once* have you or your predecessors ever bothered to get me a chair to sit in!"

Smiling down at the belligerent dwarf, Yesu calmly replied, "You must forgive me, Emissary Harshtone, but you stand so close to the ground I assumed a chair would be unnecessary." The comment invoked immediate chuckles from both dwarves and monks alike as all those assembled sat cross-legged on the mat.

Eloquently rebuked for his remark, Emissary Harshtone grumpily joined the others on the mat. Crossing his legs, the old dwarf mumbled under his breath, "It probably won't be necessary after today." The comment left Yesu with the inclination the reason behind his guests' visit wasn't a pleasant one.

Turning his attention to other matters, the monk looked towards Emissary Harshtone and initiated polite conversation. "So, how was your journey beneath the mountains?" he inquired.

The emissary pulled out an intricately crafted pipe, a little tobacco, and some matches from his pocket. Lighting the pipe, he inhaled deeply before blowing a small cloud of smoke into the air. The smell of tobacco mixed with the room's already present incense to create an interesting aroma.

"Dull and aggravating," the old dwarf replied after a moment. "I swear I don't know what the gods were thinking when they created donkeys, but the first thing I do when I die is ask them why in the world they would plague our lives with such a *stupid* animal." Yesu waited for the dwarf to finish his rant, a subtle smile creeping across his features. Fortunately, it didn't take long. "Aside from our beasts, the journey went pretty well. We were even able to stop by Shale on our way here."

The emissary's words gained Yesu's attention. Shale was the only imperial settlement located anywhere near the monastery. Trade with the town's residents had served as the lifeblood for much of the Nung-Dow's community. Sadly, that exchange had trickled to a halt almost a year ago. Clinging to a faint hope, Yesu asked, "And how are your kinsmen in Shale doing?'

Emissary Harshtone snorted. "What kinsmen? After the mines went barren, there's been no reason for anyone stick around. The town's probably been deserted for several months now."

"Except for the kobolds," exclaimed Strongstrike. "We drove a bunch of them away while searching the town."

Yesu leaned forward. "Why were there kobolds in an otherwise abandoned town?"

A grim look came over Emissary Harshtone's face. "They were scavenging goods to sell to the orcs."

A hushed tone came over those who sat at the table, and a serious expression crossed Yesu's face. "Did you see any orcs during your travels?" the monk asked quietly.

"No," the emissary replied.

A wave of tension quickly dissipated from the room. As it did, the sliding doors were opened, and two women entered the dining hall. One woman carried a tray of small cups skillfully dispersed in front of all those assembled. The second woman carried a tray that held both a teapot and a bottle of saké.

While the monks chose their beverages and thanked the women, their dwarvish counterparts grumbled in disgust. "This is what we get to quench our thirst? Piss water or soggy," complained Emissary Harshtone.

Yesu looked at the dwarf and shook his head while letting out a quiet sigh. "What sort of beverages do you normally enjoy?"

"Ever heard of Dead Dwarf's Brew?" exclaimed Emissary Harshtone with a grin. "You take half a mug of ale, pour three different types of poison in it, light it on fire, and down it right after you blow out the flames."

The monks all looked at the old dwarf with various expressions of disbelief. One of them couldn't help but ask, "Forgive me, milord, but can dwarves truly stomach such a lethal brew?"

Emissary Harshtone boasted. "I'm still sitting here, aren't I?"

Dinner conversation proceeded along more pleasant lines well into the night. As the meal concluded, the monks and dwarves dispersed to attend to their evening activities. Leaving the main building, Yesu and Emissary Harshtone went for a nighttime stroll around a pond located at the center of the monastery. A full red moon dominated much of the night sky. Surrounding it were countless stars that reminded those who looked upon them just how big the universe truly was.

Moving at a relaxed pace, the monk and the dignitary passed by several stone lanterns that illuminated their path and stopped by an odd-looking plant, which appeared to be a huge head of lettuce with a big pink and white flower at its center that grew around a thorn-covered branch. After a brief period of silence, Emissary Harshtone looked up at Yesu and solemnly asked, "So, how is he?"

Yesu stared into the distance. "Not well," he replied in a manner reflecting the question. "The master's maladies shift between physical and mental distress almost daily."

Emissary Harshtone looked towards the ground. "I was afraid you were going to say that," the old dwarf replied quietly. "It's going to make what I have to say just that much harder." Yesu nodded for the emissary to continue, and he did. "The problem the empire is facing is the local orcs have grown in strength while, at the same time, the value of these mountains has diminished. Shale was the only town worth defending in this area, and now that it's dried up, the empire sees no more reason to be here."

Yesu's tone was flat as he said, "You wish to abandon us."

Emissary Harshtone shot a sharp look at the human. "It's not like we have a whole lot of choice in the matter. The oracle hasn't issued any new prophecies in over a year! And without his help, I've had a damndable time trying to convince the emperor this monastery needs protecting."

"What do you propose?" the monk asked.

Emissary Harshtone sighed. "I've been sent here to ask you and your people to relocate to another part of the empire before it's too late…and before you say no, I'm also supposed to inform you that *all* imperial troops will be leaving these mountains at the end of the month."

Yesu stopped walking, nodded, and pointed to a small wooden tower with a long golden bell hanging inside it. "Do you see that bell tower?" the monk asked. "At the start of every new year, the master chooses an exceptional child to ring that bell and begin a new period of prayer and celebration for my people. This is the first year he has decided not to initiate the bell ringer's ritual. His decision has forced us all to realize we will not survive to the year's end."

Emissary Harshtone knew the importance of rituals to Nung-Dow, and the relevance in not fulfilling them. "You know you're all going to die, yet you still choose to stay here. What in the world is wrong with you people?"

Yesu tried to explain, "We stay because the master foresees us fulfilling a greater purpose by doing so."

"Well, what about your families?" asked the dwarf. "Does the oracle foresee them getting butchered for this mysterious purpose as well?"

"No," replied Yesu. "That is why you are here. Emissary Harshtone, I humbly ask that you and your fellow dwarves escort our women and children safely to another part of the empire."

The old dwarf's jaw dropped. "You *can't* be serious. You expect me and what few guards I have to drag a bunch of women and children through orc infested territory while you and the other monks just sit back here and wait around to die!"

"Yes," replied Yesu. "My destiny lies here with the master. If you choose to let our families accompany you to a safer place, then I can *assure* you everyone will reach their destination unharmed. If you leave them here with us, then they shall perish."

Emissary Harshtone growled. "For someone who hasn't issued any prophecies for a while, the oracle sure picked a damn time to start seeing the future. I suppose you already know my decision then."

Sharing some insight, Yesu said, "Life is a combination of choice and fate, and the choice you make will determine my people's fate. However, I also know who you are as a person, which is why my brothers and I have spent the past month packing up belongings and saying goodbye to our loved ones."

The old dwarf scowled, then sighed. "Do you really think what you're doing is actually going to matter?"

Yesu looked down at his longtime friend. "Yes. We give our lives now, hoping the lives of many others will be spared by our actions."

Staring off into the distance, Emissary Harshtone quietly uttered, "I hope you're right."

Chapter Thirteen

Ontar and Echo heard their horse panting as they rode it down a long stretch of dirt road through the Wistwind Plains. Carrying two riders on a hot summer's day had nearly pushed their animal to the point of exhaustion. Fortunately, the increased number of travelers had helped to slow its pace and match the stride of the horse being ridden by Kit, Hatch, and Wink. Coming up behind an ox-driven wagon moving sluggishly, Ontar and Kit were forced to pull the reins of their respective mounts to slow them down to a canter. Ahead of them, they could see a growing line of people heading towards the gray stone walls of Ranig.

"Are the roads to Ranig always this busy?" Ontar asked Hatch from beneath his full helmet. Sweltering in a heavy suit of armor, he longed to grab a drink from one of the city's taverns and sit in the shade for a while.

Hatch raised his hand to keep the sun out of his eyes. "Yes, unfortunately. The city has a large farmers' market that is always busy during festivals."

"Which means we get to sit here and bake," Wink grumbled as she fought with Whiskers for space in the hood of Kit's cloak.

Looking over her shoulder, Kit said, "Oh, don't be so grumpy. Tell you what. Once we get inside the city, you and I can hit the candy shops."

Perking up noticeably, Wink replied, "Really! You promise?"

"I promise," Kit said with a smile.

"Just be careful not to get lost in the crowds," Hatch warned. "Ranig can be a dangerous city if you aren't careful."

"Why do you say that?" Echo asked. The last thing she wanted was to be caught off guard by some sort of hidden threat.

Hatch elaborated, "Because the ruling magistrate is about as corrupt a man as you will ever meet. The city's various factions bought him off ages ago, and his guards put their interests well before the rule of law."

"So, how many factions are there?" Echo inquired.

Hatch crinkled his brow as he thought. "Wealthy nobles, city temples, the slave and mages' guilds, and I think your friends at the Bloody Side have a presence here as well."

Echo's eyes widened. "He's getting money from five different groups!"

"Six if you count what he collects normally through taxes," Hatch added.

"Ohy, I'm in the wrong line of work," Echo said with wide eyes.

Ontar thought about this for a moment. "It also means we could be up against skilled personal guards instead of the regular authorities."

"When's that ever been an issue?" Echo asked with a grin.

"Good point." Ontar shrugged.

It was almost an hour before the party finally reached the city's gate. Flanked by some round towers with guards moving between their parapets, Echo and Hatch grew leery of the crowd that passed through its open doors and hid their features by pulling up the hoods of their cloaks. Echo's reason for this was because Sibeia's war with the Illamine provoked people's hostility towards any elf who dared to traverse too deep into these lands. Hatch, on the other hand, didn't want anyone to recognize him as a former mage lord and try to alert the guards.

Feeling justified in her concern, Echo saw four Sibeian guards that spread out along the city gate and inspected merchant carts while collecting fees from travelers. Frowning, Echo looked over at Hatch and asked, "Why are those guards taking money from people?"

"The city usually tries to collect a toll from travelers during festivals," Hatch replied in a manner that obviously expressed his distaste of the practice.

"What sort of festival is taking place here today?" Ontar asked.

Ignoring the surprised looks from some nearby eavesdroppers, Hatch said, "It's the ceremony of Salvations Sacrifice, which is held each year by the Order of Kardok. You see, when a person dies, their soul travels to a place called the Twilight Palace for judgment. If that person paid homage to the god of death during their life, then they are allowed to enter the spirit realm. Those who didn't are often cast into the Dungeon of Eternal Torment to suffer for all eternity."

Ontar vaguely recalled hearing something about this ceremony. "Isn't this all part of some ritual for human sacrifice?"

Hatch nodded. "Yes, a maiden is sacrificed at the Temple of Kardok in a pool of blood gathered from those who seek to gain the god's favor."

"And they want us to pay for that!" Echo exclaimed. "Well, forget it. I'm going to save my soul *and* my money."

Leaving Ontar to guide their horse, Echo dismounted and sauntered up to the wagon in front of them. Driven by a farmer who was clearly irritated at the guards who were about to inspect his wares, Echo spotted a basket full of onions sitting up high near the back of the cart. Thinking quickly, she drew an arrow from her quiver and jabbed it into the basket. Jerking the projectile free with a quick tug, Echo watched as three onions fell onto the ground before her. Returning her arrow to its quiver, Echo picked up the onions and stepped back as the guards inspected the farmer's goods.

Nibbling on some of the fruits and vegetables they found during their examination, the guards jumped off the farmer's wagon and charged him with a modest fee. After being paid, they waved him through the gate and into the city. Seeing her chance, Echo held the onions in front of her and shouted, "Excuse me, sir…sir!" Running past the guards, Echo came up to the side of the farmers wagon and presented him with the onions. "I think you dropped these."

"Well, thank you," said the farmer as he took the onions. Shooting a nasty look back at the guards, he loudly proclaimed, "It's nice to know that at least someone's honest around here." Reaching into the wagon behind him, the farmer pulled out a carrot and offered it to her. "Here, have a snack. It's on me."

"Thank you," Echo replied as she took the carrot. Walking along the cobblestone street, she leaned against the side of a nearby building and waited for the rest of her companions to join her.

Continuing on with their assigned duties, the guards ordered the rest of the party to pay a toll for passage through the city's gate. Grudgingly doing so, the group emerged onto the streets of

Ranig and found they were absolutely bustling with people. Since no one had an immediate destination in mind, they all decided to dismount from their horses and meet up with Echo.

Pulling off his helmet to get a breath of fresh air, Ontar saw the deceptive dabbler smugly eating her carrot and said, "I can't believe that worked."

Echo was about to give a smartass reply when she noticed the people around her had all stopped walking and were now looking towards the sky. Following their gaze, she glanced upwards just in time to see the shadow an enormous creature as it swept over the crowd and briefly blotted out the sun. Unabashedly staring at the underside of a sky whale, Echo was awestruck by its majesty as it slowly floated over the surrounding buildings.

Considered by some to be an oversized beast of burden Orla had round green eyes and a sleek white body with a long sharp horn that smoothly protruded from her snout. Hanging from this horn was a large white banner that fluttered in the breeze and depicted the elaborate golden knot of Sibeia. In marked contrast to the color of her hide, Orla's flippers and tailfin were covered in bright orange feathers. These appendages seemed to be used for maneuverability. A series of four huge chains could be seen wrapped around the sky whale's body, and they apparently held something onto the creatures back. As Orla passed overhead, the citizens of Ranig watched her depart, then returned to their regular duties.

"That's what you want us to take on!" Ontar exclaimed as he looked over at Hatch.

Hatch waved his hands in a calming gesture. "Not exactly. Remember, our goal is to eliminate the guards who live in the manor on Orla's back. However, before we can even attempt this, I need to go and enlist the help of an old friend. While I'm gone, why don't the rest of you go and attend the Salvations Sacrifice ceremony."

Kit frowned. "Grandpa, you know I'm not going to do that."

"Well, you should at least consider it," Hatch grumbled.

Curious, Echo asked, "Why aren't you going to participate in the ceremony, Kit?"

Elaborating, Kit said, "Because a ranger like myself has been allowed to draw upon Mirsha's power when casting a spell. In exchange for this gift, I have pledged my soul to eternally serve the nature goddess once I have died. This spare's me from Kardok's judgment..."

"And forever denies you the everlasting peace that comes from admittance into the spirit realm," Hatch finished.

"Which is a sacrifice, Dad, and I gladly made a long time ago," Kit added.

"Great!" Wink exclaimed. "So, if you aren't going to the ceremony, then can we *please* go get some candy? I can't catch a changeling without the proper bait."

Echo gave the pixie a skeptical look. "Yeah, I'm sure that's why you want the candy."

"Either way, I'll take you," Kit replied as she took her horse by the reins and walked over to Ontar. "I was going to go stable my horse while Grandpa's gone and wondered if you'd like me to do the same for yours."

Ontar handed her the reins of his animal. "Sound's good to me."

Annoyed with being unable to sway his granddaughter, Hatch said, "Very well. Why don't we all meet back here after the ceremony."

Agreeing to this plan, the party split up to go their separate ways.

Finding where the ceremony was going to take place proved to be a fairly easy task for Ontar and Echo. City criers routinely rang small bells while shouting out directions to a steady line of people who headed towards the same destination. Passing by street performers, beggars, and merchants, Echo's keen pointed ears picked up on a chorus of singers that could be heard roughly a block over from where they were walking. Giving Ontar a nudge, the two took a side road to see where the music was coming from.

What they found was a large, cross-shaped building made out of plain gray stone. Built with pillared archways that helped support the two-story structures overhanging parapets Ontar noticed that a number of scantily-clad women and shirtless muscular men were standing intermittently between the columns. Echo focused on the front of the building where a prominent wooden stage displayed a talented choir of lightly-dressed humans all singing to the movements of a sweaty conductor who stood before them.

Entranced by the tragic undertones of their music, Echo shoved her way into the crowd watching them. When the song came to an end, she joined in the thunderous applause that erupted from the audience as the conductor turned around and took a courteous bow.

"Thank you...thank you one and all. I've worked hard to whip this choir into shape, and I'm proud to say that this is definitely their best show yet. On behalf of Ranig's slavers' guild, I hope that everyone here can enjoy the festival, and I'd like to remind you that all our performers are available for purchase at the end of today's activities."

As the conductor turned around to begin another song, Echo moved away in disgust. It was absolutely amazing to her how callously humans could treat each other. Wishing to get away from this place, she looked around and realized Ontar wasn't by her side. Scanning the area, she spotted him talking to one of the slave women who posed outside the guildhall.

Ontar thought he made a real connection with the sexy young woman who was erotically waving two oversized fans to keep herself cool. A long chain that shackled her ankle to the archway was clear evidence she was a slave, but if he could get her behind one of those pillars, then perhaps he could help *ease* her life of servitude for a little while.

Moving close to the woman, Ontar asked, "What would you say if I told you that a single moment of passion could erase a lifetime of hardship?"

Closing one of her fans and using it to seductively lift his chin, the slave said, "Why cling to a single moment when you have the chance to be with me forever?"

"She makes a good point," came a masculine voice from behind Ontar. Turning around, he saw a man in brown leather armor with curly black hair and a whip coiled on his weapon belt.

"Well, maybe she does," Ontar said to the slaver with a smile. "What kind of coinage are we talking about to free this lovely lady here."

"Gold always gets things going," the slaver replied.

"Gold!" Ontar repeated. Gold was a little out of his price range. "I don't think I can part with that kind of money, but what if I were interested in taking just an hour of her time?"

The slaver thought a moment. "Why don't you swing by the guild after today's festivities, and we can discuss the matter?"

"ONTAR!" Echo exclaimed as she stomped up to the horny warrior. "Have you no shame?"

"Not since I was a teenager," he shot back.

Echo's eyes narrowed as she reached out with one hand and grabbed him by the ear. Jerking the big oaf down to her level, she angrily said, "We're going." Not bothering to wait for a reply, she proceeded to drag him back towards the main street and away from this den of filth.

◆◆◆

Hatch felt out of place walking down the busy streets of Ranig. Remembering former days of glory when he would have been escorted by guards past throngs of excited citizens, he now felt like just another sad old man ignored by those around him. Considering how much time he had devoted to the people of Sibeia, he found it terribly depressing that, in a mere five years, he had been all but forgotten. Putting such thoughts aside, Hatch decided to focus on the task at hand as he finally reached his destination.

The Temple of Anthalos was an immense structure built out of solid gray stone. A broad stairway, which led up to its entrance, had three big metal bowls equally spaced on either of its sides that held a raging fire within them. Stationed between these bowls were six paladins with gray capes and white surcoats that had the emblem of a burning torch in front of an open book centered on their chests.

A similar emblem was depicted on a large banner which hung between two of the six golden minarets that lined the front of the temples roof. Supporting this roof were long rectangular columns of reddish-brown stone, each with different words of wisdom inscribed in large golden letters on them. Bowing his head. Hatch climbed the stairs as he passed by the paladins and went through the towering archway that made up the temple's entrance.

Stepping onto the polished brown tiles of the temple's foyer, Hatch saw the room had three large archways along each of its walls that led to other parts of the building. The air was cooler here, which made Hatch believe that a spell was in place to keep the temple at a continuously comfortable temperature. In the center of the foyer was a beautifully crafted podium with a young man in white robes standing behind it.

The acolyte smiled as he saw Hatch. "Welcome to the Temple of Anthalos. May the god of knowledge enlighten you during your visit with us."

"That you," Hatch managed to get out before the enthusiastic acolyte started speaking again.

"Our temple has many services available to those in need. Behind me is the worship hall where you can pray, quietly reflect, or receive information about joining our order from one of our many clerics. To your left is the infirmary should you suffer from some sort of ailment, and to your right is the library if you are interested in literature or wish to enroll your child in a formal education."

"Do I look like someone who needs to educate their child?" Hatch grunted. The young man quickly blushed, and Hatch dismissed the comment with a wave of his hand. "I think I shall head to the worship hall," he added politely before walking past the acolyte.

The hall looked exactly as Hatch remembered it, with rows of long wooden pews leading up to a large dais that had an eloquently designed golden altar placed upon it. Behind the altar was a towering statue of Anthalos, who looked like a bearded man in a robe with his hood up. In the statue's left hand was an open book, while the right hand held up a torch whose light was actually a glowing sphere of dull white energy. The sphere's light touched the chamber's side walls, which were intermittently covered with large long scrolls written in different colors of ink and stained-glassed windows depicting various important scholars.

Scanning the room, Hatch noticed the worship hall appeared to be scarcely populated at this time of day. Fortunately, one of the few people who were there just happened to be the cleric he was looking for. Watching as the middle-aged man with short blond hair humbly bowed his head in prayer, Hatch decided to sit quietly in the pew behind him. Clad in a hooded white robe, the cleric wore a brown leather weapon belt the same color as his boots. Dangling from his neck was a simple golden pendant that bore the symbol of Anthalos on it.

Speaking after an appropriate amount of time, Hatch said, "Excuse me, good cleric, is it possible for Anthalos to forgive an old man who had once lost his way in life."

Finishing his prayer, the cleric turned around and replied, "Redemption can come to any man whose journey has led to enlightenment."

Hatch smiled. "Ah, Chairbis, I see that Anthalos's wisdom continues to flow through you."

"It does, and I see that *you* have managed to escape the dungeon meant to be your tomb," Chairbis pointed out.

"Yes, well, it appears the gods have given me a second chance to do some good in this world. Provided, of course, that you'd be willing to help me."

Chairbis shook his head. "I can't help you, Hatch. My loyalties still lie with the mage lord."

Scoffing at the notion, Hatch asked, "And just who is the new mage lord?"

"Shavasae," Chairbis replied.

"Ugh…I should have known," Hatch muttered. Shavasae had had been one of his most formidable rivals from the moment he joined the mages' guild. The two had competed hard for the guild's top position, and if his ex-wife hadn't managed to get Shavasae involved in a *very* public scandal, then Hatch doubted that he ever really would have stood a chance at becoming mage lord.

Dreading his next question, Hatch asked, "Does Sir Fridlum still lead Orla's guards?"

"No," Chairbis replied. "Sir Havens leads them now. Sir Fridlum felt terrible about what happened to you and resigned his position shortly after you were found guilty of treason."

Hatch felt his temper flare. "That bastard should have felt far more than guilty for what he did to me!"

Staying completely calm, Chairbis said, "Hatch, it wasn't his fault. You were financing a rogue knight trying to overthrow the government."

"I never would have let it get that far," Hatch protested.

Chairbis gave Hatch a dubious look. "Well, you didn't exactly stop him from killing the harvest lord now, did you?"

"That was an accident!" Hatch argued.

"But encouraging Sir Temas to kill the golden lord next was not," Chairbis pointed out.

Hatch pounded his fist on the pew in front of him. "No, it wasn't! That arrogant jackass had no right to take my wife from me. Can you imagine how utterly destroyed I was by that?"

A couple people in the worship hall were surprised by Hatch's outburst, and Chairbis made a quieting gesture with his hands. "Hatch...Lady Alean left you of her own accord, and you know it. Your desire for revenge had become all-consuming, and while Sir Fridlum had sworn an oath to protect you, he also had an obligation to Sibeia. Going to the warrior lord was really his only choice."

Hatch felt himself getting teary-eyed. "I know...and I've had five years to think about what I've done. Maybe that's why I want to try and make things right."

"What do you mean?" asked Chairbis.

"I'm traveling with a group of people who have inadvertently released a demon from the Ha-Ress era. If it's as dangerous as I think it is, then we'll need advice from the Nung-Dow oracle on how to defeat it," Hatch explained.

Chairbis frowned. "And you need Orla to reach the oracle."

"Yes," Hatch said with a hint of trepidation. "But I can't take her without your help."

Chairbis shifted uncomfortably where he sat. "Hatch, you can't ask me to do this. I would be marked as a traitor by the government."

Hatch nodded in understanding. "I'm not asking you to attack Shavasae, or to even get involved in the upcoming conflict. All I'm looking for is a way to get on Orla undetected."

"So that you can seek vengeance against those who wronged you," Chairbis stated.

"Perhaps a long time ago," Hatch admitted. "But, right now, I'm here for a greater purpose, and I would never risk my granddaughter's life just to settle a personal vendetta."

Chairbis was surprised by this revelation. "Kit's here?"

Hatch knew that Chairbis had always been very close to his family, and the fact that Kit traveled with him carried a great deal of weight with the cleric. "Yes, she is, and she believes in our cause just as much any of my other travel companions."

Mulling over this new information, Chairbis said, "I need to pray before I can make a decision on whether or not I should help you. Do you mind waiting here while I ask Anthalos for guidance?"

"Not at all," said Hatch. "May the god of knowledge reveal the right path for you to tread upon." *And may that path be the one we're already traveling down,* he thought. Hatch had already told Chairbis of the party's plans, and if the cleric didn't go along with them, then things could get very ugly very fast.

❧ ❧ ❧

"Ohy, yea! Ohy, yea! The Salvations Sacrifice ceremony is about to commence," shouted one of several criers as Echo and Ontar joined a crowd of people filing into the city square.

The Order of Kardok had set up wooden posts around the area that had long, black banners with the emblem of an encircled red skull with flaming eye sockets on them. This symbol was also present on the black surcoats of the orders paladins whose matching capes hung from their armored shoulders while they organized people into long lines that surrounded a large stage in the center of the square. Ontar noticed their gear was similar to what the paladin he had fought in Miltus wore, and he wondered if they had the same type of training?

Standing on the stage with hoods up and silver pendants dangling around their necks were at least a dozen black-robed clerics. Talking casually with each other, they were careful to steer clear of a decadent wooden throne where an official of some importance sat. The man was bald and had a white goatee. Echo could have sworn that he wore something around his neck, but at her current distance, she could only make out that he held a long wooden staff with a golden crescent at its top that held a small round crystal in it.

Ontar's focus was drawn to the imposing white knight with short red hair that stood next to the man. Leaning close to Echo, he whispered, "I bet that's the mage lord and his guardian."

Echo was about to answer him when she felt someone step on her foot. Looking to her left, she saw a rather plump woman drenched in sweat standing next to a slender man that was probably her husband.

Seeming rather flustered, the woman said, "Oh, I'm sorry. I get so nervous standing in crowds."

"That's alright," Echo said absently. She was about to speak with Ontar when the woman blurted out, "I don't know why they have to have the ceremony on such a wretchedly hot day like this?"

Echo grew quickly annoyed. "I couldn't tell you."

Seeing Echo's reply as an invitation, the woman said, "Well, *I* think that it's because…"

This started a long, one-sided conversation that didn't stop until a booming voice from nowhere said, "Citizens of Ranig! We have gathered here today to pay homage to the god of death. We do this in the hopes that he will take pity on our souls and grant us eternal peace when our lives in this world have ended."

Looking for the source of the omnipresent voice, Ontar and Echo realized the mage lord had cast some sort of spell when standing up to address the crowd. His speech was short and to the point, giving them hope the ceremony wouldn't take all afternoon. Unfortunately, this hope was immediately dashed when, afterwards, a cleric of Kardok stepped forward and used a similar spell to say:

"Greetings one and all. I see you have come here to pay homage to the Lord of Darkness, but are any of you truly worthy of his blessing?"

The question was the start of an extremely long sermon that proceeded to demean the crowd for their weakness, invoke guilt over the human sacrifice committed on everyone's behalf, and play up people's fears of the afterlife. As this took place, the citizens quietly whispered amongst themselves while standing under the grueling sun and swatting at flies.

When the sermon was done, a handful of young acolytes carrying offering plates moved among the lines of people collecting money for their order. Behind them were clerics who carried sharp daggers and decorative ceremonial bowls. When an acolyte approached Echo, he said, "This is an offering to the Lord of Darkness. Pay or be turned away."

Echo didn't like being forced to pay for her salvation, but she also didn't want to have gone through such an annoyingly long sermon for nothing. Handing over some copper coins, she heard the acolyte say, "When the cleric asks you a question, the only answer is *yes*." The young man then moved over to Ontar and repeated his instructions.

Echo watched as the cleric came next. Standing in front of the man whose wife wouldn't shut up earlier, she waited as the cleric asked him a series of questions. Once the questions were answered, the husband held out his hand, and the cleric used the tip of his dagger to prick one of his fingers. He then squeezed that finger until a couple drops of blood dripped into his bowl.

Seeing this caused the plump woman to panic. "Oh...oh! I don't think I can do this. I don't thi..."

Echo saw the woman faint, and she nimbly caught her in mid-fall. The cleric was obviously surprised by Echo's reflexes and briefly caught sight of her pointed ears as his acolyte ran over and asked, "Should we take her out of line?"

The woman's husband helped Echo prop up his wife. Angrily looking at the acolyte, he said, "We didn't come all this way for nothing!" He then told the cleric, "Now, you're going to prick her and get this over with."

Amused by the husband's brash attitude, the cleric took his dagger, pricked the woman's finger, and collected a few drops of blood. Afterwards, he raised his hand near her head and cast a spell. Moments later, the woman woke up and stood by her own accord. Looking around, she asked, "Oh, what happened?"

"You made an ass of yourself, that's what happened," grumbled her spouse.

Continuing on with the ceremony, the cleric stepped in front of Echo. Bowing her head so her hood would hide any facial features, Echo waited for the cleric to ask his questions.

"Do you fear death and its almighty master?" asked the cleric.

"Yes," Echo replied.

"Are you ready to humble yourself before Kardok during the time of judgment?"

"Yes."

"Do you willingly spill your blood to fuel the fires that will engulf an innocent?"

"Yes."

"Then give me your hand," demanded the cleric. Echo lifted her left hand, and he immediately studied it. No cuts, no scars, and no blemishes of any sort. Normally, the cleric would have found this to be quite odd for someone whose attire was as rugged as Echo's, but in this case, it merely confirmed she was actually an elf! Realizing his opportunity, the cleric acted quickly to avoid suspicion.

Taking his dagger, he pricked her finger and bled it out while saying, "You have given both your blood and a piece of your soul to the dark god. May he show mercy upon you when your time has finally come."

Echo watched the cleric move on to Ontar, who removed one of his gauntlets and slipped it into the upside-down helmet under his arm. There was something unsettling about this evil holy man, and she wanted to get away from him as soon as possible. The moment Ontar finished giving homage, Echo grabbed his hand and led him through the procession out of the square.

As they left, the cleric signaled for a nearby paladin named Kethal to join him. Stopping in-between a line of people the cleric said, "The woman in the green cloak is an elf. Take another man with you and bring her to me. She will make an excellent sacrifice."

Echo overheard the cleric's comment and looked back nervously to see two paladins with their shields out following her through the crowd. Initially, she thought she might be able to lose the men among the massive throngs of people, but with Ontar lumbering along behind her, she highly doubted it. Instead, she said, "Ontar, I think we're being followed."

Ontar looked back and saw the paladins shadowing them. Slipping on his gauntlet and helmet, he said, "We'll take to the streets and see if they trail us."

Leaving the city square, Echo and Ontar casually glanced behind them as they walked down a busy street. Just as Echo feared the paladins were keeping pace with them.

Thinking of a strategy, Ontar said, "If we fight them in the open, it will attract the city guards, and if what Hatch said earlier is true, then the paladins would probably gain the upper hand. Keep your eyes peeled for a spot where we can face them."

It didn't take long for Echo to find a suitable location. A rundown four-story apartment building with yellow walls and wooden framework definitely seemed like the best place to duck into. The building was sorely missing shingles, shutters, and even a door. This meant that anyone who lived there probably didn't want to draw any more attention to themselves than they had to. Pointing the place out to Ontar, the two passed through an open doorway that led into the building.

Ontar stepped into a long wooden hallway with doors on either side of it. At the end of the hall was a stairway leading up to the next level. Pointing ahead of him, he said, "If we go up those stairs, it will give us a chance to ambush them."

"Good idea," Echo replied. Drawing forth their weapons and shields, they went up the stairs and waited for the paladins to arrive.

Moments later, the dark paladins, Kethal and Rythe, entered the building and drew their swords. Looking at the stairs, Rythe said, "It looks like there's only one place they could have gone."

"I say we soften them up and take them down," Kethal replied with a grin. Rythe nodded in agreement, and the two simultaneously cast a spell by uttering the words, "Come here!"

Ontar and Echo suddenly felt an invisible force slam them into the floor next to the stairs. More shocked than harmed by the attack, they scrambled to get to their feet. Walking slowly down the hallway, the paladins snickered at the sound of the dual *thuds* from the ceiling above. Enjoying themselves, they cast their spells a second time.

Slamming into the floor *again*, Echo said, "They're using magic to pull us towards them."

"Well, let's give them what they want," Ontar stated. "We'll rush them on my mark." Trying to predict when the paladins would cast their next spell, Ontar shouted, "Now!" as he and Echo both charged down the stairs towards their enemies.

The paladins hadn't expected such a brash move, and they had already cast their spell for a third time before realizing what was about to happen. Ontar felt the invisible force drastically increase his momentum as he raised his tower shield and collided into Rythe with all the power of a charging bull. This sent the paladin tumbling along the ground, and Ontar moved in quickly to finish the man off.

Echo didn't quite have Ontar's bulk when magically charging her paladin. Bracing himself, Kethal successfully managed to stay on his feet when her shield bashed into his. Hoping to get in a second attack, Echo swung her sword at the paladin's leg, but he parried the strike and prepared for one of his own.

Drawing upon his dark powers, Kethal shouted the word, "Tense!"

Looking on in horror, Echo felt her weapon arm suddenly lock up. Pressing his advantage, Kethal thrust his sword at the beleaguered elf, who dodged the blade but was left unable to retaliate.

Backing away from the evil paladin, Echo heard him cast his spell a second time, and she grunted in frustration when her right leg abruptly became immobile. Raising her shield, Echo barely blocked a second attack strong enough to knock her off her feet.

Ontar witnessed Echo's plight and immediately came to her aid after dispatching his enemy. Spinning his morning star vertically in the narrow hall, he attacked the paladin from behind with a lethal blow to the back of the man's neck. As Kethal died, his power over Echo faded, and she found she had regained her mobility.

Wiping his weapon on the paladin's cape, Ontar said, "We should leave here. I don't think it will take too long before the buildings residents decide to call the guards."

Standing up, Echo sheathed her sword and said, "I'm ready when you are."

Wary of onlookers, Ontar and Echo tried to leave the apartments with as much discretion as possible.

⊰⊱⊰⊱⊰⊱

It was late in the afternoon when the party reunited near the city's gate. Kit, Wink, and Hatch were all engaged in casual conversation when Ontar and Echo showed up. Warily eyeing the gate guards, Ontar removed his helmet and said, "Well, we just got our first good look at the mage lord and, in all honesty, he doesn't seem so tough."

"Appearances can be deceiving," Hatch cautioned. "But now is not the time and place to discuss such things."

"Grandpa's right," Kit added. "Let's look for a place to stay for the night while you tell us about the ceremony."

Setting off down the street, Ontar and Echo informed the group about what happened while simultaneously seeking out every single inn or tavern the city had to offer. Every place they stopped was filled with travelers, and not a single vacant room could be found. Hungry, the party decided to go to a two-story tavern with a hanging sign above the door that depicted a red-faced demon with a chicken leg in its mouth that read: "The Hungry Demon."

The tavern was packed when the party entered, and they had to wait for almost half an hour before a round wooden table finally opened up. Service was extremely slow as serving wenches frantically ran around trying to fill people's orders. As they waited, Ontar turned to Hatch and said, "Since it doesn't look like we'll be getting our food anytime soon, I figure I'd ask you if your old friend will be able to help us accomplish our objective?"

Hatch folded his hands on the table in front of him. "Yes, although he won't be there in person. Tomorrow at dawn, we're supposed find a tower crane near some warehouses that will have several crates outside of it. All we have to do is hide in the empty crates with the emblem of Anthalos on them, and the rest will be taken care of."

"I knew Chairbis wouldn't let us down," Wink said as she casually strolled along the table's top with Whiskers at her side.

"I've heard you mention that name before," Echo pondered. "Who is this guy, and how do you know we can trust him?"

Kit smiled. "Chairbis is a family friend who helped bring my parents together."

Eager to speak up, Wink turned on her heel towards Echo and said, "When Thove and I first started adventuring, I convinced him to track down a changeling rumored to be in the village of Habed. Thove found it impersonating the brother of a local girl and tried going after it. Unfortunately, the wicked changeling escaped after throwing the girl down a well.

"That girl was my mother," Kit added, "and Dad took her to the nearest shrine he could find to heal her injuries."

"Which happened to be run by Chairbis," Wink explained. "It wasn't hard for a cleric like him to make Saren well, and once he did, Thove fell madly in love with her."

"Ugh…I remember that time," Hatch said with a chuckle. "When Thove and Saren started getting serious, he wanted me to reward Chairbis for saving his beloved. So, when Orla's resident cleric passed away, I decided to select him to fill the position, and he's been grateful ever since."

As conversation about Chairbis died down, a young serving wench carrying a large platter of food and drinks came up to the table and said, "Sorry about the wait. It's just been crazy around…" The wench's eyes almost popped out of her head when she saw Wink pacing the table in front of her. She'd never seen a pixie before and being in the presence of one now caught her completely by surprise.

Realizing she was being gawked at, Wink squeaked in her most menacing voice. "FEED ME! Or I shall CONSUME YOUR SOUL!!!"

The expression on the wench's face was priceless, and everyone around the table burst into laughter. Shaking his head merrily, Hatch halfheartedly raised a scolding finger and said, "Now, Wink, behave yourself." Blushing over her part in the joke, the serving wench giggled as she passed out people's meals. Afterwards, she sheepishly left the party so they could eat their dinner.

Being the first to finish her meal, Kit went up to the bar to enquire about a room for the night. Returning to the table with a grim expression on her face, she sat down and said, "I've got bad news. It looks like there isn't a single room available."

Shoulders slumping Wink asked, "Well, now what are we supposed to do? Sleep on the street?"

"Not a chance," Echo said as she searched the dining hall for people who were dressed like travelers. It didn't take her long to find a table with three men sitting at it. Two of these men played dice while the third was passed out, with his head lying next to four empty tankards.

Standing, Echo walked over to the men's table and crouched down low next to their unconscious friend. The drunk's breath reeked of alcohol as she asked his friends, "Hey, is he alright?" while subtly sliding her hand down into his coin pouch.

Glancing up from their game, one of the men said, "Yeah, Flod just doesn't know how to hold his liquor."

Echo sighed. "Ah that's a shame. I thought he was kind of cute just sleeping there like that." Returning to her table, Echo heard the dice players taunt their passed-out friend about the opportunity he just missed. Sitting down, she held up a plain-looking key with a number on it and said, "We're in room nine."

"Good," Ontar replied. "When we get there, we can discuss what our strategy for tomorrow will be."

It was getting late into the evening by the time the party finished discussing their plans to take over Orla. Their room felt cramped with so many people in it, but at least they had a place to stay for the night. Hatch slept in the bed with Wink, while the rest of the group curled up on the floor with blankets. Echo leaned against the door to their room and quietly fingered a song on her flute until she felt tired. Putting the instrument away, she knelt by Ontar and lightly shook his shoulder. "Ontar, I'm going to meditate. Keep an ear open for the door okay."

Ontar groggily mumbled something as he pulled his blanket tightly around himself.

Echo wasn't sure if he had heard her but, at the moment, she felt pretty safe. So, sitting in a meditative position she exhaled slowly and closed her eyes.

Half an hour later, a loud pounding could be heard on the door to the party's room. Trying hard not to fall over, Flod knew that someone had taken his key thanks to what his friends had said. Drunkenly staring at the door's number with blurry, blood-shot eyes, he loudly bellowed out. "Hey...HEY, this is *my* room. You go sleep in the hall!"

Wink tossed and turned as she heard the drunk pound on the door again. Putting her hands over her ears, she said, "Onnie, can you take care of that?"

Groggy and in a bad mood, Ontar got up and made his way towards the door. It was bad enough that he had to sleep on the floor *and* get up at the crack of dawn to go kill Sibeians. The fact that some idiot couldn't even give him a full night's rest was more than he could tolerate.

Flod heard movement from inside the room and stopped pounding on the door. Ready for an argument as he saw the doorknob turn, he said, "Who do you think you..."

Making a fist, Ontar threw open the door and punched the drunk square in the nose. Grunting as blood flowed from his nostrils, Flod dropped to the ground like a stone while Ontar slammed the door shut and went back to sleep. Pissing himself as he went unconscious, Flod decided that sleeping in the hallway wasn't so bad after all.

Chapter Fourteen

"Onnie…Onnie, it's time to wake up," Wink said as she stood next to the sleeping warrior's head.

Ontar squeezed his eyes shut and tried to pretend she wasn't there. The night had passed too quickly, and as his companions awoke to prepare for the battle ahead, all he could think about was how much he wanted to have just *one* extra hour of sleep.

Wink moved in close to Ontar's face. "Onnie, if you don't wake up, I'll bite your nose."

She's bluffing, Ontar thought until he felt two tiny hands touch his face. Opening his eyes, Ontar saw the sideways pixie lean in and open her mouth widely. Sitting up before she could do anything, Ontar caught the amused grins of everyone around him.

"Told you I could get him going," Wink said to Echo as she walked over towards Ontar's backpack and armor. "Now, get your gear together. You're holding us up."

Following her orders, Ontar promptly gathered his equipment and slipped Wink into the hood of his cloak. Once the party was ready, Kit opened the door to their room and saw a foul-smelling drunk with a bloody nose and soiled pants passed out in the hallway. Trying to slip around the disgusting man, she looked over at Echo and asked, "Isn't this the guy whose key you took last night?"

"Yup," Echo said as she crouched down and swiped what little was left from the drunk's coin pouch. After all, she felt it was better for her to take the coinage then have him waste it on more beer.

Moving on, the party passed through the tavern's deserted dining hall and stepped out onto the quiet city streets.

◆◆◆

Echo loved this time of morning. The sky was a deep shade of blue just begging for the dawn's colorful arrival. Wishing that Favin was here, she wondered what it would have been like to stroll with him down the streets of a human city.

Being the most familiar with Ranig's layout, Hatch led the party towards the city's labor ward. Running across few people who were up at this time of day, Hatch felt confident the group could reach their destination safely, provided, of course, they didn't run across any guards out on patrol. Fortunately, the massive number of travelers who attended the Salvations Sacrifice ceremony were sure to keep the local authorities busy for quite some time.

Arriving at the labor ward, the party found several large buildings that dominated this part of the city. Passing by a flour mill, Echo heard the tired groans of slaves working a tread wheel, while off in the distance, a local brewery could be seen opening its doors for business. Between these buildings were a series of warehouses Hatch was able to navigate with ease.

Traveling down a garbage-strewn alleyway, the party didn't stop until they came to a street that led to the tower crane. Peeking out from behind the corner of an unoccupied granary, Hatch saw a round, four story, gray stone tower whose brown shingled roof had a wide base that ended in a long narrow point. Sticking out from the narrow part of the roof was an old wooden crane, its hoist ropes swayed lightly in the breeze. Stacked near a door at the base of the tower was a big pile of crates watched by a bored city guard.

Floating in close proximity to the crane was Orla. The enormous sky whale appeared to be half-asleep as it waited to take on cargo. Focusing on the crates, Hatch saw the ones furthest from the tower had been painted with a black emblem of a burning torch in front of an open book. Recognizing these belonged to the Order of Anthalos, he turned to his companions and said.

"The crates with the black markings are the ones we're supposed to use to get on Orla. Our only problem is there's a guard watching them, and if we don't act quickly, then they'll be loaded up without us."

Thinking of a distraction, Kit said, "I might have a spell that could help us."

Intrigued by his granddaughter's resourcefulness, Hatch replied, "By all means."

Casting her spell, Kit listened for the first sound of movement. It didn't take long before the scamper of paws could be heard at the far side of the ally. Looking towards the noise, the party saw a smelly stray dog approaching them. Getting down on one knee, Kit heard Whiskers squeak frantically from within her hood as she reached out with both hands and stroked the matted brown fur on the animal's neck.

"Oh, who's a good boy?" she asked. "Can you help us distract that nasty guard?"

The dog's tongue wagged as it licked her face with excitement. Sensing his willingness to help, Kit said. "Alright, boy, go for it!" Standing so she could peek out from the ally, Kit watched as the dog headed towards the tower crane.

The guard on duty was learning against a crate when he saw the dog approach. "Hey there, boy. Have you come to keep me company?"

Wagging his tail, the dog responded with a bark as it trotted up to the guard. Reaching out to pet the animal, the guard was shocked when the stupid mutt tried to bite it. "Little shit!" he exclaimed as he stumbled backwards. The dog growled and snapped at him. Drawing his short sword, the guard said, "I'll show you!" The dog immediately backed off and ran down the street with the guard following him in hot pursuit.

"Now's our chance!" Hatch said as the party made their way towards the crates.

Throwing open their wooden tops, everybody climbed into a different crate and pulled the lid shut. Seconds later, the guard returned to his post, shaking his head, and sheathing his sword. It was just going to be one of those days.

Ontar felt cramped as he huddled in his crate next to Wink. Fortunately, a knothole in the wood allowed them to look outside and see the vibrant colors that filled the sky at dawn. It wasn't long after sunrise they heard the sound of two masculine voices near their hiding spot. Ontar and Wink took turns peeking through the hole as they saw two busy men standing next to them.

One of these men was quite old, and he squinted while looking over a piece of parchment he held. Being of scrawny build, the old man's head was bald on top with shoulder length gray hair at the sides. What hair he did have was the same color as his neatly-kept jerkin, which he wore over a plain white shirt. This shirt was tucked into some deep blue pants, worn with a pair of brown boots.

Wink immediately identified this person and whispered to Ontar, "That's Houge. He's Orla's chief slave and has served under four different mage lords through the years."

Houge finished going over his list, then told the crane master, "These crates are a last-minute addition to our cargo. We need to have them brought onboard Orla as soon as possible."

"That shouldn't be a problem," the crane master replied as the two headed back towards the tower.

Not long afterwards, the tower cranes hoist ropes were lowered to begin transport. Ontar saw each of his companions' crates carefully being lifted out a sight, one after another. Soon, he felt a jostling motion, followed by the sensation of slowly rising off the ground. Fascinated by what was happening, he looked through the crates hole and saw that he was now above the city's skyline. This was followed by an extremely close-up view of Orla and the manor, which rested on her back.

Held in place by four huge chains that attached to the buildings base, the mage lord's manor resembled the upper half of a ship without masts or sails. Built out of a sturdy brown wood, the manor's lower level seemed to have nothing remarkable about it whatsoever. The upper level had a number of small windows for travelers to peer through. In fact, a rather large window could be seen towards the rear of the building, while the back of the manor had a magnificent bay window with a square stone chimney set at its side. Towards the front of the manor was a small, stained-glass dome next to a second chimney that might have been considered a third story. Below this story, the manor's main level gave way to a railed deck that reminded Ontar of the bow of a ship. It was here that the crates were being carefully set down and unloaded.

Waiting to see what would happen next, Ontar witnessed two masculine slaves emerge from some double doors at the rear of the deck who began taking the assembled crates inside the manor. Wearing little aside from some shabby blue pants and brown boots, the slaves were as big as Ontar, and their sweat-covered bodies teemed with tight rippling muscles. Wink drew Ontar's attention to the slave on her left who had long wavy blond hair and said, "That's Vrok." She then inclined her head towards the second slave with short brown hair and a beard saying, "The other one's Gorev. They handle most of the heavy labor here on Orla."

Hmm. They're built like warriors, Ontar thought before adding, *then again, maybe I'm built like a slave.* Pondering this thought, he and Wink waited while the two slaves brought in Orla's cargo. When the time came to take their crate, Vrok grunted as he and Gorev lifted them up saying, "Ugh...these crates for Chairbis just keep getting heavier."

As they started to move, Wink whispered to Ontar. "Don't worry, Onnie. I'll love you no matter how heavy you get."

"Oh well, pass the pie," Ontar retorted.

It was difficult for Ontar to see much once their crate was brought inside the manor. Wooden hallways illuminated by golden candlelit sconces were about all he was able to make out. At one point, he could tell they were being taken down a flight of stairs but, otherwise, he had no idea where they were until the slaves set them down in some sort of darkened storage room.

From here, he heard the clanging of pots and pans followed by the succulent aroma of masterfully cooked food.

Within this room, the party quietly hid while different slaves went in and out opening the various crates around them. Then a subtle vibration in the floor told them that Orla was on the move, and their time to strike was approaching fast.

◆ ◆ ◆

Wink hugged her knee's as she sat in a crate next to Ontar. Watching him squirm with anticipation was extremely arousing, and she considered whispering something dirty in his ear. However, before she could succumb to that temptation, she heard a squeaking outside their crate and realized that it was Whiskers giving her a signal.

Looking at Ontar, she stood up and said, "It's time."

Gently picking her up, Ontar lifted the lid of their crate and set her on the floor of the storage room. Watching him put on his full helmet before crouching back down, Wink knew he was itching for a fight. Turning towards her mousy little friend, she said, "Come on, Whiskers, we've got work to do."

Moving quietly towards the side of a large open doorway, Wink and Whiskers took a quick peek into Orla's kitchen and saw that it was bustling with cooks and slaves trying to go about their duties. Everything was exactly as she remembered it from the jar-covered preparation table in the center of the room to the hanging pot rack and bread baskets above it. Looking along the kitchen's right wall, Wink saw a baking oven positioned next to a blazing stone hearth that had two cook pots near an empty spit, which were all placed beneath a low hanging cauldron. Ironically, there was also an enchanted icebox back by the kitchens exit that helped to keep food fresh when it wasn't being prepared.

To Wink's left was a magic sink that would always fill up when the appropriate spell word was uttered, and just past it was a cupboard whose lower doors contained a vast variety of dishes. Coming up with a wicked idea, Wink motioned for Whiskers to discreetly follow her over to the cupboard.

Mrs. Pulb lifted her rolling pin from the flattened dough in front of her and grabbed a rag to wipe sweat from her brow. The kitchen was always busy at this time of day, and if she didn't remember to pace herself, then she'd almost certainly wind up passing out from exhaustion. Setting down the rag, she was about to start working again when she saw something move out of the corner of her eye. Looking down towards the floor, she saw an upside-down cup slowly sliding around the cupboard as if it were moving under its own power.

"Rats," she muttered to herself as she leaned down towards the cup and raised her rolling pin. The little vermin always found their way onto Orla when the cargo came in, and the quicker she could kill this one the better. Reaching to lift the cup, Mrs. Pulb was totally unprepared for when Wink bust out from behind the cupboard door and shouted, "Boo!"

Laughing as Mrs. Pulb gave a surprised screech, Wink knew her prank had worked perfectly. A plump woman who kept her graying black hair pulled back in a bun, Orgee Pulb was always a fun target for Wink's mischief. Wearing a patterned violet dress with a white apron and brown shoes, Mrs. Pulb never held a grudge when getting caught up in a practical joke, but that didn't stop her from getting mad when something like this happened.

Raising her rolling pin, she glared at Wink and shouted, "Oh, you little sneak! I swear I'm going to make a stew out of you."

"What in the world is going on?" asked a masculine voice as Mr. Pulb came over to check on his wife. As he did so, his brown boots kicked the small sliding cup across the floor and caused it to smack into a table leg which, of course, made Wink laugh all the harder.

Resembling his wife in many ways, Loben Pulb was a paunchy middle-aged man with a black square moustache and a receding hairline hidden beneath his toque. A consummate professional, he constantly wore a white apron over his light blue shirt and black pants. Giving the pixie an odd look, he asked, "Wink, what are you doing here?"

"Me?" Wink inquired as she went to pull the cup off Whiskers. "Oh, I'm just here to save you all from a bloody massacre."

"What!?" Both Pulbs exclaimed in shock and confusion.

Wink scratched Whiskers' ears as thanks for being such a good sport. "Pick us up and gather the slaves. I'll explain everything as we go."

Mr. and Mrs. Pulb had spent years with Wink on Orla, and all joking aside, they knew the pixie would never endanger herself by approaching them unless she had a damn good reason. So, bending down, they each picked up one of the miniature mischief makers and slipped them into the pockets of their aprons. The Pulbs then had the remaining slaves follow them out of the kitchen.

Chairbis exited his shrine and stepped out onto a long red carpet with golden tassels that covered the second-floor hallways on Orla. He prayed that he had made the right decision by helping Hatch and loathed the loss of life that was sure to follow when the former mage lord made his move. Alas, he couldn't ignore the threat that a demon might pose to the world. So, with Anthalos's blessing, he made his choice.

Lost in thought, Chairbis almost didn't notice that Mr. and Mrs. Pulb came down the corridor towards him. It was odd for the two of them to be out of the kitchen at this time of day, and they both looked a little pale as they passed by the stairway guards. Studying them carefully, Chairbis saw a slight movement coming from within the pockets of their aprons.

Wink, he thought as they headed towards their room. The time for change had come, and he was not about to stop it from happening. Opening the door to his chamber, Chairbis hoped that Hatch knew what he was doing, for if he didn't, then the consequences for everyone would surely be dire.

The butt of Malir's spear repeatedly thumped along the wooden floor as he marched briskly towards the kitchen. He was a guard *not* a slave! And yet, for some reason, when Dolsch wanted wine, *he* was the one chosen to get it because, *of course,* every slave on Orla seemed to *magically* disappear the moment any real work needed to be done. Stomping into the kitchen, Malir was about to demand that someone bring him the wine when he suddenly realized the entire room was empty.

"Hello?" he called out uncertainly. Malir saw a cauldron on the hearth starting to bubble over and noticed there was partially-made food strewn across at least half of the preparation table. *Where in the world is everyone?* he asked himself as he made his way towards the storage room. Peering over a host of crates in this darkened chamber, he uttered, "Is anyone in here?"

Ontar heard the guard's footsteps come to a stop just in front of him and knew that it was time to act. Throwing off the lid to his crate, he rose to his full height and looked down at the slack-jawed man. Grabbing the guard by the top of his pot helmet, Ontar slammed his face over and over again into the corner of the crate until he heard his enemy's skull crack.

The brutal onslaught was a signal for Echo and Kit to leap out of their own hiding spots and prepare for battle. Running through the kitchen with weapons drawn, they dashed down a long corridor towards a stairway at its far end. Echo ran a little bit faster than Kit, but her companion was more familiar with the manor's layout. Spotting an open doorway coming up on their side, Kit shouted, "Left!" as they both bolted into the room.

Echo noticed what appeared to be an armory that had four equally-spaced posts wrapped in rope to form a square in the center of the room. Standing in the middle of this sparring ring were two bare-chested guards training with swords and shields. One guard noticed Echo right away, while the other had his back to her. Taking her sword, Echo easily cut the ropes with one quick stroke.

Barely a step behind the elf, Kit's hands squeezed her sword as she swung it at the guard who was just turning around to face her. The man dropped like a stone, and his sparring partner was scarcely able to shout, "Intruders," before Echo was upon him.

Cursing the guard's quick thinking, Echo thrust her blade at the man, hoping to take him out in a single strike, but thanks to his lack of armor, he was actually fast enough to dodge her attack and counter with a blow to her shield while shouting, "Intruders!" for a second time. Capitalizing on the guard's preoccupation with her companion, Kit made a vicious cut along the man's back. Seeing her nemesis stiffen in pain, Echo raised her blade and finished him off.

Hatch and Ontar both heard the guard's warning cries as they advanced down the hallway and prepared for reinforcements. Focusing on the stairway ahead of them, Hatch raised his hand and cast a spell just as two spear-wielding guards leapt off the steps and charged towards them. A triage of firebolts assailed the guards, with the man on the left receiving one in the gut and a second in the face, scorching his flesh to the bone and giving him an agonizing death. The third firebolt hit the remaining guard's right leg, causing him to stumble.

Spinning his morning star, Ontar went after the wounded guard with steely determination. Attempting to defend himself, the guard thrust his spear towards his assailant. Knocking it aside with his weapon, Ontar saw the guard wince when the blow inadvertently put pressure on his wounded leg. Pressing his advantage, Ontar took his unbalanced opponent down with a successful attack to his remaining good leg. Death came shortly afterwards.

Moments later, Echo and Kit emerged from the armory only to have Ontar shout, "Get back!" Heeding his command, they returned to the chamber with Ontar and Hatch behind them. Facing the armory's open doorway, Ontar said, "The narrow stairs are a death trap. Let's face our enemies here so we'll all have room to fight them."

Hearing the sound of footsteps overhead, the party could tell they wouldn't have to wait long before their next battle.

⚜ ⚜ ⚜

"Report!" Sir Havens demanded as he stormed down a small, second-floor hallway. Armed with a mace in one hand and a shield in the other, he saw that to his left was a guard who dutifully blocked off the top of a stairwell. On his right was the manor's main corridor, where a fat ranger with long gray hair and a beard stood waiting for him.

Nervous with anticipation, Dolsch replied, "The intruders have taken control of the bottom floor and killed anyone who's gone to face them."

"Do we know anything about them?" Sir Havens inquired.

Dolsch shook his head. "No, but they haven't advanced any further, so I suspect they're waiting for us to come to them."

"Where's Chairbis," the white knight demanded.

Shifting uncomfortably, Dolsch glanced back down the corridor and said, "He's locked himself in his room and didn't answer when I knocked."

Sir Havens scowled when he heard this. "Well, now, we know how the intruders got on Orla. I'm sure Shavasae will deal with this treachery later. Right now, though, I want you two to follow me." Doing as they were told, Dolsch and the guard followed Sir Havens down the stairwell.

Cautiously stepping out onto an intersecting hallway, the three men proceeded down the corridor in front of them until they were just outside the manor's armory. Familiar with the ranger's heavy breathing, Hatch called out, "Dolsch, you fat swine, come out where I can see you."

"It's Hatch," Dolsch whispered to Sir Havens.

Familiar with the former noble, Sir Havens pointed to the guard and quietly replied, *"You two keep him distracted while I use my powers to both warn Shavasae and deal with Hatch."*

Approaching the armory's doorway with a guard at his side, Dolsch asked, "Hatch!? What are you doing?"

Hatch felt a pang of guilt upon seeing his old friend. An amazingly-skilled ranger in his youth, Dolsch had actually adventured with Hatch on several occasions before he became mage lord. When Thove was a teenage noble looking for a purpose to his life, Dolsch and Wink were there to take him on hunting expeditions and share stories of their early adventures with his father. Thove would later receive much of his training from Dolsch and admired him dearly as a mentor.

So, when the time was right, Hatch recruited him to serve as navigator onboard Orla. Sadly, as the decades passed, Dolsch let the good life get the best of him, and he soon grew fat and lazy. Afraid of losing his cushy position once Hatch was arrested for treason, Dolsch chose to testify against him during his trial. Alas, the time had now come for him to answer for that betrayal.

Hatch gave his former friend a determined look. "Dolsch, we've come to take control of Orla. Stand aside, and we won't have to hurt you."

Dolsch nervously glanced at the guard by his side. "No, Hatch. Your time as mage lord is over. Even if I can't defeat you, Sir Havens surely will, and between him and Shavasae, you won't stand a chance."

"Wanna bet," Ontar threatened.

Dolsch swallowed hard. "Please, if you surrender now, I'm sure that Shavasae will still be merciful."

"I'm sorry, but surrender is not an option," Hatch stated sadly.

Shoulders sagging and eyes lowered, Dolsch quietly uttered, "I see." Seconds later, his head snapped up to reveal that his eyes had changed to resemble those seen only in animals. Letting out an inhuman roar, he surged forward while lifting his fists above his head and bringing them down hard onto Ontar's shoulder plates. Shocked by this sudden attack, Ontar grunted as he dropped to his knees in pain.

Echo wasn't about to let Dolsch's sneak attack go unanswered as she swung her sword over Ontar's head and slashed the ranger's right arm. It was a move that should have sliced the man's appendage clear off but, instead, it left only a shallow cut. Apparently, whatever spell Dolsch had cast upon himself had somehow made his flesh a great deal thicker.

For a moment, Kit just stared at Dolsch's attack. Fortunately, the guard she faced did exactly the same thing. However, when she realized that he was distracted, Kit raised her sword and swung it at him with all her might. The guard barely lifted his spear in time to parry the attack. He then countered with a feeble jab she was easily able to dodge.

Ontar couldn't believe he had been brought to his knees by a *ranger* of all people. Squeezing the shaft of his dangling weapon, he punched Dolsch square in his oversized gut! Much to his surprise, Ontar found that his gauntlet barely even scratched the man. Clearly enraged, Dolsch growled and backhanded Ontar into the side of a wall.

Seeing the battle play out before him, Hatch knew that Dolsch had channeled the spirit of a bear to help him defeat his enemies. Thinking back to his childhood, he remembered a counter spell that Wink taught him as a boy to help him deal with such animals. Wishing there could have been another way, Hatch cast his spell knowing full well that it would lead to his old friend's demise.

A moment later, the corridor behind Dolsch filled with the tantalizing aroma of fresh-cooked salmon. An internal battle of wills immediately raged within the ranger as his bear spirit longed to go find food while his human soul knew that turning his back on their enemies was suicide! Unable to control the bear's primal instincts, Dolsch was forced to cancel his spell and fight Hatch as nothing more than a pathetic old man.

Echo could tell that something had changed in Dolsch when his eyes returned to normal and his arm bled more profusely. Backing away from her, Dolsch tried to draw a sword from his weapon belt to defend himself. Unfortunately, he barely managed to free his blade before Echo ran him through.

The ranger's death seemed to unnerve his remaining companion. Kit noticed that her enemy had decided to fight more defensively, and the two locked weapons as she tried to gain the upper hand. Worried the guard might be strong enough to push Kit back, Ontar rose and swung his morning star into the man's hip. Falling with a yelp, the guard was immediately dispatched by Kit.

Devastated by Dolsch's death, Hatch failed to notice the white knight staring at him from the doorway. Grabbing his head and shuddering, he looked up and said, "Damn you, Havens."

Kit was immediately concerned. "What's wrong?"

"He blanked my mind," Hatch growled. "I can't think of a single spell."

"It wouldn't matter even if you could," Sir Havens taunted. "Shavasae has already summoned air elementals to defend him on the deck. Any attempt at harming him would only lead to your demise."

Ontar spun his morning star. "Some of us don't *need* magic to fight our battles."

Sir Havens snickered. "I suppose not when you have two women to do your dirty work for you."

Echo and Kit angrily raised their blades at the insult, but Ontar shook his head. "Stay back! I'll handle this worm in warrior's armor myself."

"Face me if you dare," said the white knight as he adopted a battle stance.

If I can defeat you, then I can defeat Lydon, Ontar thought before uttering a battle cry and charging towards his opponent while trying to strike Sir Havens's weapon arm. Jerking the appendage back just in time to avoid the blow, the white knight lifted his mace and smashed it into Ontar's already injured right shoulder. Wincing from the pain, Ontar struggled to keep hold of his weapon.

Sparing his arm from additional injury, Ontar lifted his tower shield and attempted to slam it into the white knight. Anticipating this maneuver, Sir Havens sidestepped Ontar's rush and attacked him from behind. Fortunately, Ontar's backpack absorbed most of the impact, but he still found himself stumbling forward. Whirling around, he saw Sir Havens come at him again and spun his morning star in a wide circle to keep the white knight at bay.

Ontar could tell something was wrong. There was no way a man in a full suit of armor could dodge his attacks twice. It was almost as if Sir Havens could predict what he was going to do next before he did it. Then Ontar realized that *he could*! White knights were basically glorified mentalists who could use their powers to learn what an enemy was thinking. Coming up with a strategy, Ontar thought *leg, leg, leg, leg…LEG!* before swinging his weapon straight at the white knight's unprotected head.

Years of combat training were all that saved Sir Havens from certain death. The arc of his enemy's weapon was clearly not directed at his leg, and he tried to lean back in a haphazard attempt at dodging. Ontar's morning star still managed to make contact, though, cracking his jaw and tearing a hole in his cheek. Raising his shield, Sir Havens struggled to block Ontar's next attack.

Groaning in pain, Sir Havens knew he had to think of something quick. He still had three other opponents to take out after this one, and if he took another hit like that, then his task would be next to impossible. So, he utilized a spell that would help even the odds.

Ontar couldn't quite fathom what happened next. His strategy had helped him land a solid blow against the white knight, but before he could capitalize on it, his opponent's mace became a deadly blur that crashed mercilessly into his right side. Instinctively raising his shield, Ontar felt two more rapid impacts before he suffered a bone-shattering strike to his knee.

Echo and Kit's eyes widened in disbelief as Ontar fell. Using a speed spell, the white knight continued to pummel him even after he had hit the floor, and if they didn't do something quick, then their companion would surely perish! With swords at the ready, their simultaneous battle cries rang out as they raced towards Sir Havens.

The world seemed to move somewhat slower for the white knight as he saw Echo and Kit's valiant charge. Having more time to think of ways to dispatch his enemies, Sir Havens saw the morning star lying next to the warrior he had just defeated and came up with a plan. Sliding his mace along the ground, he struck the weapon and sent it tumbling towards Echo. Grunting as Ontar's morning star hit her foot, Echo was briefly knocked off balance by the attack.

Kit had hoped the white knight's sneak attack on Echo would leave him open to a strike from her. Unfortunately, he was still able to parry her weapon and countered with two direct blows to her sword in a deliberate attempt at disarming her. Echo then tried to get him with a back attack, but she wasn't quite quick enough, and he managed dodge out of the way. Much to Echo's horror, her blade instead slashed Kit's forearm, delivering a shallow cut to her companion. Seizing on Echo's shock, Sir Havens used his mace to batter her shield.

Hatch could tell the women were in trouble and tried to think of a way to help. Improvising with what he had, he removed his cloak and carefully snuck behind his enemy. This wasn't difficult to do considering the white knight's preoccupation with Echo and Kit. Waiting for just the right moment, Hatch threw his cloak over Sir Havens, then got out of the way as fast as he possibly could. Momentum from the white knight's speed spell caused the cloak to push against his face and obscure his vision.

Blinded while still moving extremely fast, Sir Havens tripped and fell. Pawing at the garment, he managed to pull it back just in time to experience Echo and Kit's full wrath! Mercilessly hacking at the white knight from multiple angles, the two continued their attack until both of their swords were caked in his blood.

Panting heavily, Echo ran over to Ontar's unconscious body and pulled off his full helmet. Bringing a pointed ear close to his mouth, she said, "He's still breathing!"

Kit and Hatch quickly joined her with the old wizard saying, "Don't worry. If you can handle Shavasae, then Kit and I will get Chairbis to heal Ontar."

"What!?" Echo exclaimed as she stood up. "You don't need two people to go fetch a cleric."

"Grandpa, I'm not going to leave Echo to fight the mage lord by herself," Kit stated.

Hatch pointed to her arm. "But you're injured."

Holding her sword in one hand, Kit used the other to cover her wound. Casting a simple healing spell, she removed her hand to reveal the injury had become scabbed over. "I'm no cleric, but this was hardly more than a scratch."

"Shavasae can hit you with spells that will do far worse than that," Hatch argued.

"Not if you told us how to fight him," Echo countered.

Looking deep into Hatch's eyes, Kit said, "Grandpa, now is not the time to treat me like a child."

Hatch reluctantly admitted she was right. "Air elementals can be defeated by disrupting their flow of wind. The longer you can hold your weapon within them, the weaker they become."

"Thank you for trusting me," Kit said before noticing that Hatch's gaze had fallen to Dolsch's dead body. "Are you going to be alright?" she asked.

Hatch patted her hand and sighed. "Your father will never forgive me for this."

Kit refused to believe that. "Dad knew this was a possible outcome from the moment you told him of our objective. As long as our motives remain pure, I'm sure he won't hold it against you."

"I hope you're right," Hatch said as he privately wondered if stopping Zattermox was really worth the death of a former friend.

✦✦ ✦✦ ✦✦

Taking the stairwell up to the manor's second floor, Kit led Echo down a hallway in front of the main corridor that had two wooden doors off to their right. Opening the first wooden door (since the second led to a latrine), they stepped into a broad rectangular room that could have passed for a dining hall. Sparsely decorated, the room had a stone fireplace along its wall near the door while its left corner had a small spiral staircase leading up. Positioned along the far wall were the large double doors the party was originally brought in from. Placed in the center of this room was a big round dining table and chairs that had been centered beneath an eloquent golden chandelier.

"Shavasae lies just beyond those doors. Are you ready to face him?" Kit asked.

"With Ontar unconscious and Hatch unable to use his magic… sure, what's the worst that could happen?" Echo replied.

Kit shook her head. "Trust me, you don't want to know."

Crossing the dining hall, the two hesitantly pushed open its large double doors. Kit felt a gust of wind blow through her hair and whip Echo's braids as they stepped out onto the manor's railed deck. Hovering in front of them on a flying carpet was the Mage Lord of Sibeia. Having caught a glimpse of him during the Salvations Sacrifice ceremony, Echo noted that up close he wore a circular gold medallion, which depicted a man's face gnashing his teeth in agony, and a red rose-like ring set within a golden band on his left hand. Floating about a foot away from the carpet's corners were four, man-sized entities that resembled tornadoes with upside-down counterparts fused together to create an air elemental.

Sitting cross-legged on the carpet, Shavasae pointed his unique staff at them and said, "I assume that you two are the murderous hags sent to assassinate me."

Echo didn't even bother explaining their motivations. "Listen well, old man. We're giving you one chance to fly out of here alive. I suggest you take it."

Shavasae scoffed at her warning. "A person of my power will never cower before the likes of you."

Upon this statement, the four air elementals at his side descended towards Echo and Kit. Sprinting forward to meet her enemy, Echo jabbed her sword at one of the elementals the moment it came within striking distance and tried to hold it in place. The chaotic winds surrounding her blade briefly slowed before once again picking up speed.

Kit didn't like the odds they were up against. The mage lord and his minions clearly had superior numbers, which meant that if she and Echo were going to stand a chance, then they'd have to quickly eliminate as many of the elementals as possibly. So, raising her sword, she boldly attacked Echo's opponent and dispersed its wicked winds with a single mighty blow.

The three remaining elementals were unmoved by the loss of their companion. Soaring into Echo, the first elemental tossed her clear across the manor's deck and into part of its railing. Lying amongst scattered bits of broken wood, she shook her head while trying to get to her feet. Kit fared little better as a second elemental flung her into a wall by the double doors. The last elemental also went after Kit and sent her tumbling back down the middle of the deck.

Shavasae was pleased with the effectiveness of his elementals, and he cast a spell to hasten their enemy's demise. Echo stood up just in time to see a light blue dot appear beneath her feet. Guessing that it was a spell, she ran from the dot seconds before a thin beam of continuous energy shot up from where she stood. Spotting two more dots close to her position, Echo dodged the rising beams as she sprinted across the deck.

Impressed with her dexterity, Shavasae had two of his deadly beams move against Echo and sent the third after Kit. Bruised and dizzy, Kit saw two air elementals and a beam of light heading her way. Praying for a miracle, she rapidly backed away from the oncoming enemies. Much to her delight, Kit noticed the beam of light collide with one of the elementals, causing them both to instantly vanish.

Echo, however, faced a much more difficult situation with two beams moving side by side towards her, and an elemental situated further back. Attempting a risky maneuver, Echo tried running between the beams to attack the elemental. Her plan would have worked had the mage lord not moved them closer together at the last moment. Turning sideways, Echo mentally cursed as she felt one of the beams shred her backpack and scatter its contents before they both made their way off the manor's deck.

Keeping a distance from its enemy, the air elemental drew in pieces of broken railing and hurled them at Echo. Holding her shield in front of her, Echo heard the noisy bits of debris slam against it as she continued her advance. Coming within sword's length of the elemental, she dodged a large hunk of wood and thrust her blade into the entity's whirling body. A gust of wind buffeted her face as the air elemental dissipated.

Attempting a similar attack against her enemy Kit plunged her sword into the air elemental's midsection. The elemental's winds did slow for a second, but much to Kit's surprise, its blustery body moved in to envelop her. Caught in a spinning maelstrom, Kit quickly grew nauseous and vomited. Expecting to be thrown somewhere, Kit shuddered when she felt a charge in the air around her. Suddenly, a dozen tiny lightning bolts struck her at once.

Echo felt a stinking line of warm vomit hit her back shoulder and heard the sound of Kit's sword slide across the deck. Turning around, she saw the last air elemental carelessly drop her unconscious companion onto the ground in a heap. Raising her sword, Echo sprinted towards the entity and jabbed at it with all her might. Having expended most of its energy on Kit, the air elemental was easily eliminated by Echo's onslaught.

"Bravo," said the mage lord as he glanced at a small bit of vomit on his carpet. "You've proven to be quite entertaining, but I have other matters to attend to, so I'm afraid you'll have to die."

Where the fuck is Hatch! Echo thought as she dropped her shield, sheathed her sword, and cast aside the tattered remnants of her backpack. Grabbing her longbow, she drew an arrow from her quiver and took aim.

"Oh, please," the mage lord snickered as Echo fired her bow. Raising the first two fingers of his left hand, he halted the arrow in midair barely inches from his face. Undaunted, Echo reloaded her bow, but as she did, Shavasae twirled his fingers, so the floating arrow was now facing her. He then sent the projectile whizzing back towards its original owner with a frightening speed.

Echo was just about to fire again when Shavasae's arrow pierced her leather armor and lodged itself deep into her shoulder. Recoiling from the pain, Echo's shot went wide as she struggled with her injury. Shavasae then pointed the top of his staff at her and caused the crystal at its head to briefly flash before a lightning bolt leapt towards her. Reliving a personal nightmare, Echo was rendered unconscious by the sheer power of the mystical strike.

Refusing to waste his time on fallen foes, Shavasae lifted the Staff of Light and caused its crystal to illuminate with a pure white glow. He then raised his left hand near the staff's head and began an incantation that made its glow brighten and expand beyond the crystal until it formed a huge sphere of crackling energy, which covered the entire top of the staff. Sighing, Shavasae was afraid he wouldn't complete his spell before his other enemies showed up.

Feeling confident, he called out, "Hatch! Sir Havens's last thoughts to me revealed you were here. I have defeated your peons with ease, so, if you truly think you're the greater wizard, then come forth and *prove it*."

Silence filled the air for a heartbeat. Playing up the drama of the situation, Hatch emerged from the manor's opened doors and stepped into full view of the mage lord. Shavasae frowned upon seeing his old rival. Wearing the garments of a peasant, Hatch seemed both older and scrawnier since his time as mage lord. Spending five years in a dungeon had obviously taken its toll on him.

"You were a fool to come here, Hatch. My powers have only gained since obtaining this position while yours have surely languished. Do you really think you can defeat me?"

Bowing his head, Hatch said in a low voice, "Your time has come, Shavasae."

Offended by his predecessor's arrogance, Shavasae snarled. "No! My time is *now!*"

Pointing his staff at Hatch's head, Shavasae sent the oversized shockbolt careening towards him. Expecting Hatch to try and dodge, Shavasae watched as his spell fragmented into five smaller shockbolts that were supposed to prevent any type of evasion. Hatch didn't even flinch. Surrounded by the hovering spheres of energy, he did nothing but give Shavasae a blank stare.

Nervous that this quiet confidence was a sign Hatch was about to cast something really nasty, Shavasae unleashed a lightning bolt from his staff and simultaneously had the shockbolts hit his rival at once. A blinding flash of light exploded where Hatch stood. Expecting to see nothing but the charred remains of his predecessor, Shavasae was shocked to see Hatch was completely unharmed.

Repeating his former threat, Hatch said, "Your time has come, Shavasae."

Hatch was amazed by Shavasae's mastery of the Staff of Light. Flying well behind his rival's lower left side, he had almost finished his incantation when the mage lord unleashed his horrible wrath upon Hatch's illusionary image. Timing was everything, and while he felt guilty about what happened to Kit and Echo, he knew Chairbis could heal them. Unfortunately, it took time for his trap to be properly set (and to find a window he could slip out of). Not many people knew Hatch had the power fly. In fact, flying carpets had mostly made that type of magic obsolete in Sibeia, but Hatch had always had an interest in studying overlooked spells, and it was a pastime that was about to pay off.

Completing his incantation, Hatch hurled a massive fireball directly at his distracted foe. Catching sight of the blazing spell at the last moment, Shavasae attempted to move his carpet out of the way before it was too late, but the fireball exploded too close to his position, and its brilliant flames completely consumed him. Shavasae's flying carpet was incinerated, and his blackened corpse fell unceremoniously to the manor's deck. The mage lord was dead!

Hatch breathed a sigh of relief. With the demise of his nemesis, a sense of vindication washed over him. He *was* the superior wizard, and while he didn't officially have the title, deep down, Hatch still felt like *he* was the mage lord. Wishing he could savor

this moment, Hatch remembered that Kit and his other companions were severely wounded and needed his attention, but he had
one last thing to do before returning to the manor.

Orla watched with mild curiosity as Hatch flew by her face
and slid the white Sibeian banner off her horn. Dropping the
bulky fabric, he saw the wind whip it about as it fell from the sky.
Hatch had wasted far too much of his life serving a country that
had turned against him. He now had a greater purpose to fulfill,
and it was time to put his past behind him.

Chapter Fifteen

Ontar tossed and turned as he fought to get comfortable. Dreaming about being struck over and over again by a blunt object, he thrashed about until, finally, his eyes popped open, and he sat up in what appeared to be a lavish, over-sized bed. Realizing he was not alone, he saw that Kit and Echo slept on either side of him, all three dressed in white nightgowns.

Kit looked positively angelic as a rainbow of different colors dazzled her features from above. Alas, this splash of color did nothing to hide the smell vomit on her breath. Lying on his other side, Echo whimpered and shifted repeatedly in her sleep. Ontar knew that this type of recuperation wasn't natural for elves and wondered how she got to be this way in the first place?

Taking in his surroundings, Ontar found that he was in a spacious round room with a colorful stained-glass dome for a ceiling. On either side of the bed was a nightstand with a candlestick that had a stained-glass cover over it. To his left was an artistically crafted wardrobe next to a privacy screen that looked more like a painting than anything else. A little past the screen was a descending spiral staircase that allowed entrance into the room.

A glance to his right revealed an overstuffed bookcase placed close to a comfy looking chair with violet and gold cushions on it. A short distance away from the chair was a cluttered writing desk that had packed cubby holes built into it. Along the desk's bottom right side was an open treasure chest filled with valuable coins.

While the chest certainly caught Ontar's attention, his focus was quickly drawn towards the rear of the room where a cleric sat at a small chess table with two chairs.

"Don't be alarmed," the cleric said. "My name is Chairbis Genestov, and I restored you to health after your battle against the white knight."

"I-I failed," Ontar said despondently. "I couldn't defeat him."

Chairbis was quick to change that emphasis. "You survived against an enemy who required three of your companions to finally bring down. Few warriors can boast of such an accomplishment."

"But those few warriors would be stronger than I am," Ontar countered while thinking, *Lydon would be one of them.*

Unaware of how badly Ontar was shaken, Chairbis said, "Some people think that strength comes from within but, personally, I have found that a man's strength comes from those who choose to support him."

Ontar knew that Chairbis was trying to raise his spirits, but he really wasn't in the mood. So, instead, he changed the subject. "Support comes in many forms, which might explain why Hatch sought you out to help us get on Orla?"

Chairbis felt a pang of guilt over the bloodshed that he helped cause. "Yes…and now that you're awake, I shall fetch him for you." Standing up, Chairbis moved over to the spiral staircase and called out, "Houge! Could you tell Hatch that one of his companions has risen?"

"As you wish," came an elderly voice from below.

Realizing he hadn't introduced himself, Ontar stated his name and said, "Thank you for healing me."

Chairbis acknowledged his gratitude with a smile. "Think nothing of it. Hatch should be here shortly to answer any questions that you might have about the previous battle."

The sound of footsteps coming up the staircase seemed to indicate that Hatch was already here, but upon closer scrutiny, Ontar realized that it was actually Houge carrying Wink up to greet him.

"Onnie!" The pixie squealed as Houge set her on the foot of the bed. Running towards her beloved warrior, Wink squeezed his rock-hard abdomen and said, "I was *so* worried about you. With all those blows you took to the head; I was afraid the white knight had bashed your brains into pudding. Quick! Tell me how many times you've wanted to kiss me since we've been together?"

"Kiss you?" Ontar asked a little confused.

"I knew you were thinking about it!" exclaimed Wink. "That's why I'm having Trigen build a house for me so that we can always be next to each other from now on."

Ontar was lost. "Who's Trigen?"

"If I may," offered Houge. "Trigen Brovis is Orla's master carpenter. He and the other servants await your arrival downstairs upon your earliest convenience."

The added commotion from Wink and Houge's appearance roused Kit from her slumber. Stretching as she sat up, Kit opened her eyes and smiled at who she saw. "Chairbis!" she stated merrily as she got out of bed and gave a big hug to the blushing cleric. "I can hardly believe it's you. It seems like ages."

"Well, at least five years," Chairbis added as he returned her embrace.

Looking over the cleric's shoulder, Kit spotted Houge and went to greet him in a similar fashion. "Houge, I should have known you'd be here. The manor would have fallen apart without you."

Houge's slender arms gave Kit a light squeeze. "I'm afraid you give me far too much credit, milady."

"Only what you deserve," Kit said with a grin. "So, where's Grandpa?"

"I'm right here," Hatch said as he came up the stairs. Having returned to his rightful place on Orla, Ontar noticed that Hatch now dressed in the regal garments befitting of a mage lord. Wearing a sleeveless red kaftan over a white robe with black trim, the only possessions he kept from his previous attire were some brown boots and a weapon belt. He also had acquired some new artifacts, with a gold medallion hanging around his neck, a rose-like ring on his left hand, and an impressive looking new staff.

"Now, that's how a wizard should look," Wink said as she stood by Ontar.

Chairbis was far more concerned with Echo's condition than Hatch's arrival. The elf had been thrashing about violently in bed and muttered incoherently. As those gathered focused their attention on her, Chairbis approached just in time to see her sit up and start to scream!

Echo quickly saw that everyone present was staring at her, and there was a cleric close by. "Who are you?" she asked.

"My name is Chairbis Genestov—" the cleric began before she interrupted him with her next question.

"Where are my clothes?"

Houge tried to alleviate her concerns. "Your garments have been taken to be cleansed and mended. As have yours," he said to Ontar and Kit.

"What about the rest of my equipment?" Echo inquired eagerly.

"Your possessions will be made available to you the moment you have need of them," Hatch replied.

Echo saw that Hatch now wore some of the mage lord's artifacts. Focusing on the staff used against her, she asked, "Why in the world are you carrying that?"

Hatch took a second to study the weapon. "The Staff of Light has been wielded by the Mage Lords of Sibeia for countless generations," he explained before lifting his left hand. "Just like the Rose Ring."

Echo was intrigued. "And the medallion?"

"The Medallion of Minds is worn by each of the six lords of Sibeia as a symbol of our...*their* rule over the country," Hatch tried to gloss over his mistake. "The medallions offer protection from the control and influence spells that could be utilized by the white knights."

Chairbis leaned in close to Echo. "I hope you don't mind my asking, but my healing spells have never invoked nightmares before. Did something happen to you in your battle with Shavasae I should know about?"

Echo looked down and blushed a little. "He threw lightning from his staff at me."

"Why's that different from any of the other spells you've been hit with?" Wink wondered.

Well, there's no point in hiding it now, Echo thought. "When I was a little girl, I tried to cross a rope bridge during a thunderstorm and watched as it got struck by lightning."

"That's terrible!" Kit said. "Were you hurt?"

Echo nodded. "I was in a coma for over a week. The town cleric said I was lucky to be alive."

"He must have been quite a powerful healer to save you from such an injury," Chairbis noted.

"He was," Echo acknowledged. "But I also am able to recover from my wounds far faster than most other elves. Unfortunately, the incident left me with a crippling fear of lightning."

"Which would explain why you acted the way you did when I used my death cloud on Fort Vakid," Hatch mused.

"Exactly," Echo said as she got out of bed and spotted the treasure chest. "Oh, I knew it!" she said to herself as she crossed the room and knelt to scoop up a handful of coins. "I knew there was a reason we were doing all this." Standing up and tossing the coins into the air, she joyfully cried out. "We're *rich!*"

"Yes, but we have to use this money responsibly," Hatch added.

Echo turned to him and scowled. "What do you mean?"

Hatch expanded on his statement, "Why don't we all go downstairs so I can show you what this bounty will be going towards."

Distracted by his earlier loss, Ontar almost didn't notice when Wink shouted, "HEY!" as he got out of bed and walked away from her.

Wink watched him with concern as he came back to scoop her up onto his shoulder. "Onnie, are you alright?"

Letting out a little sigh, Ontar replied, "No…"

Having reclaimed his private chamber, Hatch led the party down a small spiral staircase into the dining hall. Standing next to the room's large table were Mr. and Mrs. Pulb, alongside a tanned, middle-aged man whose stubble matched his short, slightly greasy, graying brown hair. Wearing dirty, worn-out clothes,

Trigen's attire consisted of a sleeveless tan shirt with black pants and brown boots. Chairbis quietly took his place with the other three before Hatch introduced them as Orla's invaluable long-time servants.

Following their initial greeting, Wink impatiently asked the carpenter, "Hey, Trigen, have you finished building my house yet?"

Trigen gave her an exasperated look. "Wink, I've spent all afternoon stitching up leather armor and banging the dents out of shields. Do you really think that I've had time to build you a house?"

"Where are your priorities, man!?" Wink squealed.

Ontar didn't want to discuss what was bothering him with Wink, so he decided to try and change the subject before it even came up. "Wink, you deserve the best house that Trigen can build. So, why don't we give him the time he needs so that he can do the job right."

"Oh, Onnie, you're always thinking of me, aren't you?" Wink replied as she playfully touched his cheek. "But I still want to be sure the house gets built."

"Alright...alright." Trigen said as he waved his hands. "Now, do you want a free-standing house or one that's mounted to the wall?"

As the three discussed the matter in more detail, Mrs. Pulb looked Echo over and said, "I've never cooked for an elf before. What can we prepare to make your first meal on Orla a special one?"

Echo was instantly delighted with the idea of having her own personal chef. "My mother used to make me a dish with honey roasted walnuts in it. Do you think that's something you could do?"

Mr. Pulb chuckled. "I think we might have some walnuts tucked away in the storage room. That is unless you've got some more friends hiding back there."

The comment got a laugh from everyone assembled, and shortly afterwards, the servants departed to go about their duties. Those who remained were given a proper tour of the manor by Houge.

❧❧❧

Passing through the first part of a familiar hallway, the party turned down an elegant corridor in front of some descending stairs and saw a line of doors on either side of them.

"These are the quarters for guests and servants of the mage lord," Houge explained. "As the newest residents of the manor, each of you have been given your own room to arrange as you see fit. If you would prefer a different room then, please, don't hesitate to let me know."

Echo had never had her *own* room before. Such things were considered either a luxury among her people or a sign that somebody lived alone. At Houge's inclination, Echo opened the door and found an average-sized chamber with a window that had a magnificent view of the sky outside. The windows curtains were blue in color and seemed to fit well with the red, black, and white quilt on the bed. A beautifully designed nightstand, with a candlestick on it, matched a chest at the foot of the bed and a wardrobe along the wall. Hanging inside the wardrobe's open door was a full-length mirror with an intricate golden frame.

While the room was truly splendid, what really caught Echo's attention was a brown, leather armor dummy by the window that had Spirit Slayer and a pile of other equipment at its base. Amongst this pile was a new backpack, which Echo picked up and inspected to see that it contained all of her former possessions.

Noticing the pleased expression on her face, Houge said, "The backpack belonged to one of our former guards. When I saw that yours had been destroyed during your battle with the mage lord, I decided to collect what items I could find and fill this one in its place."

Reaching into the backpack, Echo fondly withdrew her slender wooden flute and said, "Thank you, Houge."

Bowing slightly, Houge humbly replied, "You're welcome, milady."

❦ ❦ ❦

As it turned out, most of the manor's rooms were virtually identical to each other, with the one exception being the type of equipment left by the armor dummy. When Ontar and Wink entered *their* room, he found a disturbingly familiar mace resting on his bed.

"What's this?" he asked Wink as he sat her next to the weapon.

Wink was distracted with trying to find the best spot to put her house. "Huh? Oh, that's Sir Havens's mace. Hatch thought you might want it to remember how badly he kicked your ass in battle." Somehow, Ontar doubted that, but Wink continued, "It's mildly enchanted if you want to keep it."

Picking up the mace, Ontar could still remember the pain of having it slammed into different parts of his body. Depressed by his loss, he looked down at the pixie and said, "Wink, would you mind continuing the tour without me? I'd like a little time to think about the battle I just had with Sir Havens."

"Why? Wink wondered. "He's dead and you're not. What else is there to think about?"

"The fact that I wasn't the one who killed him," Ontar stated.

Wink shrugged. "Big deal. From what I heard, he used magic to defeat you. If it had been a fair fight, you would have beaten him easily."

"But not all my enemies will fight fair," Ontar argued. "If I can't find some way to even the odds against a sneaky opponent, then my next battle might be my last."

Wink paced the bed while thinking. "Alright. Well, Sir Havens used magic to beat you in combat. Maybe if you used magic, too, then that would balance out your chances of survival."

Ontar shook his head. "I can't use magic, and the only enchanted items I possess are this mace and my morning star. Neither of which is all that powerful."

Snapping her fingers, Wink asked, "What about Spirit Slayer? I bet you could kill a dozen white knights at once with a blade like that."

Ontar gave the pixie a curious look. "Isn't that sword best used against undead?"

Wink shook her head. "No, Onnie. Hatch says that magic swords are stronger, lighter, and sharper than regular ones. So, I think that Spirit Slayer would be a great weapon no matter who you're up against."

"But Echo needs that sword to maintain her standing in the Bloody Side," Ontar argued. "There's no way she would ever give it up."

Wagging a finger, Wink said, "You have just as much right to that blade as she does. Why not use it until she needs it?"

Ontar turned thoughtful. "Hmm. You raise a good point."

"Of course, I do," Wink replied as she raised her arms and waited for Ontar to pick her up. "Now, let's get back to the tour before Houge leaves us behind.

Unaware of any plans being devised, Kit and Hatch stood outside the door of what she presumed to be her room. However, before she could open it, Hatch said, "I hope you don't mind sharing a space, my dear. Unfortunately, the chamber's current resident simply refuses to leave."

A puzzled expression crossed Kit's face. "Should I pick a different room?"

"Only if you absolutely can't stand living in this one," Hatch replied cryptically.

Curious, Kit opened the door and saw a little white mouse sitting on a plate in the middle of her bed, eating tiny bits of cheese and various other crumbs. "Whiskers!" she gleefully exclaimed as she sat on the bed and scooped him up. "Has Grandpa been spoiling you?"

"Well, I had to spoil someone while you were asleep," Hatch answered with a wry grin.

"You're terrible," Kit teased as she stroked Whisker's fur.

"Perhaps," Hatch admitted. "But Whiskers isn't the only animal seeking your attention."

"Oh?" Kit muttered.

Tilting his head, Hatch said, "Come, let me show you."

Gathering back in the corridor, the party followed Hatch down to its far end where two open doorways revealed a study to their left and a small shrine (where Chairbis prayed) on their right. Ahead of them was a large door that Hatch went to open, but before he did, he pulled Houge aside and asked him to assemble the slaves in the manor's lower level.

As Houge departed, Wink leaned across Ontar's broad shoulder and asked Kit. "Do you remember what's in this room?"

"Yes, I do," Kit replied as she held Whiskers close to her. It had been a long time since she had ventured into the crystal room. Her most memorable occasion was back when she was ten years old. Having successfully completed her first hunt, Kit's father had taken her onboard Orla to celebrate. Together with Dolsch, Wink, her father and grandfather, Kit had been allowed to communicate directly with Orla. It was an experience that she'd never forget.

Opening the door, Hatch led the party into a room with outward diagonal walls that had a huge map of the Rashben Region on one side and Sibeia on the other. At the back of the room was a magnificent bay window that offered a view of Orla's enormous feathered tailfin swaying freely in the light of the setting sun. In the center of this room a wooden, throne-like chair with flattened red cushions faced the group. Hovering waist-high in front of that chair was a large diamond-shaped crystal with a pure white glow.

Addressing his fellow companions, Hatch said, "This is the crystal room. From here, we can guide Orla across the heavens."

"There's no *we* in this," Wink pointed out. "Kit's the only one who can communicate with animals, and *she* is the only one who can navigate Orla."

Kit looked down at the floor nervously. Of course, what Wink said was true, but Kit never imagined that she'd ever be taking Dolsch's place. For all she knew, Orla might crash into a tree the moment she tried to take control.

Hatch attempted to allay her fears. "Yes, Kit has been given an enormous responsibility, but I'm sure that she'll amaze us all with how quickly she can accomplish this task." Gesturing towards the crystal with his staff, Hatch said to her. "Why don't you give it a try?"

Kit hesitantly handed Whiskers over to Ontar. Approaching the crystal, she reached out to touch it, only to have a thin arc of blue electricity zap her hand.

Whiskers squeaked in alarm, and Echo trembled at its sight. Unnerved by the crystal, she moved back by the chambers door and said, "I'm sorry. I can't watch this." As she exited the room.

Inspecting her hand, Kit felt a slight tingle but otherwise seemed to be unharmed. Reaching out for a second time, multiple arcs of electricity leapt out at her before she finally touched the crystal. A brief second of déjà vu came over Kit as she recalled this moment from her childhood. Closing her eyes, she saw a brilliant orange sky with bright pink clouds illuminated by the golden glow of a slowly setting sun. It was a view that only Orla could share with her, and she was almost overwhelmed by it.

In the midst of this majestic scene, Kit clearly heard her grandfather's voice. "Congratulations, my dear. You have just started to form a bond with Orla, and over time, that bond will grow and flourish...but, for now, we have important matters that need tending to. As you know, sky whales have an inherent sense of direction. We need you to tap into that sense and guide Orla towards the Chapskin Empire as fast as she can possibly fly."

Kit slowly shook her head. "I don't know if I can. This is all so new to me."

Hatch put a hand on her shoulder. "Trust me, it will come to you, but it might take a little time. If you don't mind, I'll finish the tour with Ontar and Echo, then come back to check on you."

"Yes," Kit replied as her voice took on a dreamlike tone. "That sounds like a good idea."

Motioning for the others to follow him, Hatch led the group out of the crystal room. Just as he was about to leave, Ontar detected an anxious skittishness coming from Whiskers and decided to set the mouse on the floor. Watching as it scurried over to be by its master, Ontar had to admit that Kit certainly had a way with animals.

❖❖❖

Continuing their tour, the party exited a stairway that led down to the manor's lower level. Finding the bodies of dead guards had been removed while their blood had been mopped off the floor, the group crossed a small second hallway and stopped before a line of six slaves who stood along the left side of a long corridor, with Houge at their head.

Clearing his throat, Houge said, "Milords and ladies, it is with great pleasure that I introduce to you the slaves of Orla."

Going down the line, Houge started with Gorev and Vrok, then moved on to the three female slaves that Wink had seen working in the kitchen. Clad in similar attire, the women wore long blue dresses with brown shoes. Covering these dresses were white aprons that matched the bonnets on their heads. Looking the three over, Ontar decided to use eyebrows and age to define their features. The first woman in line was Sasty. She had black hair and appeared to be in her late forties. Next was Milsa. Ontar quickly noticed she was a rather attractive twenty-year-old with plain brown hair and a sad smile. The youngest of the slaves was a blonde-haired girl named Nissie, who was probably somewhere in her mid-teens.

Finishing his introduction, Houge went into detail about each slave's duties. Afterwards, he waited for questions, then politely took over in leading the tour. Guiding the party towards Trigen's workshop, he inadvertently sparked Wink's fury when she discovered the carpenter wasn't there working on her house.

This began a search through the manor's lower level that took the group past the armory they had seen earlier, the cramped quarters of both the slaves and former guards, then onwards to a small dining room for Orla's serving class. Here, Trigen was found quietly finishing some pottage and drinking a little bit of ale.

Subjected to Wink's relentless prodding, whining, and complaining, Trigen returned to his workshop to continue building her house. Making their way back to the stairs, Hatch asked Wink, "Could you make sure Ontar and Echo are seated at the dining hall in time for dinner? I have a matter which must be discussed with the slaves before I can join you."

Echo was suspicious about what Hatch wanted to *discuss* with the slaves. Unaware of her companion's apprehension, Wink said, "No problem. Come on, everybody. Dinner awaits."

As Ontar climbed the stairs, Echo got close to his shoulder and asked Wink, "What does Hatch plan on saying to the slaves?"

Wink shrugged. "He's probably just asserting who's in charge now and what he expects from them."

"Do you foresee any of them rebelling against us?" Echo fretted.

"Of course not," Wink chuckled. "They can't control Orla, and if we didn't replenish the manor's food supply, they'd starve to death."

Echo frowned when she heard this. "So, basically, they live on a flying dungeon."

"Trust me, when compared to other slaves, this is practically paradise," Wink asserted.

Letting out a disappointed sigh, Echo said, "Somehow, I don't think they'd see it that way."

❈·❈·❈

Returning to the dining hall, the party found that its central table had been set with fancy silverware and goblets, which surrounded a big pastry castle that served as its centerpiece. Motioning for Ontar to set her down on the table, Wink said, "I bet you've never seen a dungeon serve something like this."

Echo frowned. "It looks a little small to feed all of us."

Laughing when she heard this, Wink said, "Don't be silly. That's not even the first course."

Suddenly finding the perfect time to bring up a subject that had been bothering him, Ontar said, "Hey, Echo, before we eat, can I ask you something?"

"Sure," Echo replied.

"My failure to beat the white knight has shown me that I need a weapon that can give me an advantage over my enemies," Ontar explained. "I was hoping you could let me use Spirit Slayer until the time comes where we have to relinquish it to the Bloody Side."

Echo shook her head. "No. That blade is my key to redemption within the guild, and if I gave it to you now, then I'm afraid you wouldn't let it go when I needed it back."

"Onnie's not a thief!" Wink asserted.

"Don't make that sound like it's a bad thing," Echo teased. "Truthfully, though, the more time and energy Ontar invests in training with Spirit Slayer, the less likely he'll want to part with it."

Stung by her denial, Ontar said, "Echo, what if using Spirit Slayer is the only way I can beat Lydon?"

"Lydon isn't a god," Echo argued. "And if we face him *together*, then I know we'll be victorious."

"*If* we face him together," Ontar countered. "People can easily get separated in battle. If that happens, I want to know that I can take him by myself."

"Then maybe you should train harder so that you won't need Spirit Slayer," Echo stated.

Wink couldn't believe what she was hearing. "So, what's the point of having such a powerful sword if no one intends to use it?"

"I didn't say I wouldn't use it. I just plan on giving it to the Bloody Side when the time is right," Echo replied.

Ontar scoffed when he heard this. "*You* want to use Spirit Slayer? But that's such a waste. In your hands, it would only enhance your skill a little bit. In mine, I could lay waste to anyone who opposed me."

Echo didn't like Ontar's condescending attitude. "It's my sword, and I can do what I want with it."

"You wouldn't even have that sword if Onnie and Hatch didn't help you get it," Wink retorted. "The least you could do is share it, you greedy bitch."

Echo's temper flared. "My *greed* is the only reason we rescued you and Hatch in the first place."

"Yeah, and it also caused you to release a demon that could be wreaking havoc even as we speak," Wink declared.

Rolling her eyes, Echo said, "Don't be so dramatic."

Ontar sided with Wink. "It's not dramatic if it's true."

"Fine, maybe it is true," Echo snarled, "but at least I'll have a sword that can beat my enemies. Unlike some big whiny baby who cries just because he lost a fight!"

Stomping up to Echo with anger in his eyes, Ontar glared at the elf and asked, "What did you call me!?"

"She called you a big whiny baby," Wink said vindictively.

Echo stood defiant. "That's right I did."

Striking back hard, Ontar said, "I wonder if Searce ever insulted her companions the way you did just now."

"I-I don't know," Echo replied hesitantly.

"That's probably because unlike you, she didn't need other people to carry her weight," Ontar continued. "Searce never fucked up with the Bloody Side the way you did. She's smarter, more skilled, and prettier than you'll ever be. In fact, the only reason people even give two shits about you is because of *her*."

Trembling with rage, Echo felt tears come to her eyes as she said in an icy voice, *"Drop dead, you asshole!"* Turning around, she stormed out of the dining hall without looking back.

Coming down the hallway, Hatch saw Echo's reddened face and asked, "Echo, are you alright?" Ignoring him completely, Echo continued to her room.

Entering the dining hall, Hatch looked to Ontar and Wink for answers. "What's wrong with Echo?"

"I don't want to talk about it," Ontar said as he followed the elf's example and left the room.

Hatch's eyes narrowed as he glared at Wink. "What did you do?"

Wink gave him an indignant look. "What makes you think I did anything?"

"Because I've shared a lifetime of nasty arguments with you, and this looks like one of them," Hatch replied.

"Those arguments taught you how to stand your ground..." Wink began before recounting what just happened.

When she had finished, Hatch let out a sigh and said, "So, you came up with the most disruptive answer you possibly could to Ontar's problem, then fanned the flames of anger when things didn't go your way."

"Well, it sounds really bad when you say it like that," Wink grumbled.

"That's it," Hatch declared. "Tonight, you're sleeping in the laundry basket."

"You can't do that!" Wink retorted over the familiar punishment.

Towering over the pixie, Hatch declared. "I could do far worse if I wanted to."

Wink crossed her arms and said, "Fine, but don't bother looking to me for help in patching things up with those two."

Lowering her to the floor, Hatch replied, "Trust me, that thought was the furthest thing from my mind." Watching her skulk out of the dining hall, he thought, *Kit's help, on the other hand, might be useful right now.*

❖❖❖

The candlestick on Echo's nightstand burned almost as bright as the anger she felt towards Ontar. Playing a fast tune on her flute as she sat on her bed, Echo barely even noticed that evening had descended on Orla. Lost in a flurry of music, she was about to start her next song when she heard a knock at the door. "Who is it?"

"It's Kit," came the response.

"Come in," Echo said as she tried to compose herself.

Entering her room with a bowl of sliced pears dipped in cream, Kit said, "You missed dinner, so I thought I'd bring you a snack."

Setting aside her flute, Echo took the bowl and said, "Thanks. I didn't mean to miss dinner, but I probably wouldn't be very good company right now."

Kit leaned against a nearby wall and said, "I heard about your fight with Ontar."

"That greedy bastard couldn't have cared less about Spirit Slayer when I first got it. Suddenly, he loses one fight and thinks that it's the only thing that will make him a better warrior. Talk about pathetic!" Echo asserted as she bit into a cream-covered pear.

"We all try to cope with defeat in our own way," Kit argued. "Ontar just isn't handling it very well."

Echo angrily took another bite. "That's no excuse for taking it out on *me!* He said that I'd be nothing without Searce. As if

I'm not reminded of that every time I try to do something for the Bloody Side."

"Echo, I know what it's like to be stuck in someone else's shadow," Kit began. "My own father didn't even think that I could make it this far without him, yet, here I am, standing tall and proud while being ready to take on the world."

"Yeah, but you only have to hold yourself against his standard. I, on the other hand, have an entire thieves' guild constantly comparing me to my aunt," Echo lamented.

Kit wagged a finger and said, "Echo, your aunt might be a formidable dabbler, but that doesn't mean her accomplishments outweigh yours."

"I failed my first mission for the Bloody Side and have to give them a valuable sword just so I don't lose my membership. Not exactly a prestigious start to my illustrious career," Echo grumbled.

"But look at how things have gone since then," Kit countered. "Not only did you find the legendary sword, but you also broke a former mage lord out of a heavily guarded dungeon and went on to *steal a sky whale!* I mean, that's practically the stuff of legends right there."

Echo smirked when she heard this. "That is pretty impressive. Of course, Searce never failed like I did, but she also never tried anything this ambitious at my age, either."

"Which is why you're probably in better standing with the Bloody Side than you even realize," Kit concluded.

"That may be," Echo admitted, "but I still promised to bring them Spirit Slayer, and Ontar knew that before we even started hunting for the blade."

Seeing that Echo wouldn't back down on her claim to the sword, Kit suddenly came up with an interesting idea. "Ontar wants the sword because he doesn't think that he could beat Lydon without it. What if there was a way to prove that he could?"

"How?" Echo wondered.

"We ask the oracle," Kit explained. "If you or Ontar is destined to kill Lydon, then he should be able to tell us how it happens."

"But what if we're not?" Echo fretted.

Kit shrugged. "Then, at the very least, he won't want Spirit Slayer anymore."

Seeing the logic in Kit's plan, Echo secretly hoped she or Ontar would have a chance to kill Lydon. She owed it to their families...and especially to Favin.

⧫⧫⧫

Approaching Ontar's door at the same time that Kit entered Echo's room, Hatch knocked politely and said, "Ontar, its Hatch. May I come in?"

"Yeah, that's fine," Ontar replied before Hatch slipped into the room and closed the door behind him.

"I thought we might grab a bite from the kitchen since you missed dinner," Hatch began before noticing Ontar sat on the side of his bed with a small ragdoll in his hands. "Hmm. Far be it from me to judge, but I do find it a little peculiar to see a grown man playing with dolls."

Ontar chuckled when he heard this. "It belonged to my sister Kearsta. She used to pretend that it was a damsel trapped in a tower and that we were the only ones who could rescue her. I kept it to remind me of what I lost after Lydon butchered my family."

Nodding in understanding, Hatch slowly sat down next to Ontar on the bed. "Sometimes, it helps to have a reminder of why we do the things we do."

"And I've done some pretty shitty things since I started traveling with Echo," Ontar admitted. "You know I've never considered myself to be a bad person, but that was before I realized just how far I'd go in order to get my revenge."

"Well, I can tell you right now, there's nothing sweeter than getting back at one's enemies," Hatch acknowledged. "However, you must be careful not to let vengeance consume your life. When my wife left me, I went down a path that brought a nation to its knees before leading to my imprisonment. The years I lost in the aftermath of that decision will never be recovered."

Shaking his head, Ontar said, "I don't want to waste my life hunting Lydon. That's why I need Echo's Bloody Side contacts to track him down for me."

"Those contacts won't help you unless Echo gives Spirit Slayer to the guild," Hatch pointed out.

Ontar squeezed Kearsta's doll in frustration. "I know, and I know it was wrong of me to lay claim to the sword after we already agreed that Echo should have it. But using that blade is the only thing I can think of that would give me an advantage over Lydon."

Scratching his chin, Hatch turned thoughtful. "Let's try looking at things from another angle. What is it about Lydon that makes him so fearsome in a fight?"

"I'd say his skill in using two swords at once," Ontar replied.

"Well, why don't you adopt a similar fighting style using weapons you're comfortable with and beat him at his own game?" Hatch wondered.

Ontar quickly objected. "His skill in that area would be far superior to mine."

"Maybe at first," Hatch conceded, "but don't forget that we regularly face a vast array of enemies with no sign of that changing any time soon. What better way to hone your craft than by practicing on them?"

"You know, my cousin Yorus used to say that experience was always the best teacher," Ontar stated as he slipped the ragdoll into the drawer of his nightstand. "Maybe it's time to stop mourning his loss and start listening to what he had to say."

Hatch smiled. "Wise words are often recalled when one least expects it."

Standing up, Ontar said, "That may be, but it's hard to recall much of anything on an empty stomach. So, let's go find the kitchen while I'm still wise enough to do so."

⊰⊱⊰⊱⊰⊱

The next morning proved to be an interesting one for Ontar as he awoke to the sound of knocking at his door. Last night's dinner with Hatch had been a mishmash of treats followed by some fairly substantial drinking. Cringing at the smell of alcohol, which still lingered on his breath, Ontar remembered that Hatch needed a slave's help to reach his room and that he called upon Sasty to get him there. Thankfully, Ontar was able to stagger back under his own power, but that still didn't mean he wanted to get up the following day.

Answering the door, he was surprised to see Vrok standing there with some clean clothes folded over his muscular arms. Taking the clothes, Ontar almost laughed when the slave offered to help him get dressed. Politely refusing, Ontar closed the door and began the process of getting changed for the day. Tightening his headband, it was strange for him to wear little more than a shirt with some pants. If it weren't for the dagger in his boots, he'd be completely defenseless. Yet, this was all he would ever need to wear on Orla, and it was something that would take a little time to get used to.

Another knock at the door came just as Ontar had finished making his bed, prompting him to exit his room and see who it was. Greeting a casually-dressed Echo and Kit in the main corridor, he couldn't help but ask, "Kit…Echo, what are you doing here?"

"I thought we could all get breakfast together," Echo replied.

"Well, I'm glad you're here," Ontar stated when he saw the elf wasn't still mad at him. "Echo, I'm sorry I let my temper get the better of me last night. Spirit Slayer is your sword, and I had no right to expect you'd turn it over to me."

"Well, I'm sorry, too," Echo began. "You survived in battle against a white knight, and instead of being grateful you're still alive, I ridiculed you instead. I'll try to watch my tongue a little harder next time."

Kit smiled when she heard this. "I'm glad to see you two can overcome your differences. However, we *did* miss dinner last night, and if also we skip breakfast today, I think that Mr. and Mrs. Pulb will start throwing the food at us instead of serving it. So, I suggest we get on our way."

Heading towards the dining hall, the party found that Vrok and Milsa were standing outside the chambers open door holding a washbasin and a towel, respectively. Unaccustomed to formal etiquette, Ontar and Echo watched Kit wash her hands before going to eat and hastily followed suit. Entering the hall, they found that its central table had been set, with Wink and Whiskers sitting at its center. Scolding them, the pixie said, "It's about time you three showed up. I started to get hungry."

Standing at the far side of the chamber were Houge, Gorev, and Nissie. Each approached the dining table and pulled out chairs for the new arrivals. Once the party was seated, Houge said, "Breakfast shall be served momentarily," before leaving with the other slaves to go fetch it.

"So, have you come to your senses about Spirit Slayer?" Wink asked Echo.

Echo gave the pixie a nasty look. *"Actually,* Ontar just said he doesn't want it."

"What!" Wink exclaimed.

Smirking at her reaction, Ontar said, "I thought I might try practicing two weapon combat instead."

"If that's even necessary," Kit added while setting her hands on the table so Whiskers could climb on them. "Echo and I thought we could ask the oracle how Lydon dies so that we know what we might actually need to fight him."

Ontar's face brightened. "Hey, that's a good idea."

Smacking her forehead, Wink said, "I can't believe this. Are you saying Hatch made me sleep in the laundry basket for nothing!"

"I guess so," Echo replied smugly.

"Oh…where is that weaselly wizard!" Wink demanded.

Descending the spiral staircase from his chamber, Hatch replied, "Right here."

"You've got a lot of nerve making me sleep in the laundry!" Wink growled.

Houge pulled out a chair for his master while Hatch replied, "Quit complaining. You've slept in places far worse than that, and even then, the slaves were still there catering to you."

"Catering to us all," Echo added with a clearly bothered look on her face.

Picking up on her tone, Kit asked, "Did the slaves do something to upset you?"

Echo noticed the slave's expressions and replied, "No, it's just the fact that we have slaves at all, which doesn't sit well with me."

"Oh, not this again," Wink groaned.

"I see," Hatch said before addressing the slaves, "Houge, would you and the others please excuse us for a moment."

"Of course, milord," Houge replied before he and the other slaves left the room.

Turning his attention back to the elf, Hatch stated, "The slaves on Orla have a far easier life than many others in their position."

"But it's a position they should be able to choose for themselves. Why not free them so they can follow their own path in life?" Echo argued.

Hatch rubbed his eyes with a long sigh. "Where? If I had released them in Sibeia, then they would have just been captured and enslaved to a different set of masters."

"So, why don't we free them in a kingdom that doesn't have slavery?" Echo asked.

Having never given the matter much thought, Kit asked, "Who would we get to maintain the manor's upkeep here on Orla?"

"Well, it's not like we couldn't clean things up around here ourselves," Wink replied sarcastically.

Hatch scowled at the pixie's remark. "Is that really how you want to spend your time when we're not risking our lives during travel?"

"No," Ontar stated sternly. "Echo, I constantly had to do menial tasks in a tavern until I was skilled enough in combat to make a living at it and, honestly, I don't want to go back to that unless I absolutely have to."

Echo could understand where Ontar was coming from. Collecting branches for basket weaving, watching over travelers' children, and manning her father's stall were all a prelude to her eventually becoming a dabbler. She'd worked hard to put such boring duties behind her, and she didn't like the thought of returning to them.

"Ontar, all these slaves have ever known is the hard labor that we've toiled to get past. Don't they deserve something more?" Echo argued.

Hatch leaned over and touched Echo's arm. "They aren't going to miss what they never expected to have in the first place. Now, I know you're against the practice of slavery, but let's take some time to see what the benefits are before we cast them away. I say that maybe after a month, we all get together with Kit and Wink to decide their future then."

"That seems fair," Echo finally agreed. Keeping slaves for a little while probably couldn't hurt anything. Perhaps after enough time, she'd even convince the others to grant them their freedom. All she would have to do is find a way to prove they'd earned it.

Chapter Sixteen

Echo sat in the middle of the manor's deck and played her flute to the sound of wind gusting past her. The sun was warm, and the sky was clear as she finished her tune and basked in the mid-morning light. Feeling connected to the world around her, Echo detected the faint scent of pine in the air and decided to see where it was coming from. Standing, she tucked her flute into her belt and moved towards the front of the deck, resting her hands on the railing. Looking out past Orla's horn, she saw a sight more magnificent than anything nature had ever revealed to her before.

Mountains…massive monuments of majestic gray stone rose from the earth to dazzle the landscape beneath her. This was the first time that Echo had ever seen the imposing peak's that dominated much of the Chapskin Empire. The pine smell she detected earlier came from the sprawling evergreen forests that sprouted up from around their base and expanded into scenic valleys filled with crystal clear lakes and streams.

Echo had no idea how long she stood there admiring the view, but the sound of the manor's large double doors opening caused her to turn around and see Trigen step out onto the deck carrying an old wooden toolbox and a handsaw. Behind him, Gorev held some spindles and a few pieces of smooth long wood under his arms. Surprised to see Echo standing there, Trigen stopped and said, "Excuse me, milady, I didn't mean to disturb you. We're just here to fix the deck railing."

Looking over at a gaping hole in the railing, which occurred when an air elemental tossed her into it, Echo shook her head and said, "You're not disturbing me. In fact, I'd enjoy the company."

"Is that so?" Trigen asked as he set his toolbox down near the hole. Gorev mimicked the carpenter's actions with his own bundle before Trigen said, "I see you've been admiring the Crimson Ranges. They're quite a sight from up here, aren't they?"

Echo glanced back at the mountains and frowned. "Why do they call them the Crimson Ranges? They look grayer to me."

"It's from all the blood that's been spilled there." Trigen explained. "The dwarves have had to fight all sorts of creatures to protect their human subjects who farm down in the valleys."

Echo vaguely remembered encountering a dwarf once before during her travels. "I can't believe that a race like the dwarves would surround themselves with so much natural splendor."

Trigen snorted then positioned his handsaw over a broken bit of railing. "They don't. The dwarves live inside the mountains, not on them."

Oh, what a waste, Echo thought as Trigen started sawing. Watching the Crimson Ranges from above was an excellent way to learn the lay of the land, and she thought Ontar might want to have some idea on what they were heading into. Leaving Trigen to his work, she entered the manor in search of her absent companion.

⊰⊱⊰⊱⊰⊱

Sounds of combat resonated throughout the manor's lower level as Echo made her way towards the armory. Having trained here with Ontar on multiple occasions since their arrival on Orla, Echo wasn't too worried until she heard the snarling cries of some unfamiliar creature coming from up ahead. Drawing a dagger from her boot, she passed through the armory's open doorway and looked to see what was causing all the ruckus.

The creature she encountered was a monster known for frequently plaguing elvish towns and villages. Crouched in the center of the room was a forest troll with mottled green skin and sharp yellow teeth. A menacing sight to behold, the troll had lanky arms and legs, which would have put her at just under rib height and were well-proportioned with its strong yet wiry physique. Possessing a long, pointed nose and ears, the troll had bushy black hair that stood practically on end.

Alarmed by the troll's presence, Echo saw Ontar in the sparring ring attacking his oversized opponent with only a mace in one hand and a morning star in the other. Ready to join her comrade, Echo was stopped by a bony old hand that rose in front of her. Looking to her right, she saw Houge holding a towel over his arm next to Vrok, who carried a washbasin. Lowering his hand, the elderly slave said.

"Don't be concerned, milady. The battle is only a ruse."

Taking a moment to observe things more carefully, Echo noticed that Wink was jumping around the sparring rings exterior, excitedly cheering Ontar on. Hatch could be seen behind the troll, staring at it intently but taking no real action against it. The troll was far too big to fit in the ring, and its body passed back and forth through the surrounding ropes while the top of its head disappeared into the ceiling from time to time. *It's an illusion,* Echo realized as she calmly sheathed her dagger.

Waiting for Ontar to finish his training, Echo leaned against the armory's doorway along a short wall illuminated by torch-lit sconces. Looking past the sparring ring towards the chamber's far end, Echo saw a line of leather dummies wearing chain armor and weapon belts. On either side of the dummy line were archery targets, with two barrels full of arrows and crossbow bolts located near both herself and Houge. To her left, Echo saw a wall covered with weapons racks containing spears, maces, swords of different sizes, and daggers next to a collection of bows and crossbows. The wall to her right had a long shelf for pot helmets over several small wooden stands that held normal-sized shields painted with the emblem of Sibeia on them.

Ontar grunted irritably as the illusionary troll's clawed hands swiped through his head. Clearly frustrated, he lowered his weapons and said, "Enough."

Following Ontar's order, Hatch caused the troll to disappear with a simple wave of his hand.

Concerned by Ontar's reaction Wink asked, "What's wrong, Onnie? You were doing so well."

Ontar looked down at the pixie in disbelief. "Are you serious? If that had been a real troll, it would have ripped my face off."

"Perhaps you should stick with fighting real opponents," Echo observed as she walked towards the sparring ring. "Or at least training with them. That way you can get pointers on how to improve your technique."

Sliding his mace and morning star into the weapon belt around his waist Ontar ducked beneath the sparring ring's ropes. "Are you volunteering?"

Echo shrugged. "Why not? I've been itching to practice with Spirit Slayer anyways, and there's really no point in having an ancient sword if I don't intend on using it."

Ontar frowned slightly when he heard she was going to use the sword instead of him but chose to say nothing as Echo continued speaking, "Before we do any of that, though, I wanted to let you all know that we've arrived at the Crimson Ranges. Would anyone here be interested in catching a view of the mountains with me?"

"I would…I would," Wink squeaked as she ran over to Echo. "They say that if you shout at the mountains long enough, they'll eventually start shouting back, which is something *you* should already be pretty good at."

"Well, maybe I am," Echo said in reference to her name. Scooping up Wink, she turned to Ontar and asked, "Are you coming, too?"

Leaning over Vrok's washbasin, Ontar dipped his hands into the water and said, "Yeah, just let me clean up first."

Satisfied with his answer, Echo and Wink left the room, with Hatch following behind them.

The oracle stared at a long match held in his frail fingers as its flame flickered and died. Its purpose fulfilled, he set it down next to one of the hundreds of tea lights whose warm glow brightened his underground chamber. Heading towards a simple mat at the back of the room, the oracle contemplated how *his* purpose in life was about to be completed.

Blessed with the power to see how choice and fate worked hand in hand, the oracle knew that if he had fled this place earlier with the women and children, he would have extended his life by another seven years. Unfortunately, those years would have been spent living meagerly off the dwarves' charity. This would then be followed by his last three years of existence being plagued by painful physical and mental deterioration.

Having faced choices like this countless times over the course of his life, the oracle decided instead to embrace a fate that would end his existence in a terribly violent fashion. It was not an easy path to follow, but the great god Anthalos had given him the power to make one last stand against the forces of darkness. Hopefully, the knowledge he possessed would save the lives of countless others.

Sitting cross-legged on his mat, the oracle heard the clamor of his executioners above him. Knowing Echo would hear his message before he died, he calmly prayed for those who would be killed trying to secure their meeting.

Hatch sat on a comfortable chair in his private chamber, reading a journal written by Shavasae. The deceased mage lord offered valuable insight into what was happening in Sibeian politics, which Hatch couldn't help but be curious about. Alas, most of the information was fairly mundane such as when Shavasae visited his son after the Salvations Sacrifice ceremony in Ranig.

However, one of the few things Hatch shared in common with his successor was their mutual hatred of his ex-wife, Lady Alean. This was because Alean had learned, in his youth, that Shavasae had improperly prepared a potion of stallion extract to help him increase his sexual prowess. What resulted was a single night where he actually tried to procreate with a mare. Decades later, Alean decided to reveal this information to the wives of several members on the council of magi during their deliberations to decide who should be the next mage lord.

Building on what she had learned, Alean added that Shavasae bore a hybrid offspring, who he killed when the mutant tried to find his father. Afraid of losing to his rival, Hatch had a horse's head buried in a shallow grave at the mages' guild's courtyard. The scandal that erupted following the head's discovery destroyed Shavasae's chances at becoming mage lord, even though he was the superior spell caster.

Ashamed of the means he rose to power, Hatch noted that, today, Alean tried to weave a new web of deceit between her husband, the golden lord, and his son from a former marriage. Shavasae suspected Alean wanted Thove to inherit the golden lord's wealth and eventually replace him as one of Sibeia's rulers. Hatch shook his head, knowing full well his son didn't want that kind of life. Unfortunately, defending the boy's decision to become a ranger was what ultimately led to the destruction of his marriage.

Turning a page in the book, Hatch heard an excited cry come from the spiral staircase.

Popping her head up into view, Kit shouted, "Grandpa, grab your things. I found it!"

Slipping a brown satchel over his shoulder and grabbing his staff, Hatch readied himself for whatever fate had in store for him.

Kit stood at the far end of the manor's deck and proudly gazed out over the Crimson Ranges. It was almost noon, and the mountains here were far more rugged than when Orla first crossed into the empire. Lacking any signs of water or vegetation, a few scattered clouds could be seen drifting in-between some high rocky peaks dotted by snow. The only thing that drew Kit's eye away from all this natural beauty was an isolated plateau off in the distance.

Built behind an elaborate wall at the top of a mountain was the Nung-Dow monastery. At her current distance, Kit could tell the monastery consisted of one large building next to a handful of smaller ones. Constructed with an unfamiliar design, the buildings each had multi-tiered roofs covered in orange ceramic tiles and flared eaves.

Thank you, Mirsha, for guiding me here, Kit thought. She had prayed every night the goddess would help her bond with Orla, and she'd learn how to use the sky whale's instinctive abilities to find this place. Triumphant in her accomplishment, Kit turned around just as the manor's large double doors opened to reveal her companions.

Ontar and Echo were the first to emerge, clad in full battle gear and equipment. Behind them was Hatch, who went to stand by his granddaughter. Ontar took a second to inspect his full helmet before placing it on his head.

"Wow, Trigen did a great job at mending my armor."

"I know," Echo agreed. "It feels almost like new."

"Step aside, people, we're coming through," Wink commanded from the doorway.

Moving to one side, Ontar and Echo saw Gorev and Vrok carrying out a long rolled up carpet, with Wink sitting cross-legged in the middle of it. "Onward!" The pixie cried as the slaves set the carpet down on the deck. Echo found Wink's behavior to be obnoxious and put one of her boots on the carpet to unroll it. Screeching as she tipped over, Wink made several other indignant noises when Gorev and Vrok continued to unfurl the rug on top of her.

Ontar watched Wink squirm free and skulk her way over to Hatch. Looking down at the carpet, he asked, "What's this for?"

"It's to transport you from Orla to the monastery," came a voice from inside the manor. Joining the others on deck, Chairbis added, "And I'm the one who will take you there."

Echo had seen this before. "Is this like the flying carpet the mage lord had used?"

"Yes," Chairbis replied. "I'll be using it to drop you off wherever you need to go."

Ontar cocked his head towards the cleric. "It doesn't sound like you'll be joining us in our travels. How will we get ahold of you?"

"With this," Kit replied as she pulled a green gem out of her coin pouch. "It's linked to the crystal that I use to control Orla and will allow me to find you no matter where you decide to go."

"So, you won't be joining us either then?" Ontar asked.

Kit's shoulders drooped. "No. Grandpa says that someone needs to stay on Orla in case of an emergency. Since I'm our only navigator, I guess it makes sense that I stay behind."

Echo could tell that Kit was disappointed. "Hmm. Maybe we could take turns staying on Orla?"

Not terribly keen on that idea, Hatch took hold of the green gem and slipped it into his coin pouch. "Well, at the moment, Ontar, Echo, and I are the ones ready for departure, so why don't we all have a seat on the carpet."

"Hey, when was the last time you've been to the oracle?" Echo wondered.

Hatch looked a little sheepish. "Actually, I've never been to the oracle before. Sibeia's last war with the empire made it dangerous for me to do so while serving as mage lord."

Ontar had heard this story before. "Well, there's a big surprise. So, tell me, Hatch, is there any country that Sibeia hasn't gone to war with?"

Shrugging, Hatch replied, "I guess as long as they keep winning, then probably not."

Kit didn't realize that her grandfather had never seen the oracle before. "Do you still think the oracle will see us if he knows that we're from Sibeia?"

Wink thought of a simple solution. "We just won't tell him."

"Somehow, I think an *oracle* might be able to figure it out," Kit spouted.

Hatch made a dismissive gesture with his hand. "Whether he knows where we came from or not, it doesn't change the reason why we're here in the first place."

"Then let's go!" Wink prodded.

Reaching down, Hatch picked the pixie up and put her in the pocket of his kaftan. "Of course. I doubt that any of us could ever get very far without you."

"Even if we wanted to," Echo muttered to Ontar.

Sitting on the carpet, the party watched Chairbis place his hands on the intricately woven material and concentrate. An unsettling feeling came over Ontar and Echo as they felt the carpet slowly rise off the deck. Kit stood next to the slaves and waved as her companions flew away from Orla and off towards their next destination.

Making their way towards the monastery, the party decided to land outside the structures walls as a sign of respect to the Nung-Dow. Landing on a rocky plateau, the party bid farewell to Chairbis and took in their surroundings. Catching the group's initial attention was a big stone statue that resembled the upper half of a dragon's head with its mouth open. Distinct in its design, the dragon had a squared snout with long whiskers carved into its side. Sharp teeth shadowed what appeared to be a passage that descended deep inside the mountain.

Beyond the dragon was a high stone wall lined with tall ladders positioned by an elaborate gateway whose roof looked like the tops of other buildings located within the monastery.

Supporting the front part of the roof were four dark red pillars placed on either side of a long set of steps. Next to the outermost pillars were two bronze statues of what appeared to be fierce sitting lions. The steps themselves led up to a pair of large wooden double doors.

Tilting her head, Echo strained to hear what sounded like masculine chanting coming from somewhere inside the monastery. Not noticing her companion's thoughtful expression, Wink pointed to one of the gateways outer pillars that had a small bell and rope attached to it.

"Hey, there's a bell. We can use it to let people know we're here."

"Wait!" Ontar said as he held up his armored hand. The ladders on the wall had bothered him from the moment he saw them. The Nung-Dow would have no need for such things to enter their own monastery unless... "Those are siege ladders. Arm yourselves!"

Ontar and Echo barely had a chance to draw their weapons and shields before a mass of dark green warriors rose up from behind the wall to level their crossbows at them. The orcs were broad-shouldered barbarians with heavily muscled bodies and oversized jaws that had two yellow tusks sticking upwards. Possessing little uniformity amongst them, the orcs wore scattered pieces of armor and helmets ranging from plate mail to bare chests. Only their brown leather loin cloths, boots, and weapon belts gave them even the remotest sign of civilization.

Having only seconds to react, Hatch uttered a single spell word right before the orcs unleashed their volley. A deadly barrage of bolts seemed destined to end the old wizard's life, but as they fell upon him, an invisible barrier appeared to deflect every projectile that came his way. Capitalizing on Hatch's spell, Echo nimbly jumped behind him and used his magic in conjunction with her own shield for defense. Devising his own means of protection, Ontar shifted his tower shield in front of him just in time to see three random bolt heads harmlessly puncture its face.

"Get behind the dragon's head!" Ontar ordered while keeping his shield in front of him.

Reaching the protective head, Hatch told Wink to call Chairbis. Turning towards their point of arrival, Wink cast her ventriloquism spell and issued a wordless cry for help. Joining their companions, Ontar and Echo crouched down and set their backs against the stone. Glancing at the bolts in her shield, Echo asked, "Who's attacking us?"

"Orcs," Hatch replied. "They're one of the races who live in these mountains."

"Where are the dwarves?" Ontar asked, hoping against hope for reinforcements.

Hatch watched a bolt whiz over his head. "I don't know?"

Echo's sensitive pointed ears detected the sound of a crossbar being slid into a new position, followed by the creak of hinges. "The monasteries gate is opening!"

Searching the skies, Wink pointed and said, "I see Chairbis!"

Getting a bird's eye view of the party being pinned down by orcs, Chairbis brought the flying carpet in low beneath the ledge of the plateau so as not to attract crossbow fire.

Ontar noticed the number of bolts passing over head diminished. This was followed by multiple battle cries indicating the orcish warriors were swiftly approaching. Gauging where Chairbis was probably located, Ontar shouted, "Let's move!"

Raising shields and dodging bolts, the party raced towards the edge of the mountain. Behind them was a horde of battle-crazed orcs eager to butcher their prey. As their hearts pounded with uncertainty, the group engaged in an act of sheer insanity as they all leapt off the mountain at once.

The fall was short but terrifying. Hovering beneath the party on the flying carpet, Chairbis caught his fleeing comrades before they plummeted to their deaths. Peering over the ledge, the orcs saw how their adversaries made their escape and threw weapons at them. Chairbis barely managed to maneuver the carpet past two deadly spears and an ax before he began the return trip to Orla.

❧❦❧❦❧❦

Houge poured some wine into Kit's goblet as the party sat in the dining hall and told her of their orcish encounter. Snacking on a plate of crispels before dinner, Ontar summed up what he had seen of the orcs.

"If they reacted that violently to our arrival, then there's a good chance the oracle and his followers are already dead."

Echo disagreed, "Not necessarily. I could have sworn I heard chanting coming from somewhere within the monastery."

Skeptical of what she had heard, Ontar asked Hatch, "Do you think the orcs would have taken prisoners?"

Hatch furrowed his brow. "It doesn't seem likely, but then again, what little I know about them comes from reports dating back to Sibeia's invasion of the empire."

Interested in hearing an old war story, Ontar asked, "Did the orcs play much of a role during the invasion?"

"Not initially," Hatch explained. "When Sibeia first went to war with the empire, it was primarily fought against the dwarves and their horrible war machines. Our forces were eventually able to defeat them, but it was a hollow victory. We had absolutely no idea what the dwarves had strived to contain deep beneath their mountains."

"It was the orcs, wasn't it," Wink blurted out.

Hatch took a bite of crispel. "Yes…along with goblins, trog-lodytes, and a whole host of other nasty creatures that dwelled beneath the earth. It had taken everything our forces had just to defeat the dwarves. Unfortunately, when the other races at-tacked us, they successfully managed to drive our troops from the mountains. They then butchered the human farmers in the valleys until the dwarves regrouped and took back everything they had lost during the invasion."

Kit set her goblet on the table next to Wink. "What we have to consider is the oracle might have foreseen the orcs arrival and planned accordingly. If Echo heard chanting from within the monastery, then maybe there's still hope the orcs didn't kill everyone who lived there."

Grabbing the goblet's rim and tipping it enough to get a drink, Wink wiped her mouth and said, "Echo's the one who heard the chanting. Maybe she should sneak in and check it out."

Echo scowled. "Excuse me! I don't remember volunteering to enter an orc-infested monastery."

"But you're the only one with the skills to pull it off," Ontar noted.

Dammit, he's right, Echo thought. "Fine, I'll go but, Hatch, I want *you* manning the carpet in case there's trouble."

"Agreed," Hatch said softly.

The Crimson Ranges seemed to have a much more appropriate name at night when the moon's full red light tinged the moun-tains hard rocky surface. Soaring past the peaks on a flying carpet, Echo and Hatch flew at a low altitude to keep from be-ing spotted by the orcs. Preferring to travel under the cover of darkness, Hatch relied on Echo's keen vision to avoid colliding with any shadowy stones. Letting out a yawn, he regretted taking a nap earlier that evening. All it did was made him tired when the time finally came to begin their mission.

Arriving at the monastery's mountain, Hatch had the carpet rise up until it was just below the ledge the party had jumped off earlier. Nervous about what she had to do; Echo clarified with Hatch. "You'll still be here after I've found the oracle, right?"

"I won't leave from this spot," Hatch assured her.

Hoping that he kept his word, Echo took a deep breath and casted her spell of shadow self. Appearing to be a living shadow, Echo stood on the carpet and reached out to grab the ledge. Pulling herself up, she climbed onto the plateau and made a mad dash for the stone dragon's head. Reaching it without incident, she peeked out from behind cover and saw the monastery's high stone wall still had the siege ladders resting against it. *Well, it worked for the orcs,* Echo thought as she quietly moved towards one of the ladders. Watching for sentries along the wall, she climbed up the ladder and onto the battlements.

Crouching down to avoid detection, Echo peered into the courtyard and saw it was littered with the bodies of what appeared to be human monks. Dressed in orange tricivara robes with sandals, the dead monks were all bald with tan skin and slanted brown eyes. Orcs could be seen walking along paths flanked by partially extinguished stone lanterns near exotic trees that grew among the monastery's wall and garden.

Seeking entrance to the courtyard, Echo spotted a staircase protruding from the far-left wall slightly obscured by a tree. Sitting at the base of the stairs were two orcs engaged in casual conversation. Echo knew she'd need to sneak past them if she wanted to gain access to the monastery grounds.

Creeping over to the top of the steps, Echo made sure the orcs backs were to her as she made her descent. Doubting she could take both of them in a sneak attack, she decided to jump off the stairs when she reached a point she could land without hurting herself. Hitting the ground with a *thud*, Echo noticed the orcs immediately stood up upon hearing her. Slipping behind a tree, she held completely still as the orcs drew their weapons and searched the area. Muttering suspiciously to each other, one of the orcs proceeded to climb the stairs and check on the battlements while the other held firm at his post.

Scanning the area from where she hid, Echo spotted a number of dark red buildings with wooden framework that characterized the monastery grounds. Focusing on the largest of these buildings, she saw a flight of wooden stairs leading up to a covered porch with railings. At the center of the porch was an open doorway with two orcs standing guard on either side of it. Listening carefully, Echo heard the faint sound of chanting coming from within the structure.

Keeping low to the ground, she moved from tree, to stone lantern, to the far corner of the monastery's main building, all while avoiding detection. Grateful this wasn't a military structure; Echo found a large open window she could peek through to see if there were any orcs on the other side. Confident the coast was clear, she climbed through the window and into the building. Standing in a hallway with a clean wooden floor and a colorful unlit lantern hanging overhead, Echo noticed the monastery's interior walls were comprised almost completely out of white paper panels. Struggling to hear the sound of monks chanting, she was forced to deal with the loud laughter and conversation from nearby orcs. Following the sound of their brutish voices, she tried to learn the layout of this place.

Silently approaching a doorway on her right, Echo stayed close to the ground as she peeked into what looked to be some sort of dining hall. Dominating the room was a long wooden table with short legs resting of top of a big straw mat. The room's panels were decorated with ink landscape paintings smeared with blood, while a wooden wall at the head of the table had a shredded scroll hanging from it, and a small built-in platform at its base. Shattered porcelain and dead flowers covered the platform as the faint glow of a swinging lantern from above cast light onto the orcs in this chamber.

Drunk and rowdy, the orcs had small bottles littering the table amongst the disgusting remnants of their dinner. Passed out or sitting cross-legged on the floor, the orcs complained about the type of food available and how easy their conquest of the monastery was. The only part of their conversation that interested Echo's was how the orcs had mentioned a *pathetic* group of prisoners being held on the second floor. Hoping the oracle was among them, Echo listened just long enough to learn where the stairs to the upper level were before dashing across the doorway without being detected.

Skulking quietly along the corridor, she saw that it made a sharp right turn directly ahead of her, and as she poked her head around the corner, she found it led to a long hallway that crossed in front of an open staircase. The only thing that kept her from this staircase was a partially closed sliding door off to her right, which resembled the walls it was attached to. Quietly sneaking up to a room that could only be described as a kitchen, Echo peered inside and saw a heavily-bruised monk lying bound and naked on a preparation table.

Standing next to him was a mean-looking orc, who leaned close to his captive's face and said, "This is your last chance for freedom, little sun bunny. If you don't want to die like the others, then you better tell me where the oracle is hiding."

"I will never reveal such knowledge to a savage like you," the monk stated.

"Savage!" The orc snarled as he grabbed a knife off the table. "So, you wish to be civilized about this…fine." Taking the knife, the orc stabbed it into the monk's gut. As the poor man screamed, the orc went over to a nearby hearth and used a rag to pick up a steaming teapot. Walking back over to the monk, he said, "Why don't we discuss it over tea!" Sticking the teapot's spout into the monk's wound, the orc poured its scalding hot liquid directly into his captive's stomach.

Echo gritted her teeth as she tried to block out the monk's bloodcurdling scream. Advancing down the corridor, she quickly climbed the stairs while trying to get the horrific scene out of her mind.

The monastery's second level had much better lighting than the first, and Echo could clearly hear the sound of chanting coming from the corridor to her left behind a sliding door with two orcs guarding it. The chanting behind the door jumped in volume as the orcs noticed her strange shadowy figure and shouted, "Intruder!"

Echo saw an orc in plate armor with a sword and shield start to charge her, but he stopped after noticing that his companion had mysteriously disappeared behind the now open door they guarded. Exploiting his distraction, Echo rushed in with her blade and severed the orc's weapon hand. Howling in agony as her shadow spell wore off, the orc tried to bash Echo with his shield, but she sidestepped the attack and tripped him. Falling face first onto the ground, the orc's life ended with Echo running him through.

Taking a moment to see if anyone was coming, Echo was quickly unnerved when the loud chanting that had filled the hallway abruptly stopped. Cautiously approaching the open doorway, she saw a large room with small windows and soft mats on the floor that reminded her of sleeping quarters. Filling this room were solemn-looking monks who stood around the corpse of the remaining orcish guard.

A voice from within the crowd said, "Greetings, Echo…we've been expecting you."

The assembled monks stepped back to reveal one amongst their number who had blue prayer beads covering his left hand. Figuring that he was their leader, Echo entered the room and asked, "Are you the oracle?"

The monk smiled. "No. My name is Yesu, and my order has followed our master here from the Li-Chu Region to serve him in his hour of need."

"Can you take me to him?" Echo asked eagerly.

Before Yesu could reply, three orcs appeared outside the doorway, with one of them entering the room carrying a huge war hammer. Shifting his gaze between Echo and the dead guard, the orc demanded to know, "What's going on here?"

Yesu calmly moved past Echo and faced the orc. Staring into the eyes of his captor, Yesu's fist moved with a speed and skill honed by years of dedicated training. Echo heard the orc gasp as he dropped his bulky weapon onto the floor. Clutching his throat with both hands, he desperately tried to breathe through a crushed windpipe but died seconds later.

Following their leader's nonverbal cue, the monks let out a frenzied battle cry and charged at the remaining orcs. Yesu turned towards Echo and said, "Come. The master awaits."

Initially, the monk's zeal to defeat their tormentors aided them in slaying the orcs on the monastery's upper level. However, as they descended the stairs towards the building's main floor, they encountered much stiffer resistance. The orcs had superior armaments and greater numbers. Once they overcame the notion their prisoners were a bunch of passive weaklings, they counter-attacked with gory enthusiasm.

Slowly proceeding down a main level corridor, Echo stayed close to Yesu as one of the monks ahead of them engaged an orc in leather armor with a shield in one hand and an ax in the other. Raising his leg in a high kick, the monk's powerful blow crumpled the orcs shield. Unfazed, the orc swung his ax deep into the monk's side just as his foot touched the ground.

Watching the monk fall, Echo swung her sword at his attacker, but the orc parried her blade, and the two briefly locked weapons. Joining the fight, Yesu sidestepped Echo and delivered a gut-busting punch to the orc. As the brute doubled over in pain, Yesu used his hand to deliver a fatal chop to the back of his opponent's neck.

Focusing on the enemy they had just defeated; Echo was shocked when a bare-chested orc with a horned helmet and spear burst through the paper wall to her right and thrust his two-handed weapon deep into Yesu's ribs. Listening to her guide cry out as he dropped to the floor, Echo took her sword and made a bloody slash along the orcs left arm. Spinning towards her, the orc stabbed at Echo with the spear in his right hand. Deflecting the blow off her shield, Echo thrust her blade into the orcs right shoulder. Wounded in both arms, the orc lost hold of his weapon as Echo launched a series of devastating attacks that eventually did him in.

Filled with a sense of loss and urgency, Echo knelt by Yesu as he struggled to speak, "The master is located in a shrine to the south of this building. He is hidden beneath the statue. Look to the candles to find your way."

Echo wished she could do more to help the man, but the orcs had the upper hand in this conflict, and it wouldn't be long before there weren't any monks left to stall them. Touching Yesu's prayer beads, she said, "May Kardok take pity on you."

Finishing her brief goodbye, Echo stood up and quickly fled the monastery through one of the many open windows she had initially entered in from.

❖❖❖

Once again finding herself darting behind different objects for cover, Echo left the embattled monastery behind her as she made her way towards the Nung-Dow's shrine. Crouching behind a lit stone lantern, she came across a red square building with columns reinforcing its sides. The columns supported a bronze-colored roof that resembled a fat cone with a pointed top. A wooden staircase led up to the shrine's open doorway, but two bronze statues resembling monks had been tipped over on top of it.

Echo saw that it was completely black inside the shrine and knew that she'd need something to see with. Reluctantly sheathing her sword, she slid her backpack down on one shoulder and pulled out a torch. Sticking it into a stone sconce, Echo lit the torch and repositioned her equipment. Afraid the added light would make her an easy target for orcs, Echo ran towards the shrine, climbed up its stairs, and entered the building without difficulty.

Feeling a little more comfortable inside the shrine, Echo noticed the structure had a high ceiling supported by tall red pillars decorated in golden designs. Looking down at the smooth wood floor, Echo saw more smashed vases and dead plants littering the buildings walls. Centered at the back of the shrine was a beautifully adorned dais that had three tall candlesticks on each side of what would have been a huge golden statue. Unfortunately, the orcs had destroyed most of the figure, leaving only its base still intact.

Approaching the dais, Echo remembered Yesu saying the oracle was hidden somewhere beneath its statue. Since the sculpture itself was destroyed, she decided to look for a secret entrance. Putting away her shield, Echo leaned in to examine the dais's candlesticks. Reaching out, she grabbed one and gave it a light tug. Echo heard a slight clicking sound as she pulled it up less than an inch. Repeating the gesture until all the candlesticks were in their new positions, a loud *clang* emanated from beneath the dais, and she could now see that it swayed.

Using her foot to shove the rolling dais out of her way, Echo saw a dark hole in the ground with a spiral staircase that descended deep into the mountain below. Proceeding down the stairs, she saw the faint flickering of a light much like her torch that grew brighter as she reached her destination. Coming to the end of the stairs, Echo entered into a gray stone chamber filled with hundreds of tea lights covering both the floor and several wall-mounted shelves.

Sitting cross-legged on a plain straw mat was an elderly monk whose presence seemed to exude both serenity and wisdom. Clad in a yellow tricivara robe with golden trim and embroidery, he clutched a string of red prayer beads in his left hand as he stroked his long white goatee. Gesturing to a second mat in front of him near a dirt-filled urn he said.

"At last you have arrived. Please, be seated. We have much to discuss."

Echo shook her head. "There's no time. Orcs have invaded the monastery and are killing everyone in sight."

Unconcerned, the oracle casually stated that. "The orcs will not disturb us until *after* we have finished our conversation."

Echo was outraged by his cavalier attitude. "There are people out there dying to protect you!"

"And I will not abandon them," the oracle replied firmly. "But you must remember that everyone in this monastery knew what was coming. The ones who chose to flee have already done so. Those who remained here are well aware of what their fate will be."

It was hard for Echo to understand why someone would choose a violent death if they could avoid it. "So, why didn't you just join those who fled?"

The oracle smiled. "Because this is my only chance to speak with someone capable of altering destiny."

Echo had never considered herself to be all that important, but what the oracle said piqued her interest. So, she extinguished her torch in the urn and sat down on the mat next to him.

Continuing on, the oracle said, "In the realm of the gods is a stream whose waters reveal the passage of time. As an oracle, I have spent my life gazing into these waters and divining people's fate…that is, until the stream turned black."

"Who would be capable of doing such a thing?" Echo asked.

"Kardok," the oracle answered. "The Lord of Darkness is about to gain enormous power, and he will use that power to prevent the other gods from seeing how he obtained it."

Echo didn't like the sound of that. "If Kardok's blackened the time stream, then how can you prevent what's about to happen?"

The oracle was impressed by her question. "By peering along the water's edge, I was able to learn of your encounter with a cruel necromancer by the name of Narcos."

Echo nodded. "Yes, he sought out a smoke demon called Zattermox who offered us powerful treasures in thanks for releasing him."

"One of those treasures is an ancient demonic artifact known as the Crown of Darkness," the oracle warned. "It can be found at the heart of Vakerdurn's Maze in Coronas."

"What will Zattermox do with the crown?" Echo wondered.

"He will use it to assist Kardok in overthrowing his fellow gods," the oracle warned.

Echo was puzzled. "Why would a demon help a god? Evil or not, the two should still hate each other."

"Because Kardok will reward Zattermox with dominion over all things," the oracle replied.

Echo thought this conversation was taking a turn towards the unbelievable. "Can Kardok really do that?"

"He already has," the oracle answered sadly. "Kardok felt threatened when I first learned of Zattermox, so he afflicted my mind and body with horrible maladies that left me incapacitated. He then sent forth the orcs to murder those who resided within this monastery."

Taking note of the oracle's condition, Echo asked, "So, how were you able to recover from Kardok's attack?"

With a knowing smirk, the old man said, "Anthalos was able to heal me so that I may reveal to you all that I have learned. He also instructed me to give you this." Reaching behind him, the oracle pulled out a huge brown book with golden corners and a matching emblem depicting a dragon's head on its cover. Inscribed below the head was a single word...*Dragona*.

"Dragons are the only creatures who know how to directly enter a god's presence. If you are unable to stop Narcos from obtaining the Crown of Darkness, then you must warn them of the demon's intentions and ensure they do not share their sacred knowledge with anyone."

Echo took the torso-sized book in both hands. As she did, the sound of deep, angry voices could be heard overhead.

Straightening a little, the oracle said, "Our time together has come to an end."

"Wait!" Echo began as her mind raced. "A friend and I are on a quest for vengeance—"

The oracle cut her off. "I'm sorry, but the time stream's water is shrouded in darkness, and I can see no more. Now, please stand in the right-hand corner of this room by its entrance. When the orcs attack me, you will be able to sneak past them. Make your way to the pond located at the center of the courtyard. From there, a bloomlyn will help you escape."

What's a bloomlyn? Echo wondered as she followed the oracle's instructions.

The orcs footsteps thundered as they made their way down the spiral staircase. Eager to slay their evasive foe, they had just reached the oracle's chamber when all of his tea lights went out simultaneously. The stupid human didn't realize orcs could see perfectly well no matter how much light there was, and they were anxious to show him just how futile his actions really were.

Echo held the Dragona under her left arm while she used her right hand to trace an escape along the wall. Listening to the orcs slaughter a helpless old man was truly heartbreaking, but at least his death would not be in vain. Quietly making her way to the stairs, Echo was eventually able to flee the shrine and return to the courtyard.

It wasn't hard for Echo to find the courtyard's pond. Reflecting the moonlight off its calm waters, Echo couldn't help but appreciate the irony considering the chaos going on around her. Looking for anything that might be able to help her, she came across an enormous head of lettuce with a big pink and white flower at its center that grew around a thorn-covered branch.

Trying to figure out if this was a bloomlyn, Echo was surprised to see the flower rise and crown the head of a strange-looking plant creature. Watching the thorn branch descend like a sword into the slender right hand of the bloomlyn, Echo noticed that its nine-foot stem took on a vaguely feminine shape. At the base of the plant was a pile of kettle-sized peaches cupped within its lettuce leaves.

Holding one of these odd peaches in her other hand, the bloomlyn looked down at Echo and sadly stated, "I see that you possess the Dragona. Does this mean the master has perished?"

"Yes. I'm afraid so," Echo acknowledged.

The bloomlyn sighed. "It's a terrible thing to witness the ones you care about die before your very eyes. I had wanted to help the Nung-Dow stand against the orcs when they first attacked the monastery, but the master requested that I stay hidden until your arrival. I hope you realize the importance of the information he has given you."

Echo definitely grasped the severity of the situation and nodded.

The bloomlyn was about to say something further when she spotted three orcs staring at them off in the distance. Angered by their presence, she shouted, "Hey, you stinkin' worms. Over here!" She then tossed one of her oversized peaches their direction. Echo watched as the fruit smashed into the ground and exploded with a lethal barrage of sharp black seeds that tore through the orcs' armor and flesh.

Picking up a second peach and offering it to Echo, the bloomlyn said, "Take this and go. I shall keep the orcs distracted for as long as I can."

Clearly nervous as she took the giant fruit, Echo struggled to balance it in one arm while carrying the Dragona in the other. Aware there were more orcs on the way, she wobbled off, barely being able to manage her load. As Echo departed, the bloomlyn grabbed another peach and readied herself for battle.

Returning to the wall where she had first entered the monastery, she spotted two familiar orcs guarding the staircase to the battlements. The orcs easily caught sight of her standing in the open and prepared themselves for a fight. Holding her peach, Echo didn't think she was strong enough to toss it like the bloomlyn had while still maintaining a safe distance. So, instead, she set it on the ground and rolled it towards them.

The orcs suspected the fruit was deadly and dodged past it as they ran towards her. What they didn't count on, though, was the huge peach hitting the stairs behind them and exploding anyways. Hundreds of painful seeds pierced their backs, killing one orc instantly while leaving the other paralyzed.

Climbing up the stairs onto the battlements, Echo angrily cursed when she saw the orcs had knocked down all of their siege ladders. Adding to her misfortune, she found that one of the orcs responsible for her dilemma was still present and spoiling for a fight. Spinning a morning star above his head and carrying a shield, the chain-clad orc uttered a loud battle cry as Echo drew her sword.

Just as the battle was about to commence, a small crackling sphere of pure white energy slammed into the orc's shoulder. Knocked off balance by the shockbolt, the orc howled as he fell off the wall and plummeted towards the courtyard below. Echo looked over to see where the bolt came from and saw Hatch lower his glowing staff as he hovered by her side on the flying carpet.

Dipping below the wall to keep from being targeted by crossbows, Hatch shouted, "I heard the sound of combat and came to see if you were alright."

Echo sheathed her sword and leapt from the wall onto the carpet. Clutching the Dragona, she said, "Let's get out of here. I'll tell you what happened later."

Agreeing wholeheartedly, Hatch flew the carpet away from the monastery and back towards Orla.

Chapter Seventeen

dire mood had befallen the party as they joined Echo for breakfast that morning. Hatch had decided to sleep in while Ontar, Wink, and Kit sat around the table listening intently to the elf's account of what had occurred at the Nung-Dow monastery. After sharing news of the monk's tragic end at orcish hands, Echo asked Houge to fetch the sleeping wizard so she could reveal to everyone what the oracle had told her.

The oracle's words haunted the group as they discussed what should be done. Aware of Narcos's growing threat, Echo and Hatch urged Kit to find Vakerdurn's Maze as quickly as possible. Feeling that time was of the essence, Kit led her companions to the crystal room and directed them to a huge map of the Rashben Region hanging on the wall. "Does anyone know where in Coronas we'd find Vakerdurn's Maze?" she asked of those assembled.

"Here," Ontar said as he walked up and pointed to a spot on the map. "In the Ambril Plains."

Kit stared at the map and noticed the plains were far to the southeast of where Ontar had said he was originally from. "Have you ever been there?"

"No," Ontar admitted. "But everyone in my kingdom knows about Vakerdurn's Maze. Its legend spans countless generations."

Hatch grew curious. "What can you tell us about it?"

Ontar slowly paced the room with Wink on his shoulder. "From what I've been told, Vakerdurn was a vicious minotaur that attacked numerous villages with a horde of monsters at his side. Apparently, he enjoyed releasing the slaves he captured out into the wild so that he could hunt them for sport. During one of these hunts, he discovered an ancient treasure trove and used its riches to build a complex maze of unmatched size and danger."

"Let me guess," Echo speculated. "Once the maze was built, he used it to continue his slave hunts."

"He didn't need to," Ontar explained. "You see, the artifacts he sold attracted countless treasure hunters who braved the maze in search of the few remaining relics Vakerdurn vowed to keep for himself."

"Like the Crown of Darkness," Echo added ominously. "You wouldn't happen to know what other relics remain there would you?"

Ontar shook his head. "I didn't even know about the crown until you told me. Although, I do think Zattermox mentioned something about a mirror during our last encounter?"

Wink grew curious about Vakerdurn's treasure herself. "So, Onnie, did you ever think of entering the maze to find your fortune?"

"I never had a chance," Ontar explained. "When Vakerdurn's Maze became a part of Coronas, it was viewed as a danger by the local peasants. Taking action, King Deltrum ordered all but one its entrances sealed and had a dungeon built around the maze's only remaining passage. From then on, Deltrum's Dungeon was used to imprison some of the kingdoms' worst criminals. Whenever the dungeon filled up, its prisoners were shoved into Vakerdurn's Maze to face a deadly assortment of traps and monsters."

Having been a prisoner himself not so long-ago, Hatch sympathized with the poor souls who were forced to traverse Vakerdurn's Maze as punishment for their crimes. "What a horribly inhumane practice. Has anyone ever managed to escape from the maze?"

"No," Ontar uttered.

"Then I guess we'd better make sure Narcos isn't the first," Wink said with a touch more optimism than what the rest of her companions actually felt.

"I just wish the oracle could have told us if we'd be able to stop Narcos in time," Kit fretted.

Disappointed for a different reason, Ontar said, "Even if he couldn't tell us that, I still would have liked to learn about Lydon's fate."

"Me too," Echo added. "But alas, Kardok had robbed him of his ability to see the future."

"That may be, but it didn't stop him from preparing for it," Hatch noted. "Why else would he make sure to give us the Dragona?"

Thinking back to the book, Echo quietly said, "I just hope that we won't actually have to use it."

Marcain started to feel like a rambling storyteller the way Zattermox kept up his steady barrage of questions during their journey to Vakerdurn's Maze. Sitting in the back of a noisy cart with the knowledge-hungry demon, Marcain had been given the task of enlightening his foul-smelling companion while Narcos drove them to their next destination. The experience proved to be an interesting one. Initially speaking to Eragosh about the world he used to know, Zattermox eventually moved on to ask Marcain about how the surrounding lands evolved into what they were today. Thankfully, Marcain's noble upbringing gave him the education he needed to answer most of Zattermox's questions, and even pose some of his own.

"So, why did your former master feel the need to conquer our realm instead of ruling like a god in his own?"

Zattermox snickered at the human's ignorance. "Xoj'Nahell is hardly a place that anyone would actually *want* to rule. Slime-filled swamps, ash-covered wastelands, and oceans of lava make life a constant struggle for the demons who dwell there. Starvation is common, forcing many of us to feed on each other just to survive!"

"It sounds like a wretched place," Marcain remarked.

Agreeing with him, Zattermox said, "It is, which is why many demons will follow a powerful overlord in the conquest of other worlds."

Marcain grabbed the cart's railing as it went over a bump in the road. "With demons so eager to march on other worlds, I'm surprised there's anyone left on Xoj'Nahell."

"Ah, but the overlords always want to replenish the ranks of their armies," Zattermox explained. "You see, when demons conquer a world, they usually kill their victims and devour the bodies. Afterwards, an overlord will send scavengers to collect the bones and dump them in the swamp. Once there, the slime will coat these bones and begin the process of creating a new demon."

Finding little of value in his minion's conversation, Narcos preferred to listen to the steady rhythm of his nightmare's hooves as he galloped down a long dirt road through the Ambril Plains. It was still fairly early in the morning when he first caught sight of Vakerdurn's Maze. Looming over the grassland like some impenetrable fortress, the maze's towering walls were made out of a tan colored stone with a row of polished brass spikes at its top. The only place where the spikes were absent was at a small segment in the wall which had been sealed off at roughly the same time that Deltrum's Dungeon had been built. Nowhere near the dungeon itself Narcos eagerly followed the road up to this sealed portion and brought his steed to a halt.

So, this is where Zattermox protected his master's treasures, the necromancer thought. *I certainly hope for his sake that my journey here has not been a waste of time.* Glancing back at the smoke demon, he said, "Look well onto your former home, slave. The Crown of Darkness resides within its walls, and I demand that you fetch it for me."

"Forgive me, master, but the entrance has been sealed off," Zattermox pointed out.

"Then turn into a cloud and fly over it," Narcos demanded.

"And just how is he supposed to carry the crown out in that form?" Marcain asked.

Narcos was quickly growing to detest the young lord. "I suppose I'll have to conjure up some undead to accompany him. Marcain do you know if there's a cemetery nearby?"

Marcain shook his head. "No. From what I remember, the only structure around here is Deltrum's Dungeon which serves as the maze's main entrance."

Frowning when he heard this, Narcos said, "Fine. If I can't dig up the dead, then I'll just have to create some of my own."

"How do you intend to do that?" Zattermox wondered.

"A little distraction goes a long way..." Narcos began.

"Kendap, what's that?" asked a spear-wielding guard as he stood next to a flagpole on the roof of Deltrum's Dungeon. Pointing out past the building's parapets, he called attention to a peculiar-looking creature that galloped along the maze's exterior wall.

Alarmed by the blue flame that made up the nightmare's mane, Kendap replied, "Dammit, Irgis, how am I supposed to know?"

"You don't think that one of the monsters got out, do you?" Irgis wondered.

Kendap shook his head. "I don't think so. From what I can tell, it's pulling a cart with two people in it."

Bringing his cart to a stop outside the dungeon, Narcos saw that it was little more than a square keep with rounded towers at its corners that happened to blend seamlessly into the maze's exterior wall. Two long, hanging banners that displayed the emblem of Coronas flanked either side of the keep's wooden double doors and extended up to the roof where two guards watched him.

A little unnerved by the traveler's appearance, Kendap shouted, "Halt! Who goes there?"

Surrounded by tall prairie grass, Narcos wiped sweat from his brow as the day grew warmer while Marcain swatted at noisy insects. "My name is Narcos Melador," the necromancer replied. "And I am here to collect your dead."

"We have no dead," Kendap yelled from above.

"Not yet...but you will," Narcos stated.

Irgis scowled when he heard this. "Is that some sort of threat?"

Snickering at the question, Narcos replied, "It's not a threat, just a fact."

"Well, you can take your facts and shove them up your ass," Irgis retorted.

Afraid of what would happen if Narcos and Zattermox were allowed to carry out their plans, Marcain shouted, "Ignore Narcos and alert your troops! There's a demon sneaking into your dungeon even as we speak!"

Narcos gave the noble an angry look and immediately said, *"Eragosh!"* causing Marcain's face to go blank.

"What demon?" Kendap asked.

"You'll find out soon enough," Narcos replied.

Kendap exchanged a look with Irgis and said, "I don't know what's going on, but I think I'd better tell Sir Cyphus about it."

Irgis agreed, "Good idea. I'll keep an eye on Narcos to make sure he doesn't try anything."

Focused entirely on Narcos's appearance outside the dungeon, the guards failed to spot the sinister cloud of smoke that drifted over the maze towards their position. Reaching the structure with ease, Zattermox used his gaseous form to waft through an arrow slit in one of the building's towers and make his way over to a spiral staircase that descended down to the dungeon's bottom floor. Advancing along the building's main corridor, Zattermox was quickly spotted by a husky servant woman who had followed her nose to the awful-smelling cloud. Letting out a shriek, she immediately fled from the demon and went to seek out Sir Cyphus.

Unconcerned by her actions, Zattermox made his way to the dungeon's foyer, where two guards had heard the woman's scream and had gone to make sure the buildings doors were still sufficiently barred. Clutching their spears in both hands, the guards could do nothing to stop Zattermox from enveloping them in his deadly smoke. Listening to the men cough as their eyes watered, Zattermox knew that time was of the essence and shifted back into his solid form. He then lowered his head and rammed into one of the guards from behind, impaling him on his sharp black horns.

Gazing at the smoke demon through bleary eyes, the second guard tried to attack Zattermox with his spear, but at the last moment, the demon grabbed his injured companion by the hips and spun him around just in time to get stabbed through the heart by the spear's head! Pushing the dead guard onto the weapon's point so that it would be hard to remove, Zattermox dislodged himself from his first victim so that he could attack the second by slashing the man's throat with his clawed fingers. Choking as he grabbed at his mutilated neck, the guard fell to the ground and died in a pool of blood.

Triumphant, Zattermox raced to the chamber doors and slid out their crossbar before opening them. Entering the dungeon with his sword at ready, Eragosh heard footsteps heading his way and prepared himself for battle. Following behind him was Narcos, who stopped and grinned at the dead bodies on the floor. Raising a hand over the corpses, he uttered an incantation that caused them both to shudder before slowly picking themselves up off the ground. Directing them to stand next to Eragosh, the necromancer thought, *This fight just got interesting.*

"I don't like games," Sir Cyphus declared as he sat in the dining hall and listened to Kendap's encounter with Narcos. A bald, clean-shaven man clad in the armor and surcoat of a Coronasian knight he had a beautiful enchanted war hammer strapped to his back and absently played with the plume of a visored helmet, which rested on the table. "It almost seems like this Narcos person is trying to goad us into a fight."

Kendap agreed, "I just wonder if what his companion said about a demon was true?"

"The easiest way to find that out is to conduct a search of the dungeon," Sir Cyphus remarked. Not that he really expected to find anything. Deltrum's Dungeon was hardly of any strategic value. The prisoners brought there usually got shoved into the maze shortly after their arrival so the troops who escorted them could quickly return home. This meant that, on average, the dungeon only had about ten men who were stationed there on a regular basis.

"What should we do about Narcos?" Kendap wondered.

"Call his bluff," the knight replied. "Tell him that we don't have time for idle threats, and that if he doesn't move along, then we'll throw him into the maze."

Kendap was about to say something further when a servant woman burst into the dining hall and exclaimed, "Milord! There's smoke in the corridors!"

Standing up, Sir Cyphus asked, "Is there a kitchen fire?"

The woman rapidly shook her head. "No! It's just a cloud of smoke. I think it probably blew in from outside?"

Kendap immediately tensed. "Could that be the demon we were warned about?"

Picking his helmet off the table and putting it on his head, Sir Cyphus drew forth his war hammer and said, "If it is, then we better track it down before it hurts someone!"

Just then, Irgis dashed into the chamber with an alarmed look on his face. "Milord, I just saw Narcos and his companion enter the dungeon!"

"What...how?" the knight inquired in disbelief.

Irgis said, "From what I heard, a demon killed the door guards before allowing his master inside. Three more men had gone to stop them, but they were all cut down by the same skilled swordsman who had tried to warn us before."

So, is the swordsman with us or against us? Sir Cyphus thought. With only four guards left, the knight had to decide quickly or risk losing the dungeon altogether. "Summon our remaining men here to the dining hall. We've got to take a stand while we still have a chance!"

❧❧❧

Narcos hated when he had to follow behind zombies. Slow and stupid, they relentlessly pursued their enemy's life-force until it was extinguished. Aside from being frightening, their single greatest advantage was they could be raised in large numbers with relative ease. Of course, they weren't terribly skilled in a fight, but that's what Eragosh and Zattermox were for. Together, the trio followed their five zombie guards down a corridor and into the dungeon's dining hall.

Seeing the chamber's long table had been pushed to one side, Narcos noticed that Sir Cyphus stood with a line of four nervous guards, who anxiously held their weapons at ready. Armed with an impressive-looking war hammer, the knight said, "Halt! I am Sir Zatik Cyphus, and I demand to know why you're attacking this dungeon?"

Lifting a hand to stop his minions from advancing, Narcos replied, "I'm here to end your miserable lives so that your souls can serve me in reaching the treasure at the heart of Vakerdurn's Maze."

"You stupid fool. There's no treasure at the end of the maze… only death!" Sir Cyphus claimed.

"He lies!" Zattermox snarled.

"Do I?" Sir Cyphus asked innocently. "If you want, I can let you into the maze right now and you can see the truth for yourself."

Narcos smirked at the knight's bravado. "Why would I bother entering the maze when I can have fodder like you do it for me?"

Clutching his war hammer in both hands, Sir Cyphus slammed it into the table, causing its surface to splinter as the weapon's head flashed with glowing white runes. "My men and I won't go down without a fight!"

"But you *will* go down," Narcos asserted before telling his minions to, "Kill them."

Letting out a sinister laugh, Zattermox turned into a cloud of smoke that immediately drifted over the knight and his men. Coughing and bleary-eyed, the guards had trouble fighting against the advancing zombies unaffected by the smoke. Soon, their horrified cries could be heard throughout the dining hall as the undead ripped them apart!

Cursing his enemy's strategy, Sir Cyphus struggled to see a zombie clawing at his chest. Thankfully, the wretched corpse couldn't pierce his armor, allowing him the chance he needed to retaliate. Slamming the top of his war hammer into the zombie's gut, Sir Cyphus pushed it out of the smoke cloud with enough force to knock it over. Able to see once more, the knight raised his enchanted weapon and used it to brutally crush the zombie's skull!

Keenly aware that Sir Cyphus was the only opponent worth fighting, Eragosh swung his sword at the knight while he was still focused on the zombie. Stumbling backwards in a failed attempt at dodging, Sir Cyphus cried out as his adversary's blade pierced his armored arm, leaving a long bloody cut from knuckle to shoulder. Quick to retaliate, Sir Cyphus made a wide swing and struck Eragosh's sword with his enchanted weapon. Much to everyone's surprise, this caused the blade to shatter as if it had been made of glass!

Unwilling to concede the fight just yet, Eragosh dropped the hilt of his now useless sword and waited for the next attack to come. Sir Cyphus let out a fierce battle cry as he went after his enemy, but the knight's attack lacked precision since he could only carry his weapon with one hand. Easily dodging the blow, Eragosh kicked him back into Zattermox's smoke cloud, where three zombies pounced upon the poor man and rapidly brought about his demise.

With the fighting over, Zattermox reverted back into solid form and exclaimed, "The dungeon is ours! Now, only the maze awaits."

Narcos's shoulders drooped a little. "That may be, but a long journey and brief battle have left me exhausted. Tonight, we'll use the dungeon to rest and recover so that tomorrow we can carry out the rest of my plans."

Zattermox bowed humbly. "Of course, master. It is an exceptionally wise move to keep our strength up for the days ahead."

Ignoring the flattery, Narcos walked up to Eragosh and saw that he looked down at the war hammer Sir Cyphus used. Noticing that its glowing runes had faded from view, he asked, "Can you use it?"

Eragosh shook his head. *"No."*

"Pity," Narcos mused. "It looks like we'll have to find you a new blade."

Setting about the task of making themselves comfortable, Narcos, Zattermox, and Eragosh prepared for whatever trials awaited them when they finally decided to enter Vakerdurn's Maze.

Chapter Eighteen

arcain shook his head in sorrow as he strolled over the bloodstained floor of a dining hall littered with the bodies of its defenders. Holding a sword that he had picked up from the dungeon's armory, he stopped by a narrow window whose early morning light had fallen on the dead men and said, "You poor bastards. I shudder to think what Narcos has in store for you." Snickering as he slid the blade into his scabbard, he quickly added, "Then again, you might be thinking the same thing about me."

Unsure of how many dead he was responsible for, Marcain was reminded of the guards who used to protect him, and how he had always taken their presence for granted. Looking back, Marcain realized just how many things had simply been handed to him. Wealth, power, and freedom were all carelessly cast aside for the dream of a simple life with the woman he loved. But then Ontar and Echo destroyed that dream while Narcos turned his life into a nightmare.

Despising his "master" with every fiber of his being, Marcain learned Narcos had drained his powers the previous day and allowed death to reclaim the zombies that had killed Sir Cyphus and his men. This was of small comfort to Marcain, who had been given the lowly task of making meals for Narcos and his pet demon upon learning the dungeon's servants had escaped during the battle. Never wishing for poison more in his life, Marcain knew that after his earlier betrayal the necromancer had given Eragosh greater control of his body to keep any such treachery from happening again, and thus, he was forced to carry out his duties no matter how much he loathed them.

Detecting a foul but familiar stench, Marcain turned to see Zattermox enter the chamber, with Narcos right behind him. Taking a second to admire his handiwork, Narcos asked, "Have you finished your search?"

"Yes, the dungeon is completely secure," Marcain replied.

"I see," Narcos observed before turning to Zattermox. "And are you ready to retrieve the Crown of Darkness?"

Zattermox nodded. "With some assistance I will be."

"Then I will call upon the dead to aid you in your task," Narcos declared before raising his arms up to cast a spell on six of the corpses scattered across the chamber. Watching with interest, Marcain saw that each of these cadavers' shadows twisted and moved about independently from their body of origin. Rising off the ground to greet their new master, these shades possessed an almost mannish figure, with glowing red eyes, slender arms, and a long, wispy tail where its legs would have been.

Zattermox grinned as he saw the undead floating before him. Narcos had laid waste to an entire dungeon for nothing more than a handful of shades. Such a careless disregard for human life would be considered amusing by even the cruelest of demons, and it spoke volumes of the necromancer's dark nature.

Unaware of his minion's approval, Narcos said, "You now have the assistance necessary to accomplish your task. Return to me with the crown or don't bother coming back at all. Is that understood?"

"Yes, master," the demon replied before turning into a cloud of smoke. Floating out the nearest window with the shades at his side, Zattermox diligently made his way towards Vakerdurn's Maze.

⁂

Finally free from Narcos's scrutiny, Zattermox and his entourage drifted out across the sky only to be shocked by the sheer scope of maze. *Damn…just how many artifacts did that stupid minotaur sell off?* the demon wondered.

Below him, the maze stretched out like an all-encompassing city with a massive garden, pristine pool, and several odd-looking buildings dispersed randomly amongst its endless twists and turns. Drawn to the maze's most prolific structure, Zattermox headed towards an imposing castle that he felt certain was built over Da Shō's vault. Determined to reach his destination, the distracted demon didn't even realize that he was being watched.

Rising from deep within the maze, Argoth had seen the smoke demon come his way and was intrigued by the shades that accompanied him. Anyone who could command the undead would make an excellent addition to his assortment of slaves, and all he had to do was extend the *invitation*.

Zattermox had made good progress on reaching the castle when he came across a big round monster with dull red skin and six small black horns that curved upwards from near the top of its head/body. Glaring at him with its large central eye, the *seeker* opened his drooling, oversized mouth to reveal a nasty set of long sharp teeth. The drool itself coated two lengthy tentacles that dangled at the sides of its chin. "Greetings, demon. I am Argoth, the master of this maze, and I've come…"

Refusing to waste time on this arrogant fool, Zattermox passed through Argoth with little concern.

Blinking away the smoke that blurred his vision, Argoth whirled about to face the insolent demon and said, "I will not be ignored!" Emphasizing his point, Argoth's central eye flashed with a bright yellow light that caused one of the shades to suddenly vanish. Cursing as he came to a stop, Zattermox told the remaining undead to continue on towards the castle without him.

Satisfied that he had garnered the demon's attention, Argoth repeated himself, "As I was saying, I am Argoth, the master of this maze, and I've come to offer you an opportunity to serve me as one of my followers."

Zattermox's voice snickered from within the smoke cloud. "Master of this maze? Odd, you don't look like a minotaur."

Argoth didn't appreciate the sarcasm. "I killed the last of Vakerdurn's line ages ago. A fate you might share should you refuse to swear loyalty to me."

"I don't think so," Zattermox said dismissively. "My ambitions are far greater than to serve the likes of you." Feeling certain that his shades had made it to the castle, Zattermox decided to join them.

"Then prepare to die!" Argoth said as he opened his mouth and inhaled.

As his gaseous form was sucked into Argoth's gaping maw, Zattermox was shocked by the notion that he could actually be consumed by this creature. Unwilling to go down without a fight, he shifted into solid form and immediately plunged towards

Vakerdurn's Maze. Laughing heartily, Argoth descended in hot pursuit.

The ground came up fast for Zattermox, and he briefly changed into a smoke cloud to avoid impact. Turning solid again before Argoth got too close, Zattermox found himself standing on a wide stone path between two walls. Initially expecting to just drift over to the castle entering the maze itself had never been a part of his plan, and he would now be forced to see what the prisoners in Deltrum's Dungeon had to endure.

Deciding to play with his victim, Argoth used his tentacles to whip drops of acid at the smoke demon. Hearing the vile fluid hiss as it splattered all around him, Zattermox ran. Excited by the thrill of the chase, Argoth cast a spell to keep things interesting.

Zattermox had just turned a sharp right when he saw a long straight path in front of him. Moving as fast as he could, he tried to put some distance between himself and Argoth when, all of a sudden, he slammed straight into an invisible wall! Falling flat on his ass, Zattermox cried out in pain as a large drop of acid burned his back. Getting up, he saw that random segments of the maze's wall had disappeared from where he stood.

Groping an invisible portion of the wall to see if it was real or not, Zattermox suffered a second acid attack that hit him in the upper arm. Trying to think of a way out of this mess, he noticed the base of an invisible wall could still be seen along its foundation. So, by keeping his eyes on the ground, he could tell the difference between a branch in the path and a false opening. Testing his observation, Zattermox sprinted back along his former route and made two successful turns without hitting anything. Disappointed with the demon's ingenuity, Argoth canceled his invisibility spell.

Coming to a new section of the maze, Zattermox saw the walls in this area had spikes sticking out of them, with multiple skeletal bodies scattered across the ground. Debating on how to handle this trap, Zattermox saw a dagger among the dead and knew what he had to do.

Argoth closed in on the demon just as he stepped on a cobblestone that triggered the spike trap. Turning into smoke right before the piercing walls hit each other, Zattermox drifted over to the dagger and waited. It took a couple minutes for the trap to reset itself, and Argoth hovered impatiently overhead, trying to spot his prey.

As the walls parted, Zattermox shifted into his regular body, grabbed the dagger, and threw it at Argoth. The blade stuck right in the corner of the monster's eye, causing him to yell while trying to pull it out with a tentacle. Becoming a smoke cloud, Zattermox ignored Argoth's coughing threats as he passed through and above his enemy. Retaking his solid form in an interesting new position, Zattermox appeared upside-down over Argoth and fell directly on top of him. Stiffening his neck as his horns pierced the seeker's hide, Zattermox then used his clawed hands to grab at the monster's flesh in order to brace himself for what was about to come next.

Shooting across the maze in an uncontrolled fury, Argoth spun about wildly while he tried to grab the demon with his tentacles. Acting in desperation, Argoth turned himself upside-down and dragged his upper half along the labyrinth's floor. Shifting into a smoke cloud, Zattermox watched as four of his enemies' horns splintered along the ground before he collided with one of the maze's walls.

Floating above his stunned nemesis, Zattermox heard the howling of at least three ferocious creatures off in the distance and said, "I certainly hope that, as master of this maze, you command the loyalty of your subjects, because if you don't, then whatever's coming this way is about to have an easy meal."

Confident that Argoth was beaten, Zattermox wasted no more time on him as he rose into the sky and made his way towards the castle.

◆◈◆◈◆

Echo tightened her grip on Spirit Slayer as she stood in the armory's sparring ring. Facing her with a mace in one hand and a morning star in the other was Ontar. The two had trained for over an hour, and both were tired.

Outside the ring, Wink cheered. "Come on, Onnie. She can't take much more of this. Just one more attack, and you'll finish her off."

"Thanks," Echo muttered as she swung her sword at Ontar's head. Parrying the strike with his mace, Ontar sent his morning star breezing past her left side in an attack that would have smashed into her abdomen.

Skipping along the ring's edge, Wink sang, "Blow to the side. Echo just died. Echo just died from a blow to the side."

"Oh, will you SHUT UP!" Echo yelled as she lowered her blade. "That was *not* a fatal blow!"

"No, it wasn't," Ontar said as he abandoned his battle stance. "But if you had put more force behind your initial attack, then you could have thrown me off balance when I parried your blade. Then I wouldn't have been able to counter with my morning star."

Echo was getting frustrated with all of Ontar's so-called *advice*. "Ugh…will someone please spare me the lectures. What little training you've had with a two-handed sword does not automatically make you an expert."

"That may be, but I *still* have had more training with it than you," Ontar argued.

Cautiously entering the armory, Milsa passed by her fellow slaves and interrupted their squabbling. "Excuse me, milord and lady, but Kit has sent me to inform you that we've arrived at Vakerdurn's Maze."

"Good," Echo replied hotly as she addressed Ontar and Wink. "This will give me the perfect opportunity to show you two what I can really do with this sword once I'm free from your constant criticism." Not waiting for their response, Echo ducked under the sparring ring's ropes and stormed out of the room.

"What a bitch," Wink grumbled as she looked up at Ontar.

"I just hope she can handle herself as well as she thinks she can with that thing," Ontar replied.

Facing a beautiful sunset, the party clambered onto a flying carpet and hovered away from Orla. Sitting at the front of the carpet was Chairbis, with Ontar and Echo behind him dressed in full battle gear. Hatch sat at the back of the carpet while Wink peeked out of his kaftan's pocket. Together, they flew over Deltrum's Dungeon and gawked at the majesty of the maze beneath them.

Ontar felt a little sad when he saw the Coronasian flag fluttering on a pole over the dungeon's keep. Yorus had been the one to tell him about Vakerdurn's Maze in the first place, and now that he was here, he couldn't help but wonder what his cousin would have said had he lived to learn of Ontar's exploits. Alas, all Ontar knew was the world was a darker place without him in it, and that Lydon would pay dearly for killing him!

Approaching the maze's castle, Chairbis brought the carpet to a halt when he saw that it crawled with angry gargoyles! The vaguely mannish creatures had clawed fingers and skin the color of stone. Spreading leathery wings which sprouted from their backs their hideous faces snarled at the party with sharp teeth while two curved horns protruded from their brow.

"Uh-oh. I don't think those gargoyles like that we're here," Wink stated as a flock of the winged monsters leapt off their perches and flew towards the group.

"Well, this is the most likely spot where the Crown of Darkness resides, and we can't leave here without searching it," Hatch replied. Raising his arms, he cast a simple spell, which caused the wind around the carpet to suddenly die. Unable to catch an updraft, the gargoyles howled in fury as they slowly glided down into the maze.

"Looks like your spell took care of the fliers," Ontar noted. "But there's still a lot more of them lurking on the roof."

"Not for long," Hatch said as he recited his second incantation. This time, the party saw a cluster of flaming dots appear high above them in the twilight sky. Watching as a trail of fire formed behind these dots, the group witnessed a blazing rain of death that bombarded the castle in a relentless assault. Many of the gargoyles screamed and scattered as their bodies were scorched by the attack.

"Now, *that's* a powerful spell," Echo exclaimed in admiration. "Let's just hope that my magic can prove just as useful." Closing her eyes, she uttered an incantation that gave her a vision of a gray metal crown whose face looked like a skull with a band of crisscrossing bones. Opening her eyes, Echo pointed and said, "The treasury is located at the uppermost part of the castle. If we land on the roof, it will allow us the easiest chance at reaching it."

Following the elf's advice, Chairbis brought the flying carpet down on top of the castle in the midst of a dozen charred gargoyle bodies. Drawing weapons, the party had barely stepped off the carpet when they heard the angry growls of their winged foes as they clawed up the sides of the building.

Clutching the hilt of Spirit Slayer, Echo ran towards the noise just as one of the gargoyles popped its head over the parapets. Swinging her sword, she decapitated the monster in one swift motion and sent its body plummeting. Unfortunately, a second gargoyle rose next to it and swiped at her with its claws. Echo felt the leather greave on her left arm split and backed away before suffering serious injury.

Hatch could also hear the gargoyles coming and cast a spell even before others came into sight. This caused a series of cracks to form on the ramparts in front of him just as two of the hideous creatures pulled themselves into view. The stone abruptly gave way beneath their weight, and the gargoyles flapped their wings in vain as the rubble came crumbling down on top of them.

Unused to being in such a dangerous situation, Chairbis stood on the flying carpet and watched as a gargoyle climbed onto the castle's roof and lunged at him. Timing the creature's advance perfectly, he caused the carpet to rise seconds before the gargoyle could make an attack. Hovering over his infuriated enemy, he then cast a spell to neutralize its threat once and for all. Convulsing as the cleric's power washed over it, the gargoyle's movements slowed to a stop. Robbed of the magic that had given it life, the helpless creature stared vacantly ahead and became a statue once more.

Situated among the charred remains of his enemies, Ontar held his morning star and tower shield at ready as a gargoyle leapt over the parapets and made a mad dash his direction. Tracking the monster's footwork, Ontar took a decisive step backwards over one of the many corpses littering the ground. Moving too fast to stop itself, the gargoyle tripped on the body and slammed headfirst into his shield. Noticing the gargoyle's horns had punctured his barrier, Ontar lowered the shield and forced his enemy to bow before him. He then broke the gargoyle's back with a blow from his weapon.

Facing the last remaining gargoyle, Echo swung Spirit Slayer in a downward arc, hoping to split her adversary in two, but the monster dodged her attack, and she struggled with the cumbersome sword to pull it back up in time to defend herself. Seizing on her slower reactions, the gargoyle sprang at Echo, knocking her to the ground and digging its claws deep into her shoulders. It then turned its head and bit savagely into her neck!

Echo felt the gargoyle's teeth pierce the sides of her throat, and she quickly slid Spirit Slayer across its stomach in a blow that managed to rend a shallow yet painful cut. The gargoyle recoiled from its injury, but not before severely tearing at her flesh. Gasping for breath, Echo felt her warm blood pouring from the wound and immediately blacked out.

A battle cry filled with rage and concern erupted from Ontar as he saw what had happened. Despite their earlier dispute, Echo remained both a friend *and* his key to finding Lydon. Spinning his morning star as he ran forward, Ontar knocked the gargoyle off Echo in a single blow. Reeling from attacks to both its ribs and stomach, the gargoyle tried to shield itself with its wings. Unrelenting in his assault, Ontar broke the creature's wings with his first attack, then crushed the side of its skull with a second.

Wink saw that Echo lay unconscious in a growing pool of blood and shouted, "Chairbis, hurry. Echo's hurt!"

Lowering the flying carpet to the ground, Chairbis raced to Echo's side and dropped to his knees. Placing his hands on her chest, he urgently cast a spell that stopped her from bleeding out. He then touched her neck and cast a second spell to heal the gruesome wound. Relieved to have dealt with the worst of her injuries, he moved on to magically mend the gash in her shoulder. Then, with one last incantation, he stabilized her condition and made sure she breathed regularly. Exhausted by his work, Chairbis sat back in his bloodstained robes and sighed.

"Will she be alright?" Ontar asked as he knelt and put an armored hand on the cleric's shoulder.

Chairbis nodded. "Yes, but she's in no condition to continue on."

"I see," Hatch said with concern. "Would you be able to stay with her if we chose to enter the castle?"

"Of course," Chairbis replied, even though he really would have preferred taking her back to Orla.

"Good," Ontar said as he stood up to withdraw his morning star and shield. Leaning over Echo, he picked up Spirit Slayer and brought the blade close to his helmet. "Echo intended on using this sword to defeat Zattermox, and when she wakes up, I don't want her to be disappointed."

Zattermox was startled when he heard the screams of gargoyles being scorched on the roof above him. Roaming the treasury with three shades at his side, he initially entered the chamber by wafting under its door after a couple of mechataur had managed to destroy two of his minions. Finding the treasury had four golden torch stands placed at its corners (but no windows), he saw that it also displayed a tapestry depicting an angry bull's head on a yellow background over two crossed battle axes. This tapestry hung limply from the far wall near an open chest filled with gold and jewels, which sat in the center of the room. The sight of the chest almost made Zattermox sick. How in the world could so many of the artifacts held within Da Shō's vault be gone!?

Fortunately, Vakerdurn had placed the demon's most valuable relics on pedestals at the corners and back of the chest. Among these were an elegantly crafted silver hand mirror and a purple vial that held a pale glowing liquid in it, the items easily recognized as the Mirror of Corruption and Blood of the Overlord. As impressive as these artifacts were, though, it was the Crown of Darkness on the last pedestal that really caught Zattermox's attention.

The only problem was getting them to Narcos. The door to the treasury was sealed by magic, and neither Zattermox nor the shades could remove the solid relics by the same means they had entered the room. A solution to this predicament occurred to Zattermox when he heard combat coming from outside the chamber's door. If someone outside could gain access to the treasury, then it might offer an opportunity for him to swipe the artifacts and run.

Planning an ambush Zattermox placed all three demonic relics on one pedestal and instructed the shades to hide within its shadow. He then closed the chest, turned into a cloud of smoke, and slipped inside through its keyhole. Once this was done, it all became a waiting game.

❖❖❖

The loud sound of cracking stone filled the castle's normally quiet corridor as a chunk of its ceiling magically collapsed from above. Utilizing his landing spell, Hatch, Wink, and Ontar all dropped down onto the building's rubble-strewn floor and took a second to observe their surroundings. Standing in front of an arched window, the party saw two broad flights of stairs on either side of them that led further down into the building. Looking ahead, they noticed a long corridor illuminated by torch-lit sconces that had an artistically crafted wooden door at its far end.

Centered on this door was a golden, bestial face whose stern expression would make anyone think twice about of approaching it. Silently flanking the foreboding entrance were two mechanical beings that resembled bull-headed suits of armor built in the shape of brass minotaur's. These mechataurs possessed glowing yellow eyes and had an ax and sword installed where their hands would have been.

Cautiously advancing down the corridor, the party was startled when the golden face suddenly said, "Halt! You who have successfully traversed the perils of Vakerdurn's Maze, know this. I am your last obstacle before obtaining treasures undreamed of. As guardian, I applaud your efforts in making it this far and know the sacrifices you've endured must have been great. With so few who have ever reached this point, take solace in the fact that your journey is finally at an end. Present to me the Ring of Vakerdurn and his bounty shall now be yours."

"What ring?" Ontar asked uncertainly.

"It's probably some treasure from deep within the maze," Wink speculated. "You have to remember that, for most people, making it to this point would be considered the achievement of a lifetime."

Hatch sighed. "There's always a price to pay for going against the order of things."

"Well, I guess this price is ours," Ontar said as he raised Spirit Slayer and told the door. "We do not possess the Ring of Vakerdurn."

The guardian uttered a single word. "Tragic."

With that being said, the mechataurs fired beams from their eyes, which hit Ontar and Hatch with enough force to knock both men flat on their backs. The mechanical monsters then lifted their weapons and advanced towards their enemies. Knocked about the inside of Hatch's pocket before he hit the floor, Wink pulled herself up in time to see that both of her companions were stunned by the mechataurs' attacks. Thinking quickly, she uttered a spell to give her friends a fighting chance.

Prepared to hack the helpless humans into pieces, the mechataurs were forced to stop when a wall they had never seen before suddenly appeared out of nowhere. Recovering from their adversary's beam attack, Ontar was relieved to see Wink's illusionary wall as he slowly clambered to his feet. Leaning on Spirit Slayer for balance, he then went over to help Hatch up. As he did, he looked down at the pixie and said, "Thanks for the spell. Things could have been a lot worse right now if it weren't for you."

Wink blushed. "Oh, Onnie, I could never let them hurt you."

"Well, they haven't been defeated quite yet," Hatch pointed out. "Ontar, are you ready?"

Ontar got into battle position. "I'm ready."

Prepared for the fight to commence, Wink canceled her illusion. Lowering the top of his staff, Hatch unleashed a lightning bolt the moment his opponent came into view. Electricity danced around the mechataur's metallic form as its eyes lost their glow and went black. Stiffening as it fell, the mechataur hit the ground face first with a loud *clang*.

Squaring off against his own adversary, Ontar thrust Spirit Slayer up the mechataur's snout and in-between its eyes. Initiating a surprise maneuver, the mechataur disarmed Ontar by rotating its head backwards and inadvertently throwing Ontar against the wall. It then made a blind chopping motion with its ax arm while wildly swinging its sword.

Pulling back while leaving his blade wedged in the mechataur, Ontar watched as Hatch cast another spell. Witnessing a rapid change in coloration, he saw that an orange hue had come over Spirit Slayer, which brightened until it was white hot! The searing two-handed sword melted its way down the mechataur's armored body with little resistance. Reaching chest level, the blade caused enough damage to render the automaton inoperable. Shortly afterwards, Spirit Slayer returned to its normal color, and Ontar hesitantly retrieved the weapon without getting burned.

Perturbed by the loss of its protectors, the guardian boldly stated, "You shall not pass." The moment those words were uttered, a hidden trap door opened to reveal a pit beneath the party that caused them all to plummet down a long dark shaft.

Keeping his wits about him, Hatch ignored a scream from Wink and cast a landing spell on Ontar. The bulky warrior slowed in his descent as his companions whizzed past him. Repeating his spell with similar results, Hatch felt his momentum decrease as he dodged two nearby mechataurs who continued their plunge into darkness.

"Whew, that was scary," Wink said as she clung to Hatch's pocket.

"So, what happens now?" Ontar asked from above.

"We go up," Hatch replied as he uttered another incantation. Flying upwards, he took hold of Ontar's arm and, together, they rose out of the shaft.

Landing in front of the guardian, the party once again heard its proclamation. "You shall not pass!" Disagreeing with that assessment, Hatch cast a spell which caused the door's stone framework to crack and crumble into dust. "NO!" cried the guardian as Ontar pushed it over. Stepping onto the now useless hunk of wood, the party victoriously entered the treasury.

Triumph, however, quickly turned into trepidation when Ontar saw the etchings along Spirit Slayer's blade brighten with a bluish light, accompanied by a deep crimson glow from the ruby in its hilt.

Watching the sword with interest, Wink unexpectedly detected a foul aroma in the air and crinkled her nose. "Eww, what stinks?"

Ontar held his blade at ready. "It's Zattermox, and if this sword is any indication, he's probably not alone."

"Then we had better be ready for him," Hatch said as he cast a spell. The party felt a strong breeze blowing at their backs, which Hatch hoped would protect them from the vile demon's smoke.

Zattermox couldn't believe the same group of adventurers who had released him from Uch-na-Mach now faced him here. He couldn't even imagine how they learned of his whereabouts, but it didn't matter. Their arrival provided the perfect opportunity for him to accomplish his task. Taunting Hatch from within the treasure chest, he said, "Very clever, old man, but that spell won't be enough to save you."

Exploiting the element of surprise, a shade emerged from the shadow of a pedestal and swiped at Hatch with one of its ethereal hands. Groaning in pain, the wizard felt like his left forearm had been sliced open. As it turned out, though, the wound was magical in nature, and it left only a shadowy mark on the afflicted appendage.

Ontar refused to give the shade a chance to strike. Swinging his two-handed sword, he caused his enemy to dissipate with a single blow. Its eradication also caused the mark on Hatch's arm to fade.

Using the conflict to their advantage, two more shades arose from their hiding places, grabbed the demonic artifacts by their shadows, and exited the treasury by flying past the party. Taking their bounty through the hole in the ceiling, the undead successfully fled from the castle.

Zattermox laughed. "You fools just ensured my rise to power."

"Not if we kill you first," Ontar retorted angrily.

"Go ahead and try," the demon gloated. "The more time you waste on me the better."

Hatch thought things through, then turned to Ontar. "We have to stop those shades from reaching Narcos."

Ontar knew what would happen if the Crown of Darkness ended up in the necromancer's hands. "Let's go," he said grudgingly.

Hatch didn't even wait to cast his spell.

The walls of Vakerdurn's Maze looked black to Chairbis as a dull rosy haze on the horizon gave way to the darkness of evening. Catching a glimpse of the full red moon as it rose, Chairbis briefly examined Echo's unconscious form before he felt a rush of air off to his right, accompanied by the sudden appearance of Hatch, Wink, and Ontar.

Illuminating his surroundings, Hatch made the crystal at the head of his staff glow with a bright white light. Adopting a serious tone, the old wizard said, "Chairbis, we need you to stop some shades with your magic while I fly the carpet."

Chairbis watched as everyone sat on the carpet around both himself and Echo. "What's going on?"

Hatch explained their encounter with Zattermox while they flew off in the same direction as the shades. Gauging the brightness of Spirit Slayer's runes, Ontar was able to locate the undead that would have otherwise been invisible in the night sky. Shining his light on their elusive foes, Hatch saw they made their way back towards Deltrum's Dungeon.

Determined to complete their mission, one of the shades gave the Crown of Darkness to its companion who already held the other demonic artifacts. It then whirled about and attacked the party. Hatch saw the undead coming and fired a lightning bolt at it, but the shade was able to dodge and get within striking distance of the carpet. Unfortunately, that happened to be exactly when Ontar swung his mighty blade and cleaved the undead out of existence.

Holding a torch as he stood on the roof of Deltrum's Dungeon, Marcain had been instructed to alert Narcos the moment Zattermox and his shades returned. Startled by the sight of Hatch's lightning bolt, Marcain saw that a single shade carried the artifacts the necromancer was looking for, and that it was being chased by a flying carpet with some very familiar enemies on it.

"Narcos! They found us. I don't know how, but they found us!" Marcain yelled.

Emerging from a trap door near the flagpole, Narcos looked in the direction of the party and said, "I've come too far to fail now." He then cast a spell that caused a shadowbolt to appear in his hand right before he hurled it at them.

Chairbis uttered an incantation that caused the last shade to vanish just as it passed over Deltrum's Dungeon. Much to the party's horror, the artifacts it carried landed along the roof's edge, well within sight of Narcos. Hatch was just about to use his magic to keep the necromancer away from them when a shadowbolt struck him in the shoulder. Crying out as he lost concentration, the old wizard was barely able to guide the flying carpet into a crash landing on the dungeon's roof!

Diving out of the way, Narcos and Marcain successfully managed to avoid getting struck by the falling carpet. Slowly getting back up, the two saw that just about all their enemies were scattered across the roof, unconscious. Marcain glanced at Narcos and said, "I can't believe you defeated all of them with a single spell."

"Their defeat means nothing to me," Narcos replied as he went to retrieve the demonic artifacts. Examining the Mirror of Corruption and Blood of the Overlord, he saw that, even though both relics had been dropped, they still appeared to be in decent shape. Slipping them into his satchel, he then asked, "Where is the Crown of Darkness?"

Scanning the roof, Marcain quickly pointed at something with his sword. "Hey, what's that?"

Anxiously standing near the edge of the roof, Wink had been spared the same fate as her companions thanks to Hatch taking most of the impact when they fell. Being the first to spot the crown, she made a mad dash for it while Narcos collected the other artifacts. Now that she held it in her hands, she couldn't help but give the two men a cocky little smile. "Me? My name's Wink, and I'm the pixie who's just about to ruin your night." Lifting the crown, she then spun around twice before throwing it over the dungeon's parapets and into the maze below.

Narcos squeezed his staff with fury before snarling. "Eragosh...I want you to kill every last one of them, starting with the pixie." Not waiting for a response, Narcos turned around and exited the roof via its trap door.

"Oh, shit!" Wink exclaimed as a change in demeanor washed over Marcain.

Dropping his torch, Eragosh sprinted towards the pixie, with his blade at ready, and slashed at her the moment she was in range. Having dealt with angry humans on more than one occasion, Wink dodged the attack by running under Eragosh's legs.

Seeking help from her companions, she raced towards Ontar's sprawled out form and grabbed him by the collar of his cloak. "Wake up, Onnie, PLEASE!"

Coming up behind the frightened pixie, Eragosh swung his blade in an attempt to cut her in half. Thankfully, at the last moment, Spirit Slayer rose to block the attack. Rotating into a crouched position, Ontar parried a second strike from Eragosh, then countered with a wide swing that forced his adversary back. "Why don't you try picking on someone your own size?"

Eragosh raised his sword in a knight's salute. *"I knew the man who used to wield that blade. Do not disgrace his memory with it."*

Rising into a battle stance, Ontar replied, "If I can defeat you, then I can defeat Lydon."

Unsure of who Ontar was talking about, Eragosh simply ignored the warrior's last words and went in for the attack!

❧❧❧

Infuriated by the actions of an insignificant pixie, Narcos stormed into the dungeon's dining hall, knowing full well that he would need some help if he was to enter the maze. Having left the dead guards where they were for exactly that reason, he lifted his arms and cast a spell on the corpses around him. Shuddering as their bodies moved once more, ten zombies slowly got to their feet and prepared to follow their master's will.

Urging his minions to keep up, Narcos led them through the dungeon and up to a large double door with a heavy crossbar that served as the entrance to Vakerdurn's Maze. Ordering the zombies to remove the crossbar, Narcos cast a spell while touching his temple, which allowed him to see through the upcoming darkness unhindered. Finishing their initial task, the zombies pulled open the dungeon's doors so they could join their master in his search for the crown.

The stars in the sky shone brightly over the maze's high, spiked walls as Narcos saw a long straight passage that stretched to an intersection at its far end. Lying on the ground about halfway to the intersection was the Crown of Darkness. Leery about any possible traps, Narcos sent the zombies ahead of him to fetch the relic. This caution proved to be well founded when he heard what sounded like multiple growls.

Stepping into view from the far end of the passage was a massive Doberman-like dog whose body was almost as tall as the walls at its sides. Possessing three vicious heads and a long black snake for a tail, the Cerberus snarled and barked at the zombies as they shambled towards the crown. Unsure how the undead would fare against such a ferocious beast, Narcos ordered them all to, "Hurry!"

Going on the attack, the Cerberus ran and pounced on its victims just before they reached the crown. Two zombies were knocked to the ground and impaled by the beast's sharp paws, while three others were snapped up by the Cerberus's various heads and mauled. Undeterred, two more zombies stepped on their crushed comrades and either bit or clawed at the dog's front legs with their grimy nails. Three additional zombies walked under the beast and made their way towards its hind legs, but the snake that served as its tail bit deeply into one of them before flinging it against a wall. Preparing another spell, Narcos had to make sure his undead continued fighting until they accomplished their task.

"Chairbis…Chairbis, you have to wake up!" Wink pleaded as she slapped the unconscious cleric's face and pulled on his nostrils. "Onnie's hurt and needs help!"

Breathing heavily, Ontar kept both hands on Spirit Slayer as he faced off against Nanst Eragosh. The battle was not going well as blood trickled out of little cuts in his breastplate. Using a weapon that he was only modestly familiar with, Ontar struggled to fend off Eragosh, who was highly skilled in his weapon of choice and didn't have armor to slow him down. Utilizing his greater speed, Eragosh was able to stab Ontar in his upper leg before falling back to avoid getting hit by Spirit Slayer's greater reach.

Groaning, Ontar knew that an injured leg would give him balance difficulties in combat that Eragosh could easily exploit. Thinking of a strategy to counter this weakness, Ontar stumbled towards his nemesis and swung his blade in a blow that Eragosh easily parried. Utilizing his greater size and strength, Ontar locked swords with Eragosh and pushed him towards the edge of the roof.

Afraid of being knocked over by his opponent or shoved off the roof, Eragosh unleashed his secret weapon. Unprepared for what happened next, Ontar was caught off guard by a ghostly pair of hands that briefly emerged from Eragosh's waist and swiped at his hips with cold, spectral fingers. Letting out a painful cry as frostbite struck his legs, Ontar fell to the ground and watched in horror as Eragosh raised his sword and prepared to finish him…but the blow never came.

Standing defiantly with Wink at his side, Chairbis's voice seemed to echo as he finished conducting his exorcism. Violently shuddering while the divine power of Anthalos filled his very being, Marcain looked up to see Eragosh's ghost floating peacefully above him. No longer concerned with mortal affairs, Eragosh merely nodded to those he'd come to know before fading into the darkness of the night.

Relieved to see the fight was over, Wink tugged on the bottom of Chairbis's robe and said, "Look, the ghost is gone! Now's your chance to go heal Onnie."

"No," Marcain declared as he pointed his sword at the cleric. "Take one more step and I'll run you through."

Chairbis gave the nobleman a curious look. "What are you doing? You're free from Narcos's control. We don't have to be enemies."

"You don't understand," Marcain stated coldly. "I was forced to serve Narcos because of Eragosh, but Ontar and Echo did it by choice. They killed my friends and set the stage for Narcos to murder my beloved."

Stomping her foot in frustration, Wink exclaimed, "You idiot. They're trying to redeem themselves by going after Narcos before he gets ahold of the Crown of Darkness. You should be fighting with us instead of against us!"

"Narcos doesn't know that Eragosh has been purged from my body," Marcain explained. "After I end their lives, I will exact my vengeance on him as well."

"No…you won't," Ontar said as he leaned on one arm while using the other to slash at Marcain with Spirit Slayer."

Screaming in pain as his foot was chopped off, Marcain fell to the ground right next to Ontar, who then took his sword and stabbed the young lord through the heart! Watching the life fade from his opponent's eyes, Ontar quietly said, "I'm sorry to have wronged you," right before he died.

Rushing to the wounded warrior, Chairbis knelt and began casting healing spells on his injuries. Wink was quick to join them while joyfully saying, "You did it, Onnie. Now, Narcos doesn't have anyone left to protect him."

Ontar heard the distant sounds or tortured moaning on the wind and quietly replied, "I wouldn't be so sure."

❧❧❧

Narcos felt his powers draining as he struggled to control what remained of the zombies. A brutal beast like none he'd ever seen before, the Cerberus had torn six of them to pieces, leaving him with only four left to carry out his will. Giving as good as they got, though, theses undead had used their superior numbers to rend long bloody gashes along the Cerberus's front paws that forced it to limp when it moved. They also killed the snake that served as the creature's tail, while its middle canine head couldn't stop vomiting up rotting chunks of zombie flesh.

Realizing that his minions weren't strong enough to kill their foe, Narcos devised a strategy to help him retrieve the Crown of Darkness. This involved sending two zombies in to continue their attack on the Cerberus's front paws while the remaining zombies climbed up the beast's now lifeless tail to strike at its back. Barking ferociously, two of the Cerberus's heads easily sunk their teeth into the zombies that approached, while the third howled when it realized that more of their foul ilk had managed to climb onto its backside. Twisting violently, the Cerberus tried to shake off its attackers so that it could destroy them.

Hoping the zombies would distract the beast just long enough to accomplish his objective, Narcos ran up and retrieved the Crown of Darkness off the ground where it had fallen. Aware of what he'd done, one of the Cerberus's heads tried to snap at him, but he retreated along the passage without injury. Clutching the crown in his hands, Narcos felt its power by touch alone and immediately placed it upon his brow.

No words could describe the unstoppable torrent of black magic that poured out from the crown. Gasping as unseen energies filled his body, Narcos realized that such an artifact would serve as an eternal reservoir for his incantations, and that he would no longer need to call upon Kardok to cast a spell. Tapping into this new source of magic, he raised his arms and called forth a legion of the damned.

Having just finished ripping asunder the last of the zombies, the Cerberus saw what appeared to be the reddish glow of ten transparent skeletons whose bodies faded into a haze just below their ribs. Rising from the remains of the zombies, these phantoms hovered menacingly next to Narcos as if to challenge the Cerberus to attack them. Tired from its previous battle, the big beast barked menacingly at the new undead before turning around and fleeing back into the maze.

Lifting his hand in a gesture to the phantoms, Narcos instructed them to, "Rise up and destroy my enemies."

◆◆◆

"Chairbis…Chairbis, what's happening!?" Ontar asked as he stood on freshly-healed legs and saw a deep red glow that enveloped all of Vakerdurn's Maze.

Interrupting the cleric before he had a chance to speak, Wink said, "I think I already know."

Following her gesture, the party saw a phantom rise from Marcain's body and extend its ghostly arms before flying straight at Ontar. Still armed with Spirit Slayer, Ontar was able to eliminate the vengeful menace with a single swing of his blade.

"Phantoms," Chairbis stated. "Narcos must have used the crown to raise an army of them. Hurry! Let's get Hatch and Echo back on the carpet. We have to get out of here before it's too late!"

Moving their unconscious companions onto the flying carpet, Ontar, Chairbis, and Wink quickly took to the sky in the hopes of escaping from their newfound enemy. Eager to prevent this from happening, the phantom's swarmed around them.

Attempting to dodge their deadly foes, Chairbis guided the carpet through increasingly difficult aerial maneuvers while trying to find an opening in their ranks. Wary of the chance they'd be attacked from behind, Ontar moved on his knees to the rear of the carpet and attempted to mount a defense. Holding Spirit Slayer, he swung the blade at the first undead to come within range, cleaving it completely out of existence. A second phantom tried taking a swipe at Ontar with its outstretched hand, but he parried the attack with his weapon, causing the appendage to briefly vanish before its owner fell back behind the others.

Striking out at the growing number of undead, Ontar saw the phantoms were about to overtake the party when he shouted, "Left!" Heeding the warrior's command, Chairbis had the carpet make a hard left and watched as a dozen undead flew past. Hacking at them as they did, Ontar decimated as many of their numbers as he could. "There's too many of them," he shouted as the next wave of adversaries started their approach.

Spotting a large creature beneath them, Chairbis replied, "Not for long," before having the carpet dive towards the maze.

As the party descended, a phantom rose through the fabric and raked Ontar's back with its ghostly hands. Crying out from the burning sensation that blistered his skin, Ontar twisted about and thrust Spirit Slayer through both the undead and its entry point.

"Don't kill the carpet!" Wink shrieked as the rug shuddered following the phantom's disappearance.

"Hold on tight!" Chairbis warned as he surged towards a huge black dog with three heads standing in a spacious portion of the maze.

Circling above the confused animal, the party cringed as they got close enough for the Cerberus to snap at them. Following in their wake was a large number of phantoms who remembered losing their lives to this beast and started attacking it! Multiple howls went up from the Cerberus's heads as more and more undead sought to enact their revenge. Making one last pass over the dying canine, the party was relieved to see their diversion had attracted most of their enemies away from them. The few phantoms that still tried to fulfill their original task met a harsh end at the tip of Ontar's sword.

Exhausted from their encounter, the group said little as they flew back to Orla. Narcos and Zattermox had won this night, but they still managed to defeat Marcain and escape from the phantom horde. Taking solace in the fact they had *all* survived the perils of Vakerdurn's Maze the group quietly contemplated what their next move might be?

Narcos couldn't help but feel a little conflicted as he stood on the roof of Deltrum's Dungeon and looked down at Marcain's corpse. Surrounded by a few phantoms, he always felt that Marcain was a treacherous waste of space that should have died a long time ago. Eragosh, on the other hand, had been a loyal servant who surprised him by failing to kill his enemies. The two had been quite useful in helping him acquire the Crown of Darkness, but now, their purpose was at an end, and it was time to move on to other matters.

Faced with a mystery over the hand mirror and vial the shades had delivered, Narcos wished that Zattermox were there to provide some background on the remaining relics. Thankfully, he didn't have to wait long before he saw a small cloud of smoke drifting his direction across the sky. Waiting impatiently for Zattermox to take solid form, Narcos asked, "Where have you been?"

Seeing the Crown of Darkness on his *master's* head, Zattermox grinned as he got down on one knee and said, "Forgive me, master. I had to contend with those who would deny you what is rightfully yours."

"Well, you obviously failed in the attempt," Narcos said while thumping the butt of his staff on Marcain's body. "Between you and this worthless piece of garbage, I had to take the crown myself."

"Were you able to kill the ones who tried to stop us?" Zattermox wondered.

Narcos shook his head. "No, they fled once I summoned the phantoms. Do you know how they were able to find us?"

"Maybe Marcain left a clue during their previous encounter," Zattermox suggested.

Scowling at the idea, Narcos grumbled, "Little bastard probably would do something like that. Either way, he's gone, and my enemies are defeated. So, now that you're here, why don't you tell me about the other artifacts the shades retrieved?"

Looking around anxiously, Zattermox asked, "Where are the artifacts?"

Narcos gave the smoke demon a curious look. "They're in my satchel."

Zattermox breathed a sigh of relief. "Good. I'll have use for them later."

"Oh, you think so, do you?" Narcos inquired.

"*Yes*...I do," Zattermox replied with a twisted smile. "And as punishment for questioning me, I want you to stab your hand on my horn."

"Arrogant little..." Narcos began, but then he stopped himself and watched in horror as he unwittingly raised his left hand, walked over to Zattermox, and impaled it upon one of the demon's horns.

Screaming as he withdrew the wounded appendage, Narcos glared at Zattermox, who stood up and laughed at him! Looking back at the phantoms for help, Narcos shouted, "Kill him!"

The phantoms did nothing.

Getting his laughter under control, Zattermox said, "Don't even try. The phantoms are more inclined to obey me now than you."

"What are you talking about?" Narcos snarled.

This was the moment that Zattermox had been waiting for. "Didn't you know? *He who wears the Crown of Darkness is master of the dead…and a slave to its makers.*"

"No!" Narcos shouted frantically as he tried to remove the crown. Alas, his efforts proved to be in vain.

Speaking with a newfound authority, Zattermox told the necromancer. "Quit wasting your time trying to remove that crown and listen to what I'm about to say. First off, from now on, *I* am your absolute master, and you will obey my commands to the best of your ability. Second, you cannot betray me or withhold any information regarding treachery against me. Finally, from now on, you are incapable of ending your own life and will never be able to encourage others to do so for you. Is that understood?"

With those words, Narcos knew that he would have to spend the rest of his life enslaved to another. The Crown of Darkness had utterly destroyed his free will, and all he could do was despondently mutter, "I understand."

"Good," Zattermox said as he walked towards the roof's trapdoor. "Now, don't lose those artifacts. Their use will be essential for me to complete my plans." Not bothering to look back at his new slave, Zattermox thought of how he had awoken in this world with nothing but a handful of enemies who wanted him dead. Yet, through his own cunning, he was not only able to beat these foes, but also lay claim to a crown whose power would eventually help him to rule the realm forever. Grinning at this accomplishment, he couldn't help thinking, *I win.*

www.ingramcontent.com/pod-product-compliance
Lightning Source LLC
Chambersburg PA
CBHW030907300726
48970CB00001B/45